中文详注剑桥莎士比亚精选

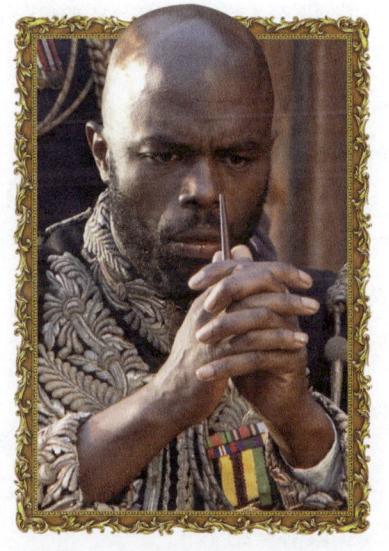

奥赛罗

OTHELLO

原版创始主编：[英] 瑞克斯·吉布森（Rex Gibson）
原版主编：[英] 瑞查德·安褚斯（Richard Andrews）
[英] 维姬·维南德（Vicki Wienand）
原版编注：[英] 珍·科尔兹（Jane Coles）
总主编：陈国华
分册主编：段素萍

北京语言大学出版社
BEIJING LANGUAGE AND CULTURE
UNIVERSITY PRESS

社图号 20197

Cambridge School Shakespeare: Othello [Third edition] [978-1-107-61559-5] was first published by CAMBRIDGE UNIVERSITY PRESS in 2014. All rights reserved.

This Simplified Chinese edition for the People's Republic of China is published by arrangement with the Press Syndicate of the University of Cambridge, Cambridge, United Kingdom.

© Cambridge University Press & Beijing Language and Culture University Press 2020.

This book is in copyright. No reproduction of any part may take place without the written permission of Cambridge University Press or Beijing Language and Culture University Press.

本书版权由剑桥大学出版社和北京语言大学出版社共同所有。本书任何部分之文字及图片，如未获得出版者书面同意，不得用任何方式抄袭、节录或翻印。

This edition is for sale in the People's Republic of China (excluding Hong Kong SAR, Macao SAR and Taiwan Province) only.

此版本仅限在中华人民共和国境内销售。

北京市版权局著作权合同登记图字：01-2020-4090 号

图书在版编目（CIP）数据

中文详注剑桥莎士比亚精选．奥赛罗／陈国华总主编；段素萍分册主编． -- 北京：北京语言大学出版社，2020.12

书名原文：Cambridge School Shakespeare：Othello

ISBN 978-7-5619-5801-8

Ⅰ.①中… Ⅱ.①陈… ②段… Ⅲ.①悲剧－剧本－英国－中世纪 Ⅳ.① I561.33

中国版本图书馆 CIP 数据核字（2020）第 230381 号

中文详注剑桥莎士比亚精选：奥赛罗
ZHONGWEN XIANG ZHU JIANQIAO SHASHIBIYA JINGXUAN: AOSAILUO

项目策划：李　亮	责任编辑：孙冠群
封面设计：乔　剑	排版制作：北京创艺涵文化发展有限公司
责任印制：武晓东	

出版发行：**北京语言大学出版社**
社　　址：北京市海淀区学院路 15 号，100083
网　　址：www.blcup.com
电子信箱：service@blcup.com
电　　话：编辑部　8610-82301019/0178
　　　　　发 行 部　8610-82303650/3591/3648
　　　　　北语书店　8610-82303653
　　　　　网购咨询　8610-82303908
印　　刷：北京博海升彩色印刷有限公司

版　次：2020 年 12 月第 1 版	印　次：2020 年 12 月第 1 次印刷
开　本：787 毫米 ×1092 毫米　1/16	印　张：16.75
字　数：491 千字	
定　价：85.00 元	

PRINTED IN CHINA

序

由于观察角度不同，评判标准不同，关于哪个国家哪位诗人或小说家的成就最大，世人可能难以达成一致；可是说到剧作家，大家的共识是，莎士比亚不仅是英语国家有史以来最伟大的剧作家，也是全世界最伟大的剧作家，在知名度、影响力和传世作品的数量上，没有任何一位剧作家可以与之比肩。正是由于其公认的文学成就和人文精神，在过去400多年里，莎士比亚戏剧的演出在英语国家和许多非英语国家经久不衰，莎剧的阅读和鉴赏已成为这些国家英文教学的必选内容。

莎剧进入中国，已经有100多年历史，莎士比亚全集已经有了四个中文译本。不懂英文的人可以通过译本来欣赏莎士比亚剧作。然而文学作品的语言，尤其是诗歌的语言，具有相当程度的不可译性，而几乎所有莎剧的大部分台词都是素体诗（blank verse）。例如《哈慕雷》（*Hamlet*）里主人翁的名言"To be, or not to be, that is the question"，不论怎样译，都难以完全再现原文的深刻内涵和形式特点。要想真正欣赏莎士比亚的语言和戏剧艺术，还得阅读其英文原作。最早由剑桥大学出版社出版的这套莎剧精选，收录了最受读者和观众喜爱的14部剧目，涵盖莎剧的各个类别，以其独具匠心的设计和编排，成为所有英文原版莎剧中最适合英语学习者阅读、最适合戏剧爱好者排演的莎剧选集。

本选集的创始主编瑞克斯·吉布森（Rex Gibson）在本书引言（Introduction）里指出："不论做什么，都要记住，莎士比亚写下他的剧本是为了演出、观看和享受的。"秉承这一宗旨，这一新版莎剧选集有四个鲜明的区别性特点：

一、书的开本和页面的宽高比例特别适合学校的老师和学生以及剧团的导演和演员在排练莎剧时把书打开，拿在手里，随时参阅，而且左边页面上有许多有关排演活动的建议。

二、书中配有大量世界各国莎剧演出的彩色剧照，为莎剧爱好者和剧团排演莎剧提供了灵感。

三、书的正文部分打开后，右页是未经删减、原汁原味的剧本原文，左页是多种不同栏目，包括导演技巧（Stagecraft）、剧中语言（Language in the play）、人物分析（Characters）、主题分析（Themes）、写作练习（Write about it）及词语注释等。每幕之间（本幕回顾）和最后一幕后（本剧回顾）有与剧情相关的各种思考题。

四、在剧本之后有各种针对全剧的专题论述，以《哈慕雷》为例，包括视角与主题（Perspectives and themes）、人物分析（Characters）、《哈慕雷》的语言（The language of *Hamlet*）、《哈慕雷》的演出（*Hamlet* in performance）、笔论莎士比亚（Writing about Shakespeare）、笔论《哈慕雷》（Writing about *Hamlet*），还有一份莎翁年表（William Shakespeare 1564–1616）。

左页上的栏目对于解读和排演莎剧特别有帮助，剧本后面的专题论述对于撰写有关莎士比亚的文章特别有帮助，而参加莎剧排演，背诵台词，撰写论文，又是提高英语水平的极好途径。

为了方便更多的中国读者阅读、欣赏、排演莎士比亚原作，北京语言大学出版社携手剑桥大学出版社，将这套莎剧精选引入中国。我有幸应邀担任这套书的中文版总主编，组织起一个团队，对原版进行一定程度的改编和汉化，以适应中国读者的需求。我们不仅将原版提供的关键注释基本译成了中文，而且针对中国英语学习者和莎剧爱好者阅读理解上的难点，主要做了以下四件事：

一、参考 The Oxford Dictionary of Original Shakespearean Pronunciation (David Crystal 2016)、Oxford Dictionary of Pronunciation for Current English (Clive Upton 2003) 和 Shakespeare's Names: A Pronouncing Dictionary (Helge Kökeritz 1950)，给每个剧本前面人物表里的人名加上了国际音标。为了便于读者识别，我们将第一本发音词典里一般中国读者不认识的个别音标替换成了大家熟悉的近似音标。

二、为左页顶端的剧情简介添加中文译文。

三、左页中以及剧本后面论文部分里有一些具有挑战性的词和术语（如tableau），我们为其中的大部分添加了相应的中文释义。

四、适当增加了原版里没有的词语注释。

给剧中人物的名字加了国际音标之后，我们发现，现有莎剧中文译本里一些人名的中文译名与原文的读音差别较大且互不相同。根据定名不咎、译音循本、音义兼顾、音系对应的原则，我们给出了新译名。根据前两个原则，我们将剧本 Julius Caesar /ˈdʒuːlɪəs ˈsiːzə(r)/ 译成《儒略·恺撒》，而没有采用《尤利/力乌斯·恺撒》《裘利/力斯·凯撒》《居里厄斯·恺撒》等现成译名中的任何一个，因为从公元前1世纪到公元16世纪西方使用的儒略历（Julian calendar）就是以这位 Julius Caesar（拉丁文读音是 /ˈjuːlɪ.ʊs ˈkae̯sar/）命名的。根据音义兼顾的原则，我们将剧本 Hamlet /ˈ(h)amlət/ 译成《哈慕雷》而不是《哈姆莱特》或《哈姆雷特》，因为"慕雷"比"姆莱"或"姆雷"更适合用来给男子起名，结尾的辅音 /t/ 在实际说话中往往不发音。根据音系对应的原则，我们借鉴了曹禺的译法，将剧本 Romeo and Juliet 译成《柔密欧与茱丽叶》，没有将 Romeo 译成更常见的"罗密欧"，因为"柔 /rou/"比"罗 /luo/"更接近原名 Romeo /ˈroːmɪoː/ 的读音；同时我们将 Juliet /ˈdʒuːlɪət/ 译成"茱丽叶"而不是"朱丽叶"，因为这样做不容易让人误以为这个女孩姓"朱"。

这套经过改编并且带中文注释的《中文详注剑桥莎士比亚精选》不仅可以用作中国高中和大学的英文教材，而且适合中国所有具有较高英语能力的莎剧爱好者阅读和欣赏，将戏剧从书中提升到自己心中，将剧本从课堂搬演到戏台。

相信《中文详注剑桥莎士比亚精选》会带给中国广大英语爱好者一个惊喜。

陈国华

2020年5月于英国剑桥家中

Contents 目录

Introduction 引言	iv
Photo gallery 剧照精选	v

Othello 《奥赛罗》

List of characters 人物表	1
Act 1 第 1 幕	3
Act 2 第 2 幕	49
Act 3 第 3 幕	93
Act 4 第 4 幕	145
Act 5 第 5 幕	185
Perspectives and themes 视角与主题	222
Characters 人物分析	223
Coroner's investigation 验尸官的调查	228
The language of *Othello* 《奥赛罗》的语言	230
Race and culture in *Othello* 《奥赛罗》里的种族和文化	233
Critics' forum 评论家论坛	238
Othello in performance 《奥赛罗》的演出	240
Writing about Shakespeare 笔论莎士比亚	246
Writing about *Othello* 笔论《奥赛罗》	248
William Shakespeare 1564–1616 莎翁年表	250
Acknowledgements 鸣谢	251

Introduction 引言

This *Othello* is part of the **Cambridge School Shakespeare** series. Like every other play in the series, it has been specially prepared to help all students in schools and colleges.

The **Cambridge School Shakespeare** *Othello* aims to be different. It invites you to lift the words from the page and to bring the play to life in your classroom, hall or drama studio. Through enjoyable and focused activities, you will increase your understanding of the play. Actors have created their different interpretations of the play over the centuries. Similarly, you are invited to make up your own mind about *Othello*, rather than having someone else's interpretation handed down to you.

Cambridge School Shakespeare does not offer you a cut-down or simplified version of the play. This is Shakespeare's language, filled with imaginative possibilities. You will find on every left-hand page: a summary of the action, an explanation of unfamiliar words, and a choice of activities on Shakespeare's stagecraft, characters, themes and language.

Between each act and in the pages at the end of the play, you will find notes, illustrations and activities. These will help to encourage reflection after every act and give you insights into the background and context of the play as a whole.

This edition will be of value to you whether you are studying for an examination, reading for pleasure or thinking of putting on the play to entertain others. You can work on the activities on your own or in groups. Many of the activities suggest a particular group size, but don't be afraid to make up larger or smaller groups to suit your own purposes. Please don't think you have to do every activity: choose those that will help you most.

Although you are invited to treat *Othello* as a play, you don't need special dramatic or theatrical skills to do the activities. By choosing your activities, and by exploring and experimenting, you can make your own interpretations of Shakespeare's language, characters and stories.

Whatever you do, remember that Shakespeare wrote his plays to be acted, watched and enjoyed.

Rex Gibson
Founding editor

This new edition contains more photographs, more diversity and more supporting material than previous editions, whilst remaining true to Rex's original vision. Specifically, it contains more activities and commentary on stagecraft and writing about Shakespeare, to reflect contemporary interest. The glossary has been enlarged too. Finally, this edition aims to reflect the best teaching and learning possible, and to represent not only Shakespeare through the ages, but also the relevance and excitement of Shakespeare today.

Richard Andrews and Vicki Wienand
Series editors

This edition of *Othello* uses the text of the play established by Norman Sanders in **The New Cambridge Shakespeare.**

Othello tells the story of a black army general who has secretly married the white daughter of a leading politician. Will their marriage survive in the face of racism, jealousy and a struggle for power?

▲ Othello has no idea that his trusted ensign (standard-bearer [掌旗官]), Iago, is plotting against him. Iago says he is angry that Othello has promoted his younger colleague Cassio to the rank of lieutenant (副将，副官) instead of him, but we never know exactly why Iago hates Othello so much.

▶ Iago enlists the help of a local gentleman, Roderigo, to stir up trouble for Othello and Desdemona. They tell Desdemona's father about the secret marriage, and spread racist lies.

▲ Meanwhile, a Turkish fleet threatens the island of Cyprus, and Othello is sent to command the Venetian (威尼斯的) forces.

▶ Othello is hailed as a 'noble and valiant (英勇) general!' A terrible storm scatters and destroys the Turkish invasion fleet, and Othello lands safely in Cyprus.

Othello is reunited with Desdemona, and he takes up official duties as commander of the occupying forces in Cyprus.

Othello is unaware that Iago is watching their every move. He plans to destroy Othello by suggesting that Desdemona is having an affair with the handsome Cassio.

Iago tricks Cassio into getting drunk at a barracks (兵营) party. After Cassio is involved in a drunken brawl (斗殴), Othello dismisses him from office and promotes Iago in his place.

Meanwhile, Iago tells his wife Emilia to steal Desdemona's handkerchief – an antique love token (定情信物) given to her as a wedding gift by Othello. Iago later places it in Cassio's lodgings, as supposed evidence of Desdemona's adultery (通奸).

▲ Iago continues to whisper poisonous lies, rousing Othello's jealousy and convincing him that Desdemona is unfaithful.

◄ All the while, Iago pretends to be Desdemona's friend and confidant (知己), maintaining his 'honest Iago' façade (表象).

▶ Eventually, Iago's lies and tricks move Othello to a jealous rage: 'jealousy: / It is the green-eyed monster which doth mock / The meat it feeds on'.

▼ Othello attacks Desdemona, refusing to listen to reason.

▲ Only after he has killed Desdemona does Othello discover the truth about her innocence. Grief-stricken and full of remorse (懊悔), Othello kills himself. Iago is arrested.

List of characters 人物表

OTHELLO /əˈθeloː/ (奥赛罗) A black army general in the service of the Duke of Venice
DESDEMONA /ˌdezdɪˈmoːnə/ (黛丝荻牟娜) Othello's wife, daughter of Brabantio
IAGO /iːˈɑːgoː/ (伊阿苟) Othello's ensign (standard-bearer)
EMILIA /eˈmɪlɪə/ (艾蜜丽叶) Iago's wife, companion to Desdemona
CASSIO /ˈkasɪoː/ (卡修) Othello's lieutenant
BIANCA /bɪˈaŋka/ (碧昂卡) in love with Cassio

DUKE OF VENICE (威尼斯公爵)
BRABANTIO /braˈbansɪoː/ (布拉班修) A Venetian senator, father of Desdemona
RODERIGO /ˌrɒdəˈriːgoː/ (若德瑞苟) A Venetian gentleman, in love with Desdemona
GRATIANO /ˌgratsɪˈɑːnoː/ (格拉奇阿诺) Brabantio's brother
LODOVICO /ˌlɒdəˈviːkoː/ (劳德维寇) Brabantio's relative

MONTANO /mɒnˈtɑːnoː/ (芒塔诺) Governor of Cyprus

SENATORS OF VENICE (威尼斯诸元老)
GENTLEMEN OF CYPRUS (塞浦路斯诸绅士)

CLOWN (小丑) Servant to Othello

HERALD (传令官)
MESSENGER (信差)
MUSICIANS, SOLDIERS, ATTENDANTS, SERVANTS (乐师、士兵、随从、仆人)
SAILOR (水手)

The action of the play takes place in Venice and Cyprus.

Two men are in the middle of an argument. Roderigo accuses Iago of cheating him. Iago is angry about failing to gain the promotion that has gone instead to Michael Cassio.

剧情简介：两个男人正在争吵。若德瑞苟指责伊阿苟骗他。伊阿苟很生气，因为自己未得提拔，而麦克尔·卡修却获晋升。

Stagecraft 导演技巧

A dramatic opening (in pairs)

In the theatres of Shakespeare's time, there was no electric lighting and no stage curtain. The playwright had to signal the start of the play by means of a dramatic opening scene. Here, the noisy audience would be silenced by two men in the middle of a heated argument, accompanied by much swearing.

a Read this opening conversation (lines 1–34) aloud. Try reading it in several different ways and decide which sounds best. Can you bring out differences between the two characters? Discuss which words in the script give you clues as to how they should be spoken. For example, look carefully at the use of pronouns: in Shakespeare's day, 'thou' indicated familiarity, or suggested that the speaker was addressing someone socially inferior; 'you' was a more polite or respectful form of address.

b Movie and theatre directors have chosen various ways to begin the play. Think about how you might want to set the scene – for example, how could you suggest to an audience that this opening scene takes place in Venice? Consider the ways the actors might enter the stage or screen, and what sound and lighting effects might imply a street at night.

c The play opens halfway through an argument. Make up what you think Iago and Roderigo have been saying before the play begins. Improvise (即兴表演) the full argument, making sure that your dialogue ends on the first line of the play.

d Imagine you are preparing to direct a performance of *Othello*. Start a Director's Journal and record your ideas (advice for actors, costume sketches, set designs) as you read through the play.

1 Tush 闭嘴；得啦；呸
2 'Sblood = By God's blood（字面意思为"以上帝的血保证"，骂人话，可译为"该死的"）
3 Abhor me 您可以恨我
4 In personal suit 亲自求情
5 Off-capped 脱帽致敬
6 bombast circumstance 冠冕堂皇的理由
7 epithets of war 军事术语
8 Non-suits my mediators 回绝为我求情的人
9 Certes = Certainly （说真的）
10 Forsooth = For sure （的确）
11 arithmetician 理论家（讽刺下文中的麦克尔·卡修 [Michael Cassio] 是纸上谈兵的空头理论家）
12 Florentine 佛罗伦萨（Florence）人
13 almost damned 就要下地狱（取自当时的一句谚语，大意是娶个漂亮老婆注定会戴绿帽子，因此耽误终生）
14 squadron 一班士兵
15 devision 排兵布阵
16 spinster 老处女
17 togèd consuls 身穿长袍的议员（togèd = togaed；toga是古罗马男人穿的一种袍子）
18 prattle 空谈
19 had the election 被选中

1 Michael Cassio – why does Iago dislike him?

Iago explains why he believes he has not been promoted to the rank of lieutenant (lines 8–27).

- Look carefully at the way Iago describes Cassio (lines 19–26) and pick out four key phrases that suggest why Iago is jealous of him. Compare your phrases with those of other students. How many do you have in common?

Othello, the Moor of Venice

Act 1 Scene 1
Venice   A street at night

Enter RODERIGO *and* IAGO.

RODERIGO   Tush[1], never tell me, I take it much unkindly
That thou, Iago, who hast had my purse
As if the strings were thine shouldst know of this.
IAGO   'Sblood[2], but you will not hear me.
If ever I did dream of such a matter, 5
Abhor me[3].
RODERIGO   Thou told'st me thou didst hold him in thy hate.
IAGO   Despise me if I do not: three great ones of the city,
In personal suit[4] to make me his lieutenant,
Off-capped[5] to him; and by the faith of man, 10
I know my price, I am worth no worse a place.
But he, as loving his own pride and purposes,
Evades them with a bombast circumstance[6],
Horribly stuffed with epithets of war[7],
And in conclusion, 15
Non-suits my mediators[8]. For 'Certes'[9], says he,
'I have already chosen my officer.'
And what was he?
Forsooth[10], a great arithmetician[11],
One Michael Cassio, a Florentine[12], 20
A fellow almost damned[13] in a fair wife,
That never set a squadron[14] in the field,
Nor the devision[15] of a battle knows
More than a spinster[16], unless the bookish theoric,
Wherein the togèd consuls[17] can propose 25
As masterly as he. Mere prattle[18] without practice
Is all his soldiership. But he, sir, had the election[19],

Iago continues to complain about 'the Moor' and the system of promotion. He says he pretends to be a faithful officer, but follows Othello only to serve his own purposes.

 剧情简介：伊阿苟继续抱怨"那个摩尔人"和提拔机制。他说自己装作一个忠于职守的军官，追随奥赛罗只是为了达到自己的目的。

Characters 人物分析
First impressions of Iago (in small groups)

a Read the script opposite aloud several times, sharing out the lines between all members of the group (hand over to the next person at each full stop, question mark or exclamation mark).

b On a large, plain piece of paper, write 'Iago' in the centre (see the diagram below). In the script, look for the key statements that Iago makes about himself. What words reveal something about his character or motivation? Write these quotations on the second layer of the diagram. On the outer layer, explain in your own words what you believe each quotation tells us about him.

c When you have finished, join together with other groups and compare your sheets. Explain how and why you chose your particular quotations.

d Pool your ideas to produce one final diagram for display on your classroom wall.

1 heathen 异教徒
2 lee'd 被占上风（航海术语）
3 debitor and creditor 借方和贷方（这里用来讽刺对方因精于算计而获得上司赏识）
4 counter-caster 算数的；会计（counter是古人用来计数的一种铁质或骨质算筹，cast的意思是"计算"）
5 his Moorship's ancient 摩尔大人的掌旗官（摩尔人 [Moor] 指北非肤色较黑的阿拉伯人，his Moorship的叫法带有讽刺意味；ancient = ensign）
6 Preferment 晋升，提拔
7 letter 举荐信
8 affection 交情
9 old gradation 按老规矩逐级提拔
10 affined 有必要，应该
11 knee-crooking knave 卑躬屈膝的奴仆
12 doting … bondage 甘心为奴
13 nought = nothing
14 provender 草料
15 cashiered 抛弃；撤职
16 trimmed … duty 假装忠诚
17 lined their coats 装满他们的腰包
18 Do themselves homage 只为自己着想
19 complement extern 外在表现
20 daws 寒鸦（羽毛基本是黑色，被视为一种傻鸟）

	And I, of whom his eyes had seen the proof	
	At Rhodes, at Cyprus, and on other grounds	
	Christian and heathen[1], must be lee'd[2] and calmed	30
	By debitor and creditor[3]; this counter-caster[4],	
	He, in good time, must his lieutenant be,	
	And I, God bless the mark, his Moorship's ancient[5].	
RODERIGO	By heaven, I rather would have been his hangman.	
IAGO	Why, there's no remedy. 'Tis the curse of service;	35
	Preferment[6] goes by letter[7] and affection[8],	
	Not by the old gradation[9], where each second	
	Stood heir to the first. Now sir, be judge yourself	
	Whether I in any just term am affined[10]	
	To love the Moor.	
RODERIGO	I would not follow him then.	40
IAGO	O sir, content you.	
	I follow him to serve my turn upon him.	
	We cannot all be masters, nor all masters	
	Cannot be truly followed. You shall mark	
	Many a duteous and knee-crooking knave[11],	45
	That doting on his own obsequious bondage[12],	
	Wears out his time much like his master's ass	
	For nought[13] but provender[14], and when he's old, cashiered[15].	
	Whip me such honest knaves. Others there are	
	Who, trimmed in forms and visages of duty[16],	50
	Keep yet their hearts attending on themselves,	
	And throwing but shows of service on their lords,	
	Do well thrive by them; and when they have lined their coats[17],	
	Do themselves homage[18]. These fellows have some soul,	
	And such a one do I profess myself.	55
	For, sir,	
	It is as sure as you are Roderigo,	
	Were I the Moor, I would not be Iago;	
	In following him, I follow but myself.	
	Heaven is my judge, not I for love and duty,	60
	But seeming so for my peculiar end.	
	For when my outward action doth demonstrate	
	The native act and figure of my heart	
	In complement extern[19], 'tis not long after	
	But I will wear my heart upon my sleeve	
	For daws[20] to peck at. I am not what I am.	65

Iago suggests a way of taking revenge against Othello. They shout in the street outside Brabantio's house, and tell him the news that he has been 'robbed'.

 剧情简介：伊阿苟提出了一个报复奥赛罗的办法。他们在布拉班修宅邸外的街上大喊，告诉布拉班修他"被抢劫"的消息。

Stagecraft 导演技巧

'BRABANTIO [*appears*] *above at a window*' (in pairs)

Below is a photograph of Shakespeare's Globe (莎士比亚环球剧场) in London, which was built towards the end of the twentieth century as a replica (复制品) of the theatre in which Shakespeare's company worked in Elizabethan and Jacobean times (伊丽莎白一世和詹姆斯一世时代). Notice that the theatre has a deep 'thrust' stage (凸出舞台), with two exits at the back and a balcony above.

- Talk together about how you would stage lines 68–93, first on the stage of Shakespeare's Globe and then in a modern acting space (for example, in a drama studio). Think about the use of lighting and consider any props (道具) that seem appropriate.
- As an extension to this activity, talk together about what you think might be the main challenges of directing a play on the stage at Shakespeare's Globe.

1 **owe** = own
2 **incense** 激怒
3 **though that** = though
4 **vexation** 苦恼，麻烦
5 **timorous** 可怕
6 **dire** 恐怖
7 **Signior** 先生（意大利语）
8 **wherefore** = why
9 **Zounds** = By Christ's wounds（"该死"，骂人话，字面意思是"以基督的伤口发誓"）
10 **tupping** 交配
11 **snorting** = snoring（打呼噜）
12 **devil** 魔鬼（古时的宗教绘画中，魔鬼通常是黑色的，这里暗指奥赛罗）
13 **grandsire** = grandfather

RODERIGO	What a full fortune does the thick-lips owe[1],
	If he can carry it thus!
IAGO	Call up her father:
	Rouse him, make after him, poison his delight,
	Proclaim him in the street, incense[2] her kinsmen,
	And though he in a fertile climate dwell,
	Plague him with flies: though that[3] his joy be joy,
	Yet throw such chances of vexation[4] on't
	As it may lose some colour.
RODERIGO	Here is her father's house; I'll call aloud.
IAGO	Do, with like timorous[5] accent and dire[6] yell,
	As when, by night and negligence, the fire
	Is spied in populous cities.
RODERIGO	What ho, Brabantio! Signior[7] Brabantio, ho!
IAGO	Awake! What ho, Brabantio! Thieves, thieves!
	Look to your house, your daughter, and your bags!
	Thieves, thieves!

BRABANTIO [*appears*] *above at a window.*

BRABANTIO	What is the reason of this terrible summons?
	What is the matter there?
RODERIGO	Signior, is all your family within?
IAGO	Are your doors locked?
BRABANTIO	Why, wherefore[8] ask you this?
IAGO	Zounds[9], sir, you're robbed; for shame, put on your gown;
	Your heart is burst; you have lost half your soul;
	Even now, now, very now, an old black ram
	Is tupping[10] your white ewe. Arise, arise;
	Awake the snorting[11] citizens with the bell,
	Or else the devil[12] will make a grandsire[13] of you.
	Arise, I say!

Brabantio suspects that the two men are drunk. He learns Roderigo's name, but not Iago's. Iago tells Brabantio that Desdemona and Othello are having sexual intercourse and that his descendants will be mere animals.

剧情简介: 布拉班修怀疑这两个人喝醉了。他问了若德瑞苟的名字，但没问伊阿苟。伊阿苟告诉布拉班修，黛丝荻牟娜和奥赛罗正在发生关系，布拉班修的后人将因此沦为动物。

Language in the play 剧中语言

Verse and prose (韵文和散文) (in pairs)

Brabantio and Roderigo speak in **blank verse** (无韵诗；素体诗) (a poetic style of writing that does not rhyme). Each line usually has five main beats (节拍) or stresses. But when Iago interjects (插话) at line 109, the script switches to prose. Read the information about verse and prose in 'The language of *Othello*' on page 230, then suggest why Shakespeare has Iago speak in prose here. Consider:

- the different social status of the three characters
- what each of the men is saying
- the context of the scene as a whole.

1 Freeze the action (in threes)

There are three men on stage when Brabantio asks the question 'What profane wretch art thou?'

- Decide where each man is positioned at this point. Who is visible to whom? Then create a tableau (定格；活人画) (a freeze-frame) of this moment. Think carefully about facial expressions and ways of standing/crouching. Other groups should try to guess who is who in your frozen picture.

2 Who is Roderigo?

When Roderigo introduces himself (line 96), Brabantio is not pleased to see him ('The worser welcome' [更不欢迎]). He reminds Roderigo that on a previous occasion he ordered him to stay away from his house and his daughter (lines 97–9).

- What might have happened in the past to cause this reaction from Brabantio? Carefully read lines 96–105 and prepare a short improvised drama in modern English, depicting the incident that led to Roderigo being banned from the house.

▶ What gestures might Brabantio use to express his displeasure?

1 reverend 尊贵
2 charged 命令
3 distempering draughts 扰乱心智的狂饮（指喝醉酒）
4 malicious bravery 耍酒疯
5 start 惊扰
6 My spirit and my place 我的脾气和地位
7 grange 农舍，田庄
8 ruffians 无赖，流氓
9 Barbary horse 巴巴利马（北非巴巴利海岸地区产的一种名马）
10 nephews 外孙（下一行的 cousins 同义）
11 coursers 赛马
12 jennets 吉耐马（一种西班牙矮马，巴巴利马的一个变种）
13 germans 本家，亲戚
14 profane wretch 满嘴脏话的家伙
15 making ... backs 交配

BRABANTIO	What, have you lost your wits?	
RODERIGO	Most reverend[1] signior, do you know my voice?	
BRABANTIO	Not I; what are you?	95
RODERIGO	My name is Roderigo.	
BRABANTIO	The worser welcome;	

BRABANTIO   The worser welcome;
I have charged[2] thee not to haunt about my doors;
In honest plainness thou hast heard me say
My daughter is not for thee. And now in madness,
Being full of supper and distempering draughts[3],   100
Upon malicious bravery[4] dost thou come
To start[5] my quiet.

RODERIGO   Sir, sir, sir –

BRABANTIO   But thou must needs be sure
My spirit and my place[6] have in them power
To make this bitter to thee.

RODERIGO   Patience, good sir.   105

BRABANTIO   What tell'st thou me of robbing? This is Venice;
My house is not a grange[7].

RODERIGO   Most grave Brabantio,
In simple and pure soul I come to you.

IAGO   Zounds, sir; you are one of those that will not serve God if the
devil bid you. Because we come to do you service and you think   110
we are ruffians[8], you'll have your daughter covered with a Barbary
horse[9], you'll have your nephews[10] neigh to you, you'll have
coursers[11] for cousins, and jennets[12] for germans[13].

BRABANTIO   What profane wretch[14] art thou?

IAGO   I am one, sir, that comes to tell you your daughter and the Moor   115
are now making the beast with two backs[15].

BRABANTIO   Thou art a villain.

IAGO   You are a senator.

Roderigo tells Brabantio that Desdemona has run away to live with Othello. Brabantio leaves to check if the story is true, saying he has already dreamt of such a thing happening.

剧情简介：若德瑞苟告诉布拉班修，黛丝荻牟娜已私奔到奥赛罗的住处。布拉班修动身去核实这一说法，口中说道他已经梦见发生这样一件事了。

1 'a gross revolt' (in small groups)

Roderigo tells Brabantio that Desdemona has run away from home to get married without her father's permission. Several of Shakespeare's plays include young people rebelling against their parents' wishes (most famously *Romeo and Juliet*). Generally speaking, in the comedies they are eventually forgiven, while in the tragedies the situation ends in disaster.

- Talk together about stories you have read, and movies or television shows you have seen, that include a similar plot element. How is the family split resolved in those storylines?

2 The chain of being (by yourself)

In medieval England, people believed that God assigned all humans a specific place in society. This meant that people had to accept whatever social status they were born into; it also meant that young people were expected to obey their parents without question. By Shakespeare's time, however, this belief was being challenged.

- Carry out some research of your own into this 'chain of being'. Write some notes about the way in which an Elizabethan audience might view Desdemona's decision to run away and marry without her father's knowledge. How might those views differ from modern perspectives on the issue?

Language in the play 剧中语言
Roderigo's references (in pairs)

In lines 119–39, Roderigo refers to Desdemona in positive terms ('fair'), whereas he uses derogatory (贬义) language to speak about Othello ('gross clasps', line 125).

a List all the words or phrases Roderigo uses in the script opposite to refer to Desdemona and Othello. Write down what these words and phrases mean.

b We have not yet met Desdemona or Othello. Talk together about the way the audience's expectations are being shaped at this point. Record your ideas and then review them when you reach the end of Act 1.

1 answer = answer for（说清楚；为……负责）
2 beseech 恳请，恳求
3 odd-even 刚过午夜
4 dull watch 深更半夜
5 gondolier 贡多拉船夫（贡多拉 [gondola] 即威尼斯小划船）
6 gross clasps 恶心的拥抱
7 lascivious 淫荡
8 saucy 无礼，鲁莽
9 trifle with your reverence 戏弄您老人家
10 extravagant and wheeling stranger 四处流浪、居无定所的外乡人
11 Straight = Immediately（立即，马上）
12 Let loose on me 控告我
13 Strike on the tinder 打燃火绒（旧时的取火工具）
14 taper 蜡烛
15 meet 合适
16 wholesome 有好处
17 gall 惹恼，烦扰
18 check 责难
19 cast 开除，免职
20 embarked 奉命
21 With such loud reason 带着（元老院）如此高调的支持

BRABANTIO	This thou shalt answer[1]; I know thee, Roderigo.	
RODERIGO	Sir, I will answer anything. But I beseech[2] you	
	If't be your pleasure and most wise consent	120
	(As partly I find it is) that your fair daughter,	
	At this odd-even[3] and dull watch[4] o'the night,	
	Transported with no worse nor better guard,	
	But with a knave of common hire, a gondolier[5],	
	To the gross clasps[6] of a lascivious[7] Moor:	125
	If this be known to you, and your allowance,	
	We then have done you bold and saucy[8] wrongs.	
	But if you know not this, my manners tell me,	
	We have your wrong rebuke. Do not believe	
	That from the sense of all civility	130
	I thus would play and trifle with your reverence[9].	
	Your daughter, if you have not given her leave,	
	I say again, hath made a gross revolt,	
	Tying her duty, beauty, wit, and fortunes	
	In an extravagant and wheeling stranger[10]	135
	Of here and everywhere. Straight[11] satisfy yourself.	
	If she be in her chamber or your house,	
	Let loose on me[12] the justice of the state	
	For thus deluding you.	
BRABANTIO	Strike on the tinder[13], ho!	
	Give me a taper[14]; call up all my people.	140
	This accident is not unlike my dream;	
	Belief of it oppresses me already.	
	Light, I say, light! *Exit*	
IAGO	Farewell, for I must leave you.	
	It seems not meet[15] nor wholesome[16] to my place	
	To be produced, as if I stay I shall,	145
	Against the Moor. For I do know the state,	
	However this may gall[17] him with some check[18],	
	Cannot with safety cast[19] him; for he's embarked[20]	
	With such loud reason[21] to the Cyprus wars,	

Iago slips away, not wishing to be identified as a trouble-maker. Brabantio discovers his daughter is indeed missing. He goes off with Roderigo to seek assistance from neighbours and the police.

剧情简介：伊阿苟溜走，因为他不想被视为搬弄是非的人。布拉班修发现女儿真的不在，便和若德瑞苟一起去寻求邻居和巡夜的帮助。

Characters 人物分析

'the Moor' (in small groups)

Throughout the whole of this first scene no one has used Othello's name, although all three men have referred to him several times.

a Collect all the terms used to describe Othello in Scene 1. Copy the table below and add to it to record your findings. Decide what aspect of Othello is being highlighted in each instance – is it a complimentary (称赞的) term or an insulting one? In each case, note down what these descriptive terms tell you about the speaker.

Term used	Aspect of Othello	Spoken by?	What does it say about the speaker?
'the Moor' (line 40)	His ethnicity or 'race'	Iago	He's trying to take away Othello's individuality.
'the thick-lips' (line 67)	His physical features (stereotype [刻板印象])		He is being racist and purposely insulting.
'stranger' (line 135)	He was not born in Venice	Roderigo	

b When you have completed your table, compare your ideas with those of other groups.

1 stands in act 还在进行
2 fathom 本事，能力
3 life 生计，饭碗
4 show … love 打着尊崇上级的旗号和招牌
5 Sagittary 人马旅店
   (Sagittarius是希腊神话里一个暴躁、淫荡的怪物，人首马身，手持弓箭，人们常将其与性欲联系起来)
6 raisèd search 唤醒的搜查队
   (raisèd = roused)
7 despisèd time 荣誉扫地的余生
8 Past thought! 难以置信！
9 charms 魔咒；春药
10 property 性质，本性
11 apprehend 逮捕
12 discover him 找到他
13 deserve your pains 答谢您这番辛劳

Write about it 写作练习

Describing Othello

- Using the information you gathered for the activity above, write a paragraph analysing the language by which Othello has been introduced during Scene 1.
- Write a second paragraph, suggesting why a dramatist might want to delay the entrance of the main character until the audience has heard a significant amount about him from other characters in the play.

Which even now stands in act[1], that, for their souls, 150
Another of his fathom[2] they have none
To lead their business; in which regard,
Though I do hate him as I do hell's pains,
Yet, for necessity of present life[3],
I must show out a flag and sign of love[4], 155
Which is indeed but sign. That you shall surely find him,
Lead to the Sagittary[5] the raisèd search[6],
And there will I be with him. So farewell. *Exit*

Enter Brabantio in his nightgown, and SERVANTS *with torches.*

BRABANTIO   It is too true an evil. Gone she is,
And what's to come of my despisèd time[7] 160
Is nought but bitterness. Now Roderigo,
Where didst thou see her? O unhappy girl!
With the Moor, say'st thou? Who would be a father?
How didst thou know 'twas she? O she deceives me
Past thought![8] What said she to you? Get more tapers, 165
Raise all my kindred. Are they married, think you?

RODERIGO   Truly I think they are.

BRABANTIO   O heaven! How got she out? O treason of the blood!
Fathers, from hence trust not your daughters' minds
By what you see them act. Is there not charms[9] 170
By which the property[10] of youth and maidhood
May be abused? Have you not read, Roderigo,
Of some such thing?

RODERIGO   Yes, sir, I have indeed.

BRABANTIO   Call up my brother. O that you had had her!
Some one way, some another. Do you know 175
Where we may apprehend[11] her and the Moor?

RODERIGO   I think I can discover him[12], if you please
To get good guard and go along with me.

BRABANTIO   Pray you lead on. At every house I'll call;
I may command at most. Get weapons, ho! 180
And raise some special officers of night:
On, good Roderigo; I'll deserve your pains[13].

Exeunt

Iago, pretending to be Othello's faithful supporter, warns Othello that Brabantio will attempt to break up the marriage. Othello is confident that his service to Venice and his noble descent will make all well.

剧情简介：伊阿苟假装成奥赛罗的忠实支持者，警告他布拉班修将设法拆散他的婚姻。奥赛罗自信他为威尼斯立下的功劳及其高贵血统能摆平一切。

1 Iago's version (in pairs)

In lines 6–10, Iago tells of the conversation he had with Roderigo.

- Talk together about how this version compares with what was actually said in the previous scene. You could draw up two columns on a sheet of paper. In the first column, write down the key items of information given here by Iago; in the second column record how it was presented in Scene 1.

Write about it 写作练习

Opinions of Othello (by yourself)

We have heard a lot about Othello from other characters. Now we meet him for the first time, in the second scene of the play.

- Look closely at Othello's lines 17–28. Think about what he says and the way he says it. Does your impression of Othello differ now from the opinion you had formed based on the words of Iago, Roderigo and Brabantio in Scene 1? Write a paragraph analysing the language of Othello's first full speech in the play, and explaining what it suggests to you as a viewer or reader.

Stagecraft 导演技巧

'Enter OTHELLO' (in small groups)

a If you were directing a production of the play, what effect would you want to create with Othello's entrance? In Trevor Nunn's 1990 Royal Shakespeare Company (RSC) production, the imposing figure (仪表堂堂的形象) of Othello (played by opera singer Willard White) was framed in a doorway illuminated by brilliant light. He was dressed in smart military uniform. In Janet Suzman's 1987 Market Theatre of Johannesburg production, the physically slight figure (瘦小的身材) of John Kani (playing Othello) was leaning against a wall, dressed in a flowing white shirt and brushing a rose against his lips. What impression do you think each of these directors was trying to make?

b Create a tableau of the stage direction 'Enter OTHELLO, IAGO and ATTENDANTS with torches'. Compare your ideas with other groups and talk about the effects of each tableau.

1	stuff	本质
2	contrived	蓄意
3	I … service	有时我不够心狠，于事无益
4	yerked	猛刺
5	prated	胡扯，吹牛
6	scurvy	卑鄙
7	fast	牢牢，坚定
8	magnifico	大官，显贵
9	in … potential	利用自己强大的影响力
10	grievance	不满
11	give him cable	让他为所欲为
12	spite	怨恨
13	signiory	（威尼斯）大议会
14	provulgate = promulgate	（宣扬）
15	royal siege	王族地位
16	demerits	功绩
17	unbonneted	有礼貌（bonnet 的意思是"帽子"，unbonneted 的字面意思是"脱帽"）
18	unhousèd	无家室拖累
19	circumscription and confine	限制和拘束
20	For the sea's worth	即使给我所有的海底宝藏
21	yond	那边

Act 1 Scene 2
Venice   Outside the Sagittary

Enter OTHELLO, IAGO *and* ATTENDANTS *with torches.*

IAGO	Though in the trade of war I have slain men,	
	Yet do I hold it very stuff[1] o'the conscience	
	To do no contrived[2] murder. I lack iniquity	
	Sometimes to do me service[3]. Nine or ten times	
	I had thought to have yerked[4] him here, under the ribs.	5
OTHELLO	'Tis better as it is.	
IAGO	Nay, but he prated[5],	
	And spoke such scurvy[6] and provoking terms	
	Against your honour,	
	That, with the little godliness I have,	
	I did full hard forbear him. But I pray, sir,	10
	Are you fast[7] married? For be sure of this,	
	That the magnifico[8] is much beloved,	
	And hath in his effect a voice potential[9]	
	As double as the duke's. He will divorce you,	
	Or put upon you what restraint and grievance[10]	15
	The law, with all his might to enforce it on,	
	Will give him cable[11].	
OTHELLO	Let him do his spite[12];	
	My services which I have done the signiory[13]	
	Shall out-tongue his complaints. 'Tis yet to know –	
	Which, when I know that boasting is an honour,	20
	I shall provulgate[14] – I fetch my life and being	
	From men of royal siege[15], and my demerits[16]	
	May speak unbonneted[17] to as proud a fortune	
	As this that I have reached. For know, Iago,	
	But that I love the gentle Desdemona,	25
	I would not my unhousèd[18] free condition	
	Put into circumscription and confine[19]	
	For the sea's worth[20]. But look what lights come yond[21]!	

Cassio arrives on an urgent mission from the Duke to find Othello. He reports that war is imminent and the Senate urgently needs Othello. Iago tells Cassio of Othello's marriage.

剧情简介：卡修奉公爵急令寻找奥赛罗，向他报告战争在即，元老院紧急召见他。伊阿苟告知卡修奥赛罗的婚事。

Themes 主题分析

Appearance and reality: two-faced Janus (in pairs)

Why is it significant that Iago swears 'By Janus'?

- Stand back to back. One partner reads Iago's words in lines 1–53 aloud, pausing at the end of each sentence. The other partner speaks in each pause, saying what Iago's real thoughts might be.

1 Greetings (in large groups)

Two separate search parties come looking for Othello in lines 34–61 – one on official war business, the other pursuing a personal grievance.

- Work out how each search party might enter and how they would greet Othello and Iago. Freeze each scene at the moment of greeting, making it clear from the way the characters are looking or standing who they are and what their intentions are. Perform your tableaux for the rest of the class to guess who is who.

1. raisèd = roused (吵醒；义愤)
2. parts 天赋
3. manifest me rightly 为我证明
4. Janus 雅努（罗马神话中的门神，一头二脸，前脸面朝秋冬，后脸面朝春夏，被用来命名January）
5. haste-post-haste 火速
6. divine 卜算，猜
7. heat 紧急
8. galleys 战船，战舰
9. sequent 接连不断
10. consuls 执政官
11. Faith 说实话
12. boarded a land carrack 海盗般登上一艘宝船（boarded暗示奥赛罗的性行为）
13. lawful prize 合法战利品
14. Marry – By (the Virgin) Mary （向圣母马利亚发誓）

▼ Can you work out who is who in this image?

IAGO	Those are the raisèd[1] father and his friends;
	You were best go in.
OTHELLO	Not I; I must be found.
	My parts[2], my title, and my perfect soul
	Shall manifest me rightly[3]. Is it they?
IAGO	By Janus[4], I think no.

Enter CASSIO, *with* OFFICERS *and torches.*

OTHELLO	The servants of the duke and my lieutenant!
	The goodness of the night upon you, friends.
	What is the news?
CASSIO	The duke does greet you, general,
	And he requires your haste-post-haste[5] appearance
	Even on the instant.
OTHELLO	What is the matter, think you?
CASSIO	Something from Cyprus, as I may divine[6].
	It is a business of some heat[7]. The galleys[8]
	Have sent a dozen sequent[9] messengers
	This very night at one another's heels;
	And many of the consuls[10], raised and met,
	Are at the duke's already. You have been hotly called for,
	When, being not at your lodging to be found,
	The senate hath sent about three several quests
	To search you out.
OTHELLO	'Tis well I am found by you.
	I will but spend a word here in the house,
	And go with you. [*Exit*]
CASSIO	Ancient, what makes he here?
IAGO	Faith[11], he tonight hath boarded a land carrack[12];
	If it prove lawful prize[13], he's made for ever.
CASSIO	I do not understand.
IAGO	He's married.
CASSIO	To who?

[*Enter Othello.*]

IAGO	Marry[14], to – Come, captain, will you go?
OTHELLO	Have with you.
CASSIO	Here comes another troop to seek for you.

Stagecraft 导演技巧

Direct Othello and Brabantio (in pairs)

a If you were directing a production of *Othello*, what advice would you give to the two actors playing Othello and Brabantio at line 57 ('Down with him, thief!') and lines 59–61 (from 'Keep up your bright swords')? Experiment with ways of saying the lines. For example, should Othello sound:
- defensive
- angry and frustrated
- calm
- authoritative and in control
- scared?

Show your version to the rest of the class, then explain how you reached your decisions.

b Look at the production photographs below and on page 16. How do these productions differ in their visual presentation of Othello? Are either of them how you imagine Othello to look? If not, why not? Can you suggest another way to present Othello (perhaps think of a particular actor who might suit the part)?

1 be advised   要小心
2 Keep up   收起
3 refer ... sense   根据一切常理判断
4 curlèd darlings   烫发俊小伙
5 guardage = guardianship （监护，家人的保护）
6 sooty   乌黑
7 gross in sense   显而易见
8 disputed on   对簿公堂
9 palpable   显然
10 abuser of the world   危害社会者
11 arts ... warrant   违法的妖术
12 Subdue him at his peril   制服他，让他后果自负
13 of my inclining   站在我这边的
14 my cue to fight   我动手的信号（cue原指演出中的提示，如台词、演员上下场、灯光和音响效果等）
15 prompter   提示者
16 session   庭审

Enter BRABANTIO, RODERIGO *and* OFFICERS *with lights and weapons.*

IAGO	It is Brabantio; general, be advised[1],	55
	He comes to bad intent.	
OTHELLO	Holla, stand there!	
RODERIGO	Signior, it is the Moor.	
BRABANTIO	Down with him, thief!	
IAGO	You, Roderigo? Come, sir, I am for you.	
OTHELLO	Keep up[2] your bright swords, for the dew will rust them.	
	Good signior, you shall more command with years	60
	Than with your weapons.	
BRABANTIO	O thou foul thief! Where hast thou stowed my daughter?	
	Damned as thou art, thou hast enchanted her,	
	For I'll refer me to all things of sense[3],	
	If she in chains of magic were not bound,	65
	Whether a maid so tender, fair, and happy,	
	So opposite to marriage that she shunned	
	The wealthy curlèd darlings[4] of our nation,	
	Would ever have, t'incur a general mock,	
	Run from her guardage[5] to the sooty[6] bosom	70
	Of such a thing as thou – to fear, not to delight.	
	Judge me the world, if 'tis not gross in sense[7]	
	That thou hast practised on her with foul charms,	
	Abused her delicate youth with drugs or minerals	
	That weakens motion. I'll have't disputed on[8];	75
	'Tis probable and palpable[9] to thinking.	
	I therefore apprehend and do attach thee	
	For an abuser of the world[10], a practiser	
	Of arts inhibited and out of warrant[11].	
	Lay hold upon him. If he do resist,	80
	Subdue him at his peril[12].	
OTHELLO	Hold your hands,	
	Both you of my inclining[13] and the rest.	
	Were it my cue to fight[14], I should have known it	
	Without a prompter[15]. Where will you that I go	
	To answer this your charge?	
BRABANTIO	To prison, till fit time	85
	Of law and course of direct session[16]	
	Call thee to answer.	

Brabantio is certain that the Duke will decide in his favour. In the next scene, the Duke and Venetian senators are considering news of the Turkish threats of war on Cyprus, a Venetian colony.

剧情简介：布拉班修坚信公爵会为他做主。下一场中，公爵和威尼斯众元老商议如何应对土耳其对塞浦路斯的战争威胁；塞浦路斯是威尼斯的殖民地。

1 Setting Scene 3 – the Council Chamber

Scene 3 marks a change from private – even secret – matters to public affairs of state.

- If you were directing this scene on stage, what kind of room would you have it take place in? Consider how you would show the change of location from the previous street scene, using a bare minimum of props or sound effects. Remember that in most modern productions, scene-changing is very swift and one scene flows quickly into the next. You could sketch out a stage set and add printed images found on an Internet search.

▼ A contemporary illustration of the Duke of Venice.

1 present 紧急
2 idle 无关紧要，微不足道
3 brothers of the state 邦国的兄弟们（指同僚元老）
4 Bondslaves and pagans 契约奴隶和异教徒
5 composition 一致
6 credit 信誉
7 disproportioned 不对应，不一致
8 jump … accompt 数目对不上
9 aim 估计，揣测
10 oft = often
11 bearing up to 驶向

OTHELLO	What if I do obey?
	How may the duke be therewith satisfied,
	Whose messengers are here about my side
	Upon some present¹ business of the state 90
	To bring me to him?
OFFICER	'Tis true, most worthy signior;
	The duke's in council, and your noble self
	I am sure is sent for.
BRABANTIO	How? The duke in council?
	In this time of the night? Bring him away;
	Mine's not an idle² cause. The duke himself, 95
	Or any of my brothers of the state³,
	Cannot but feel this wrong as 'twere their own;
	For if such actions may have passage free,
	Bondslaves and pagans⁴ shall our statesmen be.

Exeunt

Act 1 Scene 3
Venice   The Council Chamber

Enter DUKE *and* SENATORS, *set at a table with lights, and* ATTENDANTS.

DUKE	There is no composition⁵ in these news
	That gives them credit⁶.
1 SENATOR	Indeed they are disproportioned⁷.
	My letters say a hundred and seven galleys.
DUKE	And mine, a hundred and forty.
2 SENATOR	And mine, two hundred;
	But though they jump not on a just accompt⁸ – 5
	As in these cases where the aim⁹ reports
	'Tis oft¹⁰ with difference – yet do they all confirm
	A Turkish fleet, and bearing up to¹¹ Cyprus.

Amid uncertainty about the size of the Turkish fleet, a sailor brings news that it is now sailing towards Rhodes. However, a senator and the Duke agree that the Turks intend to attack Cyprus.

剧情简介：大家不确定土耳其舰队的规模，此时一名水手带来消息说，舰队正驶向罗德岛。但一位元老和公爵一致认为，土耳其人意在进攻塞浦路斯。

1 The Mediterranean – the commercial empire of Venice

In the sixteenth century, Venice was a thriving commercial centre. It was also the dominant colonial force in the Mediterranean. Powerful merchants protected their commercial empire with military strength, including mercenary forces (雇佣军). Cyprus was particularly valued as a colony because it was a profitable source of sugar and cotton.

- Read the script opposite, using the map below – which shows the extent of the Ottoman (Turkish) Empire (奥斯曼帝国) – to help your understanding of the reports of the Turkish invasion plans in lines 14–46.

1. secure me 让我放心
2. main article （众多报告中的）主要一点
3. approve / In fearful sense 忧心忡忡地赞同
4. preparation 舰队
5. assay 判断
6. pageant 虚张声势
7. keep us in false gaze 干扰我们的注意力
8. importancy = importance
9. with … it 更容易攻下它（指塞浦路斯）
10. warlike brace 战备
11. wake and wage 振作起来冒险
12. in all confidence 可以确信

Write about it 写作练习

Declaration of war

Read up to line 49. The Duke and Senators conclude that the Turkish fleet is heading for Cyprus and give orders for Othello to lead the Venetian counter-attack.

- Write the formal statement published by the Duke's press office. Briefly explain the case for war against the Turks, and outline the strategic decisions made by the Senate.

OTHELLO ACT 1 SCENE 3
奥赛罗

DUKE   Nay, it is possible enough to judgement:
        I do not so secure me[1] in the error,   10
        But the main article[2] I do approve
        In fearful sense[3].
SAILOR (*Within*)   What ho! What ho! What ho!
OFFICER A messenger from the galleys.

                        Enter a SAILOR.

DUKE   Now, what's the business?
SAILOR The Turkish preparation[4] makes for Rhodes;
        So was I bid report here to the state   15
        By Signior Angelo.
DUKE   How say you by this change?
1 SENATOR   This cannot be,
        By no assay[5] of reason. 'Tis a pageant[6]
        To keep us in false gaze[7]. When we consider
        The importancy[8] of Cyprus to the Turk,   20
        And let ourselves again but understand
        That as it more concerns the Turk than Rhodes,
        So may he with more facile question bear it[9],
        For that it stands not in such warlike brace[10],
        But altogether lacks the abilities   25
        That Rhodes is dressed in. If we make thought of this,
        We must not think the Turk is so unskilful
        To leave that latest which concerns him first,
        Neglecting an attempt of ease and gain
        To wake and wage[11] a danger profitless.   30
DUKE   Nay, in all confidence[12] he's not for Rhodes.
OFFICER Here is more news.

23

A messenger from Montano, the governor of Cyprus, brings more news: the Turkish fleet, reinforced, sails towards Cyprus. Discussion of war tactics is interrupted by Brabantio's and Othello's arrival.

 剧情简介：塞浦路斯总督芒塔诺派来的信差带来更多消息：土耳其舰队得到增援，正驶向塞浦路斯。布拉班修和奥赛罗的到来打断了战术讨论会。

1 What is the Turkish fleet doing? (in pairs)

Read the messenger's words at lines 33–42 and the Duke's response at line 43. Look back at the map on page 22 and see if you can work out the Turkish war strategy. Remind yourself why Cyprus was important to both the Venetians and to the Turks.

2 Valiant Othello – the statue! (in pairs)

It has long been common practice to erect statues to commemorate military leaders who have performed 'great' deeds.

- One person becomes the sculptor, the other the 'raw material'. Create your own statue to commemorate 'Valiant Othello'. Then pose your partner into a second sculpture with the title 'foul thief' (Brabantio uses these words to greet Othello in Scene 2, line 62). How different are your two sculptures based on these descriptions?

3 Public affairs and private anxiety (in small groups)

Brabantio wants to make a formal complaint about Othello to the Duke of Venice and the Venetian Senate. Unfortunately, he raises his complaint just at the moment when the Senate is dealing with urgent matters of state. In lines 52–8, Brabantio tries to convey the extent of his grief, and ends up using the **imagery** of a flood-gate to do it (see p. 231).

- Discuss how appropriate you think it is for Brabantio to take his complaint to the Senate at this moment. If you were the Duke or a Senator, would you consider this to be a public or a personal matter?

1 **Ottomites** 奥斯曼人（即土耳其人）
2 **reverend and gracious** 尊敬的诸位元老
3 **injointed** 联合，会合
4 **restem / Their backward course** 掉转航向驶回
5 **servitor** = servant（这里是塞浦路斯总督自称）
6 **free duty** 效忠
7 **recommends** 禀告
8 **general enemy** 公敌（奥斯曼人反基督教）
9 **aught** = anything
10 **engluts** 吞噬，吞没

▼ Is Brabantio being selfish in demanding the attention of the Senate for this personal issue during a time of war?

OTHELLO ACT 1 SCENE 3

奥赛罗

Enter a MESSENGER.

MESSENGER	The Ottomites[1], reverend and gracious[2],	
	Steering with due course toward the isle of Rhodes	
	Have there injointed[3] with an after fleet.	35
1 SENATOR	Ay, so I thought. How many, as you guess?	
MESSENGER	Of thirty sail, and now they do restem	
	Their backward course[4], bearing with frank appearance	
	Their purposes toward Cyprus. Signior Montano,	
	Your trusty and most valiant servitor[5],	40
	With his free duty[6] recommends[7] you thus,	
	And prays you to believe him.	
DUKE	'Tis certain then for Cyprus.	
	Marcus Luccicos, is not he in town?	
1 SENATOR	He's now in Florence.	
DUKE	Write from us to him	45
	Post-post-haste dispatch.	
1 SENATOR	Here comes Brabantio and the valiant Moor.	

Enter BRABANTIO, OTHELLO, CASSIO, IAGO, RODERIGO *and*
OFFICERS.

DUKE	Valiant Othello we must straight employ you	
	Against the general enemy[8] Ottoman.	
	[*To Brabantio*] I did not see you: welcome, gentle signior;	50
	We lacked your counsel and your help tonight.	
BRABANTIO	So did I yours. Good your grace, pardon me:	
	Neither my place nor aught[9] I heard of business	
	Hath raised me from my bed, nor doth the general care	
	Take hold on me; for my particular grief	55
	Is of so flood-gate and o'erbearing nature	
	That it engluts[10] and swallows other sorrows	
	And yet is still itself.	

Brabantio publicly accuses Othello of abducting and seducing his daughter. Othello offers to explain what has really happened.

剧情简介：布拉班修公开指控奥赛罗劫持并诱奸了他女儿。奥赛罗主动解释事情的实际情况。

Write about it 写作练习
Brabantio's story

Legends and stories play an important part in *Othello*. Here, in lines 59–64, Brabantio composes his own version of his daughter's flight. In the form of a sinister-feeling (令人有不祥之感的) myth, write at least three paragraphs telling the story of:

- how Desdemona was charmed
- how she was stolen
- how she was 'abused'.

Language in the play 剧中语言
'Rude am I in my speech' (in groups of four to six)

a Read through Othello's speech in lines 76–94, with each person handing over to the next at a punctuation mark.

b Go through the speech again, this time reading round the group in different styles or moods. Experiment with the sound of the speech until you can agree on the style that best fits the words.

c Talk together about whether you think Othello is 'rude' (clumsy) in his speech. Find examples of his language to support your views, considering terms of address, vocabulary, style and tone. (As you read on, look particularly at Othello's speech from line 127 onwards, and think about how it contrasts with Iago's construction of Othello.)

1 'Here is the man' (in sevens)

At one precise moment (line 71), there are at least seven characters on the stage.

- Work out who they all are and discuss how each might react to the events that are unfolding.
- Present this moment as a tableau to the rest of the class and have them guess who is who.
- Once everyone has been correctly identified, class members can ask certain characters to step forward out of the tableau to reveal what their thoughts are at that moment.

---

1 **of mountebanks** 从江湖骗子那里
2 **so preposterously to err** 犯下如此荒谬的过错
3 **deficient** 头脑简单
4 **Sans** 没有，若非
5 **beguiled your daughter of herself** 迷惑了您的女儿（让她无法自拔）
6 **bloody book of law** 含有死刑的法典
7 **After your own sense** 随您意愿
8 **our proper son** 亲生儿子
9 **mandate** 命令，指令
10 **hither** = here
11 **potent** 有权势
12 **tane** = taken
13 **head and front** 最大程度
14 **pith** 力量，力气
15 **nine moons wasted** 9个月以前
16 **tented field** 军营，战场
17 **broil and battle** 战乱和打仗
18 **grace** 美化
19 **conjuration** 魔咒
20 **withal** = with

DUKE	Why, what's the matter?	
BRABANTIO	My daughter! O, my daughter!	
SENATORS	Dead?	
BRABANTIO	Ay, to me.	

        She is abused, stol'n from me, and corrupted   60
        By spells and medicines bought of mountebanks[1];
        For nature so preposterously to err[2],
        Being not deficient[3], blind, or lame of sense,
        Sans[4] witchcraft could not.

DUKE   Whoe'er he be that in this foul proceeding   65
        Hath thus beguiled your daughter of herself[5],
        And you of her, the bloody book of law[6]
        You shall yourself read in the bitter letter
        After your own sense[7], yea, though our proper son[8]
        Stood in your action.

BRABANTIO   Humbly I thank your grace.   70
        Here is the man: this Moor, whom now it seems
        Your special mandate[9] for the state affairs
        Hath hither[10] brought.

ALL   We are very sorry for't.

DUKE   [*To Othello*] What in your own part can you say to this?

BRABANTIO   Nothing, but this is so.   75

OTHELLO   Most potent[11], grave, and reverend signiors,
        My very noble and approved good masters,
        That I have tane[12] away this old man's daughter,
        It is most true; true I have married her;
        The very head and front[13] of my offending   80
        Hath this extent, no more. Rude am I in my speech
        And little blessed with the soft phrase of peace,
        For since these arms of mine had seven years' pith[14]
        Till now some nine moons wasted[15], they have used
        Their dearest action in the tented field[16];   85
        And little of this great world can I speak
        More than pertains to feats of broil and battle[17];
        And therefore little shall I grace[18] my cause
        In speaking for myself. Yet, by your gracious patience,
        I will a round unvarnished tale deliver   90
        Of my whole course of love: what drugs, what charms,
        What conjuration[19] and what mighty magic –
        For such proceedings I am charged withal[20] –
        I won his daughter.

Brabantio again accuses Othello of drugging his daughter. The Duke asks for proof. Othello suggests that Desdemona is sent for to give her side of the story. Iago goes to fetch her.

 剧情简介：布拉班修再次指控奥赛罗给他女儿下了迷魂药，公爵要求提供证据。奥赛罗提议派人将黛丝荻牟娜请来，让大家听听她怎么说。伊阿苟前去请她。

1 Perfection in a woman?

a According to Brabantio, his daughter is a perfect mixture of womanly virtues. Read his lines 94–8 and note down the aspects he seems to admire in a woman.

b Carry out some research into the position of women in Shakespeare's day. How are the views in Brabantio's speech consistent with or different from the common views of the time?

c Write a paragraph giving your own opinion of Brabantio's views. Make sure you refer explicitly to his words in your writing, and use embedded quotations.

2 'Against all rules of nature' (in small groups)

a Discuss whether you think that today's society is more tolerant of so-called 'mixed-race' marriages. What do you think your family's reaction would be if you were in a similar situation? Think of any countries where other circumstances (for example, politics or religion) might make certain relationships illicit (违法). Compare your views with other groups in your class.

b As your study of *Othello* progresses, look out for items of news (local, national or international) that involve 'mixed-race' relationships. Consider how the matter is reported. For example, commentators famously made reference to *Othello* during the 1995 trial of O.J. Simpson, an African-American sports star accused of murdering his white wife.

3 The case against Othello (in pairs)

With all the talk of criminal acts and sentencing in the script opposite, it is almost as if Othello is on trial. What exactly is the case against him?

a Take a large sheet of paper and draw two columns, headed 'Accusations' and 'Defence'. In the first column, list all the accusations Brabantio makes against Othello, using words and phrases from the script. Read on up to line 158 and add Othello's main points of defence to the chart. Who do you believe – Brabantio or Othello? Why?

b If you were directing the play, how might you increase or decrease the audience's sympathy for Brabantio's view?

---

1 **motion** 情感，欲望
2 **credit** 名声
3 **maimed** 残废的（这里指错误的）
4 **vouch** 证明，断言
5 **blood** 激情，性欲
6 **dram** 药水
7 **conjured to this effect** 通过魔法产生了这个效果
8 **wrought upon her** 施加在她身上（指诱奸她）
9 **overt test** 明显证据
10 **thin habits** 外在的表象
11 **poor likelihoods** 微小的可能性
12 **modern seeming** 平常的猜测
13 **affordeth** 应允

BRABANTIO	A maiden never bold;	
	Of spirit so still and quiet that her motion[1]	95

BRABANTIO A maiden never bold;
Of spirit so still and quiet that her motion[1]   95
Blushed at herself; and she, in spite of nature,
Of years, of country, credit[2], everything,
To fall in love with what she feared to look on?
It is a judgement maimed[3] and most imperfect
That will confess perfection so could err   100
Against all rules of nature, and must be driven
To find out practices of cunning hell
Why this should be. I therefore vouch[4] again
That with some mixtures powerful o'er the blood[5]
Or with some dram[6] conjured to this effect[7]   105
He wrought upon her[8].

DUKE   To vouch this is no proof
Without more wider and more overt test[9]
Than these thin habits[10] and poor likelihoods[11]
Of modern seeming[12] do prefer against him.

1 SENATOR But, Othello, speak: 110
Did you by indirect and forcèd courses
Subdue and poison this young maid's affections?
Or came it by request and such fair question
As soul to soul affordeth[13]?

OTHELLO   I do beseech you
Send for the lady to the Sagittary   115
And let her speak of me before her father.
If you do find me foul in her report,
The trust, the office I do hold of you,
Not only take away, but let your sentence
Even fall upon my life.

DUKE   Fetch Desdemona hither.   120

OTHELLO   Ancient, conduct them: you best know the place.
           [*Exit Iago with two or three Attendants*]
And till she come, as truly as to heaven
I do confess the vices of my blood,
So justly to your grave ears I'll present
How I did thrive in this fair lady's love,   125
And she in mine.

DUKE   Say it, Othello.

Othello tells how he was introduced to Brabantio's household. He recounts how his relationship with Desdemona began when he entertained her with the story of his life.

 剧情简介：奥赛罗讲述他如何结识布拉班修一家，回顾他如何因为给黛丝荻牟娜讲述自己的生平故事而与她结缘。

1 Othello's life story (whole class)

- As a class, read through the summary Othello gives of his life in lines 131–44, and list the incidents and strange sights that Othello describes.
- Split into small groups. Each group chooses one of Othello's descriptions from the list and prepares a short mime (哑剧) based on his words.
- Afterwards, come back together as a class and show your collective version of Othello's life story in order.

2 Two contrasting stories (in pairs)

Othello's account of his courtship of Desdemona gives a very different picture of their relationship from that told by Brabantio.

a Storyboard two scenes between Othello and Desdemona: one taken from Brabantio's version of events (lines 59–64 and 94–106) and the other illustrating how Othello claims the courtship occurred (lines 144–69).

b Discuss which version you think is true, based on your impressions of the characters of Brabantio and Othello so far. What evidence from the script do you have to support your position?

---

1 chances　遭遇，事件
2 moving accidents　惊心动魄的变故
3 by flood and field　在海上和陆上
4 hair-breadth scapes　命悬一线死里逃生（scapes = escapes）
5 redemption　赎身
6 antres　洞窟
7 idle　荒凉
8 Rough quarries　悬崖峭壁
9 Anthropophagi　食人族（同上一行的cannibals）
10 pliant hour　恰当的时机
11 dilate　仔细讲述
12 by parcels　零零碎碎
13 intentively　全神贯注

Language in the play 剧中语言
Othello's 'soft phrase of peace'

Othello claims to be a soldier who is 'little blessed with the soft phrase of peace' (line 82). Now you have read Othello's explanation of his conduct with Desdemona, what do you think?

- Write a paragraph describing the way Othello speaks in this section of the play. Add this to the other notes on language that you have made so far. As you read on, you will find further activities on Othello's language; you can add to your description as you discover more. Always try to include quotations from the script to support your viewpoint.

OTHELLO   Her father loved me, oft invited me,
Still questioned me the story of my life
From year to year – the battles, sieges, fortunes
That I have passed.
I ran it through, even from my boyish days
To the very moment that he bade me tell it;
Wherein I spake of most disastrous chances[1],
Of moving accidents[2] by flood and field[3],
Of hair-breadth scapes[4] i'th'imminent deadly breach,
Of being taken by the insolent foe
And sold to slavery; of my redemption[5] thence,
And with it all my travels' history:
Wherein of antres[6] vast and deserts idle[7],
Rough quarries[8], rocks, and hills whose heads touch heaven,
It was my hint to speak – such was the process:
And of the cannibals that each other eat,
The Anthropophagi[9], and men whose heads
Do grow beneath their shoulders. This to hear
Would Desdemona seriously incline;
But still the house affairs would draw her thence,
Which ever as she could with haste dispatch
She'd come again, and with a greedy ear
Devour up my discourse; which I observing
Took once a pliant hour[10] and found good means
To draw from her a prayer of earnest heart
That I would all my pilgrimage dilate[11]
Whereof by parcels[12] she had something heard,
But not intentively[13]. I did consent,
And often did beguile her of her tears
When I did speak of some distressful stroke
That my youth suffered. My story being done,
She gave me for my pains a world of sighs:

Othello completes the story of his courtship just as Desdemona arrives. Brabantio demands to know where her duty lies, and she answers him diplomatically, but makes it clear that she now obeys Othello before her father.

剧情简介：奥赛罗刚讲完他的求爱故事，黛丝狄蒙娜就来了。布拉班修要求女儿表明立场，她回答得很有策略，但也很明确：她现在首先听命于奥赛罗，其次才听命于父亲。

1 'She loved me for the dangers I had passed'
(in small groups)

a Improvise a short scene, using line 166 as the title, in which Othello recounts some of his dangerous adventures. Othello should narrate the tale, while others in the group act out or mime the scenes described. Experiment with different styles of presentation, both serious and comic. Afterwards, discuss whether you think this is a solid foundation for a marriage.

b What is Desdemona looking for in a man? Imagine that she has placed an advertisement in the 'lonely hearts' column of a magazine or on a dating website. Write her ad. As an extension to this activity, you could write Othello's reply to the ad.

1	passing	极其，非常
2	witness	作证
3	take … best	尽量把这一糟糕的情况处理好
4	Light on	落在
5	education	养育；教养
6	learn = teach	
7	hitherto	迄今
8	challenge	要求，索取

Characters 人物分析

'Enter DESDEMONA' (in large groups)

There are six or seven main characters on stage at this moment, as well as a number of Senators.

a Work out who each of these characters is, and then decide where everyone would be positioned on stage when Desdemona enters the scene. Freeze the action at this moment in such a way as to make it clear who's who.

b Consider the different ways in which Desdemona might make her entrance. Secretly? Defiantly? Respectfully? What is her status in this space and how might you show this in your tableau? How do other characters look at her – and what does this reveal about their individual attitudes? Try a number of versions of Desdemona's entrance and choose which one you feel is best.

c Act out lines 173–87, paying particular attention to Desdemona's movement around the stage. For example, she speaks of her 'divided duty' (line 179) to her father and to her husband. To whom does she address those lines? Does she kneel to her father, then move over to her husband? Does she speak directly to the Duke at any point? Try acting out this section in several ways. Once you have agreed on the best way of directing and acting it, share your production with the rest of the class.

　　　　　　　She swore, in faith, 'twas strange, 'twas passing[1] strange,
　　　　　　　'Twas pitiful, 'twas wondrous pitiful;
　　　　　　　She wished she had not heard it, yet she wished
　　　　　　　That heaven had made her such a man. She thanked me,
　　　　　　　And bade me, if I had a friend that loved her,
　　　　　　　I should but teach him how to tell my story,
　　　　　　　And that would woo her. Upon this hint I spake:
　　　　　　　She loved me for the dangers I had passed,
　　　　　　　And I loved her that she did pity them.
　　　　　　　This only is the witchcraft I have used.
　　　　　　　Here comes the lady: let her witness[2] it.

　　　　　　　　　Enter DESDEMONA, *Iago and Attendants.*

DUKE　　　　　I think this tale would win my daughter too.
　　　　　　　Good Brabantio, take up this mangled matter at the best[3]:
　　　　　　　Men do their broken weapons rather use
　　　　　　　Than their bare hands.

BRABANTIO　　　　　　　　　　I pray you hear her speak.
　　　　　　　If she confess that she was half the wooer,
　　　　　　　Destruction on my head if my bad blame
　　　　　　　Light on[4] the man! Come hither, gentle mistress;
　　　　　　　Do you perceive in all this noble company
　　　　　　　Where most you owe obedience?

DESDEMONA　　　　　　　　　　　My noble father,
　　　　　　　I do perceive here a divided duty:
　　　　　　　To you I am bound for life and education[5];
　　　　　　　My life and education both do learn[6] me
　　　　　　　How to respect you. You are lord of all my duty;
　　　　　　　I am hitherto[7] your daughter. But here's my husband;
　　　　　　　And so much duty as my mother showed
　　　　　　　To you, preferring you before her father,
　　　　　　　So much I challenge[8] that I may profess
　　　　　　　Due to the Moor my lord.

Brabantio grudgingly gives up his accusations against Othello. The Duke attempts to cheer him up, but Brabantio refuses comfort. The Duke appoints Othello to supreme charge of the defence of Cyprus.

剧情简介：布拉班修不情愿地放弃了对奥赛罗的指控。公爵试图让布拉班修高兴起来，但布拉班修不听他的安慰。公爵委任奥赛罗全权负责保卫塞浦路斯。

1 Brabantio as a father (in pairs)

Read Brabantio's lines 187–96 and 208–18. He wishes Desdemona was adopted, rather than his own flesh and blood. He says that he is forced to give his daughter to Othello because Othello already possesses her, and that he is giving away something very precious to him. Brabantio is glad that he has no more children because he would be tempted to hobble (捆绑两腿) them (like a horse) to stop them running away.

a Which of Brabantio's words do you find the most moving or shocking (if any)? Discuss your reactions with your partner.

b To what extent is Brabantio's attitude the same or different from that of a father in your own time and culture? Write a contemporary version of Brabantio's speech – what might a strict father say nowadays?

2 Rhyming proverbs and clichés (陈词滥调)
(in threes)

Read aloud the Duke's words (lines 200–7) to hear what his speech sounds like. He offers a series of clichés and proverbs (along the lines of 'every cloud has a silver lining') as consolation to Brabantio for the loss of his daughter. He also speaks in **rhyming couplets** (押韵二行连句，对偶句) (two lines of the same length, with rhyming endings).

a Pick out the three distinct pieces of advice that the Duke offers Brabantio. Choose one each and express it in your own words.

b What effect do these words have? How sincere do you think the Duke is? Discuss subject matter, tone and style of delivery.

c One person takes the role of the Duke, one Desdemona and one Othello. In these roles, write two or three lines expressing what your character is thinking at this point in the play.

3 Back to business – in prose

At line 219, the Duke stops speaking in verse when he begins to discuss affairs of state. Some critics argue that the reason for the switch from verse to prose is that the Duke urgently wishes to move on to what he considers to be more important matters, rather than Brabantio's private affairs.

• If you were directing this scene, how would you mark this change on stage (for example, through tone of voice, movement or the position of the characters)? Write a list of key points in your Director's Journal. What indication is there of Othello's value to the Duke and his Senators?

1 God bu'y! = God be with you! = Goodbye!
2 get 生养
3 that with all my heart 我全心全意爱着的（女儿）
4 jewel 宝贝（指自己的女儿）
5 clogs 桎梏，脚铐（拴在动物或犯人脖子或腿上限制其行动的厚重木块）
6 like yourself 以您的口吻
7 lay a sentence 下个判决（a sentence 也可以理解为"一句名言"）
8 grise 台阶
9 What … makes 命运女神打劫你毫无商量，逆来顺受可令其脸上无光
10 The robbed 被抢者
11 bootless 无益，无用
12 He … hears = He who bears nothing except the free comfort which he hears from that sentence bears the sentence well. （这里bears的意思是"感受"）
13 to sugar or to gall 使……甜蜜或痛苦
14 equivocal 模棱两可
15 bruised … ear 破碎的心是通过耳朵射穿的
16 fortitude 防御力量
17 substitute of most allowed sufficiency 能力极强的代理总督
18 opinion … effects 舆论，这一最能影响决策的力量
19 slubber the gloss 玷污（你刚当上新郎的）光彩
20 stubborn and boisterous 千难万险的

BRABANTIO	God bu'y![1] I have done.	
	Please it your grace, on to the state affairs.	
	I had rather to adopt a child than get[2] it.	
	Come hither, Moor:	190
	I here do give thee that with all my heart[3]	
	Which, but thou hast already, with all my heart	
	I would keep from thee. For your sake, jewel[4],	
	I am glad at soul I have no other child,	
	For thy escape would teach me tyranny	195
	To hang clogs[5] on them. I have done, my lord.	
DUKE	Let me speak like yourself[6] and lay a sentence[7]	
	Which as a grise[8] or step may help these lovers	
	Into your favour.	
	When remedies are past the griefs are ended	200
	By seeing the worst which late on hopes depended.	
	To mourn a mischief that is past and gone	
	Is the next way to draw new mischief on.	
	What cannot be preserved when fortune takes,	
	Patience her injury a mockery makes[9].	205
	The robbed[10] that smiles steals something from the thief;	
	He robs himself that spends a bootless[11] grief.	
BRABANTIO	So let the Turk of Cyprus us beguile,	
	We lose it not so long as we can smile;	
	He bears the sentence well that nothing bears	210
	But the free comfort which from thence he hears[12];	
	But he bears both the sentence and the sorrow	
	That to pay grief must of poor patience borrow.	
	These sentences, to sugar or to gall[13],	
	Being strong on both sides, are equivocal[14].	215
	But words are words; I never yet did hear	
	That the bruisèd heart was piercèd through the ear[15].	
	Beseech you now, to the affairs of the state.	
DUKE	The Turk with a most mighty preparation makes for Cyprus. Othello, the fortitude[16] of the place is best known to you; and though we have there a substitute of most allowed sufficiency[17], yet opinion, a more sovereign mistress of effects[18], throws a more safer voice on you. You must therefore be content to slubber the gloss[19] of your new fortunes with this more stubborn and boisterous[20] expedition.	220 225

> Othello promises to depart immediately for Cyprus, asking only that Desdemona be provided for. Neither Brabantio nor Desdemona wishes her to return to her father's house. Desdemona asks if she might accompany Othello.
>
> 剧情简介：奥赛罗应允立刻出发前往塞浦路斯，唯一的请求是将黛丝荻牟娜的生活安置好。布拉班修不想让女儿回家，黛丝荻牟娜也不愿回家。黛丝荻牟娜问是否可以随同奥赛罗赴任。

Characters 人物分析

'A maiden never bold'?

Remember, Desdemona's father said of her:

> A maiden never bold;
> Of spirit so still and quiet that her motion
> Blushed at herself
>
> Act 1 Scene 3, lines 94–6

a How well does her father really know her? Read all Desdemona's lines in the script opposite. Identify the things she says that appear to challenge both her father's description of her and the convention that a wife should not accompany her husband to war.

b Write two paragraphs outlining your thoughts about the presentation of Desdemona as a dramatic role. Provide evidence to support your ideas, including quotations from the script.

1	tyrant custom	"习惯"这位暴君
2	thrice-driven bed of down	三次筛选的羽绒床（最柔软）
3	agnise	认识，承认
4	alacrity	快感
5	disposition	安置
6	exhibition	生活开销
7	besort	合适的仆从
8	As levels with her breeding	与她的地位相称
9	prosperous	赞成的
10	charter	恩准
11	simpleness	纯真
12	downright violence	公然违抗
13	quality	本性
14	visage	面孔
15	consecrate	奉献
16	moth of peace	平静的飞蛾（吃闲饭的人）
17	bereft	被剥夺

Themes 主题分析

Appearance and reality

One of the themes that runs through the whole play is that of appearance and reality, including the difference between expected and actual behaviour. Iago pretends to be Othello's loyal ensign while plotting behind his back. Desdemona has appeared to be a dutiful daughter while marrying Othello without her father's knowledge.

- In pairs, discuss Desdemona's comment at line 248: 'I saw Othello's visage in his mind'. What do you think she means by this? What assumption might many Venetians make when they see Othello's face? Can you suggest reasons why she feels it important to make such a point at this moment?

OTHELLO	The tyrant custom[1], most grave senators,	
	Hath made the flinty and steel couch of war	
	My thrice-driven bed of down[2]. I do agnise[3]	
	A natural and prompt alacrity[4]	
	I find in hardness, and do undertake	230
	These present wars against the Ottomites.	
	Most humbly, therefore, bending to your state,	
	I crave fit disposition[5] for my wife,	
	Due reference of place and exhibition[6]	
	With such accommodation and besort[7]	235
	As levels with her breeding[8].	
DUKE	If you please,	
	Be't at her father's.	
BRABANTIO	I'll not have it so.	
OTHELLO	Nor I.	
DESDEMONA	Nor I; I would not there reside	
	To put my father in impatient thoughts	
	By being in his eye. Most gracious duke,	240
	To my unfolding lend your prosperous[9] ear	
	And let me find a charter[10] in your voice	
	T'assist my simpleness[11].	
DUKE	What would you, Desdemona?	
DESDEMONA	That I did love the Moor to live with him,	
	My downright violence[12] and storm of fortunes	245
	May trumpet to the world. My heart's subdued	
	Even to the very quality[13] of my lord.	
	I saw Othello's visage[14] in his mind	
	And to his honours and his valiant parts	
	Did I my soul and fortunes consecrate[15].	250
	So that, dear lords, if I be left behind	
	A moth of peace[16], and he go to the war,	
	The rites for which I love him are bereft[17] me,	
	And I a heavy interim shall support	
	By his dear absence. Let me go with him.	255

Othello wishes Desdemona to accompany him, and asserts that she will not distract him from his military duties. The Duke orders that they must depart that very night for Cyprus. Brabantio warns Othello of Desdemona's deceit.

剧情简介：奥赛罗希望黛丝荻牟娜陪他，坚称不会因她而疏于军务。公爵命令他们务必当夜出发前往塞浦路斯。布拉班修警告奥赛罗小心上黛丝荻牟娜的当。

1 'Let housewives make a skillet of my helm'

Othello assures the Senators that he is too mature to be swayed by sexual appetite or distracted by Desdemona's presence during a military campaign. In lines 262–70, he uses two images to emphasise this: first, that of Cupid (the god of love) blindfolding him; second, his helmet converted to a cooking pot (skillet).

- Locate the exact words in the script, then create a visual representation of both images.

2 Dramatic irony (戏剧反讽) (in small groups)

Othello says of Iago: 'A man he is of honesty and trust' (line 280). This is an example of **dramatic irony**, when the audience knows more than a character on stage. Dramatic conflict arises out of the fact that this character is unconsciously relying upon crucial information that is untrue.

- You will come across numerous other examples of dramatic irony as you read or watch *Othello*. Make a note of this example in your Director's Journal, and continue to add to this list as you read on.

Themes 主题分析
Honesty, trust and loyalty (in pairs)

Brabantio's parting words are a warning to Othello that Desdemona is untrustworthy (line 289). Othello swears that he would stake his life on Desdemona's loyalty (line 290).

- On a large sheet of paper, try ways of mapping out which characters have been explicitly described as trustworthy (and by whom), matched by those characters who have been described as untrustworthy or dishonest (and by whom). If you doubt any of these opinions, highlight these on your map and explain why.

Language in the play 剧中语言
Black versus white

The Duke comments: 'If virtue no delighted beauty lack, / Your son-in-law is far more fair than black' (lines 285–6).

- What does this suggest to you about the Duke's attitude to Othello as a black man?

1. voice 赞同，支持
2. palate 喜好，趣味
3. comply with heat 受性欲支配
4. scant 疏忽
5. light-winged toys 插着轻翅膀的玩意儿（指爱神丘比特 [Cupid] 之箭）
6. seel 合上或蒙上眼睛（原本是驯鹰术语）
7. wanton dullness （纵欲之后的）疲懒昏睡
8. speculative and officed instruments 有辨识力和负有责任的器官（指双眼）
9. disports 鱼水之欢
10. make ... helm 用我的头盔当饭锅
11. indign and base adversities 可耻、卑鄙的污名
12. Make head against 群起而攻击
13. estimation 名誉
14. import 与……有关
15. conveyance 护送

OTHELLO	Let her have your voice¹.
	Vouch with me, heaven, I therefore beg it not
	To please the palate² of my appetite,
	Nor to comply with heat³ the young affects
	In my distinct and proper satisfaction,	260
	But to be free and bounteous to her mind.
	And heaven defend your good souls that you think
	I will your serious and great business scant⁴
	For she is with me. No, when light-winged toys⁵
	Of feathered Cupid seel⁶ with wanton dullness⁷	265
	My speculative and officed instruments⁸,
	That my disports⁹ corrupt and taint my business,
	Let housewives make a skillet of my helm¹⁰,
	And all indign and base adversities¹¹
	Make head against¹² my estimation¹³!	270
DUKE	Be it as you shall privately determine,
	Either for her stay or going. Th'affair cries haste,
	And speed must answer it. You must hence tonight.
DESDEMONA	Tonight, my lord?
DUKE	This night.
OTHELLO	With all my heart.
DUKE	At nine i'the morning, here we'll meet again.	275
	Othello, leave some officer behind
	And he shall our commission bring to you
	With such things else of quality and respect
	As doth import¹⁴ you.
OTHELLO	So please your grace, my ancient:
	A man he is of honesty and trust.	280
	To his conveyance¹⁵ I assign my wife,
	With what else needful your good grace shall think
	To be sent after me.
DUKE	Let it be so.
	Good night to everyone. [*To Brabantio*] And noble signior,
	If virtue no delighted beauty lack,
	Your son-in-law is far more fair than black.	285
1 SENATOR	Adieu, brave Moor; use Desdemona well.
BRABANTIO	Look to her, Moor, if thou hast eyes to see:
	She has deceived her father and may thee.
OTHELLO	My life upon her faith!

Exeunt [*Duke, Brabantio, Cassio, Senators and Attendants*]

Othello charges Iago to look after Desdemona. Roderigo is despondent, but Iago scorns his love-sickness and argues that will and reason govern men's appetites.

 剧情简介：奥赛罗吩咐伊阿苟照顾黛丝狄蒙娜。若德瑞苟很沮丧，但伊阿苟嘲笑他得了相思病，并讲了一番意志和理性应管控住男人欲望的道理。

1 Contrasting characters (in threes)

Read the exchange between Iago and Roderigo, then try different ways of acting it out. The third member of your group should be the director. Try to distinguish between the two characters in your presentation – for example, Roderigo complains of being mortally love-sick, but Iago scorns such feelings. Remember also that Roderigo is a 'gentleman', while Iago is a professional soldier. Try reading the dialogue in a variety of styles (serious, funny, threatening) and at different paces. Which one sounds best?

Language in the play 剧中语言
Iago's garden imagery (in pairs)

Writers use imagery (see p. 231) to help create a picture or association in the reader's or listener's mind.

a How successful is Iago at creating a picture for you in lines 313–24. Does the imagery make his point clearer?

b Talk about whether you agree with Iago's view that 'our wills are gardeners' where emotions are concerned, and that love (or what Roderigo claims to be love) is 'a sect or scion'. Can love be controlled by reason? One of you argues that it can, the other that it cannot. Whose case is stronger?

Themes 主题分析
The role of women: sexist language

Some readers find the way Iago describes women to be highly offensive. Examples are derogatory terms like 'guinea-hen' (a prostitute) and his exclamation of 'A fig!', which was a contemptuous (轻蔑的，侮辱的) remark usually accompanied by a rude gesture (thrusting the thumb between the first and second fingers).

a Write down at least two bullet points explaining why you think Iago uses sexist language.

b Consider how sexist language is used to oppress women today. In your experience, how is sexist language received. Is it always challenged? Prepare notes to support a three-minute presentation to the class.

1	direction	吩咐，嘱托
2	incontinently	立即
3	betwixt = between（后文出现的'twixt是betwixt的缩略形式）	
4	Ere = Before	
5	baboon	狒狒（指傻瓜或好色之徒）
6	A fig!	屁大点儿！（表示少得可怜）
7	nettles / lettuce / hyssop / thyme	荨麻、野莴苣、神香草和麝香草（这些都是散发浓郁气味的植物）
8	gender	种类
9	corrigible authority	矫正力
10	poise	抗衡
11	preposterous	荒唐
12	motions	情欲
13	carnal stings	肉体冲动
14	unbitted	不加束缚
15	sect or scion	分支或插条（喻指情欲的幼芽）

                    Honest Iago   290
My Desdemona must I leave to thee;
I prithee, let thy wife attend on her,
And bring her after in the best advantage.
Come, Desdemona, I have but an hour
Of love, of worldly matters and direction¹   295
To spend with thee. We must obey the time.
                                        Exeunt Othello and Desdemona

RODERIGO Iago.
IAGO What say'st thou, noble heart?
RODERIGO What will I do, think'st thou?
IAGO Why, go to bed and sleep.   300
RODERIGO I will incontinently² drown myself.
IAGO If thou dost, I shall never love thee after. Why, thou silly gentleman?
RODERIGO It is silliness to live, when to live is torment: and then we have a prescription to die, when death is our physician. 305
IAGO O villainous! I have looked upon the world for four times seven years, and since I could distinguish betwixt³ a benefit and an injury, I never found a man that knew how to love himself. Ere⁴ I would say I would drown myself for the love of a guinea-hen, I would change my humanity with a baboon⁵. 310
RODERIGO What should I do? I confess it is my shame to be so fond, but it is not in my virtue to amend it.
IAGO Virtue? A fig!⁶ 'Tis in ourselves that we are thus or thus. Our bodies are our gardens, to the which our wills are gardeners. So that if we will plant nettles⁷ or sow lettuce⁷, set hyssop⁷ and weed 315
up thyme⁷, supply it with one gender⁸ of herbs or distract it with many, either to have it sterile with idleness or manured with industry, why the power and corrigible authority⁹ of this lies in our wills. If the balance of our lives had not one scale of reason to poise¹⁰ another of sensuality, the blood and baseness of our 320
natures would conduct us to most preposterous¹¹ conclusions. But we have reason to cool our raging motions¹², our carnal stings¹³, our unbitted¹⁴ lusts; whereof I take this, that you call love, to be a sect or scion¹⁵.
RODERIGO It cannot be.   325

Iago continues to persuade Roderigo that Desdemona and Othello will soon tire of one another. He tells of his hatred for Othello and urges Roderigo to join him in seeking revenge.

剧情简介：伊阿苟继续劝若德瑞苟，说黛丝荻牟娜和奥赛罗很快会彼此厌倦。他说自己恨奥赛罗，并怂恿若德瑞苟和他一起报复。

Language in the play 剧中语言
More verse and prose (in small groups)

a The dialogue in lines 297–364 is all written in prose. Discuss why Shakespeare might have chosen prose rather than verse here. Think about the situation, the content of Iago's words, and the fact that he urges Roderigo *ten times* to arrange to have a plentiful supply of cash at his disposal.

b Look back through Act 1 and locate all the occasions on which characters speak in prose. Write down the reference (the scene and line numbers) and briefly summarise what is being said and by whom. Then suggest a possible reason why Shakespeare used prose in each case.

1 perdurable 耐久
2 stead 帮助
3 Put money in thy purse 把钱装进钱袋里（谚语，意思是"要想取得胜利，准备充足的金钱"）
4 defeat … beard 戴一副假胡子改变你的容貌
5 sequestration 分裂，分离
6 luscious 可口
7 locusts 长角豆（可食，味甜）
8 acerb 苦涩
9 coloquintida 药西瓜（又称bitter apple）
10 sated 厌腻
11 sanctimony 假装神圣
12 erring barbarian 四处流浪的野蛮人
13 compassing 获得（指得到黛丝荻牟娜）
14 fast 忠诚，真诚
15 hearted 刻骨铭心
16 conjunctive 联手
17 cuckold him 给他戴绿帽子
18 delivered 产生，出生
19 Traverse! 前进！（军事指令）
20 betimes 尽早

▼ What does this photograph suggest about the relationship between Iago and Roderigo?

IAGO   It is merely a lust of the blood and a permission of the will. Come, be a man. Drown thyself? Drown cats and blind puppies. I have professed me thy friend, and I confess me knit to thy deserving with cables of perdurable[1] toughness. I could never better stead[2] thee than now. Put money in thy purse[3]. Follow thou these wars; defeat thy favour with an usurped beard[4]. I say, put money in thy purse. It cannot be that Desdemona should long continue her love to the Moor – put money in thy purse – nor he his to her. It was a violent commencement, and thou shalt see an answerable sequestration[5] – put but money in thy purse. These Moors are changeable in their wills – fill thy purse with money. The food that to him now is as luscious[6] as locusts[7] shall be to him shortly as acerb[8] as the coloquintida[9]. She must change for youth; when she is sated[10] with his body she will find the error of her choice. Therefore put money in thy purse. If thou wilt needs damn thyself, do it a more delicate way than drowning. Make all the money thou canst. If sanctimony[11] and a frail vow betwixt an erring barbarian[12] and a super-subtle Venetian be not too hard for my wits and all the tribe of hell, thou shalt enjoy her – therefore make money. A pox of drowning thyself! It is clean out of the way. Seek thou rather to be hanged in compassing[13] thy joy than to be drowned and go without her.

RODERIGO   Wilt thou be fast[14] to my hopes, if I depend on the issue?

IAGO   Thou art sure of me. Go make money. I have told thee often, and I retell thee again and again, I hate the Moor. My cause is hearted[15]: thine hath no less reason. Let us be conjunctive[16] in our revenge against him. If thou canst cuckold him[17], thou dost thyself a pleasure, me a sport. There are many events in the womb of time which will be delivered[18]. Traverse![19] Go, provide thy money. We will have more of this tomorrow. Adieu.

RODERIGO   Where shall we meet i'the morning?

IAGO   At my lodging.

RODERIGO   I'll be with thee betimes[20].

IAGO   Go to; farewell. Do you hear, Roderigo?

RODERIGO   What say you?

IAGO   No more of drowning, do you hear?

RODERIGO   I am changed.

IAGO   Go to; farewell. Put money enough in your purse.

RODERIGO   I'll sell all my land.   *Exit*

Alone, Iago reveals that he suspects his wife has been unfaithful with Othello. He begins to make plans to ruin Othello's marriage and to seek revenge on Cassio, by making Othello believe Cassio and Desdemona are lovers.

剧情简介：伊阿苟独自一人，表露他怀疑妻子与奥赛罗有染，于是心生一计，要设法使奥赛罗相信卡修和黛丝荻牟娜是情人，从而毁掉奥赛罗的婚姻，并报复卡修。

Stagecraft 导演技巧

Iago's soliloquy (独白) (in pairs)

The **soliloquy** is a dramatic convention in which a character who is alone on stage speaks his or her thoughts aloud. In Shakespeare's theatre, the speech was probably delivered from the front of the stage directly to the audience. Usually, a soliloquy reveals a character's motives or state of mind at that point in the play.

This is the first time that Iago has been alone on stage, and the first time the audience hears his version of events. Three ways in which a director could present this speech are:

- directed towards the audience
- as if Iago is talking to himself
- as a voice-over (画外音), while the actor looks pensive (心事重重) and lost in thought.

All three methods have been used in movie and television versions of Shakespeare's plays.

a Read the speech in each of the three ways listed above. For each method, consider:
  - how the actor would speak the lines
  - what movements would be required
  - in what ways you would want the audience to react
  - how it affects your interpretation of Iago's character. Is he sly, evil or manipulative? Does it draw the audience into colluding and sympathising with Iago?

b Make notes on the impact of each version as you try it out. Get together with two other pairs, present one different interpretation to one another and discuss which is most effective and why.

1 profane 亵渎
2 snipe 菜鸟（本义指一种叫沙锥的鸟）；傻瓜
3 But = Except
4 thought abroad 普遍认为
5 done my office 代行了我的职责（即"和我妻子睡觉"）
6 holds me well 器重我
7 proper 英俊，好看
8 plume up my will 实现我对荣耀的追求
9 double knavery 双重毒计
10 abuse Othello's ear 哄骗奥赛罗
11 person 俊美外表
12 dispose 风度，气质
13 framed 天生
14 engendered （计谋）生成了

44

IAGO	Thus do I ever make my fool my purse;	365
	For I mine own gained knowledge should profane[1]	
	If I would time expend with such a snipe[2]	
	But[3] for my sport and profit. I hate the Moor,	
	And it is thought abroad[4] that 'twixt my sheets	
	He's done my office[5]. I know not if't be true	370
	Yet I, for mere suspicion in that kind,	
	Will do as if for surety. He holds me well[6]:	
	The better shall my purpose work on him.	
	Cassio's a proper[7] man: let me see now;	
	To get his place and to plume up my will[8]	375
	In double knavery[9]. How? How? Let's see.	
	After some time, to abuse Othello's ear[10]	
	That he is too familiar with his wife;	
	He hath a person[11] and a smooth dispose[12]	
	To be suspected, framed[13] to make women false.	380
	The Moor is of a free and open nature,	
	That thinks men honest that but seem to be so,	
	And will as tenderly be led by the nose	
	As asses are.	
	I have't. It is engendered[14]. Hell and night	385
	Must bring this monstrous birth to the world's light.　　*Exit*	

Othello
奥赛罗

Looking back at Act 1 第1幕回顾
Activities for groups or individuals

1 Cast (为……选演员) the play

Imagine you are a movie director about to shoot a new version of *Othello*. Read through the list of characters on page 1, noting down all those who have appeared in Act 1. Decide which well-known actors you would cast in each part. In each case, explain why you have chosen them – what makes them suited to the part?

2 Disputed stories

In Act 1 Scene 3, it is clear that Brabantio believes his daughter has been charmed by Othello – unnaturally lured away from her family by 'witchcraft'. The version of events that Othello offers is that Desdemona was simply enchanted by his heroic stories, which are a mixture of travellers' tales and action-man (硬汉) adventures. Desdemona does not reveal what actually happened during her courtship, but suggests to her father that she is in control of the situation. Re-read this scene, then write four short pieces:

- Brabantio makes a formal written complaint to the Senate, disputing the Duke's ruling.
- Roderigo writes a witness statement in support of Brabantio's complaint (above). How much is really based on his first-hand experience?
- Othello writes a letter to the Duke, thanking him for his support and looking forward to representing the state of Venice in the forthcoming war with Turkey.
- Desdemona writes to her father, describing the events leading up to her marriage to Othello. She explains how she feels after hearing her father's abusive words in front of the Senate.

3 Emerging themes

- 'Thus do I ever make my fool my purse' (Act 1 Scene 3, line 365)
- 'The robbed that smiles steals something from the thief' (Act 1 Scene 3, line 206)
- 'I am not what I am.' (Act 1 Scene 1, line 66)
- 'I must show out a flag and sign of love' (Act 1 Scene 1, line 155)
- 'trust not your daughters' minds / By what you see them act.' (Act 1 Scene 1, lines 169–70)
- 'She loved me for the dangers I had passed' (Act 1 Scene 3, line 166)

In small groups, choose three of the quotations listed above. Talk together about the meanings of the lines, and the ideas that link them together. Devise a short improvisation, set in a modern context, in which you include your three quotations. Share this with the rest of the class and hold a wider discussion about the themes that seem to be emerging.

4 Iago's language

When talking candidly (坦率) to Roderigo about Othello, Iago's language is peppered (充满) with references to different kinds of animals (e.g. Act 1 Scene 1, lines 87–116).

When giving his opinions about love, he draws on garden images (Act 1 Scene 3, lines 313–55). When talking about women, he employs offensive language (Act 1 Scene 3, lines 306–47).

- Re-read the lines mentioned above and discuss with a partner the impression you have of Iago from the way he speaks at these moments. Next, locate some other moments in Act 1 when Iago talks more guardedly. Who is he speaking to and what is the context? How is his language different?

5 Venice: public and private tensions

Why does Shakespeare set Act 1 in Venice? One answer is that the original story that inspired *Othello* was set in Venice and Cyprus and that he simply copied it – but that's not the only possibility. In order to fully understand *Othello*, it is important to know something about

LOOKING BACK AT ACT 1

sixteenth-century Venice and its social and economic significance in Europe.

In Act 1, Venetian law and order is seen to operate quickly and efficiently. Iago's troublemaking is easily dealt with, as is the Turkish threat to Venetian stability. In Act 2, the setting shifts to a disputed outpost (哨所) on the edges of Venetian rule. Our introduction to Cyprus is a violent storm, where the natural boundaries between sea and sky are blurred.

- Before you read on, use the information on Venice and Venetian culture on page 237 to write several paragraphs on the tensions between 'private' and 'public' interests in the play so far. You could take each of the main characters in turn and write about their personal interests, discussing whether these conflict with their public duty.

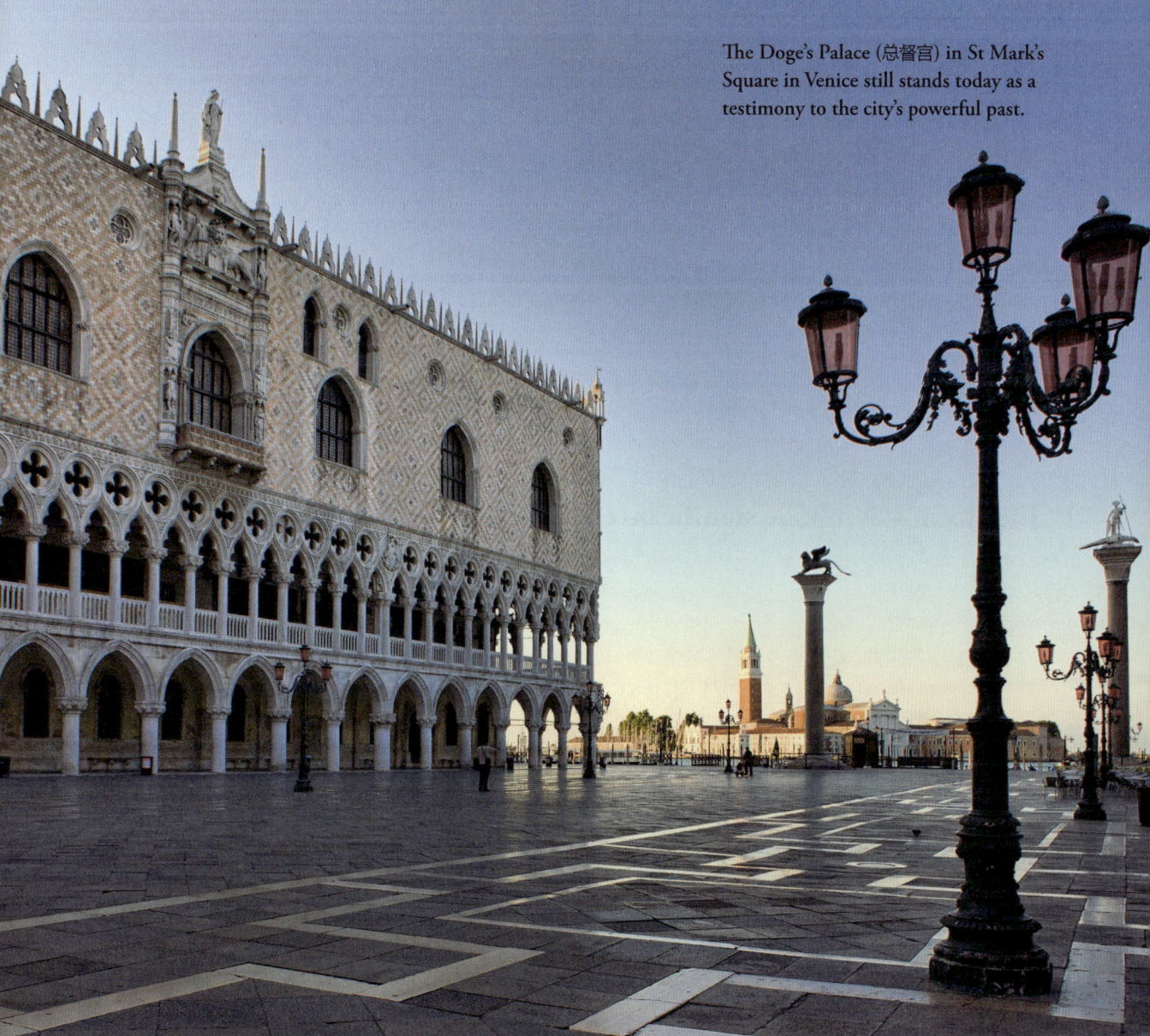

The Doge's Palace (总督宫) in St Mark's Square in Venice still stands today as a testimony to the city's powerful past.

Montano and two gentlemen discuss the terrible storm. A third gentleman brings news that the Turkish fleet has been destroyed. He reports that Cassio's ship has safely docked, but that Othello is still at sea.

剧情简介：芒塔诺与两位绅士讨论那场可怕的风暴。另一位绅士带来消息说土耳其舰队已被摧毁。他报告说卡修的船已安全抵港，但奥赛罗仍在海上。

Stagecraft 导演技巧

Staging a storm (in pairs)

As with most Elizabethan drama, there are no original stage directions for this scene specifying where it takes place ('Cyprus A quayside' has been added by later editors). Playwrights gave clues in the dialogue to convey to an audience who the characters were and where a scene was set.

a Read lines 1–29 opposite and pick out any words or phrases that provide clues as to:
- where this scene is set
- what has happened since we last saw Othello and the others depart for war with Turkey
- who these characters are.

b In your Director's Journal, write notes on how you would stage the script opposite, including:
- directions you would give the actors
- props or specific items of clothing you might use
- lighting you would like
- any sound effects you might employ.

1 high-wrought flood 汹涌的波涛
2 main 海
3 Descry 发现，辨认
4 ne'er = never
5 ruffianed 肆虐
6 ribs of oak （船体的）橡木船肋
7 hold the mortise 保持榫卯咬合
8 segregation （被风浪）冲散，吹散
9 banning 令人生畏
10 chidden billow 翻滚的海浪
11 with high and monstrous mane 像鬃毛耸立的怪兽
12 Bear 小熊星座
13 quench 熄灭
14 guards 卫星（实际为小熊星座的两颗恒星）
15 Pole 北极星
16 like molestation 如此狂暴
17 enchafèd flood 波涛汹涌的大海
18 embayed 躲进海港
19 designment halts 计策破产
20 sufferance 毁坏
21 Veronesa 维罗纳船（即维罗纳造的船，Verona 为意大利城市）；来自威尼斯（Venice）的船
22 in full commission 被委任负有全权

1 The storm – symbolic significance? (whole class)

In the original story by Giraldi Cinthio, from which Shakespeare took his ideas for *Othello*, there is no storm at all. Yet we have here a whole page of dialogue devoted to a description of it. You will also find that as the scene continues, most of the characters mention the storm several times. Presumably Shakespeare felt that a storm at this point would have some dramatic or thematic use; it certainly echoes the ominous (不祥) mood established by Iago's couplet at the end of Act 1. Some commentators suggest that the storm also has a symbolic function (as the calm before the storm, or as stormy emotions, and so on).

- Can you think of other possible symbolic functions of the storm? Discuss any ideas you have about its purpose at this point in the play. As you read the rest of this scene, keep in mind this stormy opening, and think about its effect on what follows.

Act 2 Scene 1

Cyprus   A quayside

Enter MONTANO *and two* GENTLEMEN.

MONTANO	What from the cape can you discern at sea?	
1 GENTLEMAN	Nothing at all; it is a high-wrought flood[1].	
	I cannot 'twixt the heaven and the main[2]	
	Descry[3] a sail.	
MONTANO	Methinks the wind does speak aloud at land,	5
	A fuller blast ne'er[4] shook our battlements.	
	If it hath ruffianed[5] so upon the sea,	
	What ribs of oak[6], when mountains melt on them,	
	Can hold the mortise[7]? What shall we hear of this?	
2 GENTLEMAN	A segregation[8] of the Turkish fleet:	10
	For do but stand upon the banning[9] shore,	
	The chidden billow[10] seems to pelt the clouds;	
	The wind-shaked surge, with high and monstrous mane[11],	
	Seems to cast water on the burning Bear[12]	
	And quench[13] the guards[14] of th'ever-fixèd Pole[15].	15
	I never did like molestation[16] view	
	On the enchafèd flood[17].	
MONTANO	If that the Turkish fleet	
	Be not ensheltered and embayed[18], they are drowned:	
	It is impossible they bear it out.	

Enter a third GENTLEMAN.

3 GENTLEMAN	News, lads! Our wars are done:	20
	The desperate tempest hath so banged the Turks	
	That their designment halts[19]. A noble ship of Venice	
	Hath seen a grievous wrack and sufferance[20]	
	On most part of their fleet.	
MONTANO	How? Is this true?	
3 GENTLEMAN	The ship is here put in,	25
	A Veronesa[21]; Michael Cassio,	
	Lieutenant to the warlike Moor Othello,	
	Is come on shore; the Moor himself at sea,	
	And is in full commission[22] here for Cyprus.	
MONTANO	I am glad on't; 'tis a worthy governor.	30

Cassio lands safely, but he is worried that Othello's ship has not yet reached shore. A messenger reports that another ship has been sighted, and Cassio sends for news.

 剧情简介：卡修安全登陆，但他担心奥赛罗的船还未靠岸。信差报告又发现了一艘船，卡修派人去打探消息。

1 A delayed entrance (in pairs)

In the first 171 lines of Scene 1, several characters ask the question 'Is Othello alive or dead?'

- Locate these points in the script. Talk together about what you think is the dramatic purpose of this delay before Othello's triumphant entrance, fresh from the storm. You may find it helpful to think about how Othello's entrance in Act 1 was also delayed.

1 the main … blue 大海和蓝天
2 An indistinct regard 无法分辨
3 arrivance 抵达的人
4 approve 赞美
5 bark 船
6 pilot 领航员
7 allowance 公认的经验
8 surfeited to death 太过分
9 Stand in bold cure 很可能实现
10 discharge their shot of courtesy 鸣放礼炮

Characters 人物分析

More views of Othello

Lines 1–59 contain several references to Othello.

- Find them in the script and list them on a piece of paper. For each quotation, decide whether it is a positive or a negative reference to Othello. Are the comments about Othello's professional or personal attributes (个人品质)? Consider the people making the comments, and what views each person might represent.
- Present your findings in the format of a chart or table, and compare this with the chart you drew up on page 12.

Write about it 写作练习

Front page news (in small groups)

Imagine you are a news team reporting on the destruction of the Turkish fleet and on Othello's expected triumphant return. Compile the front page of your newspaper. It might contain:

- news of the routing (溃败) of the Turkish fleet (see lines 10–24)
- a description of the storm (either as part of the main news story or as a separate weather report)
- reports of the fears for Othello's safety
- a profile of Othello, including a report on his recent marriage and interviews with witnesses/colleagues/friends.

Produce a large-format front page for your classroom wall and compare it with other groups' versions. As an additional challenge, one group could choose to write a version of events from either a Turkish or a Cypriot point of view. (A Venetian paper would be very supportive of Othello and his exploits, whereas a Cypriot or Turkish newspaper might view the events differently.)

3 GENTLEMAN	But this same Cassio, though he speak of comfort
	Touching the Turkish loss, yet he looks sadly
	And prays the Moor be safe; for they were parted
	With foul and violent tempest.
MONTANO	Pray heaven he be;
	For I have served him, and the man commands
	Like a full soldier. Let's to the seaside, ho!
	As well to see the vessel that's come in
	As to throw out our eyes for brave Othello,
	Even till we make the main and th'aerial blue[1]
	An indistinct regard[2].
3 GENTLEMAN	Come, let's do so;
	For every minute is expectancy
	Of more arrivance[3].

Enter CASSIO.

CASSIO	Thanks, you the valiant of this warlike isle
	That so approve[4] the Moor. O, let the heavens
	Give him defence against the elements,
	For I have lost him on a dangerous sea.
MONTANO	Is he well shipped?
CASSIO	His bark[5] is stoutly timbered, and his pilot[6]
	Of very expert and approved allowance[7];
	Therefore my hopes, not surfeited to death[8],
	Stand in bold cure[9].

[*A shout*] *within*, 'A sail, a sail, a sail!'

Enter a MESSENGER.

CASSIO	What noise?
MESSENGER	The town is empty; on the brow o'the sea
	Stand ranks of people and they cry, 'A sail!'
CASSIO	My hopes do shape him for the governor.

A shot [*is heard within*].

2 GENTLEMAN	They do discharge their shot of courtesy[10];
	Our friends at least.
CASSIO	I pray you, sir, go forth,
	And give us truth who 'tis that is arrived.
2 GENTLEMAN	I shall. *Exit*

35

40

45

50

55

Cassio describes to Montano the virtues of Desdemona. Iago is reported to have come ashore. Desdemona, Iago, Emilia and Roderigo are greeted by Cassio, but there is still no news of Othello.

剧情简介： 卡修向芒塔诺描述黛丝荻牟娜的美德。据报伊阿苟已经上岸。黛丝荻牟娜、伊阿苟、艾蜜丽叶及若德瑞苟受到卡修的迎接，但仍然没有奥赛罗的消息。

1 Cassio's descriptions of Desdemona (in pairs)

Cassio refers to Desdemona in several different ways. For example, the 'riches of the ship' is how he describes her as she comes ashore.

a Pick out four descriptions of Desdemona from the script opposite and write them down. Comment on the kind of language used (such as comparison or exaggeration) and the effect you think it has.

b Iago and Brabantio have already compared Desdemona to treasure (in Act 1 Scene 1, line 88 and Act 1 Scene 2, line 62). Discuss the significance of linking Desdemona with treasure. What does this use of language reveal about attitudes to women in Othello's society? Are similar terms used today? If so, how they are received?

Characters 人物分析
Impressions of Cassio

a What advice would you give an actor playing Cassio? Go through the script opposite and decide how you would like each of his speeches to be delivered.

b Look back at Act 1 Scene 1, lines 19–27, and Act 1 Scene 3, lines 374–80, and then make a list of the qualities you think Cassio possesses. Does the production photograph of Cassio below match your expectations of what this character looks like? If not, find an image that more closely represents your impression of Cassio.

1 wived 娶妻
2 paragons 胜过
3 quirks 辞藻
4 blazoning 褒扬的
5 essential vesture 天生丽质
6 ingener 造物者
7 guttered rocks 锯齿状的礁石
8 congregated sands 淤积的沙滩
9 enscarped 形成海岭
10 guiltless keel 无忧虑的船只（keel的本义是"船的龙骨"）
11 footing 到达
12 se'nnight 七天
13 Jove 乔武（即罗马神话中的主神朱庇特 [Jupiter]）
14 tall ship 大船
15 let her have your knees 向她下跪
16 Enwheel 围绕
17 tidings 消息

MONTANO	But, good lieutenant, is your general wived[1]?	60
CASSIO	Most fortunately: he hath achieved a maid	
	That paragons[2] description and wild fame;	
	One that excels the quirks[3] of blazoning[4] pens	
	And in th'essential vesture[5] of creation	
	Does tire the ingener[6].	

Enter Second Gentleman.

	How now? Who's put in?	65
2 GENTLEMAN	'Tis one Iago, ancient to the general.	
CASSIO	He's had most favourable and happy speed:	
	Tempests themselves, high seas, and howling winds,	
	The guttered rocks[7] and congregated sands[8],	
	Traitors enscarped[9] to clog the guiltless keel[10],	70
	As having sense of beauty do omit	
	Their mortal natures, letting go safely by	
	The divine Desdemona.	
MONTANO	What is she?	
CASSIO	She that I spake of, our great captain's captain,	
	Left in the conduct of the bold Iago,	75
	Whose footing[11] here anticipates our thoughts	
	A se'nnight's[12] speed. Great Jove[13] Othello guard	
	And swell his sail with thine own powerful breath,	
	That he may bless this bay with his tall ship[14],	
	Make love's quick pants in Desdemona's arms,	80
	Give renewed fire to our extinct spirits,	
	And bring all Cyprus comfort.	

Enter DESDEMONA, IAGO, EMILIA *and* RODERIGO.

	O, behold,	
	The riches of the ship is come on shore!	
	You men of Cyprus, let her have your knees[15].	
	Hail to thee, lady! And the grace of heaven,	85
	Before, behind thee, and on every hand,	
	Enwheel[16] thee round.	
DESDEMONA	I thank you, valiant Cassio.	
	What tidings[17] can you tell me of my lord?	
CASSIO	He is not yet arrived; nor know I aught	
	But that he's well, and will be shortly here.	90

While waiting for news of Othello's ship, Iago, Emilia and Desdemona pass the time in conversation. Iago makes provocative comments about wives and women.

 剧情简介：在等待奥赛罗那条船的消息时，伊阿苟、艾蜜丽叶和黛丝荻牟娜聊天打发时间。说到为人妻者和女人，伊阿苟发表了一些带挑逗性的看法。

Stagecraft 导演技巧
Cassio's kiss – dramatic possibilities (in threes)

Cassio has greeted Desdemona with a flourish and a bow (lines 84–5). Now he kisses Emilia – but he apologises first to Iago for his 'bold show of courtesy', justifying his actions on the grounds of good 'breeding' and 'manners'. This can be a dramatically fascinating moment on stage, open to a wide range of acting possibilities.

a Discuss some of these possibilities and then decide which of the following interpretations of Cassio's behaviour you most agree with:
- He's a naturally courteous man.
- Aware of Iago's jealous nature, he is being deliberately provocative.
- He's trying to be nice to everyone at a difficult moment.
- He's not very confident in social situations.
- He's deliberately patronising Emilia (she's just a common soldier's wife).
- Another interpretation (give details).

b Consider ways of acting out this moment. For example, is Cassio's kiss a courteous peck (快速轻吻), or is he taking liberties? How does Emilia react? Is she embarrassed? Flattered? Irritated?

c What about Iago? In Trevor Nunn's 1990 production, Iago is clearly jealous. He swiftly moves across to take hold of Emilia, as if reclaiming his property. Decide how you would like Iago to react. In what tone of voice does he say lines 100–2?

1 fellowship 船队
2 hark = listen
3 still = always
4 list 愿望；倾向
5 puts ... heart 把舌头往心里多放了一点儿
6 chides with thinking 在心里叱责
7 pictures 图画一样（指美丽而沉默）
8 bells 铜钟一样（指大声嚷嚷）
9 players in your housewifery 在家务上吊儿郎当
10 housewives in your beds 在床上才不愧家庭主妇
11 or ... Turk 否则我就是个土耳其鬼子（当时土耳其人是敌人）
12 You shall ... praise 您别那样"赞美"我（反话）
13 assay 尝试
14 There's one 有人

1 Friendly banter (玩笑) or pointed comments?
(in small groups)

- Read lines 100–60. How should this part of the scene be played? Is it light-hearted banter, the only tension being that of Desdemona awaiting news that her husband is safe? Or is there bitterness and tension arising out of Iago's comments about women in general and his wife in particular? (Some commentators have suggested that there is an underlying class conflict between the courtly, educated Cassio and the uneducated, lower-class Iago).

- Discuss whether you think this is an episode of friendly chatter, or one tinged (略带) with misogyny (hatred of women), domestic strife and class-based tension.

DESDEMONA	O, but I fear – how lost you company?	
CASSIO	The great contention of the sea and skies Parted our fellowship[1].	

[*A shout*] *within*, 'A sail, a sail!' [*A shot is heard.*]

But hark[2], a sail!

2 GENTLEMAN	They give their greeting to the citadel: This likewise is a friend.	
CASSIO	See for the news.	95

[*Exit Second Gentleman*]

Good ancient, you are welcome. [*To Emilia*] Welcome, mistress.
Let it not gall your patience, good Iago,
That I extend my manners. 'Tis my breeding
That gives me this bold show of courtesy.

[*He kisses Emilia.*]

IAGO	Sir, would she give you so much of her lips As of her tongue she oft bestows on me You would have enough.	100
DESDEMONA	Alas, she has no speech.	
IAGO	In faith, too much: I find it still[3] when I have list[4] to sleep. Marry, before your ladyship, I grant She puts her tongue a little in her heart[5] And chides with thinking[6].	105
EMILIA	You've little cause to say so.	
IAGO	Come on, come on; you are pictures[7] out of doors, bells[8] in your parlours, wild-cats in your kitchens, saints in your injuries, devils being offended, players in your housewifery[9], and housewives in your beds[10].	110
DESDEMONA	O fie upon thee, slanderer!	
IAGO	Nay, it is true, or else I am a Turk[11]: You rise to play and go to bed to work.	
EMILIA	You shall not write my praise[12].	
IAGO	No, let me not.	115
DESDEMONA	What wouldst thou write of me, if thou shouldst praise me?	
IAGO	O, gentle lady, do not put me to't, For I am nothing if not critical.	
DESDEMONA	Come on, assay[13]. There's one[14] gone to the harbour?	
IAGO	Ay, madam.	120

Desdemona reveals that she is joining in the conversation to take her mind off waiting for Othello. Iago continues to joke about women.

剧情简介：黛丝荻牟娜透露说，她加入谈话只是为了让自己分分心，免得等奥赛罗等得心急火燎。伊阿苟继续拿女人开玩笑。

Language in the play 剧中语言
Puns (双关语), paradoxes (悖论谜语) and epigrams (箴言诗) (in pairs)

Shakespeare's audiences were amused and fascinated by all types of language play. Find examples of each of the following:

- **Puns** These are words that sound the same but have quite different meanings. Puns were a highly fashionable form of wordplay in Shakespeare's time. In *Romeo and Juliet*, Mercutio, fatally stabbed, makes a pun: 'Ask for me tomorrow, and you shall find me a grave man.' Here, Iago puns on the words 'white' (meaning colour, wit or cleverness) and 'wight' (an old word for person or lover). The words 'fair' and 'black' are used repeatedly in this play. They are used to denote the physical colouring of Desdemona and Othello, but they also carry certain connotations (associations), which Iago is keen to exploit.
- **Epigrams** Also very popular with Shakespeare's audiences, an epigram is a concise, witty poem that often ends on a surprising turn of thought. Sardonic (讽刺) generalisations were commonly put into the mouths of down-to-earth, 'honest' characters.
- **Paradoxes** A kind of riddle, paradoxes contain ideas that are self-contradictory.

1. beguile / The thing I am　掩饰我真实的感情
2. pate　脑袋
3. birdlime　粘鸟胶，捕鸟粘网
4. frieze　羊毛粗呢
5. muse　缪斯（希腊神话里的诗神）
6. black　黑发黑肤
7. witty　有智慧
8. thereto　还，而且
9. white　小白脸
10. folly　蠢（暗指春心）
11. old fond paradoxes　老掉牙的胡说八道（fond = foolish）
12. thereunto　此外
13. foul pranks　丑事
14. heavy　愚钝
15. One … itself?　仅凭自己的美德就足以让坏人也会称赞的好女人呢？（malice意思是"邪恶"）
16. gay　衣着华丽
17. wight　人，爱人
18. chronicle small beer　记日常收支流水账
19. profane and liberal　粗俗又放肆

▼ Identify who is who in this production photograph. What line from the script opposite do you think is being spoken at this moment?

OTHELLO ACT 2 SCENE 1
奥赛罗

DESDEMONA [*Aside*] I am not merry, but I do beguile
The thing I am¹ by seeming otherwise –
Come, how wouldst thou praise me?
IAGO I am about it, but indeed my invention
Comes from my pate² as birdlime³ does from frieze⁴ –   125
It plucks out brains and all. But my muse⁵ labours,
And thus she is delivered:
'If she be fair and wise, fairness and wit,
The one's for use, the other useth it.'
DESDEMONA Well praised! How if she be black⁶ and witty⁷?   130
IAGO 'If she be black, and thereto⁸ have a wit,
She'll find a white⁹ that shall her blackness fit.'
DESDEMONA Worse and worse.
EMILIA How if fair and foolish?
IAGO 'She never yet was foolish that was fair,
For even her folly¹⁰ helped her to an heir.'   135
DESDEMONA These are old fond paradoxes¹¹ to make fools laugh i'th'alehouse. What miserable praise hast thou for her that's foul and foolish?
IAGO 'There's none so foul and foolish thereunto¹²,
But does foul pranks¹³ which fair and wise ones do.'   140
DESDEMONA O heavy¹⁴ ignorance! Thou praisest the worst best. But what praise couldst thou bestow on a deserving woman indeed? One that in the authority of her merit did justly put on the vouch of very malice itself?¹⁵
IAGO 'She that was ever fair, and never proud,   145
Had tongue at will, and yet was never loud;
Never lacked gold, and yet went never gay¹⁶;
Fled from her wish, and yet said "Now I may";
She that being angered, her revenge being nigh,
Bade her wrong stay, and her displeasure fly;   150
She that in wisdom never was so frail
To change the cod's head for the salmon's tail;
She that could think and ne'er disclose her mind,
See suitors following and not look behind;
She was a wight¹⁷, if ever such wight were –'   155
DESDEMONA To do what?
IAGO 'To suckle fools and chronicle small beer¹⁸.'
DESDEMONA O, most lame and impotent conclusion! Do not learn of him, Emilia, though he be thy husband. How say you, Cassio, is he not a most profane and liberal¹⁹ counsellor?   160

57

Iago revels in Cassio's attention to Desdemona, seeing in it a way in which he can ruin Cassio. Othello arrives safely. He and Desdemona greet each other, speaking of happiness and love.

剧情简介： 伊阿苟看到卡修关心黛丝荻牟娜心中大喜，从中看到一个能毁掉卡修的办法。奥赛罗平安抵达，与黛丝荻牟娜彼此问候，幸福洋溢，互诉衷情。

1 'an excellent courtesy!' (in threes)

Iago uses a dramatic device called an **aside** (旁白) here, speaking in such a way that the audience can hear him but the other characters on stage cannot. Elizabethan and Jacobean playwrights used asides to share characters' thoughts or intentions without revealing secrets to other characters.

- Act out Iago's aside (lines 163–71), matching the movements of Cassio and Desdemona to Iago's commentary. Where should Iago stand, and how should he say the words? Iago uses several images in his speech: a spider's web, a snare ('gyve') and, lastly, tubes for inserting enemas ('clyster-pipes')!

2 Another kiss (in small groups)

a How would you have Othello and Desdemona kiss? In Oliver Parker's 1995 movie version, it was an intensely passionate embrace, the lovers oblivious (忘记) of the public gaze. In Trevor Nunn's 1990 Royal Shakespeare Company production, it was restrained and revealed little of the couple's private life. This picture shows another version of the same moment.

b Discuss how you would differentiate between the three different kisses contained in this scene so far (one is mentioned in Iago's aside). Then show them in tableau form and ask the rest of the class to identify each one. Don't forget to include Iago – consider his position, actions, facial expressions and so on.

1 home　直白
2 relish ... scholar　当他是军人，而非文人雅士，反而会赏识他了
3 well said = well done（干得好）
4 gyve　上镣铐
5 courtship = courtesies（绅士风度）
6 kissed your three fingers　亲吻您的三个手指（当时男女间的一种文雅礼节）
7 play the sir in　假装绅士
8 clyster-pipes　灌肠管
9 Lo = Look
10 Olympus　奥林匹斯山（希腊神话中诸神的住所）
11 If ... die　如果我现在就死去
12 It stops me here　如此快乐让我窒息
13 the greatest ... make　就让它成为我们两颗心发出的最大噪声

OTHELLO ACT 2 SCENE 1
奥赛罗

CASSIO   He speaks home[1], madam; you may relish him more in the soldier than in the scholar[2].

IAGO   [*Aside*] He takes her by the palm. Ay, well said[3]; whisper. With as little a web as this will I ensnare as great a fly as Cassio. Ay, smile upon her, do. I will gyve[4] thee in thine own courtship[5]. You say true, 'tis so indeed. If such tricks as these strip you out of your lieutenantry, it had been better you had not kissed your three fingers[6] so oft, which now again you are most apt to play the sir in[7]. Very good, well kissed, an excellent courtesy! 'Tis so indeed. Yet again your fingers to your lips? Would they were clyster-pipes[8] for your sake!

Trumpets within.

The Moor! I know his trumpet.

CASSIO   'Tis truly so.

DESDEMONA   Let's meet him and receive him.

CASSIO   Lo[9], where he comes!

Enter OTHELLO *and* ATTENDANTS.

OTHELLO   O, my fair warrior!

DESDEMONA   My dear Othello!

OTHELLO   It gives me wonder great as my content
To see you here before me. O, my soul's joy,
If after every tempest come such calms,
May the winds blow till they have wakened death,
And let the labouring bark climb hills of seas,
Olympus[10]-high, and duck again as low
As hell's from heaven. If it were now to die[11],
'Twere now to be most happy; for I fear
My soul hath her content so absolute
That not another comfort like to this
Succeeds in unknown fate.

DESDEMONA   The heavens forbid
But that our loves and comforts should increase,
Even as our days do grow.

OTHELLO   Amen to that, sweet powers!
I cannot speak enough of this content;
It stops me here[12]; it is too much of joy.

They kiss.

And this, and this, the greatest discords be
That e'er our hearts shall make[13].

Othello and Desdemona go off together, leaving Iago alone with Roderigo. Iago tells him that Desdemona is in love with Cassio, because she must necessarily tire of Othello.

 剧情简介：奥赛罗与黛丝荻牟娜一起离开，留下伊阿苟和若德瑞苟。伊阿苟告诉他黛丝荻牟娜爱上了卡修，因为她必定会对奥赛罗生厌。

Language in the play 剧中语言
Imagery of music and food (in small groups)

'Making sweet music together': Iago's comment (line 191) that Othello and his wife 'are well tuned' is followed by his vow to 'set down the pegs' (to slacken the strings of an instrument). The **metaphor** (隐喻) (see p. 231) uses the harmony of music to indicate the harmony of Othello's marriage, and Iago's intention to disrupt it. Iago's speech in lines 212–28 contains more metaphors – references to food, eating and appetite.

- Read through the speeches and pick out as many examples as you can find of these metaphors. Discuss what Iago is talking about and what his language reveals about his attitude to women, love and affection.

Write about it 写作练习
Ship's log (by yourself)

Write Othello's ship's log for his journey to Cyprus. You might include some of the following:

- thoughts on setting out
- plans to defend Cyprus
- any encounters with the Turkish ships
- thoughts about Desdemona
- a description of the storm
- fears for Desdemona's safety
- feelings on reaching harbour safely.

1 Iago's argument – how convincing? (in pairs)

According to Iago, Othello is defective in 'loveliness in favour, sympathy in years, manners and beauties'. He assures Roderigo that Desdemona will quickly tire of her husband ('When the blood is made dull with the act of sport') and that she is only attracted to his 'bragging' and 'fantastical lies'.

- Read lines 212–35 to each other, taking turns to read small sections. On what evidence is Iago basing his view of their relationship? How does Iago try to convince Roderigo that he is right? Start a file noting the attempts Iago has made to manipulate people and events so far. Add to this as you continue reading.

1 well tuned 琴瑟和谐
2 set … music 放松琴弦使音乐走调
3 well desired 受欢迎
4 prattle out of fashion 不合时宜地啰唆
5 dote … comforts 高兴得昏了头
6 disembark my coffers 卸下我的箱子
7 master 船长
8 presently 立刻，马上
9 base men 出身低贱的人
10 list = listen to
11 directly 肯定，一定
12 Lay thy finger thus 把你的手指这样放着（指放在唇上，示意别出声）
13 sport（指性交）
14 satiety 满足
15 favour 相貌
16 sympathy 相似；一致
17 required conveniences 必需的相似性
18 heave the gorge 恶心，呕吐
19 pregnant and unforced position 显而易见、自然得出的假设
20 voluble 油嘴滑舌
21 conscionable 有良心；一丝不苟
22 compassing 获取
23 salt 下流，淫荡

OTHELLO ACT 2 SCENE 1
奥赛罗

IAGO [*Aside*] O, you are well tuned[1] now!
But I'll set down the pegs that make this music[2],
As honest as I am.

OTHELLO Come, let us to the castle.
News, friends; our wars are done; the Turks are drowned.
How does my old acquaintance of this isle? 195
Honey, you shall be well desired[3] in Cyprus;
I have found great love amongst them. O my sweet,
I prattle out of fashion[4] and I dote
In mine own comforts[5]. I prithee, good Iago,
Go to the bay and disembark my coffers[6]; 200
Bring thou the master[7] to the citadel;
He is a good one, and his worthiness
Does challenge much respect. Come, Desdemona,
Once more well met at Cyprus!

Exeunt [all except Iago and Roderigo]

IAGO [*To a departing Attendant*] Do thou meet me presently[8] at the 205
harbour. [*To Roderigo*] Come hither. If thou be'st valiant – as
they say base men[9] being in love have then a nobility in their
natures more than is native to them – list[10] me. The lieutenant
tonight watches on the court of guard. First, I must tell thee this:
Desdemona is directly[11] in love with him. 210

RODERIGO With him? Why, 'tis not possible!

IAGO Lay thy finger thus[12], and let thy soul be instructed. Mark me
with what violence she first loved the Moor but for bragging and
telling her fantastical lies. And will she love him still for prating?
Let not thy discreet heart think it. Her eye must be fed. And 215
what delight shall she have to look on the devil? When the blood
is made dull with the act of sport[13], there should be, again to
inflame it and to give satiety[14] a fresh appetite, loveliness in
favour[15], sympathy[16] in years, manners and beauties: all which the
Moor is defective in. Now for want of these required conveniences[17], 220
her delicate tenderness will find itself abused, begin to heave the
gorge[18], disrelish and abhor the Moor. Very nature will instruct
her in it, and compel her to some second choice. Now, sir, this
granted – as it is a most pregnant and unforced position[19] – who
stands so eminent in the degree of this fortune as Cassio does? – a 225
knave very voluble[20]; no further conscionable[21] than in putting on
the mere form of civil and humane seeming for the better
compassing[22] of his salt[23] and most hidden loose affection.

Iago assures Roderigo that Desdemona has tired of Othello, and has her eye on other men. Iago tells his plan. He urges Roderigo to provoke Cassio to anger that night. The resulting riot will ruin Cassio's prospects.

剧情简介：伊阿苟向若德瑞苟保证，黛丝荻牟娜对奥赛罗已经厌倦了，看上了其他男人。伊阿苟说出了他的计谋，敦促若德瑞苟当晚去挑衅卡修，让他发怒。随之而来的骚乱将毁掉卡修的前程。

1 'a slipper and subtle knave' (in pairs)

Read Iago's description of Cassio in lines 229–35. Pick out features that you agree are an accurate portrait of this character, and those that you think are deliberately false.

Characters 人物分析

Roderigo (in pairs)

a In discussion, sum up what you have learned about Roderigo from the play so far.

b Read lines 205–66. Roderigo seems remarkably gullible (易受骗). His protests about Iago's descriptions suggest he is besotted (痴迷) with Desdemona, yet he quickly agrees to Iago's plan. One person takes the part of Roderigo and the other steps into role as director. Advise Roderigo how he might react as Iago speaks lines 248–65, and the way he should interject (插嘴) at lines 236, 242, 254 and 263.

▶ Choose lines from the script opposite that might provide a suitable caption (说明文字) for this image of Iago (left) and Roderigo.

1 slipper = slippery （油滑，滑头）
2 stamp and counterfeit 捏造，伪造
3 green 青涩；不成熟
4 pestilent complete knave 不折不扣的流氓
5 blest condition 圣洁的贞操
6 Blest fig's end! 圣洁个毛！
7 Blest pudding! 圣洁个球！
8 paddle with 抚摸
9 mark 注意
10 by this hand 举手发誓
11 incorporate conclusion 肉体合二为一
12 watch 站岗执勤
13 I'll lay't upon you 我会给您安排任务
14 tainting his discipline 嘲笑他的武艺
15 minister 提供
16 in choler 生气时
17 haply 或许
18 truncheon 权杖
19 qualification 安抚
20 come into no true taste 不对胃口
21 prefer 促进
22 I warrant thee 我向你担保
23 by and by 尽快，立刻
24 necessaries 行李

	Why none; why none – a slipper[1] and subtle knave, a finder out of occasions, that has an eye can stamp and counterfeit[2] advantages, though true advantage never present itself; a devilish knave! Besides, the knave is handsome, young, and hath all those requisites in him that folly and green[3] minds look after. A pestilent complete knave[4]; and the woman hath found him already.
RODERIGO	I cannot believe that in her; she's full of most blest condition[5].
IAGO	Blest fig's end![6] The wine she drinks is made of grapes. If she had been blest she would never have loved the Moor. Blest pudding![7] Didst thou not see her paddle with[8] the palm of his hand? Didst not mark[9] that?
RODERIGO	Yes, that I did; but that was but courtesy.
IAGO	Lechery, by this hand[10]: an index and obscure prologue to the history of lust and foul thoughts. They met so near with their lips that their breaths embraced together – villainous thoughts, Roderigo! When these mutualities so marshal the way, hard at hand comes the master and main exercise, the incorporate conclusion[11]. Pish! But, sir, be you ruled by me. I have brought you from Venice; watch[12] you tonight; for the command, I'll lay't upon you[13]. Cassio knows you not; I'll not be far from you. Do you find some occasion to anger Cassio, either by speaking too loud or tainting his discipline[14], or from what other course you please, which the time shall more favourably minister[15].
RODERIGO	Well.
IAGO	Sir, he's rash and very sudden in choler[16], and haply[17] with his truncheon[18] may strike at you: provoke him that he may; for even out of that will I cause these of Cyprus to mutiny, whose qualification[19] shall come into no true taste[20] again but by the displanting of Cassio. So shall you have a shorter journey to your desires by the means I shall then have to prefer[21] them, and the impediment most profitably removed without the which there were no expectation of our prosperity.
RODERIGO	I will do this, if you can bring it to any opportunity.
IAGO	I warrant thee[22]. Meet me by and by[23] at the citadel. I must fetch his necessaries[24] ashore. Farewell.
RODERIGO	Adieu. *Exit*

Iago again says that he is seeking revenge because he suspects that Othello has slept with Emilia. He plans to use Roderigo to ensure the downfall of Cassio, whom he also suspects has made love to Emilia.

 剧情简介：伊阿苟再次说他要伺机报复，因为他怀疑奥赛罗已经跟艾蜜丽叶上过床了。他打算利用若德瑞苟搞垮卡修，因为他还怀疑卡修与艾蜜丽叶有了奸情。

Stagecraft 导演技巧
Direct the actor

- Read lines 267–93 and identify all the words associated with love. Then pick out words to do with sex. Explain to an actor playing Iago what the character appears to be saying in this speech. How might Iago deliver key words such as 'love', 'the Moor', 'Michael Cassio', 'revenge')?

- In your Director's Journal, summarise your thoughts by writing out two or three paragraphs of advice for your Iago. (It will help if you are able to watch two different versions of this soliloquy in performance so you can consider the differences in movement, setting and props.)

Characters 人物分析
Hot-seat* Iago (whole class)

What questions would you really like to ask Iago? A volunteer steps into role as Iago and the class questions him. Your questions might include:

- Why do you hate Othello so much?
- What did you think about Desdemona's decision to marry Othello?
- Do you enjoy being in the army?
- Do you love your wife?

The person playing Iago should base his or her answers on the script. Take turns as Iago in the hot-seat.

1. howbeit 尽管
2. absolute 纯粹
3. peradventure 或许
4. accountant = accountable （有责任的）
5. diet 满足
6. leaped into my seat 扑上了我的马鞍（seat 喻指妻子）
7. mineral 药
8. gnaw my inwards 啃咬我的五脏六腑
9. trace 追踪（打猎用语）
10. stand the putting on 按我的怂恿行事
11. on the hip 处于劣势（摔跤用语）
12. rank garb 下三烂的形式/办法
13. with my night-cap 戴着我的睡帽（以我的身份）
14. egregiously 异乎寻常地
15. practising upon 阴谋反对

*热座位，一种课堂游戏，玩法是请一位同学坐到讲台上的一把椅子上，其他同学轮番给他/她出难题，哪个问题他/她回答不出就算输。

OTHELLO ACT 2 SCENE 1
奥赛罗

IAGO That Cassio loves her, I do well believe't;
That she loves him, 'tis apt and of great credit.
The Moor, howbeit[1] that I endure him not,
Is of a constant, loving, noble nature; 270
And I dare think he'll prove to Desdemona
A most dear husband. Now, I do love her too,
Not out of absolute[2] lust – though peradventure[3]
I stand accountant[4] for as great a sin –
But partly led to diet[5] my revenge, 275
For that I do suspect the lusty Moor
Hath leaped into my seat[6], the thought whereof
Doth like a poisonous mineral[7] gnaw my inwards[8];
And nothing can or shall content my soul
Till I am evened with him, wife for wife; 280
Or failing so, yet that I put the Moor
At least into a jealousy so strong
That judgement cannot cure. Which thing to do,
If this poor trash of Venice, whom I trace[9]
For his quick hunting, stand the putting on[10], 285
I'll have our Michael Cassio on the hip[11],
Abuse him to the Moor in the rank garb[12] –
For I fear Cassio with my night-cap[13] too –
Make the Moor thank me, love me, and reward me,
For making him egregiously[14] an ass, 290
And practising upon[15] his peace and quiet
Even to madness. 'Tis here, but yet confused;
Knavery's plain face is never seen till used. *Exit*

A Herald publicly announces celebrations to mark the destruction of the Turkish fleet. These festivities also honour Othello's wedding. Scene 3 opens with Othello asking Cassio to inspect the guard at night.

剧情简介：传令官宣布庆典开始，庆祝消灭土耳其舰队。这一庆典也是为了庆祝奥赛罗的婚礼。第三场从奥赛罗命卡修晚上查岗开始。

1 The proclamation (in small groups)

a Read the Herald's proclamation aloud. Talk together about whether you would cut this or keep it in if you were directing a performance of the play. Give your reasons.

b Decide how Scene 2 might be performed. Directly to the audience? Spoken to a crowd on stage, with the Herald mingling in the audience? Or in some other dramatically effective way?

c Imagine three or four ordinary Cypriot workers pausing from their labours to listen to the proclamation. Improvise their reactions to each section of the speech.

d Suggest how the proclamation characterises both Othello's public role and his private role.

1	certain 可靠
2	mere perdition 全军覆没
3	triumph 欢庆
4	addiction 喜好，意愿
5	nuptial 婚礼
6	offices 厨房、贮藏室、酒窖等
7	full liberty of 完全尽情享用
8	honourable stop 适可而止
9	out-sport discretion 过分放纵
10	with your earliest = at your earliest convenience
11	profit 好处（这里指鱼水之欢）

Stagecraft 导演技巧

A change of atmosphere

Othello and Desdemona have had to endure the drama of appearing in front of the Senate, the tension of war and a terrifying storm at sea.

- Consider how these two characters make their entrance at this point in the play, when they are looking forward to the celebrations acknowledging their marriage. How might you show a change of atmosphere on stage? Consider: costumes (is Othello still in uniform?); lighting; music, sound effects and background noise; scenery and props. Add your ideas to your Director's Journal.

2 'Iago is most honest'

a The obvious piece of dramatic irony (see p. 38) in line 6 of Scene 3 comes soon after Iago's vow in Scene 1 to drive Othello 'Even to madness'. What effect do you think Othello's comment would have on an audience in the theatre?

b If this were a pantomime (哑剧), such a misguided comment by the hero would invite the audience to shout out to warn him! Write down what you would say to Othello at this moment if you had the chance to step out of the audience and onto the stage with the characters.

Act 2 Scene 2
Cyprus   A street

Enter Othello's HERALD *with a proclamation.*

HERALD   It is Othello's pleasure, our noble and valiant general, that upon certain¹ tidings now arrived importing the mere perdition² of the Turkish fleet, every man put himself into triumph³: some to dance, some to make bonfires, each man to what sport and revels his addiction⁴ leads him; for besides these beneficial news, it is the celebration of his nuptial⁵. So much was his pleasure should be proclaimed. All offices⁶ are open, and there is full liberty of⁷ feasting from this present hour of five till the bell have told eleven. Heaven bless the isle of Cyprus and our noble general Othello!   *Exit*   10

Act 2 Scene 3
Cyprus   A room in the castle

Enter OTHELLO, DESDEMONA, CASSIO *and* ATTENDANTS.

OTHELLO   Good Michael, look you to the guard tonight.
Let's teach ourselves that honourable stop⁸,
Not to out-sport discretion⁹.
CASSIO   Iago hath direction what to do;
But notwithstanding with my personal eye   5
Will I look to't.
OTHELLO   Iago is most honest.
Michael, good night; tomorrow with your earliest¹⁰
Let me have speech with you – Come, my dear love,
The purchase made, the fruits are to ensue;
That profit's¹¹ yet to come 'tween me and you.   10
Good night.
                        Exeunt Othello, Desdemona [and Attendants]

Iago persuades Cassio to join in the celebrations with various male friends. Cassio reveals he has a poor head for alcohol, and declines to drink further. Iago plans to make Cassio drunk and quarrelsome.

剧情简介：伊阿苟说服卡修跟几个男性朋友参加庆祝活动。卡修透露他不胜酒量，拒绝再饮酒。伊阿苟计划把他灌醉，让他跟人吵架。

Characters 人物分析

Men's talk (in pairs)

a Read the dialogue between Iago and Cassio. What differences can you detect between the two speakers in their attitudes towards women in general and Desdemona in particular?

b Act out the dialogue up to line 39 in such a way as to highlight any significant differences between the two men and the nature of their remarks. Experiment with playing Cassio in more than one way. For example, do you think that he is ill at ease with the way Iago directs the conversation?

c After you have experimented with speaking the lines, talk together about how Iago takes control of the dialogue. Do this by considering each interchange (交谈) between the two men. For example, Cassio begins by stressing 'we must to the watch', implying that they must ensure quiet and restraint among the public while Othello and Desdemona consummate their love. How does Iago avoid that order?

1 Not this hour　一小时后再说
2 cast　打发
3 Jove　乔武（即朱庇特，生性好色）
4 full of game　很会玩花样
5 sounds a parley to provocation　听到集结号了
6 alarum　冲锋号
7 stoup　酒壶，酒罐
8 fain　愿意
9 have a measure　喝一口
10 craftily qualified　偷偷掺了水
11 innovation　头昏脑涨
12 fasten … him　灌他一杯酒
13 my young mistress' dog　少奶奶惯坏的狗
14 hath … out　使之神魂颠倒
15 caroused　痛饮
16 Potations pottle-deep　人杯大杯地

Enter IAGO.

CASSIO   Welcome, Iago; we must to the watch.

IAGO   Not this hour[1], lieutenant; 'tis not yet ten o'th'clock. Our general cast[2] us thus early for the love of his Desdemona; who let us not therefore blame: he hath not yet made wanton the night with her, and she is sport for Jove[3].

CASSIO   She's a most exquisite lady.

IAGO   And I'll warrant her full of game[4].

CASSIO   Indeed she is a most fresh and delicate creature.

IAGO   What an eye she has! Methinks it sounds a parley to provocation[5].

CASSIO   An inviting eye, and yet methinks right modest.

IAGO   And when she speaks, is it not an alarum[6] to love?

CASSIO   She is indeed perfection.

IAGO   Well, happiness to their sheets! Come, lieutenant, I have a stoup[7] of wine, and here without are a brace of Cyprus gallants, that would fain[8] have a measure[9] to the health of the black Othello.

CASSIO   Not tonight, good Iago; I have very poor and unhappy brains for drinking. I could well wish courtesy would invent some other custom of entertainment.

IAGO   O, they are our friends – but one cup; I'll drink for you.

CASSIO   I have drunk but one cup tonight, and that was craftily qualified[10] too; and behold what innovation[11] it makes here. I am unfortunate in the infirmity and dare not task my weakness with any more.

IAGO   What, man! 'Tis a night of revels; the gallants desire it.

CASSIO   Where are they?

IAGO   Here at the door; I pray you call them in.

CASSIO   I'll do't, but it dislikes me.   *Exit*

IAGO   If I can fasten but one cup upon him[12],
With that which he hath drunk tonight already,
He'll be as full of quarrel and offence
As my young mistress' dog[13]. Now my sick fool Roderigo,
Whom love hath turned almost the wrong side out[14],
To Desdemona hath tonight caroused[15]
Potations pottle-deep[16], and he's to watch.

Iago gets the party going, singing drinking songs.

剧情简介：伊阿苟唱起酒歌，让庆功会热闹起来。

1 'My boat sails freely' (in pairs)

Iago's metaphor 'My boat sails freely, both with wind and stream' (line 55) echoes earlier imagery.

- Work out what Iago means by this image, and talk together about whether you think it is appropriate. Make sure you can give reasons for your decision.

Characters 人物分析

Iago: a man of many parts

Iago (third on the left in the photograph below) is a man of many parts, able to switch roles with great ease depending on who he is talking to and what he wants to achieve. In this 'party scene', he demonstrates a sociable side, and comes across as someone who is fun to be with.

- Make a list of other parts or roles Iago has played so far.

1	swelling	自命不凡
2	That … distance	极其看重荣誉
3	The very elements	特别的风气
4	flustered	灌醉
5	rouse	大杯（酒）
6	Good faith	说真的
7	cannikin	小杯（酒）
8	potent in potting	酒量好
9	with facility	轻易
10	sweats not	不流汗（指不用费力）
11	Almain	日耳曼人
12	pottle	酒罐（容量是半加仑，约3.79升）
13	do you justice	（即"跟您喝一样多"）

OTHELLO ACT 2 SCENE 3
奥赛罗

Three lads of Cyprus, noble swelling[1] spirits,
That hold their honours in a wary distance[2],
The very elements[3] of this warlike isle,
Have I tonight flustered[4] with flowing cups; 50
And they watch too. Now, 'mongst this flock of drunkards,
Am I to put our Cassio in some action
That may offend the isle. But here they come.

Enter Cassio, MONTANO *and* GENTLEMEN.

If consequence do but approve my dream,
My boat sails freely, both with wind and stream. 55

CASSIO 'Fore God, they have given me a rouse[5] already.
MONTANO Good faith[6], a little one; not past a pint, as I am a soldier.
IAGO Some wine, ho!
[*Sings*]
  And let me the cannikin[7] clink, clink,
  And let me the cannikin clink; 60
   A soldier's a man,
   O, man's life's but a span,
  Why then, let a soldier drink.
Some wine, boys!
CASSIO 'Fore God, an excellent song. 65
IAGO I learned it in England, where indeed they are most potent in potting[8]. Your Dane, your German, and your swag-bellied Hollander – drink, ho! – are nothing to your English.
CASSIO Is your Englishman so exquisite in his drinking?
IAGO Why, he drinks you with facility[9] your Dane dead drunk; he sweats not[10] to overthrow your Almain[11]; he gives your Hollander a vomit ere the next pottle[12] can be filled. 70
CASSIO To the health of our general!
MONTANO I am for it, lieutenant, and I'll do you justice[13].

The party continues and Cassio becomes drunk very quickly. He goes off to take his turn on guard, and Iago comments on his dangerous 'vice': his weakness for alcohol.

 剧情简介：庆祝会继续进行，卡修很快喝醉了。他动身去查岗。伊阿苟评价说，卡修身上的一个危险"缺点"就是爱喝酒。

1 Party photograph (in groups of four to six)

Take line 97 – 'Do not think, gentlemen, I am drunk' – and imagine freezing the action on stage. The photograph below shows one version of this moment, in the middle of what is clearly quite a wild barracks party. In what other ways might this moment be presented? Create a tableau, with each person in the group making it clear from the way they are positioned whom they represent. The rest of the class guesses who is who.

1	breeches	马裤
2	crown	克朗（过去在英国流通的银币，值5先令，1先令值12便士）
3	lown	流氓，恶棍
4	degree	地位
5	pride	奢华的穿着
6	auld cloak	旧衣服
7	by your leave	请您原谅
8	platform	炮台
9	set the watch	站岗
10	stand by	与……并肩
11	just equinox	正好抵消（equinox是昼夜平分点，这里指卡修的美德和缺点刚好抵消）
12	odd time	恰逢
13	shake	摧毁

2 Acting the drunk (in pairs)

a Acting a drunk is one of the most difficult tasks for any actor. But in lines 85–102, Shakespeare provides a script for Cassio that really does catch the rhythms of drunken speech. Take parts and read the lines, using any actions you think appropriate.

b Cassio has let Othello down by behaving unprofessionally. He also declares his social superiority when he asserts that 'the lieutenant is to be saved before the ancient'. Talk together about whether you think Cassio is displaying a less attractive side of his character here.

IAGO	O sweet England!	75
	[*Sings*]	
	King Stephen was and a worthy peer,	
	His breeches[1] cost him but a crown[2];	
	He held them sixpence all too dear,	
	With that he called the tailor lown[3].	
	He was a wight of high renown,	80
	And thou art but of low degree[4];	
	'Tis pride[5] that pulls the country down;	
	Then take thine auld cloak[6] about thee.	
	Some wine, ho!	
CASSIO	'Fore God, this is a more exquisite song than the other.	85
IAGO	Will you hear't again?	
CASSIO	No, for I hold him to be unworthy of his place that does those things. Well, God's above all, and there be souls must be saved, and there be souls must not be saved.	
IAGO	It's true, good lieutenant.	90
CASSIO	For mine own part – no offence to the general, nor any man of quality – I hope to be saved.	
IAGO	And so do I too, lieutenant.	
CASSIO	Ay, but by your leave[7], not before me; the lieutenant is to be saved before the ancient. Let's have no more of this; let's to our affairs. God forgive us our sins! Gentlemen, let's look to our business. Do not think, gentlemen, I am drunk; this is my ancient, this is my right hand, and this is my left hand. I am not drunk now, I can stand well enough, and I speak well enough.	95
ALL	Excellent well.	100
CASSIO	Why, very well then; you must not think then that I am drunk. *Exit*	
MONTANO	To the platform[8], masters. Come, let's set the watch[9].	
IAGO	You see this fellow that is gone before,	
	He is a soldier fit to stand by[10] Caesar	105
	And give direction. And do but see his vice –	
	'Tis to his virtue a just equinox[11],	
	The one as long as th'other. 'Tis pity of him.	
	I fear the trust Othello puts him in,	
	On some odd time[12] of his infirmity,	110
	Will shake[13] this island.	

Montano thinks that Othello should be told of Cassio's weakness for drink. Iago sends Roderigo after Cassio, and the two re-enter fighting. Montano tries to stop Cassio striking Roderigo.

 剧情简介：芒塔诺认为，应该告诉奥赛罗卡修有嗜酒的毛病。伊阿苟让若德瑞苟紧随卡修，二人在打斗中再次上台。芒塔诺试图阻止卡修打若德瑞苟。

Themes 主题分析

Appearance versus reality; honesty and dishonesty

Iago continues to paint a very negative picture of Cassio, alleging that his 'vice' of drunkenness occurs every night. Montano is concerned that Othello should be advised of Cassio's 'evils', because Othello's good nature sees only 'virtue' in his lieutenant.

a Write two paragraphs explaining how this exchange between Montano and Iago contributes to the theme of appearance versus reality.

b Note down at least two other examples where there has been a significant difference between appearance and reality in the play so far.

Characters 人物分析

Honest Iago? (in fours)

At line 124, Montano suggests that it would be 'an honest action' for Iago to tell Othello about Cassio's drink problem.

a This is not the first time that the word 'honest' has been used in connection with Iago. Flick back through the play and find other examples where the word 'honest' has been applied to this character. Note down the line references and the speakers, then compare your findings with those of other groups.

b Two group members take parts as Montano and Iago and act out lines 121–7, pausing at the end of key phrases or sentences. The other two become Montano and Iago's 'inner thoughts', voicing exactly what is in each character's mind during this short exchange.

1 What did Roderigo do? (in pairs)

So, what happened outside? What *did* Roderigo do or say to annoy Cassio so much?

- Consider what you know about both men. For example, Roderigo is a civilian and Cassio is an army officer; also, Roderigo is jealous of Othello's marriage to Desdemona, whilst Cassio appears to be fiercely loyal to Othello. Taking lines 130–1 as a clue, improvise the incident.

---

1 horologe a double set 时钟转两圈（即24小时）
2 put in mind 告知
3 hazard … second 冒险授予他副官职位
4 ingraft 根深蒂固
5 twiggen bottle 套着柳编的酒瓶（喻指把他打得伤痕累累，像个套着柳编的酒瓶）
6 mazzard 脑袋

OTHELLO ACT 2 SCENE 3
奥赛罗

MONTANO But is he often thus?
IAGO 'Tis evermore the prologue to his sleep:
He'll watch the horologe a double set[1],
If drink rock not his cradle.
MONTANO It were well
The general were put in mind[2] of it. 115
Perhaps he sees it not, or his good nature
Prizes the virtue that appears in Cassio
And looks not on his evils: is not this true?

Enter RODERIGO.

IAGO [*Aside to Roderigo*] How now, Roderigo?
I pray you after the lieutenant, go. 120

Exit Roderigo

MONTANO And 'tis great pity that the noble Moor
Should hazard such a place as his own second[3]
With one of an ingraft[4] infirmity;
It were an honest action to say so
To the Moor.
IAGO Not I, for this fair island: 125
I do love Cassio well, and would do much
To cure him of this evil.
[*A cry of*] 'Help, help!' *within*.
But hark! what noise?

Enter Cassio, pursuing Roderigo.

CASSIO Zounds, you rogue, you rascal!
MONTANO What's the matter, lieutenant?
CASSIO A knave teach me my duty! I'll beat the knave into a 130
twiggen bottle[5].
RODERIGO Beat me?
CASSIO Dost thou prate, rogue?
[*He strikes Roderigo.*]
MONTANO Nay, good lieutenant, I pray you, sir, hold your hand.
CASSIO Let me go, sir; or I'll knock you o'er the mazzard[6]. 135
MONTANO Come, come, you're drunk.

Cassio, incensed by Montano's accusation of drunkenness, fights him. The alarm is sounded. Othello enters to restore order and demand an explanation. Iago denies he knows who began the brawl.

 剧情简介： 卡修因芒塔诺指责他醉酒而发火，跟他打了起来。警铃响起，奥赛罗上台恢复秩序，要求解释。伊阿苟说他不知道是谁挑起的争端。

1 The fight (in small groups)

Create a slow-motion, silent version of this scene from line 128 ('*Enter Cassio, pursuing Roderigo*') to line 150 ('From whence ariseth this?') Make each character recognisable and clearly define each stage of the action. Start and end your presentation with a tableau. Remember, your movements must be slow, controlled, safe and easy to follow.

1 cry a mutiny 大喊"兵变了"
2 Diabolo 魔鬼（西班牙语）
3 rise 发生骚乱
4 carve for his own rage 因自己动怒而动刀
5 Holds his soul light 不珍视自己的性命
6 he dies upon his motion 谁敢动就得死
7 propriety 平静，安宁
8 love 忠诚
9 quarter 彼此的关系，交情
10 Divesting 宽衣解带
11 had unwitted men 让人失去理智（古人相信脱离轨道的星宿会让人发疯）
12 tilting 刺
13 speak 解释
14 peevish odds 无意义的争斗

Themes 主题分析
Honesty and dishonesty (in pairs)

At line 158, Iago is once again described as 'honest'. Design a diagram of all the uses of 'honest' in the script so far. Leave room for further additions to the list – you'll find many more as this scene progresses. Continue adding to your diagram as you read the rest of the play.

Write about it 写作练习
Iago's language

In lines 160–8, find three or four expressions that Iago knows will appeal to Othello. Write two paragraphs explaining how Iago chooses his words to suit his listeners, giving precise examples from the script opposite.

OTHELLO ACT 2 SCENE 3
奥赛罗

CASSIO	Drunk?
	They fight.
IAGO	[*Aside to Roderigo*] Away I say, go out and cry a mutiny[1].
	[*Exit Roderigo*]
	Nay, good lieutenant; God's will, gentlemen!
	Help ho! Lieutenant, sir! Montano, sir! 140
	Help, masters, here's a goodly watch indeed!
	A bell rings.
	Who's that which rings the bell? Diabolo[2], ho!
	The town will rise[3]. God's will, lieutenant, hold!
	You will be shamed forever.
	Enter Othello, and GENTLEMEN *with weapons.*
OTHELLO	What is the matter here?
MONTANO	Zounds, I bleed still. 145
	I am hurt to th'death.
OTHELLO	Hold for your lives!
IAGO	Hold ho, lieutenant, sir; Montano, gentlemen,
	Have you forgot all place of sense and duty?
	Hold! the general speaks to you; hold, for shame!
OTHELLO	Why, how now, ho! From whence ariseth this? 150
	Are we turned Turks, and to ourselves do that
	Which heaven hath forbid the Ottomites?
	For Christian shame, put by this barbarous brawl.
	He that stirs next to carve for his own rage[4]
	Holds his soul light[5]: he dies upon his motion[6]. 155
	Silence that dreadful bell: it frights the isle
	From her propriety[7]. What is the matter, masters?
	Honest Iago, that looks dead with grieving,
	Speak. Who began this? On thy love[8], I charge thee.
IAGO	I do not know. Friends all but now, even now, 160
	In quarter[9] and in terms like bride and groom,
	Divesting[10] them for bed; and then but now –
	As if some planet had unwitted men[11] –
	Swords out and tilting[12] one at other's breasts
	In opposition bloody. I cannot speak[13] 165
	Any beginning to this peevish odds[14]:
	And would in action glorious I had lost
	Those legs that brought me to a part of it.

77

Othello tries to discover who started the fight. Cassio gives no explanation. Montano pleads self-defence, and says that Iago knows as much as he does. Othello orders Iago to speak.

 剧情简介：奥赛罗试图弄清楚谁先动手的。卡修不说，芒塔诺称自己是自卫，还说伊阿苟知道的跟他一样多。奥赛罗命令伊阿苟说话。

1 Cassio's silence (in pairs)

At the start of this scene, Othello twice called Cassio 'Michael'. Here, once again, he uses Cassio's first name as he asks him to explain. This denotes a friendship and trust that will soon be lost. Why, when questioned, does Cassio choose to say nothing?

- Do you think that is the right course of action? If not, what should he have said? Discuss in pairs, then spend about five minutes writing down a possible reply for Cassio.

Language in the play 剧中语言
Black and white

Othello becomes impatient and indicates that he is on the verge of losing his temper with the brawlers (斗殴者). At line 187, he exclaims: 'passion having my best judgement collied, / Assays to lead the way.' He is saying that his rage is about to overtake his better ('best') judgement. The word 'collied' is usually defined as 'blackened', with its links with the word 'coal' ('collier', 'colliery').

- Why is black/white imagery appropriate in this play? What other examples of black and white in **binary opposition** (二元对立) have we heard so far? (Binary opposition is a term used in literary criticism to describe a pair of related terms or ideas that have opposite meanings.)

Characters 人物分析
Iago the actor (in pairs)

At lines 201–3, Iago pretends he would rather have his own tongue cut out than make any allegation (指控) against Cassio (thus revealing the identity of the guilty person).

- How should the actor playing Iago say these lines? Should he slightly overplay (夸张地表演) the moment (for example, by adopting a tone of mock innocence for the audience to enjoy)? Or do you think he should underplay (含蓄地表演) the words?
- With your partner, try acting out Iago's lines in two or three different ways. Share your most successful version with the class.

---

1 thus forgot　如此忘乎所以
2 wont　一向，惯常
3 gravity and stillness　持重和冷静
4 censure　判断力
5 spend your rich opinion　挥霍众人对您的普遍好评
6 something now offends me　我感到有点儿痛
7 self-charity　自我防卫
8 blood　愤怒
9 safer guides　理智
10 collied　变得暗淡
11 Assays　试图
12 foul rout　不文明的动粗
13 approved　证实有罪
14 twinned with me　与我是孪生兄弟
15 brimful of　充满
16 manage private and domestic quarrel　因私人恩怨大打出手
　（manage：进行，实施）
17 partially affined　偏袒
18 leagued in office　顾虑同僚关系

OTHELLO	How comes it, Michael, you are thus forgot[1]?	
CASSIO	I pray you pardon me, I cannot speak.	170
OTHELLO	Worthy Montano, you were wont[2] be civil:	
	The gravity and stillness[3] of your youth	
	The world hath noted; and your name is great	
	In mouths of wisest censure[4]. What's the matter	
	That you unlace your reputation thus,	175
	And spend your rich opinion[5] for the name	
	Of a night-brawler? Give me answer to it.	
MONTANO	Worthy Othello, I am hurt to danger;	
	Your officer Iago can inform you –	
	While I spare speech, which something now offends me[6]–	180
	Of all that I do know; nor know I aught	
	By me that's said or done amiss this night,	
	Unless self-charity[7] be sometimes a vice,	
	And to defend ourselves it be a sin	
	When violence assails us.	
OTHELLO	Now by heaven	185
	My blood[8] begins my safer guides[9] to rule,	
	And passion having my best judgement collied[10],	
	Assays[11] to lead the way. Zounds, if I stir,	
	Or do but lift this arm, the best of you	
	Shall sink in my rebuke. Give me to know	190
	How this foul rout[12] began, who set it on,	
	And he that is approved[13] in this offence,	
	Though he had twinned with me[14], both at a birth,	
	Shall lose me. What, in a town of war,	
	Yet wild, the people's hearts brimful of[15] fear,	195
	To manage private and domestic quarrel[16],	
	In night, and on the court and guard of safety?	
	'Tis monstrous. Iago, who began't?	
MONTANO	If partially affined[17] or leagued in office[18],	
	Thou dost deliver more or less than truth,	200
	Thou art no soldier.	
IAGO	Touch me not so near.	
	I had rather have this tongue cut from my mouth	
	Than it should do offence to Michael Cassio.	

> Iago gives an account of how Cassio started the affray. Asserting that Iago's honesty has made him play down Cassio's offence, Othello immediately dismisses Cassio from office.
>
> 剧情简介：伊阿苟叙述卡修如何挑起争斗。奥赛罗认为伊阿苟实诚，以为他对卡修的过错轻描淡写，故立即将卡修革职。

1 Personal feelings, public judgement (whole class)

Iago gives a falsely sympathetic account of Cassio's behaviour (lines 201–27). Othello is taken in by Iago's cunning, and confirms that his 'honesty and love' have made the report 'light to Cassio'. In dismissing Cassio as one of his officers, Othello distinguishes between his private feelings for his friend and his public judgement of his lieutenant.

a Suggest how both these aspects are implied in Othello's line 231: 'Look if my gentle love be not raised up!'

b Othello declares his intention to make an example of Cassio (line 232). Think back on the play so far. On what other occasion has a character had to balance personal feelings against public judgement?

1 To execute upon him 要处置他
2 entreats his pause 求他住手
3 fall in fright 受惊扰
4 For that 因为
5 indignity 侮辱
6 mince this matter 轻描淡写
7 myself will be your surgeon 我会为您医治

Write about it 写作练习

Iago's diary

Consider how well Iago has orchestrated (精心安排) the brawl. Do you think he would feel pleased with the way he has managed to convincingly play his part as a loyal friend to Cassio, while also seeming to reluctantly tell the truth to his commanding officer, Othello?

- Write Iago's private diary, describing the events of the day from the point that he, Desdemona and Emilia disembark (Act 2 Scene 1, line 83).
- Think about the kind of language he might use. To help you, look at his soliloquies during this act so far, where he speaks in the same type of confessional language that he is likely to use in his diary. (See Act 1 Scene 3, lines 365–86; Act 2 Scene 1, lines 267–93; Act 2 Scene 3, lines 40–6; Act 2 Scene 3, lines 303–29 and 347–53.) Don't forget that Iago also talks directly to the audience by means of asides, as in Act 2 Scene 1, lines 163–71 and 191–3.
- In his diary, have Iago think back over his speech to Othello in lines 201–27 and comment on his own words.
- At the end of the diary entry, indicate how successfully Iago believes he has set things up for his future plans.

OTHELLO ACT 2 SCENE 3
奥赛罗

           Yet, I persuade myself, to speak the truth
           Shall nothing wrong him. This it is, general: 205
           Montano and myself being in speech,
           There comes a fellow crying out for help,
           And Cassio following him with determined sword
           To execute upon him[1]. Sir, this gentleman
           Steps in to Cassio and entreats his pause[2];   210
           Myself the crying fellow did pursue,
           Lest by his clamour – as it so fell out –
           The town might fall in fright[3]. He, swift of foot,
           Outran my purpose and I returned the rather
           For that[4] I heard the clink and fall of swords   215
           And Cassio high in oath, which till tonight
           I ne'er might say before. When I came back –
           For this was brief – I found them close together
           At blow and thrust, even as again they were
           When you yourself did part them.   220
           More of this matter can I not report;
           But men are men; the best sometimes forget.
           Though Cassio did some little wrong to him,
           As men in rage strike those that wish them best,
           Yet surely Cassio, I believe, received   225
           From him that fled some strange indignity[5]
           Which patience could not pass.

OTHELLO   I know, Iago,
           Thy honesty and love doth mince this matter[6],
           Making it light to Cassio. Cassio, I love thee,
           But never more be officer of mine.   230

                   Enter Desdemona attended.

           Look if my gentle love be not raised up!
           I'll make thee an example.

DESDEMONA   What's the matter, dear?
OTHELLO   All's well now, sweeting; come away to bed.
           Sir, for your hurts myself will be your surgeon[7].
                                       [*Montano is led off*]

After Othello has gone back to bed, Cassio bemoans the loss of his reputation to Iago. Iago tells him to make an appeal. Cassio curses what drink does to men.

　剧情简介：奥赛罗回去就寝后，卡修向伊阿苟表达对自己名誉受损的懊悔。伊阿苟让他去求情。卡修咒骂饮酒害人不浅。

Language in the play 剧中语言

From verse to prose (in pairs)

After Othello and Desdemona's exit (line 238), the script changes from verse to prose for the dialogue between Cassio and Iago.

- Read the information about verse and prose in 'The language of *Othello*' on page 230, then spend five minutes discussing possible reasons for this change of style here. How might you reflect this transition on stage (for example, by a change of lighting or the movement of characters)?

1 What is 'reputation'? (in pairs)

Read lines 242–9 to each other several times. Cassio uses the word 'reputation' six times in three lines, and defines it as 'the immortal part of myself', without which 'what remains is bestial'. In contrast, Iago defines reputation as 'an idle and most false imposition, oft got without merit and lost without deserving' (lines 247–8).

a Make notes about the different ways in which Iago and Cassio regard reputation as a concept.

b Write a paragraph reflecting on the importance of reputation and self-image for each of the following: you and your friends; celebrities you are familiar with from news stories and interviews; politicians in your country.

2 Alcohol awareness campaign (in small groups)

Imagine that Cassio has been employed by the Venetian Health Education Council to make an advertisement about the dangers of alcohol abuse. Design the campaign, making sure you include some of the following:

- a clear message about the dangers of alcohol abuse
- a focus on your target audience
- a well-known celebrity (Cassio)
- a suitable logo
- a slogan (taken from the script, if possible) to help your audience remember the message
- music and/or a jingle (短曲).

Improvise a three-minute television commercial featuring Cassio's account of his own experiences at the hands of the 'invisible spirit of wine'.

1　balmy slumbers　酣睡
2　past all surgery　无药可救
3　bestial　禽兽一般
4　idle and most false imposition　无用又十分虚假的身外之物
5　repute　认为
6　cast in his mood　他一时气愤免你的职
7　policy　政治手腕
8　imperious　凶猛
9　Sue　求情
10　speak parrot　吧啦吧啦
11　fustian　胡说八道
12　nothing wherefore　不知缘由
13　It … wrath　正是因为醉酒让愤怒的恶魔钻了空子

Iago, look with care about the town, 235
And silence those whom this vile brawl distracted.
Come, Desdemona, 'tis the soldier's life
To have their balmy slumbers[1] waked with strife.

Exeunt [all but Iago and Cassio]

IAGO   What, are you hurt, lieutenant?
CASSIO Ay, past all surgery[2]. 240
IAGO   Marry, God forbid!
CASSIO Reputation, reputation, reputation! O, I have lost my reputation! I have lost the immortal part of myself, and what remains is bestial[3]. My reputation, Iago, my reputation!
IAGO   As I am an honest man, I thought you had received some bodily 245
        wound: there is more of sense in that than in reputation. Reputation is an idle and most false imposition[4], oft got without merit and lost without deserving. You have lost no reputation at all, unless you repute[5] yourself such a loser. What, man! There are ways to recover the general again. You are but now cast 250
        in his mood[6], a punishment more in policy[7] than in malice, even so as one would beat his offenceless dog to affright an imperious[8] lion. Sue[9] to him again, and he's yours.
CASSIO I will rather sue to be despised than to deceive so good a commander with so light, so drunken, and so indiscreet an 255
        officer. Drunk! And speak parrot[10]! And squabble! Swagger! Swear! And discourse fustian[11] with one's own shadow! O thou invisible spirit of wine, if thou hast no name to be known by, let us call thee devil!
IAGO   What was he that you followed with your sword? What had he 260
        done to you?
CASSIO I know not.
IAGO   Is't possible?
CASSIO I remember a mass of things, but nothing distinctly: a quarrel, but nothing wherefore[12]. O God, that men should put an enemy 265
        in their mouths to steal away their brains! That we should with joy, pleasance, revel and applause transform ourselves into beasts!
IAGO   Why, but you are now well enough. How came you thus recovered?
CASSIO It hath pleased the devil drunkenness to give place to the devil 270
        wrath[13]; one unperfectness shows me another, to make me frankly despise myself.

Iago suggests that Cassio should approach Desdemona about his reinstatement. He insists that her good nature and her influence over Othello will restore Cassio to office. Cassio accepts the advice.

 剧情简介：伊阿苟建议卡修找黛丝荻牟娜求情以谋求复职，坚称她的好性情和她对奥赛罗的影响力必能助卡修官复原职。卡修接受了这个建议。

Characters 人物分析

Cassio (in small groups)

Cassio bemoans the fact that he no longer regards himself as 'a sensible man', but how does Cassio really see himself at this point in the play?

- Read lines 242–80. Find the ways in which Cassio describes himself (for example, in lines 267, 277 and 279). Then create a tableau or a collage (拼贴画) based on the images Cassio uses.

1 Thought-track Iago (in pairs)

Iago deceitfully advises Cassio to ask Desdemona for help. Why do you think he suggests this course of action? What are his ulterior (隐藏的) motives?

- With your partner, stand back to back. One person becomes Iago and reads the speech in lines 281–95, pausing at the end of each sentence. This is the cue for the second person to voice Iago's hidden thoughts. Present what is going on in Iago's mind, explaining what he really thinks and what his future plans are. Share your ideas with the rest of the class.

Write about it 写作练习

Cassio's diary

Imagine Cassio keeps a personal journal. Write his diary entry for this evening. To help you decide what to include, consider the following questions while in role as Cassio:

- How has your life changed this evening? Give a brief description of the events that have taken place.
- How do you feel about yourself?
- Do you think Othello reacted fairly?
- What is your opinion of Iago and the advice he has given you?
- What do you hope to achieve by approaching Desdemona tomorrow?

1 **Hydra** 亥爪（希腊神话里的九头怪蛇，它的头被砍去一个马上会长出两个新头）
2 **inordinate** 过量，过度
3 **unblessed** = cursed （该死，受诅咒）
4 **ingredience** 里面装的东西（指杯子里的酒）
5 **familiar creature** 友好的精灵
6 **approved it** 证实了
7 **mark, and denotement** 所看和所记
8 **parts** 优点，品质
9 **importune** 纠缠，强求
10 **free** 宽宏大量
11 **splinter** 修复，弥合
12 **lay** 赌注
13 **freely** 完全，无保留
14 **check** 拒绝

IAGO	Come, you are too severe a moraler. As the time, the place, and the condition of this country stands, I could heartily wish this had not befallen; but since it is as it is, mend it for your own good.	275
CASSIO	I will ask him for my place again; he shall tell me I am a drunkard. Had I as many mouths as Hydra[1], such an answer would stop them all. To be now a sensible man, by and by a fool, and presently a beast! O strange! Every inordinate[2] cup is unblessed[3], and the ingredience[4] is a devil.	280
IAGO	Come, come, good wine is a good familiar creature[5], if it be well used; exclaim no more against it. And, good lieutenant, I think you think I love you.	
CASSIO	I have well approved it[6], sir. I drunk!	
IAGO	You or any man living may be drunk at a time, man. I'll tell you what you shall do. Our general's wife is now the general. I may say so in this respect, for that he hath devoted and given up himself to the contemplation, mark, and denotement[7] of her parts[8] and graces. Confess yourself freely to her, importune[9] her help to put you in your place again. She is of so free[10], so kind, so apt, so blest a disposition, that she holds it a vice in her goodness not to do more than she is requested. This broken joint between you and her husband entreat her to splinter[11]; and my fortunes against any lay[12] worth naming, this crack of your love shall grow stronger than it was before.	285 290 295
CASSIO	You advise me well.	
IAGO	I protest, in the sincerity of love and honest kindness.	
CASSIO	I think it freely[13]; and betimes in the morning I will beseech the virtuous Desdemona to undertake for me. I am desperate of my fortunes if they check[14] me here.	300
IAGO	You are in the right. Good night, lieutenant, I must to the watch.	
CASSIO	Good night, honest Iago. *Exit*	

Left alone, Iago reveals his plan to lie to Othello about Desdemona and Cassio having an affair. When Desdemona pleads for Cassio's reinstatement, it will only make things worse. Roderigo tells Iago that he's fed up.

剧情简介： 独自一人时，伊阿苟透露了自己的计谋，他会向奥赛罗撒谎，诬陷黛丝荻牟娜与卡修私通。一旦黛丝荻牟娜为卡修复职说情，只会使情况更糟。若德瑞苟对伊阿苟说自己受够了。

1 Iago's soliloquy – bare bones (in threes)

a Read through Iago's soliloquy in the script opposite (lines 303–29) in order to get the general sense. It demonstrates Iago's acute awareness that appearances can be deceptive. He uses **antitheses** (对偶) (words with opposite meanings), culminating (达到极点) in the contrasting concepts of 'virtue' versus 'pitch' (line 327).

b In your group, take one line at a time and quickly agree what you consider to be the key word in each line (for example, in the first line this might be the word 'villain'). Write down each key word (one word per line). When you have done this for the whole speech, you will have a list of twenty-seven words. This is your 'bare-bones' script.

c Keeping the words in their original order, present this new script in any ways that seem appropriate (choral speech, movement, mime, sound effects, echoing individual words). Divide up the words between each group member however you like, but make sure everyone is fully involved. Afterwards, share your presentation with the rest of the class.

▼ In this production, Iago is crouched – sinister (阴险) and threatening. How would you have Iago deliver his soliloquy?

1 Probal 有道理；站得住
2 win 说服
3 inclining 有同情心的
4 fruitful 慷慨
5 free elements 免费元素（即土壤、空气、水、火，喻指黛丝荻牟娜热心慷慨）
6 baptism （基督教）洗礼
7 seals and symbols 印记和象征（如十字架）
8 enfettered 受制于，成为……的奴隶
9 list 愿意，喜欢
10 appetite 情欲
11 function 意志
12 parallel course 相关途径（指实现伊阿苟阴谋的路径）
13 Divinity 神学
14 suggest 引诱
15 Plies 恳求
16 pestilence 瘟疫
17 repeals him 让他复职
18 pitch 沥青（喻指抹黑）
19 fills up the cry 滥竽充数
20 cudgelled 遭暴打

IAGO	And what's he then that says I play the villain,
	When this advice is free I give, and honest,
	Probal[1] to thinking, and indeed the course 305
	To win[2] the Moor again? For 'tis most easy
	Th'inclining[3] Desdemona to subdue
	In any honest suit. She's framed as fruitful[4]
	As the free elements[5]; and then for her
	To win the Moor, were't to renounce his baptism[6], 310
	All seals and symbols[7] of redeemèd sin,
	His soul is so enfettered[8] to her love,
	That she may make, unmake, do what she list[9],
	Even as her appetite[10] shall play the god
	With his weak function[11]. How am I then a villain 315
	To counsel Cassio to this parallel course[12]
	Directly to his good? Divinity[13] of hell!
	When devils will the blackest sins put on,
	They do suggest[14] at first with heavenly shows
	As I do now. For whiles this honest fool 320
	Plies[15] Desdemona to repair his fortunes,
	And she for him pleads strongly to the Moor,
	I'll pour this pestilence[16] into his ear:
	That she repeals him[17] for her body's lust;
	And by how much she strives to do him good, 325
	She shall undo her credit with the Moor.
	So will I turn her virtue into pitch[18],
	And out of her own goodness make the net
	That shall enmesh them all.

Enter Roderigo.

How now, Roderigo?

RODERIGO I do follow here in the chase, not like a hound that hunts, 330
but one that fills up the cry[19]. My money is almost spent; I have
been tonight exceedingly well cudgelled[20]; and I think the issue will
be, I shall have so much experience for my pains; and so, with
no money at all, and a little more wit, return again to Venice.

Iago bids Roderigo to be patient, and tells him they have already succeeded in disgracing Cassio. Left alone, Iago plans to make Emilia urge Desdemona to help Cassio, then to ensure that Othello sees his wife and Cassio together.

 剧情简介：伊阿苟劝若德瑞苟要耐心，说他们已经成功让卡修失势。台上剩下他一个人时，伊阿苟谋划让艾蜜丽叶敦促黛丝荻牟娜帮助卡修，还要确保奥赛罗看见妻子和卡修在一起。

Stagecraft 导演技巧

Director's notes (in pairs)

For this activity you are going to work on both parts of Iago's soliloquy, from the previous page (lines 303–29) and from the script opposite (lines 347–53). One of you takes the role of director; the other is the actor playing Iago in a new production of the play. You need to prepare this key speech in detail before rehearsals. Annotate (批注) the speech, indicating:

- how Iago should speak (think about changes of tone of voice and of pace)
- what's Iago's movements should be and the way in which he will move around the stage
- what facial expressions and gestures he should employ
- where there might be pauses and silences
- what Iago might be thinking/feeling
- where the speech is set (if that is important)
- the props (if any) that Iago should have.

Overall, consider what relationship you want Iago to have with the audience. For example, does he draw the audience in to his plans? You may wish to work with an enlarged copy of the speech, which you can annotate similarly to the example below.

1 by degrees 一步一步，慢慢
2 dilatory 逐渐
3 cashiered Cassio 让卡修丢了官
4 By th'mass 天啊
5 where thou art billeted 你的驻地
6 move 求情
7 the while 同时
8 jump 刚好那时
9 Dull 误了，坏了
10 device 大计

Turns slowly to face audience directly

Speaks quite slowly

Half smiles, then puts on an innocent look

Slight pause on this word

Make this word stand out (so many people have called him 'honest')

IAGO

As he speaks, he walks to front of stage

And what's he then that says I play the villain,
When this advice is free I give, and honest,
Probal to thinking, and indeed the course
To win the Moor again? For 'tis most easy
Th'inclining Desdemona to subdue
In any honest suit. She's framed as fruitful
As the free elements; and then for her
To win the Moor, were't to renounce his baptism,
All seals and symbols of redeemèd sin,

Speed up a little

Allow word a little emphasis

Spoken with disgust

End of question, so pause

Light and quick

IAGO	How poor are they that have no patience!	335

                What wound did ever heal but by degrees[1]?
                Thou know'st we work by wit and not by witchcraft,
                And wit depends on dilatory[2] time.
                Does't not go well? Cassio hath beaten thee,
                And thou by that small hurt hath cashiered Cassio[3].   340
                Though other things grow fair against the sun,
                Yet fruits that blossom first will first be ripe.
                Content thyself awhile. By th'mass[4], 'tis morning:
                Pleasure and action make the hours seem short.
                Retire thee, go where thou art billeted[5].   345
                Away, I say, thou shalt know more hereafter –
                Nay, get thee gone.

Exit Roderigo

                        Two things are to be done.
                My wife must move[6] for Cassio to her mistress –
                I'll set her on.
                Myself the while[7] to draw the Moor apart,   350
                And bring him jump[8] when he may Cassio find
                Soliciting his wife. Ay, that's the way:
                Dull[9] not device[10] by coldness and delay.

Exit

Othello 奥赛罗

Looking back at Act 2 第2幕回顾
Activities for groups or individuals

1 Headlines – what has happened so far?

Imagine you are a newspaper sub-editor (助理编辑). First of all, consider whether your newspaper is a tabloid (小报) or a broadsheet (大报). Once you have decided, your job is to write brief, memorable headlines for each of the six scenes in the first two acts of the play. Make your headlines as accurate as possible. Try to use some of Shakespeare's own words.

2 Epithets (绰号, 外号) and statues

An **epithet** is an adjective or describing phrase, added before a name or noun, that defines the person or thing – for example, 'honest Iago'. In Act 2, there are several epithets, which are applied to a number of different characters.

a In pairs, identify who said each of the following, then discuss what the description tells us about the speaker and the person described:

- 'the warlike Moor'
- 'brave Othello'
- 'valiant Cassio'
- 'divine Desdemon'
- 'bold Iago'
- 'the lusty Moor'
- 'virtuous Desdemona'
- 'honest Iago'
- 'good Michael'
- 'worthy (可敬的) Montano'.

b In your pairs, one person becomes a sculptor, the second person a block of marble. The sculptor must 'carve' three separate statues, choosing from the descriptions above. Swap roles and repeat the activity. Afterwards, share your statues with the rest of the class. Can they identify the statue from the list of titles above?

3 Judgements and justice

Differing notions of justice permeate (渗透) the play. In both Act 1 and Act 2, a crucial judgement is made and 'justice' is publicly dispensed (执行).

a With a partner, locate these judgements and the participants in each case. Identify the motive, the 'evidence' presented and the consequences of the ruling (裁决). What key similarities and/or differences can you find? Make notes as you work.

b On your own, write a short essay (approximately five paragraphs) examining how justice is represented in the first two acts of *Othello*. Use the notes that you and your partner generated in the activity above to support this piece of writing. Make sure that you make close references to the script, and include embedded quotations.

4 Staging the play

The pictures opposite show two different stage sets, both for outdoor performances of *Othello*. They may be rather different from how you imagined the set or from productions you have seen.

a Choose one of the sets and suggest how it might incorporate key locations that you have come across in the play so far:

- a street at night, including Brabantio's house
- outside the Sagittary
- the Council Chamber in Venice
- the storm at sea, and the quayside in Cyprus
- the herald's proclamation in Cyprus
- a barracks room in the castle in Cyprus.

b Design your own stage set, in which different locations can be suggested swiftly and without the need for major physical changes of scenery.

Cassio has hired Musicians to play for Othello and Desdemona. A Clown jokes with a Musician. Cassio sends the Clown to Emilia, to ask her to come out and speak with him.

 剧情简介：卡修聘请了乐师为奥赛罗和黛丝荻牟娜演奏。小丑与一名乐师开玩笑。卡修打发小丑去找艾蜜丽叶，请她出来和他说话。

1 The Clown and the Musicians (in threes)

Elizabethan and Jacobean acting companies always employed a comic actor, or clown. His main role was to play funny or witty parts, possibly embellishing (点缀) the script with improvised jokes. Playwrights would create a specific role in order to accommodate (照顾) the clown, even in tragic plays. One effect (for example, with the role of the Porter in *Macbeth*) was to momentarily relieve tension in the drama.

a Read the script opposite aloud, then talk together about what you think of the humour here, which relies heavily on puns and wordplay. For example, the Clown plays with the double meaning of the word 'Naples' – a joke on the nasal sound of a Neapolitan accent and 'Neapolitan disease', a venereal disease. He also generates puns around the word 'instrument', where the first reference in line 6 is to a kind of bagpipe (风笛), the second reference (line 10) to flatulence (肠胃胀气). Some people find the jokes to be rather crude and laboured (牵强), but others argue that the dramatic function of the Clown's punning is to foreshadow (预示) the misunderstandings that are shortly to happen in the play. Consider both points of view in your discussion.

b If you were directing a production of *Othello*, what popular stage or television comedian would you cast in the role of the Clown? Explain your choice.

c It was an Elizabethan custom to wake newlyweds with music outside their bedchamber. Discuss whether you would open the scene with musicians really playing on stage. In a modern production, what music would you choose, and why? Can you think of a particular song or piece of music that might have significant meaning for the characters at this point in the play?

2 Make a director's decision (in pairs)

Lines 1–27 are often cut from productions. Discuss with your partner whether you would include them in your own modern production of the play. Give at least two reasons for and against their inclusion before reaching your decision. Share your views with the rest of the class, then make some notes in your Director's Journal.

---

1 **content your pains** 答谢你们的辛劳
2 **Good morrow** 早安（这里提到旧时习俗，在新婚第二日的清晨在新婚夫妻卧室外奏乐以示庆贺）
3 **Naples** 那不勒斯
4 **speak i'th'nose thus** 这样嚷着鼻子说话（花柳病又名 Neapolitan disease，得此病者因鼻腔受损，说话时鼻音重）
5 **How, sir, how?** 先生，您这话怎讲？
6 **tail** 尾巴（暗指男性器官；乐师误以为他说的是 tale）
7 **wind instrument** 管乐器（暗指放屁的器官）
8 **for love's sake** 出于对他的爱
9 **noise** 噪声（也与 nose 构成谐音双关，指难听的鼻音）
10 **may not** = cannot
11 **put ... bag** 把你那箫装进袋子（这里是下流话）
12 **keep up thy quillets** 收起你的双关语吧；别耍贫嘴了
13 **stirring** 起床
14 **stirring** 叫床
15 **seem** 安排

Othello Act 3 Scene 1
奥赛罗

Act 3 Scene 1
Cyprus   Outside Desdemona's bedchamber

Enter CASSIO, MUSICIANS *and* CLOWN.

CASSIO   Masters, play here; I will content your pains[1].
Something that's brief, and bid 'Good morrow[2], general.'
[*They play.*]

CLOWN   Why, masters, have your instruments been in Naples[3], that they speak i'th'nose thus[4]?

1 MUSICIAN   How, sir, how?[5]

CLOWN   Are these, I pray you, wind instruments?

1 MUSICIAN   Ay, marry are they, sir.

CLOWN   O, thereby hangs a tail[6].

1 MUSICIAN   Whereby hangs a tale, sir?

CLOWN   Marry, sir, by many a wind instrument[7] that I know. But, masters, here's money for you; and the general so likes your music that he desires you, for love's sake[8], to make no more noise[9] with it.

1 MUSICIAN   Well sir, we will not.

CLOWN   If you have any music that may not[10] be heard, to't again; but, as they say, to hear music the general does not greatly care.

1 MUSICIAN   We have none such, sir.

CLOWN   Then put up your pipes in your bag[11], for I'll away. Go, vanish into air, away!

Exeunt Musicians

CASSIO   Dost thou hear, mine honest friend?

CLOWN   No, I hear not your honest friend; I hear you.

CASSIO   Prithee keep up thy quillets[12] – there's a poor piece of gold for thee. If the gentlewoman that attends the general's wife be stirring[13], tell her there's one Cassio entreats her a little favour of speech. Wilt thou do this?

CLOWN   She is stirring[14], sir; if she will stir hither, I shall seem[15] to notify unto her.

CASSIO   Do, good my friend.

Exit Clown

Iago promises Cassio that he will take Othello out of the way for a while, so Cassio and Emilia can talk freely. Emilia tells Cassio that Othello feels obliged to make an example of him, but intends to reinstate him at a convenient moment.

剧情简介：伊阿苟向卡修保证他会把奥赛罗引开片刻，这样卡修和艾蜜丽叶就能畅所欲言。艾蜜丽叶告诉卡修，奥赛罗觉得不得不这样对他，以儆效尤，但打算在合适的时候重新起用他。

1 The timescale of the play (in pairs)

Iago's opening comment, 'You have not been abed then?' suggests that this is the morning after the drunken party. The dramatic function might be to:

- give the impression that Cassio is too upset to sleep
- make the action seem to happen very quickly
- give the play continuity
- give a sense of urgency to the events
- keep the party fresh in the audience's mind
- heighten tension
- illustrate how astute (精明，狡猾) or cunning Iago is.

Critics have argued about the timescale of the whole play, which is quite difficult to follow in any naturalistic way. As you read through the rest of the play, pay attention to the passage of time and consider what sense you get of the speed of the action. Construct a timeline of events as they unfold, either individually in your Director's Journal or collectively as a class display.

1	abed 上床睡觉
2	made bold 冒昧，斗胆
3	suit 请求
4	Procure （设法）获得，取得
5	a mean 办法
6	For your displeasure 因您受处分的事情
7	stoutly 坚决
8	great affinity 很有人脉
9	might not but refuse 可能不得不将……免职
10	take … front 抓住最妥当的机会
11	bring you in again 重新任用您
12	bosom 心里话
13	much bound = much obliged （非常感激）

Characters 人物分析

Emilia: role and relationships

In the dual role of Desdemona's companion and Iago's wife, Emilia becomes an increasingly important character in the play. In this part of the scene, she takes on the dramatic function of enabling Cassio to gain access to Desdemona, thereby becoming an unwitting pawn (不明就里的棋子) in Iago's elaborate plot.

a Read all that Emilia says in the script opposite, then write a paragraph outlining your impressions of Emilia. You might want to refer back to her first appearance (Act 2 Scene 1, lines 83–204) and compare how she came across then with your opinion of her now.

b Over the next two scenes, we will learn a great deal more about Emilia's relationship with Iago. As you read or watch Act 3, make notes on the way Emilia's character develops.

2 More dramatic irony

Find at least two examples of dramatic irony (see p. 38) in the script opposite. For each, explain in what way the comment is ironic and what the dramatic effect might be.

Othello Act 3 Scene 1
奥赛罗

Enter IAGO.

	In happy time, Iago.	
IAGO	You have not been abed¹ then?	
CASSIO	Why, no; the day had broke before we parted.	30
	I have made bold², Iago,	
	To send in to your wife. My suit³ to her	
	Is that she will to virtuous Desdemona	
	Procure⁴ me some access.	
IAGO	I'll send her to you presently;	
	And I'll devise a mean⁵ to draw the Moor	35
	Out of the way, that your converse and business	
	May be more free.	
CASSIO	I humbly thank you for't.	

Exit [*Iago*]

I never knew a Florentine more kind and honest.

Enter EMILIA.

EMILIA	Good morrow, good lieutenant; I am sorry	
	For your displeasure⁶; but all will sure be well.	40
	The general and his wife are talking of it,	
	And she speaks for you stoutly⁷. The Moor replies	
	That he you hurt is of great fame in Cyprus	
	And great affinity⁸, and that in wholesome wisdom	
	He might not but refuse⁹ you; but he protests he loves you,	45
	And needs no other suitor but his likings	
	To take the safest occasion by the front¹⁰	
	To bring you in again¹¹.	
CASSIO	Yet I beseech you,	
	If you think fit, or that it may be done,	
	Give me advantage of some brief discourse	50
	With Desdemon alone.	
EMILIA	Pray you, come in;	
	I will bestow you where you shall have time	
	To speak your bosom¹² freely.	
CASSIO	I am much bound¹³ to you.	

Exeunt

Othello goes off to inspect the fortifications. In Scene 3, Desdemona assures Cassio that she will help him. Cassio expresses his gratitude.

剧情简介：奥赛罗下场去视察防御工事。在第三场，黛丝荻牟娜向卡修保证她会帮他，卡修表示感激。

Write about it 写作练习

Othello's official report

In line 1 of Scene 2, we discover that Othello has written an official report ('letters') to the Duke of Venice. In role as Othello, write this report. Firstly, think about the content, which might include:

- **Military mission** What has been the outcome of the mission to engage with the Turkish fleet and protect Cyprus from attack? Have all survived the storms at sea?
- **Current situation** What are you doing to make sure Cyprus is safe?
- **Incident involving Montano** How are you going to explain this? What changes in military personnel have there been?

What tone should you adopt as Othello (in your capacity as army general)? Find appropriate phrases from the script to include in your writing. Will you make any mention of your wedding celebration? If so, will the tone change when you turn to personal matters?

1 do my duties   转达我的敬意
2 walking   巡查
3 works   工事
4 Repair   回到
5 Bounteous   慷慨，宽厚
6 He … distance   他将只是出于策略的考虑表面上疏远你
（politic：讲策略，明智）

1 The dramatic function of Scene 2 (in pairs)

Scene 2 is very short. What dramatic purpose do you think this scene serves? Look back at the previous scene, and glance at the beginning of the next, then copy and complete the table below.

	Scene 1	Scene 2	Scene 3
Characters			
Where does it take place?			
What happens?			
How is the plot taken forward?			

What can you deduce (推断) about the function of Scene 2? Consider the following in your discussions:

- Othello's role as a military leader
- Iago's relationship with Othello
- Desdemona's whereabouts
- the time scheme
- Cassio's whereabouts
- Cyprus as a colonial outpost (前哨).

Act 3 Scene 2
Cyprus   Outside the castle

Enter OTHELLO, IAGO *and* GENTLEMEN.

OTHELLO   These letters give, Iago, to the pilot,
And by him do my duties[1] to the senate.
That done, I will be walking[2] on the works[3];
Repair[4] there to me.
IAGO   Well, my good lord, I'll do't.   [*Exit*]
OTHELLO   This fortification, gentlemen, shall we see't?   5
GENTLEMEN   We'll wait upon your lordship.

                                    Exeunt

Act 3 Scene 3
Cyprus   A room in the castle

Enter DESDEMONA, CASSIO *and* EMILIA.

DESDEMONA   Be thou assured, good Cassio, I will do
All my abilities in thy behalf.
EMILIA   Good madam, do; I warrant it grieves my husband
As if the case were his.
DESDEMONA   O, that's an honest fellow. Do not doubt, Cassio,   5
But I will have my lord and you again
As friendly as you were.
CASSIO   Bounteous[5] madam,
Whatever shall become of Michael Cassio,
He's never anything but your true servant.
DESDEMONA   I know't; I thank you. You do love my lord,   10
You have known him long, and be you well assured
He shall in strangeness stand no farther off
Than in a politic distance[6].

Cassio fears that Othello may not relent, but Desdemona again pledges her support. Othello sees them in conversation, and Iago draws attention to Cassio's hurried departure, implying furtiveness and guilt.

剧情简介：卡修担心奥赛罗可能不松口，但黛丝荻牟娜再次保证她会帮忙。奥赛罗看见他们在交谈，伊阿苟提醒他注意卡修离开得很匆忙，暗示他卡修行为鬼祟、做贼心虚。

Themes 主题分析

The position of women in the play (in pairs)

Desdemona promises Cassio: 'I give thee warrant of thy place.' She will help him back to his military position on the grounds of personal friendship.

- Briefly discuss Desdemona's role here, as friend, wife, woman and civilian. Then read on to the next page of script, and look at Activity 1 on page 100, which develops this issue further.

Stagecraft 导演技巧

Exits, entrances and movement (in small groups)

The manner and timing of characters' entrances and exits at this moment of the play are crucial to the dramatic development. In Shakespeare's day, the stage had a deep acting area with two entrance/exit doors at the back. The size of this area would make it possible for Othello and Iago to enter and pass by Cassio at a distance, allowing the remaining dialogue (notably, Iago's 'Ha! I like not that') to work theatrically. Look at the picture on page 186, which shows an Elizabethan stage similar in shape to the Globe Theatre, where *Othello* was originally performed.

- Try 'blocking' the moves of all the characters involved between line 25 and line 51 ('blocking' is working out different positions where people stand). Match the characters' movements and precise entrances and exits with lines of script. For example, decide how many lines it takes for Cassio to make his exit, and where Othello and Iago might be during those lines.

1 'Ha! I like not that' (in pairs)

a Read through lines 35–40. Annotate a copy of the script to show how Iago shapes what Othello thinks he sees.

b In role as Othello and Desdemona, read through lines 41–51. Experiment with ways in which Desdemona might speak her lines. For example, is she serious or playful?

c Discuss how chance yet again plays into Iago's hands. Consider what dramatic effect this combination of manipulation and chance creates, then add some notes to your Director's Journal.

1	nice	很少
2	breed ... circumstance	创造的机会少之又少
3	supplied	被人代替
4	doubt	担心
5	warrant	承诺，保证
6	To the last article	到底，到最后
7	watch him tame	不让他睡觉，直到把他驯服（这是驯鹰的做法）
8	board	餐桌
9	shrift	忏悔室
10	solicitor	辩护人，说情人
11	give thy cause away	放弃你的诉讼
12	do your discretion	请您酌情处理
13	languishes	郁闷，憔悴

CASSIO	Ay, but, lady,	
	That policy may either last so long	
	Or feed upon such nice[1] and waterish diet,	15
	Or breed itself so out of circumstance[2],	
	That I being absent and my place supplied[3],	
	My general will forget my love and service.	
DESDEMONA	Do not doubt[4] that. Before Emilia here,	
	I give thee warrant[5] of thy place. Assure thee	20
	If I do vow a friendship, I'll perform it	
	To the last article[6]. My lord shall never rest,	
	I'll watch him tame[7] and talk him out of patience;	
	His bed shall seem a school, his board[8] a shrift[9];	
	I'll intermingle every thing he does	25
	With Cassio's suit. Therefore be merry, Cassio;	
	Thy solicitor[10] shall rather die	
	Than give thy cause away[11].	

Enter OTHELLO *and* IAGO.

EMILIA	Madam, here comes my lord.	
CASSIO	Madam, I'll take my leave.	30
DESDEMONA	Why, stay and hear me speak.	
CASSIO	Madam, not now: I am very ill at ease,	
	Unfit for mine own purposes.	
DESDEMONA	Well, do your discretion[12].	
		Exit Cassio
IAGO	Ha! I like not that.	
OTHELLO	What dost thou say?	35
IAGO	Nothing, my lord; or if – I know not what.	
OTHELLO	Was not that Cassio parted from my wife?	
IAGO	Cassio, my lord? No, sure I cannot think it	
	That he would steal away so guilty-like,	
	Seeing you coming.	
OTHELLO	I do believe 'twas he.	40
DESDEMONA	How now, my lord?	
	I have been talking with a suitor here,	
	A man that languishes[13] in your displeasure.	
OTHELLO	Who is't you mean?	

Desdemona playfully lobbies Othello about Cassio's reinstatement. She reminds him that Cassio accompanied Othello during their courtship. Othello agrees that Cassio may come to see him at any time.

 剧情简介：黛丝荻牟娜顽皮地游说奥赛罗让卡修复职。她提醒说，奥赛罗向她求爱时，卡修一直陪着他。奥赛罗同意卡修可以随时来见他。

1 Desdemona pleads for a friend (in pairs)

Several readers of the play have commented that Desdemona shows little understanding of the responsibilities of her husband's position. She confuses personal feelings with official duties, and believes that Cassio should be pardoned for a military offence simply because he has been a good friend to them.

a Discuss how far you believe Desdemona is justified in pleading on Cassio's behalf. Share your ideas with another pair of students.

b Make a list of other occasions in the play so far when it could be said that the boundary between public and private concerns has been blurred. Does this make any difference to your thoughts about Desdemona's intervention here?

1 His present reconciliation take 立即与他和好
2 in cunning 故意
3 sooth 确实
4 trespass 过失
5 in our common reason 按常理看
6 Save 除了
7 check 责难
8 mammering on 犹豫不决
9 Hath tane your part 为您说话
10 bring him in 让他复职
11 By'r Lady 向圣母发誓

Characters 人物分析

Othello's response

Read through the exchange between Desdemona and Othello (lines 45–76), and decide what advice you would give the actor playing Othello at this point. What do you think Othello's tone would be by the time he says: 'I will deny thee nothing'? Consider the following suggestions in turn. Othello's mood is:

- weary (厌烦)
- condescending (居高临下)
- impatient
- loving and indulgent (放纵)
- anxious
- angry
- surprised that Desdemona is so assertive.

Write a paragraph outlining what you would want an actor to convey here, including precisely how he should utter line 76.

2 A private conversation? (in fours)

When you read the script on the page, it is easy to forget that characters who have fallen silent are still on stage.

- Remind yourselves who else is on stage, then step into roles as the characters present and create a tableau of the line 'I shall not dine at home'. In turn, each person should bring their character to life and express his or her thoughts at this moment in the play.

DESDEMONA	Why, your lieutenant, Cassio. Good my lord,	45
	If I have any grace or power to move you,	
	His present reconciliation take[1].	
	For if he be not one that truly loves you,	
	That errs in ignorance, and not in cunning[2],	
	I have no judgement in an honest face.	50
	I prithee call him back.	
OTHELLO	Went he hence now?	
DESDEMONA	Ay, sooth[3]; so humbled	
	That he hath left part of his grief with me	
	To suffer with him. Good love, call him back.	
OTHELLO	Not now, sweet Desdemon; some other time.	55
DESDEMONA	But shall't be shortly?	
OTHELLO	The sooner, sweet, for you.	
DESDEMONA	Shall't be tonight at supper?	
OTHELLO	No, not tonight.	
DESDEMONA	Tomorrow dinner then?	
OTHELLO	I shall not dine at home.	
	I meet the captains at the citadel.	
DESDEMONA	Why, then, tomorrow night, or Tuesday morn,	60
	On Tuesday noon, or night; on Wednesday morn.	
	I prithee name the time, but let it not	
	Exceed three days. In faith, he's penitent;	
	And yet his trespass[4], in our common reason[5] –	
	Save[6] that, they say, the wars must make example	65
	Out of their best – is not almost a fault	
	T'incur a private check[7]. When shall he come?	
	Tell me, Othello. I wonder in my soul	
	What you would ask me that I should deny,	
	Or stand so mammering on[8]. What! Michael Cassio,	70
	That came a-wooing with you, and so many a time	
	When I have spoke of you dispraisingly	
	Hath tane your part[9], to have so much to do	
	To bring him in[10]? By'r Lady[11], I could do much –	
OTHELLO	Prithee no more. Let him come when he will;	75
	I will deny thee nothing.	

Othello dismisses Desdemona, promising to grant her requests. Iago continues to drop deceptive hints about Cassio. Othello tries to find out what's on Iago's mind.

剧情简介：奥赛罗打发黛丝荻牟娜离开，承诺答应她的请求。伊阿苟继续无中生有地影射卡修。奥赛罗试图弄清楚伊阿苟到底在想什么。

1 Sowing the seeds of doubt (in small groups)

Right from Cassio's exit and Iago's accompanying 'I like not that' at line 35, Iago manages to plant ideas in Othello's mind without saying very much. His use of understatement is highly effective and suggestive.

- Share out the following quotations between the groups in your class. Each group should work out a dramatic presentation of its quote. Bring out the insidious (阴险) way in which Iago works – probing, asking questions, vaguely hinting …

    'Ha! I like not that.'
    'My lord, for aught I know.'
    'Honest, my lord?'
    'No further harm.'
    'Nothing, my lord?'
    'Think, my lord?'
    '… or if'
    'Cassio, my lord?'
    'Indeed?'
    '… acquainted with her?'

1	boon	恩惠，恩宠
2	'Tis as	= It is as if
3	peculiar	特定
4	profit	益处
5	touch your love	考验您对我的爱
6	poise and difficult weight	事关重大
7	fearful to be granted	不敢应允 / 下决心
8	Whereon	现在，此刻
9	fancies	意愿
10	Excellent wretch!	可怜的宝贝！
11	Perdition	万劫不复
12	But	如果不
13	But … thought	只是想知道
14	went between us	在我们之间传递信息
15	hideous	极其可怕

2 'Chaos is come again' – imagery, or a memory?

For Othello, falling out of love with Desdemona will be 'the end of the world'. Some Elizabethans believed that a state of Chaos existed before the creation, and that when the world ended Chaos would return. It was something to be feared, in the same way that even in the twenty-first century some people fear that a catastrophe (大灾难) (such as a comet striking Earth) will destroy the world. But consider Othello's comments at a personal level. He might mean that the effects of falling out of love will be personally catastrophic, or that personal chaos will literally return ('come again'), implying that he has experienced such a state of personal disorder once before.

- Which interpretation do you think is more likely? Or are they both equally likely? Try reading Othello's line aloud in different ways to convey the meaning you prefer.

DESDEMONA	Why, this is not a boon[1];
	'Tis as[2] I should entreat you wear your gloves,
	Or feed on nourishing dishes, or keep you warm,
	Or sue to you to do a peculiar[3] profit[4]
	To your own person. Nay, when I have a suit 80
	Wherein I mean to touch your love[5] indeed,
	It shall be full of poise and difficult weight[6],
	And fearful to be granted[7].
OTHELLO	I will deny thee nothing.
	Whereon[8], I do beseech thee, grant me this,
	To leave me but a little to myself. 85
DESDEMONA	Shall I deny you? No; farewell, my lord.
OTHELLO	Farewell, my Desdemona, I'll come to thee straight.
DESDEMONA	Emilia, come. Be as your fancies[9] teach you;
	Whate'er you be, I am obedient.

Exeunt Desdemona and Emilia

OTHELLO	Excellent wretch![10] Perdition[11] catch my soul 90
	But[12] I do love thee; and when I love thee not,
	Chaos is come again.
IAGO	My noble lord –
OTHELLO	What dost thou say, Iago?
IAGO	Did Michael Cassio,
	When you wooed my lady, know of your love?
OTHELLO	He did from first to last. Why dost thou ask? 95
IAGO	But for a satisfaction of my thought[13];
	No further harm.
OTHELLO	Why of thy thought, Iago?
IAGO	I did not think he had been acquainted with her.
OTHELLO	O yes, and went between us[14] very oft.
IAGO	Indeed? 100
OTHELLO	Indeed? Ay, indeed. Discern'st thou aught in that?
	Is he not honest?
IAGO	Honest, my lord?
OTHELLO	Honest? Ay, honest.
IAGO	My lord, for aught I know.
OTHELLO	What dost thou think? 105
IAGO	Think, my lord?
OTHELLO	Think, my lord! By heaven, he echoes me,
	As if there were some monster in his thought
	Too hideous[15] to be shown. Thou dost mean something.

Othello presses Iago to reveal his thoughts, assuring him that he knows him to be an honest and faithful man. Iago says he believes Cassio to be honest, but asks to be excused from telling his inner thoughts.

 剧情简介：奥赛罗逼伊阿苟说出他的想法，并让他放心，说自己知道他是个正直忠诚的人。伊阿苟说他相信卡修为人正直，但请奥赛罗原谅他无法说出内心的想法。

Language in the play 剧中语言
Qualified praise (in threes)

At line 126, Iago appears to be asserting his confidence in Cassio's honesty. Yet if you look carefully at the exact words he uses, he is cleverly and subtly suggesting just the opposite.

- Start with the basic statement 'he is honest' and see how Iago doubly modifies it with phrases that signal doubt. Take the following three statements and experiment with ways of presenting them to bring out Iago's qualified praise:

'he is honest.'
'I think that he is honest.'
'I dare be sworn I think that he is honest.'

Themes 主题分析
Appearance and reality (in pairs)

In lines 119–25 – shortly before Iago's breathtakingly hypocritical (虚伪) 'Men should be what they seem' – Othello talks of the 'just' man and the 'false' man. He says that both can speak in the same style or manner, but from different causes. For a 'false disloyal knave', hesitation in speech is a customary habit. For a 'just' man it arises because he is carefully weighing his words. It is ironic that Othello thinks Iago's 'stops' (hesitations) are a mark of honesty.

- Write a paragraph analysing lines 119–25 and 131–4, then write a further two paragraphs exploring the relationship between words and deeds in the play so far.

Stagecraft 导演技巧
Figures of authority

Othello's speech opposite is peppered with verbal signs that he is already filled with self-doubt (for example, in his repetition of 'I think' and his frequent use of questions or pleas for information).

- How might you direct the actors in this scene to suggest that Othello is no longer the authoritative figure he was in Acts 1 and 2? In what ways might you subtly suggest that Iago is taking control? Add your ideas to your Director's Journal.

1 **of my counsel** 是我的心腹；知道我的心思
2 **In ... wooing** 在我（向黛丝荻牟娜）求爱的整个过程中
3 **contract ... together** 皱起你的眉头
4 **conceit** 想法
5 **Show** 告诉
6 **weigh'st** 思量
7 **stops** 暂停；欲言又止
8 **tricks of custom** 惯用伎俩
9 **just** 正直
10 **close dilations** 神秘 / 秘而不宣的指责
11 **That passion cannot rule** 激情无法抑制
12 **Or ... none!** 而有些人并非如此，因为你根本看不到他们的内心！
13 **speak ... thinkings** 告诉我你的真实想法
14 **ruminate** 认真思考
15 **that ... to** 连奴隶都可以不做的事情
16 **apprehensions** 念头
17 **leets** 地方法庭
18 **law-days** 开庭日

	I heard thee say even now thou lik'st not that,	110
	When Cassio left my wife. What didst not like?	
	And when I told thee he was of my counsel[1]	
	In my whole course of wooing[2], thou cried'st 'Indeed?'	
	And didst contract and purse thy brow together[3],	
	As if thou then hadst shut up in thy brain	115
	Some horrible conceit[4]. If thou dost love me,	
	Show[5] me thy thought.	
IAGO	My lord, you know I love you.	
OTHELLO	I think thou dost;	
	And for I know thou'rt full of love and honesty,	
	And weigh'st[6] thy words before thou giv'st them breath,	120
	Therefore these stops[7] of thine fright me the more;	
	For such things in a false disloyal knave	
	Are tricks of custom[8]; but in a man that's just[9],	
	They're close dilations[10], working from the heart,	
	That passion cannot rule[11].	
IAGO	For Michael Cassio,	125
	I dare be sworn I think that he is honest.	
OTHELLO	I think so too.	
IAGO	Men should be what they seem;	
	Or those that be not, would they might seem none![12]	
OTHELLO	Certain, men should be what they seem.	
IAGO	Why then, I think Cassio's an honest man.	130
OTHELLO	Nay, yet there's more in this.	
	I prithee speak to me as to thy thinkings[13],	
	As thou dost ruminate[14], and give thy worst of thoughts	
	The worst of words.	
IAGO	Good my lord, pardon me;	
	Though I am bound to every act of duty,	135
	I am not bound to that all slaves are free to[15].	
	Utter my thoughts! Why, say they are vile and false?	
	As where's that palace, whereinto foul things	
	Sometimes intrude not? Who has a breast so pure,	
	But some uncleanly apprehensions[16]	140
	Keep leets[17] and law-days[18], and in session sit	
	With meditations lawful?	

Iago continues to seem reluctant to reveal what he claims to know about Cassio and Desdemona. He strongly defends the importance of a man's or woman's reputation, and warns Othello to beware of jealousy.

 剧情简介：伊阿苟声称知道卡修和黛丝荻牟娜的事，却继续假装不愿透露详情。他竭力强调一个男人或女人名声的重要性，并警告奥赛罗不要心生嫉妒。

Language in the play 剧中语言

Metaphors (in small groups)

Earlier, Iago dismissed Cassio's lament about loss of 'reputation'. But now he describes 'Good name', or reputation, in a man or woman as 'the immediate jewel of their souls' (lines 156–7). He uses another visual image to describe jealousy: 'the green-eyed monster which doth mock / The meat it feeds on.'

a Choose one of these metaphors and create a tableau as a physical representation of the words (remember, you are not showing a picture of what is happening on stage, but creating an interpretation of the image). Make sure everyone in the group is involved.

b For the other metaphor, create a drawing or collage that seems to you to best illuminate the sense and connotations of the words. Share both visual interpretations with the rest of the class.

c Talk together about how Iago develops each of these images through practical examples in the lines that follow (158–62 and 168–72).

1 conspire against 给……使坏
2 mak'st … thoughts 不告诉他你的想法
3 perchance 或许
4 it is my nature's plague 我生性如此，改不了了
5 jealousy 疑窦；嫉妒
6 Shapes 构建
7 conceits 构想，想象
8 scattering and unsure observance 鸡零狗碎、捕风捉影的观察
9 quiet 内心的安宁
10 immediate 首要
11 filches 窃取
12 in my custody 由我保管
13 doth … on 戏弄爪下的猎物
14 cuckold 戴绿帽子的丈夫
15 tells 计数
16 dotes 宠爱

1 Game tactics (in threes)

Iago tactically approaches his task of heightening Othello's anxiety. It is as intriguing following his verbal 'moves' as it can be monitoring a game of football, chess or snooker, where each individual move is part of a much wider game strategy.

a Read aloud lines 143–78 to familiarise yourselves with the script. Discuss the points at which Iago cleverly shapes Othello's responses, and what kinds of tactics he employs.

b One of you then becomes a commentator on the game, and the other two take the parts of Iago and Othello. Present the dialogue as if it is a game being watched by a radio or television presenter, who comments throughout on the tactics Iago uses against Othello and Othello's responses. Iago and Othello may need to briefly freeze their dialogue at pre-arranged moments so that the commentary can be heard. Remember that the 'players' might gain or lose ground during the game.

c As an extension to this activity, try beginning your commentary from line 90 of this scene.

OTHELLO	Thou dost conspire against[1] thy friend, Iago,	
	If thou but think'st him wronged, and mak'st his ear	
	A stranger to thy thoughts[2].	
IAGO	I do beseech you,	145
	Though I perchance[3] am vicious in my guess –	
	As I confess it is my nature's plague[4]	
	To spy into abuses, and oft my jealousy[5]	
	Shapes[6] faults that are not – that your wisdom then,	
	From one that so imperfectly conceits[7],	150
	Would take no notice, nor build yourself a trouble	
	Out of his scattering and unsure observance[8].	
	It were not for your quiet[9], nor your good,	
	Nor for my manhood, honesty, and wisdom,	
	To let you know my thoughts.	
OTHELLO	What dost thou mean?	155
IAGO	Good name in man and woman, dear my lord,	
	Is the immediate[10] jewel of their souls.	
	Who steals my purse, steals trash; 'tis something, nothing,	
	'Twas mine, 'tis his, and has been slave to thousands:	
	But he that filches[11] from me my good name	160
	Robs me of that which not enriches him	
	And makes me poor indeed.	
OTHELLO	By heaven, I'll know thy thoughts.	
IAGO	You cannot, if my heart were in your hand,	
	Nor shall not, while 'tis in my custody[12].	165
OTHELLO	Ha!	
IAGO	O beware, my lord, of jealousy:	
	It is the green-eyed monster which doth mock	
	The meat it feeds on[13]. That cuckold[14] lives in bliss	
	Who certain of his fate loves not his wronger;	170
	But O, what damnèd minutes tells[15] he o'er	
	Who dotes[16], yet doubts, suspects, yet fondly loves?	
OTHELLO	O misery!	

Othello assures Iago he's not a naturally jealous man. He says he is confident of his wife's virtue. Iago warns him to watch Desdemona with Cassio, as she is capable of deception.

 剧情简介：奥赛罗让伊阿苟放心，他不是天生嫉妒的人。他说他对妻子的美德有信心。伊阿苟警告他要留意黛丝荻牟娜与卡修在一起的时候，因为她有可能骗人。

1 Key words and phrases (in pairs)

a Read lines 178–206. Between you, agree on what seems to be a key word or phrase in each line. Working only with those words or phrases you have chosen, experiment with ways of presenting the exchange between Iago and Othello to express Othello's apparent confidence but underlying uncertainty, and Iago's insinuations (影射) and warning. You could 'intercut' (interweave) the two sets of key words, for example, if you feel that contributes to an understanding of the dynamics of the dialogue. Make use of the dramatic approach that seems to be most appropriate. Compare your presentation with those of other pairs, and discuss similarities or differences.

b With a digital camera, take two or three photographs as you work with the script, then upload them to a computer. Compare your group's interpretations with those of other groups. You could create a class display of 'production photos', which you can add to as you continue to read or watch the play.

▼ How well do you think this photograph conveys the relationship between Iago and Othello at this point in the play?

1 fineless 无穷无尽
2 To … suspicions 像月亮阴晴圆缺一样时刻产生新的怀疑
3 to be once … resolved 我一旦起了疑心，就立即解决
4 goat 山羊（被认为是一种特别淫荡的动物）
5 exsufflicate 夸张
6 surmises 猜疑
7 Matching thy inference 符合你的暗示
8 weak merits 微小优点
9 revolt 不忠，背叛
10 bound 有职责的
11 Wear your eyes thus 这样用您的眼神（伊阿苟会怎样眉目传情？）
12 secure 放心
13 self-bounty 自己的仁厚
14 our country disposition 我国女人的德行
15 pranks 淫荡
16 Their best conscience 她们最崇高的道德观

IAGO	Poor and content is rich, and rich enough;	
	But riches fineless[1] is as poor as winter	175
	To him that ever fears he shall be poor.	
	Good God, the souls of all my tribe defend	
	From jealousy.	
OTHELLO	Why, why is this?	
	Think'st thou I'd make a life of jealousy,	
	To follow still the changes of the moon	180
	With fresh suspicions[2]? No, to be once in doubt	
	Is once to be resolved[3]. Exchange me for a goat[4]	
	When I shall turn the business of my soul	
	To such exsufflicate[5] and blown surmises[6]	
	Matching thy inference[7]. 'Tis not to make me jealous	185
	To say my wife is fair, feeds well, loves company,	
	Is free of speech, sings, plays, and dances well:	
	Where virtue is, these are more virtuous.	
	Nor from mine own weak merits[8] will I draw	
	The smallest fear or doubt of her revolt[9],	190
	For she had eyes and chose me. No, Iago,	
	I'll see before I doubt; when I doubt, prove;	
	And on the proof, there is no more but this:	
	Away at once with love or jealousy!	
IAGO	I am glad of this; for now I shall have reason	195
	To show the love and duty that I bear you	
	With franker spirit. Therefore, as I am bound[10],	
	Receive it from me. I speak not yet of proof.	
	Look to your wife, observe her well with Cassio;	
	Wear your eyes thus[11]: not jealous, nor secure[12].	200
	I would not have your free and noble nature,	
	Out of self-bounty[13], be abused. Look to't.	
	I know our country disposition[14] well:	
	In Venice they do let God see the pranks[15]	
	They dare not show their husbands. Their best conscience[16]	205
	Is not to leave't undone, but keep't unknown.	

Iago reminds Othello that Desdemona has already deceived her father. He professes his love for Othello, but continues to drop hints about Desdemona's lack of fidelity.

剧情简介：伊阿苟提醒奥赛罗，黛丝荻牟娜骗过她父亲。他向奥赛罗表忠心，但继续影射黛丝荻牟娜不忠。

Characters 人物分析

Iago the manipulator (in pairs)

Iago continues to undermine Othello, using cunning strategies to heighten Othello's doubts. Each of Iago's speeches opposite employs a different technique of insidious persuasion.

a Consider each of these speeches in turn. Trace the way Iago puts words into Othello's mouth and thoughts into his head to create suspicion of Desdemona.

b Practise saying the lines, experimenting with physical distances between the characters. Start at far sides of the room and read through the script, raising your voices sufficiently to be heard; move closer and try again, finally moving towards each other until almost whispering into each others' ears. What works best? At what points might you move closer together and at what points would you move or turn away?

1 Why, go to then! = There you are! （哎，这就对了！）
2 seel 闭上
3 close as oak 像橡木的木纹一样紧密
4 bound 心存感激
5 Not a jot 一点儿也没有
6 moved 沮丧
7 strain 过分解读
8 grosser issues 更惊世骇俗的结论
9 larger reach 更大范围
10 vile success 恶果
11 aimed not at 并不想要
12 honest 贞洁的
13 erring from itself 迷失自我

1 Who's deceiving whom?

Iago has already commented on Venetian women's ability to deceive (lines 203–6). Now, his 'She did deceive her father, marrying you' closely echoes Brabantio's parting words in Act 1 Scene 3, lines 288–9.

- Devise a diagrammatic way of representing which characters are being (or have been) deceived by Iago at this point, and who believes they are being deceived by others. You could use the example below as a starting point. For each 'strand' (分支) of your diagram, find a relevant quotation and include that in your design.

OTHELLO	Dost thou say so?
IAGO	She did deceive her father, marrying you;
	And when she seemed to shake and fear your looks
	She loved them most.
OTHELLO	And so she did.
IAGO	Why, go to then![1]
	She that so young could give out such a seeming
	To seel[2] her father's eyes up close as oak[3]
	He thought 'twas witchcraft – but I am much to blame,
	I humbly do beseech you of your pardon
	For too much loving you.
OTHELLO	I am bound[4] to thee for ever.
IAGO	I see this hath a little dashed your spirits.
OTHELLO	Not a jot[5], not a jot.
IAGO	I'faith, I fear it has.
	I hope you will consider what is spoke
	Comes from my love. But I do see you're moved[6].
	I am to pray you not to strain[7] my speech
	To grosser issues[8] nor to larger reach[9]
	Than to suspicion.
OTHELLO	I will not.
IAGO	Should you do so, my lord,
	My speech should fall into such vile success[10]
	As my thoughts aimed not at[11]. Cassio's my worthy friend –
	My lord, I see you're moved.
OTHELLO	No, not much moved.
	I do not think but Desdemona's honest[12].
IAGO	Long live she so, and long live you to think so!
OTHELLO	And yet how nature erring from itself[13] –

Line numbers: 210, 215, 220, 225

Iago implies that Desdemona is unnatural for preferring a black man over someone of her own colour. Othello orders Iago to set Emilia to watch Desdemona. Iago advises Othello to see how Desdemona pleads for Cassio.

剧情简介：伊阿苟暗示，黛丝荻牟娜不正常，因为她喜欢黑人而不是跟她肤色一样的人。奥赛罗命令伊阿苟让艾蜜丽叶监视黛丝荻牟娜。伊阿苟建议奥赛罗观察黛丝荻牟娜如何为卡修求情。

Stagecraft 导演技巧

Stage directions: 'Going' and 'Returning'

Iago skilfully plays his victim. He even pretends to leave the stage, only to come straight back as if having a spontaneous second thought.

- Give advice to the actor playing Iago – how should he go and return? Add these ideas to your Director's Journal.

▶ Compare and contrast this image with the one on page 108. What does each image suggest about the relationship between the two characters? What has changed in the way Iago is 'playing' Othello in the picture here?

1 **bold** 直率
2 **affect** 喜欢
3 **clime** 国家
4 **Foh!** 呸！
5 **a will most rank** 一种非常臭／丑的情欲
6 **disproportion** 不得体
7 **I … her** 我说这番话并非专门针对她
8 **recoiling** 让位于，退回
9 **fall to match** 开始比较
10 **country forms** 本国同胞（指威尼斯的英俊男子）
11 **happily** 或许
12 **unfolds** 吐露
13 **scan** 考虑，深究
14 **place** 职位
15 **means** 手段
16 **strain his entertainment** 竭力主张给他复职
17 **vehement** 热切的
18 **importunity** 恳求
19 **busy** 管闲事
20 **government** 自制力

1 Natural – then and now? (in small groups)

Iago's 'in all things nature tends' (line 233) echoes Othello's 'And yet how nature erring from itself' (line 229). But is Desdemona's marriage to Othello unnatural?

- Talk together about whether you feel that in your culture, people's views on 'mixed-race' marriage have changed since Shakespeare's time. (See 'Race and culture in *Othello*' on pp. 233–7 for additional information about seventeenth-century views about black people.)

IAGO	Ay, there's the point: as, to be bold[1] with you,	230
	Not to affect[2] many proposèd matches	
	Of her own clime[3], complexion, and degree,	
	Whereto we see in all things nature tends –	
	Foh![4] one may smell, in such, a will most rank[5],	
	Foul disproportion[6], thoughts unnatural.	235
	But pardon me: I do not in position	
	Distinctly speak of her[7]; though I may fear	
	Her will, recoiling[8] to her better judgement,	
	May fall to match[9] you with her country forms[10],	
	And happily[11] repent.	
OTHELLO	Farewell, farewell.	240
	If more thou dost perceive, let me know more;	
	Set on thy wife to observe. Leave me, Iago.	
IAGO	[*Going.*] My lord, I take my leave.	
OTHELLO	Why did I marry? This honest creature doubtless	
	Sees and knows more, much more, than he unfolds[12].	245
IAGO	[*Returning.*] My lord, I would I might entreat your honour	
	To scan[13] this thing no farther. Leave it to time.	
	Although 'tis fit that Cassio have his place[14] –	
	For sure he fills it up with great ability –	
	Yet if you please to hold him off awhile,	250
	You shall by that perceive him and his means[15].	
	Note if your lady strain his entertainment[16]	
	With any strong or vehement[17] importunity[18] –	
	Much will be seen in that. In the mean time,	
	Let me be thought too busy[19] in my fears –	255
	As worthy cause I have to fear I am –	
	And hold her free, I do beseech your honour.	
OTHELLO	Fear not my government[20].	
IAGO	I once more take my leave.	*Exit*

Othello reflects that his colour, speech and age may have lost him Desdemona. He sees women's unfaithfulness as the curse of marriage. But the sight of Desdemona seems to make him reject his suspicions.

 剧情简介：奥赛罗思忖，他的肤色、言语和年纪可能已经令他失去了黛丝荻牟娜。他将女人的不忠视为婚姻的祸根。但一见到黛丝荻牟娜，他的疑心似乎又消除了。

Stagecraft 导演技巧

Othello's soliloquy: Iago's influence (in pairs)

Iago's success in troubling Othello's mind is evident. He even affects the language that Othello now begins to use.

a Read Othello's soliloquy opposite and identify the ways in which it is reminiscent (让人想起) of Iago's language and attitudes. First look at any references to creatures or animals – what kind of animals are they, and what are they used in reference to? Next, re-read one of Iago's previous speeches (e.g. Act 1 Scene 1, lines 87–93 and 110–13 or Act 3 Scene 3, lines 168–9) to remind yourself of the language Iago has used elsewhere. How does Othello's choice of image reflect Iago's growing influence over him?

b What advice would you give to an actor playing Othello at this point in the play? Would you suggest any shift in pace and tone when Desdemona comes on stage? How should this soliloquy be delivered: directly to the audience, or as if Othello is muttering (喃喃自语) to himself? Add these notes to your Director's Journal.

1 **haggard** 未驯服的鹰
2 **jesses** 束缚猎鹰的腿带
3 **Haply for** 或许因为
4 **chamberers** 客厅绅士
5 **declined … years** 上了年纪
6 **loathe** 厌恶
7 **vapour** 浊气
8 **Prerogatived** 享有特权
9 **destiny unshunnable** 无法逃脱的命运
10 **forkèd plague** 头上长角（民间的说法是，妻子不忠，丈夫就会头上长角）
11 **do quicken** 出生之时

Language in the play 剧中语言

Hawking imagery

Using trained hawks for hunting small prey was a courtly pursuit in Elizabethan and Jacobean times. Othello uses a number of hawking images in his soliloquy about Desdemona. He wonders if she will prove to be a 'haggard' (a wild hawk), in which case he will set her free ('whistle her off') and untie the 'jesses' (straps). He will 'let her down the wind / To prey at fortune' – in other words, let her go to look after herself.

• Create a design that could be used as a symbolic stage backdrop (背景), making use of this hawk or captive bird imagery.

Othello Act 3 Scene 3
奥赛罗

OTHELLO   This fellow's of exceeding honesty   260
           And knows all qualities, with a learnèd spirit,
           Of human dealings. If I do prove her haggard[1],
           Though that her jesses[2] were my dear heart-strings,
           I'd whistle her off and let her down the wind
           To prey at fortune. Haply for[3] I am black,   265
           And have not those soft parts of conversation
           That chamberers[4] have, or for I am declined
           Into the vale of years[5] – yet that's not much –
           She's gone, I am abused, and my relief
           Must be to loathe[6] her. O curse of marriage,   270
           That we can call these delicate creatures ours
           And not their appetites! I had rather be a toad
           And live upon the vapour[7] of a dungeon
           Than keep a corner in the thing I love
           For others' uses. Yet 'tis the plague of great ones, 275
           Prerogatived[8] are they less than the base;
           'Tis destiny unshunnable[9], like death:
           Even then this forkèd plague[10] is fated to us
           When we do quicken[11]. Look where she comes.

                    Enter Desdemona and Emilia.

           If she be false, O then heaven mocks itself;   280
           I'll not believe it.

Desdemona greets Othello, who claims he has a headache. She tries to bind his head with her handkerchief, but he pushes it aside. Emilia picks it up, remembering that Iago has urged her to steal it.

剧情简介：黛丝荻牟娜问候奥赛罗，奥赛罗声称自己头疼。她试图用她的手绢给他包头，他却把手绢推开。艾蜜丽叶捡起手绢，想起伊阿苟曾叮嘱她偷这手绢。

1 'I am to blame' (in pairs)

To whom does Othello address line 284? How does he say it? Try it out in a number of different ways, then decide which one is the best – and why. Discuss what reasons Othello might have to claim that he is to blame. What does he think he is to blame for?

2 Why does Iago want the handkerchief?

As Emilia holds the handkerchief ('napkin'), she reflects that Iago 'hath a hundred times / Wooed me to steal it'. Why?

- Predict what Iago might want to do with Desdemona's handkerchief.

▼ How does Emilia tell the audience about the 'napkin'? For example, consider how she describes her husband (see line 294). Is she triumphant at obtaining the handkerchief? Or should the actor suggest that Emilia has her doubts about her husband's motives?

1	generous	高贵
2	attend	等待
3	watching	值夜班；缺觉
4	napkin	手绢
5	remembrance	信物
6	wayward	反复无常，一意孤行
7	Wooed	说服
8	conjured her	要她发誓
9	reserves	带着
10	work tane out	照着图案刺绣
11	fantasy	奇思异想

DESDEMONA	How now, my dear Othello?
	Your dinner and the generous[1] islanders,
	By you invited, do attend[2] your presence.
OTHELLO	I am to blame.
DESDEMONA	Why do you speak so faintly?
	Are you not well? 285
OTHELLO	I have a pain upon my forehead here.
DESDEMONA	Faith, that's with watching[3]; 'twill away again.
	Let me but bind it hard, within this hour
	It will be well.
OTHELLO	Your napkin[4] is too little.
	[*He puts the handkerchief from him, and she drops it.*]
	Let it alone. Come, I'll go in with you. 290
DESDEMONA	I am very sorry that you are not well.

Exeunt Othello and Desdemona

EMILIA	I am glad I have found this napkin:
	This was her first remembrance[5] from the Moor.
	My wayward[6] husband hath a hundred times
	Wooed[7] me to steal it; but she so loves the token, 295
	For he conjured her[8] she should ever keep it,
	That she reserves[9] it evermore about her
	To kiss and talk to. I'll have the work tane out[10]
	And give't Iago.
	What he will do with it, heaven knows, not I: 300
	I nothing but to please his fantasy[11].

Emilia hands the handkerchief over to her husband. Iago reveals to the audience what he intends to do with it.
剧情简介：艾蜜丽叶把手绢交给自己的丈夫。伊阿苟向观众透露他打算拿它作何用途。

1 Iago and Emilia: what relationship? (in threes)

Lines 302–21 present an exchange between husband and wife. It is possible to direct it in a way that brings out very different interpretations of the relationship between Iago and Emilia. You could even make an important statement about the institution of marriage as it is presented in the play.

a One person directs the other two, who take parts as Iago and Emilia. You will have to make decisions about Iago's attitude to his wife, Emilia's own mood and the way she approaches her husband. For example, Emilia may be:

- intimidated (恐吓) by Iago
- cheerful
- confident
- desperate for her husband's attention
- frustrated
- playfully flirtatious (调情的)
- resentful and moody.

You may find it useful to know that in Elizabethan slang, 'thing' meant the female sexual organ. Does Emilia knowingly use it in this sense (line 303) or is Iago introducing the obscene (下流) meaning (line 304)? Decide at precisely what point she would reveal the handkerchief to Iago and how she would relinquish (放弃) it according to your interpretation of the mood of the exchange. How does she leave the stage at line 321?

b Afterwards, watch at least two different film or stage versions of this scene and discuss how other directors have interpreted it. For example, in Oliver Parker's 1995 movie, this is a deeply disturbing scene in which Iago virtually sexually assaults his wife.

c Write two paragraphs interpreting this dialogue in two contrasting ways chosen from the suggestions below (brief explanations of a range of different critical approaches to the play are given on p. 222).

- a feminist interpretation (which sympathetically presents an obviously oppressed Emilia)
- a fairly 'traditional' reading of the play, which focuses on the cleverness of Iago and regards Emilia as of little interest
- an approach that focuses on the interesting psychological interplay between Iago and Emilia, in which each character is playing games with the other.

---

1 a common thing 人人都用的东西
2 to th'advantage 恰好
3 import 重要性
4 Be not acknown on't 不要说你知道这事
5 holy writ 《圣经》
6 conceits 想象
7 scarce found to distaste 不觉得讨厌
8 act 作用
9 mines of sulphur 硫黄矿（指地狱）

OTHELLO ACT 3 SCENE 3
奥赛罗

Enter Iago.

IAGO	How now? What do you here alone?
EMILIA	Do not you chide; I have a thing for you.
IAGO	You have a thing for me? It is a common thing[1] –
EMILIA	Ha!
IAGO	To have a foolish wife.
EMILIA	O, is that all? What will you give me now For that same handkerchief?
IAGO	What handkerchief?
EMILIA	What handkerchief! Why, that the Moor first gave to Desdemona, That which so often you did bid me steal.
IAGO	Hast stolen it from her?
EMILIA	No, faith; she let it drop by negligence, And to th'advantage[2] I being here took't up. Look, here it is.
IAGO	A good wench! Give it me.
EMILIA	What will you do with't, that you have been so earnest To have me filch it?
IAGO	[*Snatching it.*] Why, what's that to you?
EMILIA	If it be not for some purpose of import[3], Give't me again. Poor lady, she'll run mad When she shall lack it.
IAGO	Be not acknown on't[4]: I have use for it. Go, leave me.

Exit Emilia

I will in Cassio's lodging lose this napkin
And let him find it. Trifles light as air
Are to the jealous confirmations strong
As proofs of holy writ[5]. This may do something.
The Moor already changes with my poison:
Dangerous conceits[6] are in their natures poisons,
Which at the first are scarce found to distaste[7]
But, with a little act[8] upon the blood,
Burn like the mines of sulphur[9]. I did say so.

305

310

315

320

325

330

Othello is convinced of Desdemona's infidelity. He wishes he was ignorant of it and declares he has lost interest in his life as a professional soldier. He demands that Iago provide him with hard evidence.

  剧情简介：奥赛罗相信了黛丝荻牟娜对他不忠。他但愿自己不知情，宣称已失去了当职业军人的兴趣。他要求伊阿苟提供确凿证据。

Characters 人物分析

Othello's 'general camp' speech (in large groups)

Othello laments his loss of contentment, reputation and occupation.

a One member of the group reads lines 346–58 aloud. The others listen carefully and echo any words to do with military activity.

b Divide the speech (from line 349) between group members. Each person takes one or two lines or meaningful phrases. Learn your respective chunks of text, and work out a choral version, including actions, to present your group's delivery of the speech.

c Use your experience of the activities above to discuss what the speech suggests to you about Othello at this point in the play. Is there any evidence of the 'old' Othello here (i.e. Othello as he was presented in Act 1 and the first part of Act 2)?

1 'ocular proof' (in pairs)

a Decide what Othello might be referring to when he says 'ocular proof' in line 361 ('ocular' is to do with eyes). Can you detect any inconsistencies in the way Othello is thinking? Spend three or four minutes comparing your ideas.

b On page 122, there is a picture showing one director's interpretation of how Othello performed this speech. Discuss what is happening here in the relationship between Iago and Othello. How do you think this piece of dialogue should be directed?

2 'Is't come to this?' (in pairs)

a In your own words, explain what you think the situation has 'come to' (line 364) from your own perspective.

b One of you takes the part of Iago and the other Othello. Stand back to back. Take it in turns to answer the question 'Is't come to this?', briefly explaining what your character believes or hopes the situation has 'come to'. Make sure you stay in role.

c As an extension of this activity, regroup as a class and 'hot-seat' one of your classmates as Iago. Ask questions about the way his plot is developing. What has gone well, and what (if anything) has not gone as well as he hoped? What outcome is he looking for?

1	Not poppy nor mandragora	不论罂粟或茄参（两者均有催眠、麻醉作用）
2	medicine	对……有药效
3	thou owed'st	你拥有
4	Avaunt	滚开
5	rack	拷刑架
6	sense	意识
7	general camp	整个军营的人
8	Pioners	工兵
9	plumèd	插着羽毛
10	trump = trumpet	（号角声）
11	fife	短笛（主要用于为军鼓伴奏）
12	quality	（战场的）本性
13	pomp	排场，盛典
14	circumstance	盛大仪式
15	engines	大炮
16	Jove's dread clamours	乔武发出的万钧雷霆
17	occupation	职业，生涯
18	ocular	可见
19	waked	被激起

Enter Othello.

Look where he comes! Not poppy nor mandragora[1],
Nor all the drowsy syrups of the world,
Shall ever medicine[2] thee to that sweet sleep
Which thou owed'st[3] yesterday.

OTHELLO   Ha, ha, false to me!

IAGO   Why, how now, general! No more of that.   335

OTHELLO   Avaunt[4], be gone! Thou hast set me on the rack[5].
I swear 'tis better to be much abused
Than but to know't a little.

IAGO   How now, my lord!

OTHELLO   What sense[6] had I of her stolen hours of lust?
I saw't not, thought it not, it harmed not me.   340
I slept the next night well, fed well, was free and merry;
I found not Cassio's kisses on her lips.
He that is robbed, not wanting what is stolen,
Let him not know't and he's not robbed at all.

IAGO   I am sorry to hear this.   345

OTHELLO   I had been happy if the general camp[7],
Pioners[8] and all, had tasted her sweet body
So I had nothing known. O, now for ever
Farewell the tranquil mind! Farewell content!
Farewell the plumèd[9] troops, and the big wars   350
That makes ambition virtue – O farewell!
Farewell the neighing steed and the shrill trump[10],
The spirit-stirring drum, th'ear-piercing fife[11],
The royal banner, and all quality[12],
Pride, pomp[13], and circumstance[14] of glorious war!   355
And, O you mortal engines[15], whose rude throats
Th'immortal Jove's dread clamours[16] counterfeit,
Farewell! Othello's occupation's[17] gone.

IAGO   Is't possible, my lord?

OTHELLO   Villain, be sure thou prove my love a whore;   360
Be sure of it. Give me the ocular[18] proof,
Or by the worth of mine eternal soul,
Thou hadst been better have been born a dog
Than answer my waked[19] wrath!

IAGO   Is't come to this?

Othello curses Iago if his suspicions are without foundation. Iago protests that he was only acting as a friend and asks what proof Othello requires of his wife's infidelity.

剧情简介：奥赛罗诅咒伊阿苟，他的怀疑要是无中生有，他就会下地狱。伊阿苟坚称他只是尽朋友的情分，并问奥赛罗要什么证据证明他妻子不忠。

Characters 人物分析

In two minds (in pairs)

To experience Othello's tortured, contradictory emotions, share lines 384–91 between you, speaking them as an argument between two people. Try saying the lines standing face to face, or back to back, or standing on different levels. Decide which works best and share your interpretation with the rest of the class.

Write about it 写作练习

'honesty's a fool'

Consider how far Iago's phrase in line 383 could be regarded as central to the play as a whole. Write two paragraphs outlining your views, supported by evidence from the script. You might like to structure your writing in the following way:

- For the first paragraph, outline all the characters who appear to be honest in the play, and consider what has happened to each so far.
- For the second paragraph, write about Iago. Which characters have described him as honest in the play? What do we (as readers or as viewers) know about Iago and how honest he really is? How is this ironic? Why might Iago conclude that honest people are fools?

1 probation ... loop （即无懈可击的证据）
2 For ... that 你再也不能犯下更多的罪恶遭受地狱之灾了
3 God bu'y you = God be with you （上帝与您同在；Goodbye 的前身）
4 direct 心直口快
5 profit 教训
6 sith = since
7 breeds such offence 造成这种不快
8 that it works for 它努力去争取的东西
9 Dian = Diana （荻阿娜，罗马神话中的贞洁和月亮女神）
10 begrimed 被玷污，被抹黑
11 If ... it （这里指奥赛罗想自杀）
12 satisfied 真相大白
13 supervisor 旁观者
14 grossly gape on 张着大嘴
15 topped 被人压在身下

OTHELLO   Make me to see't; or, at the least, so prove it   365
           That the probation bear no hinge nor loop[1]
           To hang a doubt on – or woe upon thy life!
IAGO   My noble lord –
OTHELLO   If thou dost slander her and torture me,
           Never pray more; abandon all remorse;   370
           On horror's head horrors accumulate;
           Do deeds to make heaven weep, all earth amazed:
           For nothing canst thou to damnation add
           Greater than that[2].
IAGO   O grace! O heaven forgive me!
           Are you a man? Have you a soul? Or sense?   375
           God bu'y you[3]; take mine office. O wretched fool,
           That lov'st to make thine honesty a vice!
           O monstrous world! Take note, take note, O world!
           To be direct[4] and honest is not safe.
           I thank you for this profit[5], and from hence   380
           I'll love no friend, sith[6] love breeds such offence[7].
OTHELLO   Nay, stay: thou shouldst be honest.
IAGO   I should be wise; for honesty's a fool
           And loses that it works for[8].
OTHELLO   By the world,
           I think my wife be honest, and think she is not;   385
           I think that thou art just, and think thou art not.
           I'll have some proof. Her name, that was as fresh
           As Dian's[9] visage, is now begrimed[10] and black
           As mine own face. If there be cords or knives,
           Poison or fire or suffocating streams,   390
           I'll not endure it[11]. Would I were satisfied[12]!
IAGO   I see, sir, you are eaten up with passion.
           I do repent me that I put it to you.
           You would be satisfied?
OTHELLO   Would? Nay, I will.
IAGO   And may. But how? How satisfied, my lord?   395
           Would you, the supervisor[13], grossly gape on[14]?
           Behold her topped[15]?
OTHELLO   Death and damnation! O!

Iago warns that it will be impossible to catch Desdemona and Cassio in the act of adultery. He reports that he has heard Cassio talk of Desdemona in his sleep. Othello threatens murder.

 剧情简介：伊阿苟警告说，不可能对黛丝荻牟娜和卡修现场捉奸。他还说听到过卡修说梦话提到黛丝荻牟娜。奥赛罗威胁说要杀人。

1 'I'll tear her all to pieces' (in pairs)

At lines 280–1, Othello says: 'If she be false, O then heaven mocks itself; / I'll not believe it.' Only 150 lines later, he vows: 'I'll tear her all to pieces!' (line 432). What has happened in the intervening five pages of script?

- Trace the stages of Iago's manipulation and record them and Othello's responses in the form of a flow diagram. Your diagram might start something like this:

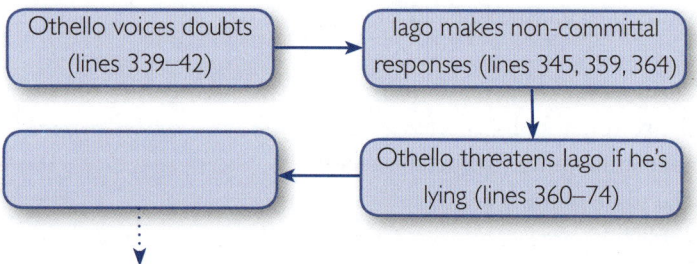

- Calculate how much time has elapsed in the time-scheme of the play. Add this dimension to your diagram.
- Discuss the dramatic effect of this timescale and write your conclusions on the diagram.

Language in the play 剧中语言
Bestial imagery (by yourself)

What effect does Iago's talk of animals on heat (lines 404–5) have on you as a reader or viewer? Read Iago's speech aloud to yourself, then write some suggestions as to how you might draw attention to the various examples of animal imagery in the play (for example, in the set design [戏台设计], use of digital projector, costumes and style of speech).

Stagecraft 导演技巧
Act it out (in pairs)

Iago graphically describes what happened during a night he spent in the barracks with Cassio (lines 411–32). Put actions to the words so that Iago creates a lifelike reconstruction of events. Try playing it in two or three different ways, using some of the following suggestions:

- make it funny – play for laughs
- make it creepy (令人毛骨悚然) and/or menacing (威胁的)
- Iago is embarrassed by the lurid (骇人的) detail
- Iago is disgusted.

---

1 prospect 场景，情景
2 bolster 同床共枕
3 More than their own 放浪形骸
4 prime 淫荡
5 monkeys （当时英国人视猴子为性欲旺盛的象征）
6 As … pride 像发情的狼一样好色
7 imputation and strong circumstances 有力的旁证
8 living 充分的，正当的
9 office 任务
10 Pricked 受驱使
11 lay with 与……同榻而眠
12 loose 不谨慎，轻率
13 gripe 握紧
14 denoted 表示
15 foregone conclusion 之前发生的事
16 shrewd doubt 十分可疑
17 thicken 巩固，增强
18 do demonstrate thinly 证据单薄

IAGO	It were a tedious difficulty, I think,	
	To bring them to that prospect¹. Damn them then,	
	If ever mortal eyes do see them bolster²	400
	More than their own³. What then? How then?	
	What shall I say? Where's satisfaction?	
	It is impossible you should see this,	
	Were they as prime⁴ as goats, as hot as monkeys⁵,	
	As salt as wolves in pride⁶, and fools as gross	405
	As Ignorance made drunk. But yet, I say,	
	If imputation and strong circumstances⁷,	
	Which lead directly to the door of truth,	
	Will give you satisfaction, you might have't.	
OTHELLO	Give me a living⁸ reason she's disloyal.	410
IAGO	I do not like the office⁹;	
	But sith I am entered in this cause so far –	
	Pricked¹⁰ to't by foolish honesty and love –	
	I will go on. I lay with¹¹ Cassio lately,	
	And being troubled with a raging tooth	415
	I could not sleep.	
	There are a kind of men so loose¹² of soul	
	That in their sleeps will mutter their affairs.	
	One of this kind is Cassio.	
	In sleep I heard him say, 'Sweet Desdemona,	420
	Let us be wary, let us hide our loves.'	
	And then, sir, he would gripe¹³ and wring my hand,	
	Cry, 'O sweet creature!' and then kiss me hard,	
	As if he plucked up kisses by the roots	
	That grew upon my lips; then laid his leg	425
	Over my thigh, and sighed, and kissed, and then	
	Cried, 'Cursèd fate that gave thee to the Moor.'	
OTHELLO	O monstrous, monstrous!	
IAGO	Nay, this was but his dream.	
OTHELLO	But this denoted¹⁴ a foregone conclusion¹⁵.	
IAGO	'Tis a shrewd doubt¹⁶, though it be but a dream;	430
	And this may help to thicken¹⁷ other proofs	
	That do demonstrate thinly¹⁸.	
OTHELLO	I'll tear her all to pieces!	

Iago claims that Cassio has Desdemona's handkerchief. Othello is overcome with jealous grief and vows revenge. To Iago's call for patience, Othello replies that his murderous thoughts will never change.

 剧情简介：伊阿苟声称卡修有黛丝荻牟娜的手绢。奥赛罗满怀嫉妒和悲伤，发誓要报复。听到伊阿苟劝他要忍耐，奥赛罗回答说，他杀人的想法绝不会改变。

1 Evidence (in pairs)

Just a few lines ago, Othello asked repeatedly for proof of Desdemona's infidelity – 'a living reason' (line 410). Now he greets Iago's comment about the handkerchief with the words: 'Now do I see 'tis true.' Yet Othello has asked for 'ocular proof' (something he could see for himself).

- Up to now, what exactly has Iago offered by way of 'proof'?

> ### Language in the play 剧中语言
> **Imagery of revenge and hatred (in threes)**
>
> **a** Express the following images through a series of two or three linked tableaux:
> - 'Arise, black vengeance, from thy hollow cell!'
> - 'Yield up, O love, thy crown and hearted throne / To tyrannous hate!'
>
> **b** Share your tableaux with another group, then select the one that both groups agree to be the most effective. Show these to the rest of the class, explaining what you think are the most successful features.

2 The tidal wave of Othello's emotions
(in large groups)

This activity (used by actors in rehearsal) will enable you to experience the relentless energy embodied in Othello's extended **simile** of the 'Pontic Sea' in lines 454–61. Work in quite a large space.

- Divide up the lines into small, meaningful chunks (lines or phrases) and distribute them amongst your group members. Memorise your lines, repeating them out loud as you walk around the available space.
- Get into a long line, not necessarily facing the same way, and link arms securely. The two students on either end must tug and pull the line around the room in opposite directions. As you are tugged around the room, say your lines in the correct order. Try performing the lines you have learnt in different ways – for example, shouting, or hissing them, or as if panting with exhaustion.

Afterwards, discuss what insights this activity has given you into Othello's state of mind at this point in the play. How does the style of his language (vocabulary, length of sentences, punctuation) reflect the intensity of his thoughts and feelings?

---

1 **yet** 仍然
2 **sometimes** 曾经
3 **speaks against** 对……不利
4 **the slave** 奴才（指卡修）
5 **fond** 愚蠢（参见第57页第136行）
6 **hearted** 我心中的
7 **fraught** 重载（指仇恨之重）
8 **aspics** 毒蛇
9 **be content** 冷静
10 **Pontic Sea** 黑海（即Black Sea）
11 **compulsive course** 势不可当的势头
12 **Propontic** 普罗庞海（即Sea of Marmora，马尔马拉海）
13 **Hellespont** 赫勒斯滂海峡（即Dardanelles，达达尼尔海峡，位于土耳其的欧亚两部分之间，连接马尔马拉海与爱琴海）
14 **capable** 宽敞；足够
15 **marble** 永恒；无情
16 **engage** 发誓

Othello Act 3 Scene 3 奥赛罗

IAGO Nay, yet[1] be wise; yet we see nothing done,
She may be honest yet. Tell me but this:
Have you not sometimes[2] seen a handkerchief 435
Spotted with strawberries in your wife's hand?

OTHELLO I gave her such a one; 'twas my first gift.

IAGO I know not that; but such a handkerchief –
I am sure it was your wife's – did I today
See Cassio wipe his beard with.

OTHELLO   If it be that – 440

IAGO If it be that, or any that was hers,
It speaks against[3] her with the other proofs.

OTHELLO O that the slave[4] had forty thousand lives!
One is too poor, too weak, for my revenge.
Now do I see 'tis true. Look here, Iago, 445
All my fond[5] love thus do I blow to heaven;
'Tis gone.
Arise, black vengeance, from thy hollow cell!
Yield up, O love, thy crown and hearted[6] throne
To tyrannous hate! Swell, bosom, with thy fraught[7], 450
For 'tis of aspics'[8] tongues.

He kneels.

IAGO   Yet be content[9].

OTHELLO O, blood, blood, blood!

IAGO Patience, I say; your mind perhaps may change.

OTHELLO Never, Iago. Like to the Pontic Sea[10],
Whose icy current and compulsive course[11] 455
Ne'er feels retiring ebb but keeps due on
To the Propontic[12] and the Hellespont[13],
Even so my bloody thoughts with violent pace
Shall ne'er look back, ne'er ebb to humble love,
Till that a capable[14] and wide revenge 460
Swallow them up. Now by yond marble[15] heaven,
In the due reverence of a sacred vow
I here engage[16] my words.

Iago swears to serve Othello, who instructs him to kill Cassio. Othello vows to kill Desdemona himself. He appoints Iago to be his lieutenant. Scene 4 opens with Desdemona sending a messenger to Cassio.

 剧情简介：伊阿苟发誓效忠奥赛罗，奥赛罗命他去杀卡修。奥赛罗发誓会亲手杀死黛丝荻牟娜。他任命伊阿苟为副官。第四场开场，黛丝荻牟娜差人去找卡修。

1 'But let her live' (in pairs)

Why do you think Iago tells Othello to let Desdemona live (line 475)? Consider the following possibilities:

- He has no quarrel with Desdemona, and/or is attracted to her.
- He seeks only Cassio's death.
- He's displaying old-fashioned courtesy towards women.
- He needs her alive to torment Othello further – and to torment her.
- He actually means the opposite; he's planting the idea in Othello's mind on purpose.
- It's all happening too quickly; it's going beyond what Iago had planned.
- He wants to appear merciful in order to aid his deception.

Rank the statements from most likely to least likely, then give reasons for your choices. Pool your ideas with the rest of the class. Are there other possibilities?

2 What does Iago mean?

Scene 3 ends on Iago's statement, 'I am your own for ever.' It could simply mean 'Thanks for the promotion, I'll serve you well.' But what other, more ominous meanings could his words carry at the end of this scene, when Iago has successfully stirred Othello to hatred, jealousy and determination to murder?

> ### Stagecraft 导演技巧
> #### Scene changes: dramatic effect
>
> An important feature of Shakespeare's plays is how scenes are often contrasted with one another. We have just witnessed a lengthy scene of sustained emotional charge, promising bloody violence and concluding with language that references scenes of damnation.
>
> - If you were directing the play, what dramatic effect would you hope to achieve at the beginning of Scene 4? Make notes about the possibilities: how quickly the scene change takes place; whether there is a change in lighting (for example, a brighter, warmer effect) or scenery; how Desdemona's mood is signalled by her entrance; and how she and the Clown speak. What might be the dramatic effect of the Clown's inability to give a straight answer to her questions?
> - In your Director's Journal, write up these notes into a plan for how to stage Scene 3, line 480 to Scene 4, line 18.

1 ever-burning lights 长明灯（即日月星辰）
2 elements 宇宙元素（这里泛指自然界的力量）
3 clip 包围，环绕
4 give up 交付，奉献
5 execution 指令；行动
6 remorse 同情
7 What bloody business ever 不管事情如何血腥（ever = soever）
8 greet 欢迎
9 vain 空洞
10 acceptance bounteous 慷慨的回报
11 put thee to't 考验你
12 lewd minx 淫妇
13 furnish me 给我提供
14 sirrah 小子（对身份低下的人的称呼）
15 lies 居住
16 one ... stabbing 说当兵的撒谎（lies是双关）是要挨刀的

IAGO	Do not rise yet.	
	He kneels.	
	Witness you ever-burning lights[1] above,	
	You elements[2] that clip[3] us round about,	465
	Witness that here Iago doth give up[4]	
	The execution[5] of his wit, hands, heart,	
	To wronged Othello's service. Let him command,	
	And to obey shall be in me remorse[6],	
	What bloody business ever[7].	
	[They rise.]	
OTHELLO	I greet[8] thy love,	470
	Not with vain[9] thanks, but with acceptance bounteous[10];	
	And will upon the instant put thee to't[11].	
	Within these three days let me hear thee say	
	That Cassio's not alive.	
IAGO	My friend is dead;	
	'Tis done at your request. But let her live.	475
OTHELLO	Damn her, lewd minx[12]! O, damn her, damn her!	
	Come, go with me apart. I will withdraw	
	To furnish me[13] with some swift means of death	
	For the fair devil. Now art thou my lieutenant.	
IAGO	I am your own for ever.	480
	Exeunt	

Act 3 Scene 4

Cyprus   A room in the castle

Enter DESDEMONA, EMILIA *and* CLOWN.

DESDEMONA	Do you know, sirrah[14], where Lieutenant Cassio lies[15]?	
CLOWN	I dare not say he lies anywhere.	
DESDEMONA	Why, man?	
CLOWN	He's a soldier, and for one to say a soldier lies is stabbing[16].	5

The Clown leaves to tell Cassio to visit Desdemona. She expresses concern about the loss of her handkerchief to Emilia. Othello greets Desdemona and comments that her hand feels hot.

剧情简介：小丑去叫卡修来见黛丝荻牟娜。黛丝荻牟娜告诉艾蜜丽叶，自己丢了手绢，感到担心。奥赛罗问候黛丝荻牟娜，说她的手摸起来很热。

Characters 人物分析

Emilia in the hot-seat (in large groups)

When Emilia lies that she knows nothing about the loss of Desdemona's handkerchief ('I know not, madam', line 20), what might be going through her mind?

- A volunteer steps into role as Emilia. The group questions her, exploring her possible motives. Try to work out where her loyalties lie. How does Emilia see her various positions as wife, employee and confidante (密友)?

1 A dramatic entrance (in fours)

At line 27, we see another dramatically charged entrance. Right on cue – just as Desdemona tells Emilia that Othello is incapable of suffering from jealousy – he enters the scene.

a In your group, three people take a role each and freeze the moment as Emilia says: 'Look where he comes.' The fourth person acts as director. Think carefully about positioning and the space between the three characters; also pay particular attention to facial expressions and the direction in which each character is looking. Once you are happy with your tableau, bring the stage picture alive and act out the next fifteen lines. End with a freeze on Othello's line, ''Tis a good hand, / A frank one'. How are each of the characters now positioned?

b Share your performance with two or three groups. At the final tableau, bring each character alive in turn and ask them to share their immediate thoughts (in role).

2 Sweaty palms (in small groups)

Othello takes Desdemona's hand and remarks that it is 'hot, and moist' – supposedly a sign of a lecherous nature. He goes on to tell Desdemona that instead of giving her 'hand' in marriage as a love match ('hearts of old gave hands') she has merely given her hand – not her heart as well (lines 41–3).

- Read lines 28–43, then improvise a scene in which the main character wrongly (and privately) suspects his or her boyfriend or girlfriend of infidelity, and all sorts of quite innocent conversations and behaviour are misinterpreted. After watching one another's improvisations, discuss how easily this kind of situation arises, and under what circumstances.

---

1 **devise** 捏造，编造
2 **lie in my own throat** 公然撒谎
3 **be edified by report** 听听有什么说法
4 **catechise** 拷问（宗教常用问答教学法；小丑这里回应上一行的 edified [受启发]）
5 **by them** 根据听到的说法
6 **moved** 说动
7 **compass** 范围
8 **crusadoes** 远征币（旧时葡萄牙为纪念十字军远征铸造的一种金币，上有十字图案）
9 **humours** 体液（这里指情绪）
10 **dissemble** 掩饰真实情感
11 **moist** 湿润（当时认为多情者的手心爱出汗）
12 **argues fruitfulness** 证明多情多子
13 **liberal** 放荡；无拘无束
14 **sequester** 抑制；远离
15 **fasting** 禁食，斋戒
16 **castigation** 反省自律
17 **exercise devout** 虔诚礼拜
18 **frank** 慷慨；开放（暗示黛丝荻牟娜行为放浪）

OTHELLO ACT 3 SCENE 4
奥赛罗

DESDEMONA   Go to. Where lodges he?
CLOWN   To tell you where he lodges is to tell you where I lie.
DESDEMONA   Can anything be made of this?
CLOWN   I know not where he lodges, and for me to devise[1] a lodging, and say he lies here, or he lies there, were to lie in mine own throat[2].   10
DESDEMONA   Can you enquire him out, and be edified by report[3]?
CLOWN   I will catechise[4] the world for him: that is, make questions, and by them[5] answer.
DESDEMONA   Seek him; bid him come hither; tell him I have moved[6] my lord on his behalf and hope all will be well.   15
CLOWN   To do this is within the compass[7] of man's wit, and therefore I will attempt the doing of it.   *Exit*
DESDEMONA   Where should I lose that handkerchief, Emilia?
EMILIA   I know not, madam.   20
DESDEMONA   Believe me, I had rather lose my purse
Full of crusadoes[8]; and but my noble Moor
Is true of mind and made of no such baseness
As jealous creatures are, it were enough
To put him to ill thinking.
EMILIA   Is he not jealous?   25
DESDEMONA   Who, he? I think the sun where he was born
Drew all such humours[9] from him.
                    Enter OTHELLO.
EMILIA   Look where he comes.
DESDEMONA   I will not leave him now; let Cassio
Be called to him. – How is't with you, my lord?
OTHELLO   Well, my good lady. [*Aside*] O hardness to dissemble[10]!   30
How do you, Desdemona?
DESDEMONA   Well, my good lord.
OTHELLO   Give me your hand. This hand is moist[11], my lady.
DESDEMONA   It yet hath felt no age, nor known no sorrow.
OTHELLO   This argues fruitfulness[12] and liberal[13] heart.
Hot, hot, and moist. This hand of yours requires   35
A sequester[14] from liberty, fasting[15] and prayer,
Much castigation[16], exercise devout[17];
For here's a young and sweating devil here
That commonly rebels. 'Tis a good hand,
A frank[18] one.

Othello asks for the handkerchief. When Desdemona denies she has lost it, Othello informs her of its magical powers and its great sentimental value. He claims it was magically made.

 剧情简介：奥赛罗问黛丝荻牟娜要手绢，她说手绢没丢，奥赛罗跟她讲手绢的魔力，讲它巨大的情感价值。他声称那手绢是用魔力织就的。

1 The myth of the handkerchief (in pairs)

Othello's description of the handkerchief's history (lines 51–71) is like a myth or folk tale.

- Read it dramatically, then experiment with retelling it as a fairy story for young children. (See p. 220 for a consideration of the dramatic significance of this handkerchief in the play as a whole.)

Write about it 写作练习
What if?

What if Desdemona had told Othello the truth at this point – that she had indeed accidentally lost the handkerchief?

- Compose the next ten to twenty lines of dialogue, in which Desdemona tells Othello about losing the handkerchief. What exactly does she say? How does Othello react? What role does Emilia play – does she confess to giving the handkerchief to her husband or not?
- Remember to lay your dialogue out like a proper play script, with the name of the character speaking on the left and the stage directions in square brackets. Don't forget that you do not need speech marks in a script.
- Write in modern English, but try to make the characters' comments sound in keeping with what you know of them and the way they relate to one another.

1 **The hearts ... hearts** （大意：从前新人结婚手牵手，表示把心也交给对方；现在我们也手牵手，但心已不属于对方了。**heraldry**：纹章）
2 **speak of** 理解
3 **chuck** 乖乖，宝贝儿
4 **salt and sorry rheum** 让人讨厌和难受的感冒
5 **charmer** 巫师
6 **amiable** 可爱
7 **hold her loathèd** 讨厌她
8 **spirits** 心思，欲望
9 **fancies** 情人，爱人
10 **wive** 娶妻
11 **take heed** 留心，注意
12 **perdition** 灾难
13 **web** 织纹
14 **sibyl** 女先知
15 **numbered ... compasses** 活了200岁
16 **In her prophetic fury** 在她灵感迷狂之际
17 **hallowed** 背后有光环，神圣
18 **dyed in mummy** 用木乃伊炮制
19 **Conserved of** 用……调配

DESDEMONA	You may indeed say so,	40
	For 'twas that hand that gave away my heart.	
OTHELLO	A liberal hand! The hearts of old gave hands;	
	But our new heraldry is hands, not hearts[1].	
DESDEMONA	I cannot speak of[2] this. Come now, your promise.	
OTHELLO	What promise, chuck[3]?	45
DESDEMONA	I have sent to bid Cassio come speak with you.	
OTHELLO	I have a salt and sorry rheum[4] offends me;	
	Lend me thy handkerchief.	
DESDEMONA	Here, my lord.	
OTHELLO	That which I gave you.	
DESDEMONA	I have it not about me.	
OTHELLO	Not?	50
DESDEMONA	No, faith, my lord.	
OTHELLO	That's a fault. That handkerchief	
	Did an Egyptian to my mother give:	
	She was a charmer[5] and could almost read	
	The thoughts of people. She told her, while she kept it,	
	'Twould make her amiable[6] and subdue my father	55
	Entirely to her love; but if she lost it	
	Or made a gift of it, my father's eye	
	Should hold her loathèd[7] and his spirits[8] should hunt	
	After new fancies[9]. She dying gave it me,	
	And bid me when my fate would have me wive[10],	60
	To give it her. I did so, and take heed[11] on't:	
	Make it a darling, like your precious eye.	
	To lose't or give't away were such perdition[12]	
	As nothing else could match.	
DESDEMONA	Is't possible?	
OTHELLO	'Tis true. There's magic in the web[13] of it:	65
	A sibyl[14], that had numbered in the world	
	The sun to course two hundred compasses[15],	
	In her prophetic fury[16] sewed the work;	
	The worms were hallowed[17] that did breed the silk,	
	And it was dyed in mummy[18], which the skilful	70
	Conserved of[19] maidens' hearts.	

Othello orders Desdemona to bring him the handkerchief. She tries to divert his attention by reminding him of Cassio's unresolved plight, but he leaves, swearing. Emilia comments unflatteringly on men.

剧情简介：奥赛罗命令黛丝荻牟娜把手绢拿给他。她试图转移他的注意力，提醒他卡修的困境还没有解决，但他骂骂咧咧地离开了。艾蜜丽叶发表了一番对男人不恭的评论。

1 Repetition (in threes)

Othello first asks Desdemona for the missing handkerchief at line 48, and he tells her to fetch it at line 81. In the following eleven lines he repeats the words 'The handkerchief' three times.

a How should Othello speak these lines? For example, each time he asks for it does he shout louder and louder, or does he get quieter and more menacing?

b Create a short mime around the action suggested by the command, 'Fetch me the handkerchief', in which 'the handkerchief' is the only phrase anyone can use (as many times as you like) in a variety of tones, volumes and moods.

2 Let's talk about Cassio! (in pairs)

a Desdemona draws the audience's attention to the fact that Othello is speaking 'startingly and rash'. Othello is clearly highly agitated about the lost handkerchief (as signalled by his frequent short or incomplete sentences), yet Desdemona persists in pursuing a conversation about Cassio. Why do you think she does this? What advice would you give to the actor playing Desdemona? Is she:

- completely naive
- bemused (感到茫然) by Othello's anger
- forceful and assertive
- irritated by Othello's behaviour
- deliberately provocative
- afraid?

b Try reading line 71 (from 'I'faith, is't true?') to line 93 in three or four different ways.

▼ Emilia (right) expounds (阐述) her philosophy concerning men in lines 97–100. She uses a food/appetite metaphor reminiscent of that used by Iago to talk about women in Act 2 Scene 1, lines 215–22. What do you think this suggests about Emilia and Iago's relationship?

1	look to't well	好生保管它
2	startlingly and rash	断断续续而且急躁
3	is't out of th'way?	找不着了？
4	put me from my suit	把我从求情这件事上岔开
5	My mind misgives	我很担心
6	sufficient	能干，称职
7	founded	建立
8	wonder	魔力
9	'Tis … man	一个男人的真面目不是一两年就能暴露出来的
10	but stomachs	只是胃口
11	belch	呕吐
12	the happiness	好运气
13	importune	恳求

OTHELLO ACT 3 SCENE 4
奥赛罗

DESDEMONA	I'faith, is't true?
OTHELLO	Most veritable; therefore look to't well[1].
DESDEMONA	Then would to God that I had never seen't!
OTHELLO	Ha? Wherefore?
DESDEMONA	Why do you speak so startingly and rash[2]?
OTHELLO	Is't lost? Is't gone? Speak; is't out of th'way?[3]
DESDEMONA	Heaven bless us!
OTHELLO	Say you?
DESDEMONA	It is not lost, but what and if it were?
OTHELLO	How?
DESDEMONA	I say it is not lost.
OTHELLO	Fetch't, let me see't.
DESDEMONA	Why so I can, sir; but I will not now. This is a trick to put me from my suit[4]. Pray you let Cassio be received again.
OTHELLO	Fetch me the handkerchief. My mind misgives[5].
DESDEMONA	Come, come; You'll never meet a more sufficient[6] man.
OTHELLO	The handkerchief!
DESDEMONA	I pray, talk me of Cassio.
OTHELLO	The handkerchief!
DESDEMONA	A man that all his time Hath founded[7] his good fortunes on your love, Shared dangers with you –
OTHELLO	The handkerchief!
DESDEMONA	I'faith, you are to blame.
OTHELLO	Zounds! *Exit*
EMILIA	Is not this man jealous?
DESDEMONA	I ne'er saw this before. Sure there's some wonder[8] in this handkerchief; I am most unhappy in the loss of it.
EMILIA	'Tis not a year or two shows us a man[9]. They are all but stomachs[10], and we all but food; They eat us hungerly, and when they are full, They belch[11] us.

Enter IAGO *and* CASSIO.

Look you, Cassio and my husband.

IAGO	There is no other way: 'tis she must do't. And lo, the happiness[12]! Go, and importune[13] her.

Cassio again asks Desdemona to plead with Othello on his behalf. She tells him he will have to be patient, since Othello seems to be behaving strangely. Iago leaves to find Othello.

 剧情简介： 卡修再次请求黛丝荻牟娜为他向奥赛罗说情。她说他接下来必须得有耐心，因为奥赛罗似乎行为古怪。伊阿苟离开去找奥赛罗。

Write about it 写作练习

'My lord is not my lord'

In line 118, Desdemona states that 'My lord is not my lord'. She is confused by the changes in Othello's manner towards her, and uses this phrase in the colloquial sense, meaning 'he's not himself'. However, in another sense it could be argued that Othello's identity has literally changed and that he is a different man than the one we encountered at the beginning of the play. His identity has been undermined by Iago, who is busy constructing a new one for him.

- Write one or two paragraphs describing the way Iago has worked on Othello through this act and has brought about these startling changes. You could write a second paragraph assessing how important the context has been in contributing towards Othello's feeling of instability (for example, think about Othello as an isolated black man living in white society; also think about his position as commander of an occupying force on a colonial outpost, and the loss of his trusted lieutenant). Prioritise (排序) the factors you believe to be important.

1 Unspoken thoughts (in threes)

Look over Iago's short interchange with Emilia and Desdemona (lines 126–34). Both Emilia and Iago know more than they reveal, yet on the surface they appear innocent. Iago falsely expresses surprise at Othello's anger. He even finds four different ways of commenting that anger is an emotion unfamiliar to Othello.

- First, play with the lines, experimenting with ways of acting them out and exploring the undercurrent (潜在的情绪) of (partially) shared knowledge between Emilia and her husband.
- Next, attempt to intercut the script with the unspoken thoughts and preoccupations of the three characters. For example, if in your initial explorations with acting out the script, you had actors exchanging significant looks, explain in each character's words what is going through their minds at that point.
- When you are happy with your intercut (交切) script, share it with other groups and discuss any similarities or differences.

1 Exist = Be myself （回归自己）
2 office 效忠
3 would not be delayed 不想耽搁
4 nor … nor = neither … nor
5 purposed merit 想取得的建树
6 in futurity 将来
7 ransom 赎回
8 But = Merely （仅仅）
9 shall … content 我将强作欢颜
10 shut … course 一心寻求其他途径
11 To fortune's alms 听凭命运的垂怜
12 thrice-gentle 最有风度
13 advocation 恳求
14 in tune 合适
15 Were … altered 假如他的相貌跟着他的脾气一起变化
16 every spirit sanctified 所有神圣精灵（即天使）
17 blank 靶心
18 of moment 重大，重要

OTHELLO ACT 3 SCENE 4
奥赛罗

DESDEMONA	How now, good Cassio! What's the news with you?	
CASSIO	Madam, my former suit. I do beseech you	
	That, by your virtuous means, I may again	105
	Exist¹ and be a member of his love,	
	Whom I, with all the office² of my heart,	
	Entirely honour. I would not be delayed³.	
	If my offence be of such mortal kind	
	That nor my service past nor⁴ present sorrows,	110
	Nor purposed merit⁵ in futurity⁶,	
	Can ransom⁷ me into his love again,	
	But⁸ to know so must be my benefit:	
	So shall I clothe me in a forced content⁹,	
	And shut myself up in some other course¹⁰	115
	To fortune's alms¹¹.	
DESDEMONA	Alas, thrice-gentle¹² Cassio,	
	My advocation¹³ is not now in tune¹⁴:	
	My lord is not my lord; nor should I know him,	
	Were he in favour as in humour altered¹⁵.	
	So help me every spirit sanctified¹⁶,	120
	As I have spoken for you all my best,	
	And stood within the blank¹⁷ of his displeasure	
	For my free speech! You must awhile be patient.	
	What I can do, I will; and more I will	
	Than for myself I dare. Let that suffice you.	125
IAGO	Is my lord angry?	
EMILIA	He went hence but now	
	And certainly in strange unquietness.	
IAGO	Can he be angry? I have seen the cannon	
	When it hath blown his ranks into the air,	
	And like the devil from his very arm	130
	Puffed his own brother – and is he angry?	
	Something of moment¹⁸ then. I will go meet him.	
	There's matter in't indeed if he be angry.	
DESDEMONA	I prithee do so.	

Exit Iago

Desdemona reassures herself that Othello must be upset by some affair of state. Emilia hopes he is not growing jealous. Desdemona prays he has no such thought in mind and leaves to seek Othello. Bianca greets Cassio.

剧情简介：黛丝荻牟娜自我安慰说，奥赛罗一定是因为什么国家大事而不高兴。艾蜜丽叶希望奥赛罗不会变得越来越妒忌。黛丝荻牟娜祈祷奥赛罗不会有这种念头，然后离开去找奥赛罗。碧昂卡问候卡修。

Write about it 写作练习

Desdemona: the public face

In the scenes with Desdemona, it is easy to forget that Othello's primary role in Cyprus is to administer Venetian rule. In Desdemona's words about 'some unhatched practice' (secret plot), she draws attention to their position as quasi-colonial (准殖民) rulers once again. Keep this political dimension in mind as subsequent events unfold.

- Up to now, what has been Desdemona's main public role in the play? Write a paragraph about Desdemona's actions and reputation in her position as a high-ranking army officer's wife and as a senator's daughter.

Characters 人物分析

Directing Desdemona (in pairs)

Desdemona assures Cassio and Emilia that 'men are not gods'. She excuses Othello's rudeness towards her on the grounds that he has a very important job to do and that personal matters must take second place to this. Talk together about what advice you would give to the actor playing Desdemona. For example, should she come across as:

- meek and mild
- fresh and innocent
- strong and independent
- world weary and cynical
- nervous and shy?

Give reasons for your decision. For an additional challenge, look back through the play so far and find examples from the text to support your reasoning.

1 Jealousy: 'a monster / Begot upon itself, born on itself'

Again, Emilia's language is an unconscious echo of Iago's. Look back to Act 3 Scene 3, lines 168–9 and read through Iago's graphic jealousy metaphor. How are the two images similar? Sketch a design based on Emilia's metaphor.

1. unhatched practice 未实现的阴谋
2. puddled 让人心绪混乱
3. wrangle （长时间）争吵
4. object 关心的事
5. endues 带来，引起
6. members 身体器官
7. observancy 温存，柔情
8. bridal 新婚之夜
9. unhandsome 笨拙
10. Arraigning 指责
11. suborned the witness 让证人作假
12. indicted 指控
13. conception 胡思乱想
14. toy 奇想
15. 'Save you = God save you（上帝保佑您，问候语，类似"早上好"）

	Something sure of state,	
	Either from Venice, or some unhatched practice[1]	135
	Made demonstrable here in Cyprus to him,	
	Hath puddled[2] his clear spirit; and in such cases	
	Men's natures wrangle[3] with inferior things,	
	Though great ones are their object[4]. 'Tis even so;	
	For let our finger ache, and it endues[5]	140
	Our other healthful members[6] even to a sense	
	Of pain. Nay, we must think men are not gods,	
	Nor of them look for such observancy[7]	
	As fits the bridal[8]. Beshrew me much, Emilia,	
	I was – unhandsome[9] warrior as I am –	145
	Arraigning[10] his unkindness with my soul;	
	But now I find I had suborned the witness[11]	
	And he's indicted[12] falsely.	
EMILIA	Pray heaven it be state matters, as you think,	
	And no conception[13] nor no jealous toy[14]	150
	Concerning you.	
DESDEMONA	Alas the day, I never gave him cause.	
EMILIA	But jealous souls will not be answered so.	
	They are not ever jealous for the cause,	
	But jealous for they're jealous. 'Tis a monster	155
	Begot upon itself, born on itself.	
DESDEMONA	Heaven keep that monster from Othello's mind.	
EMILIA	Lady, amen!	
DESDEMONA	I will go seek him. Cassio, walk here about.	
	If I do find him fit, I'll move your suit	160
	And seek to effect it to my uttermost.	
CASSIO	I humbly thank your ladyship.	

Exeunt Desdemona and Emilia

Enter BIANCA.

BIANCA	'Save you[15], friend Cassio.	
CASSIO	What make you from home?	
	How is it with you, my most fair Bianca?	
	I'faith, sweet love, I was coming to your house.	165

Bianca accuses Cassio of neglecting her. He pleads that worries have kept him away and gives Bianca the handkerchief, saying he found it in his bedroom. He asks Bianca to leave so that he may meet Othello.

剧情简介：碧昂卡抱怨卡修冷落了她。卡修辩称诸多烦心事使他无法脱身，然后把手绢交给碧昂卡，说这是在自己卧室发现的。他让碧昂卡离开，因为他要去见奥赛罗。

Characters 人物分析

Who is Bianca? (in pairs)

a What are your first impressions of Bianca, and what relationship do you think she has with Cassio? Explore this question by taking parts. Create a series of tableaux to tell the story of this scene between Bianca and Cassio. Either freeze the moment at each of the following lines, or select your own to create a sequence of five still pictures:
- ''Save you, friend Cassio'
- 'This is some token from a newer friend'
- 'I found it in my chamber'
- 'Not that I love you not'
- ''Tis but a little way I can bring you'

b After you have performed your tableaux, talk about Bianca and how she appears to relate to Cassio. Do we learn anything new about Cassio in this scene?

Write about it 写作练习

Bianca: dramatic purpose

Write at least two paragraphs exploring the dramatic purpose of this short episode with Bianca. Think about:
- the plot (does this episode further the main plot in any way?)
- themes or central ideas in the play (for example, the position of women, relationships, jealousy)
- dramatic tension (this episode comes straight after the high drama of Othello and Iago's pact [协议] to commit a double murder)
- characterisation (人物塑造) (does this episode add to our knowledge of Cassio?)
- the passage of time (Bianca's words at line 167 suggest that a whole week has passed by since the Venetian fleet arrived at Cyprus, yet Othello wanted Cassio dead within three days at the end of Scene 3).

Once you have finished, exchange your writing with another student and compare your ideas.

1 Eight score eight hours 168 个钟头（即一周的小时数）
2 dial 日晷，时钟
3 with leaden thoughts been pressed 心事重重，心情压抑
4 continuate 连续不断
5 Take me this work out 把这个花样描下来（me 无意义）
6 whence came this? 这是哪儿来的？
7 newer friend 新欢
8 To … cause 现在我知道你为何冷落我了
9 like enough 很可能
10 And think it no addition 我认为对我没什么好处
11 womaned 有女人陪着
12 bring me 陪我
13 be circumstanced 随遇而安

BIANCA	And I was going to your lodging, Cassio.	
	What! Keep a week away? Seven days and nights?	
	Eight score eight hours¹? And lovers' absent hours	
	More tedious than the dial² eight score times!	
	O weary reckoning!	
CASSIO	Pardon me, Bianca.	170
	I have this while with leaden thoughts been pressed³;	
	But I shall in a more continuate⁴ time	
	Strike off this score of absence. Sweet Bianca,	
	Take me this work out⁵.	
BIANCA	O Cassio, whence came this?⁶	
	This is some token from a newer friend⁷.	175
	To the felt absence now I feel a cause⁸.	
	Is't come to this? Well, well.	
CASSIO	Go to, woman!	
	Throw your vile guesses in the devil's teeth	
	From whence you have them. You are jealous now	
	That this is from some mistress, some remembrance.	180
	No, by my faith, Bianca.	
BIANCA	Why, whose is it?	
CASSIO	I know not neither; I found it in my chamber.	
	I like the work well. Ere it be demanded –	
	As like enough⁹ it will – I'd have it copied.	
	Take it and do't, and leave me for this time.	185
BIANCA	Leave you? Wherefore?	
CASSIO	I do attend here on the general;	
	And think it no addition¹⁰, nor my wish,	
	To have him see me womaned¹¹.	
BIANCA	Why, I pray you?	
CASSIO	Not that I love you not.	
BIANCA	But that you do not love me.	190
	I pray you, bring me¹² on the way a little,	
	And say if I shall see you soon at night.	
CASSIO	'Tis but a little way that I can bring you,	
	For I attend here; but I'll see you soon.	
BIANCA	'Tis very good; I must be circumstanced¹³.	195

Exeunt

Othello 奥赛罗

Looking back at Act 3 第3幕回顾
Activities for groups or individuals

1 Iago's tempting

At the beginning of Scene 1, Othello is in control of himself; by the end of Scene 4, he seems to be verging on insanity. This activity concentrates on the insidious way in which Iago works upon Othello's mind.

a Get together in large groups. Each group member learns one or two of the following lines:

1 'Ha! I like not that.'
2 'Cassio, my lord? … so guilty-like'
3 'Did Michael Cassio … know of your love?'
4 'Honest, my lord?'
5 'I dare be sworn I think that he is honest.'
6 'I think Cassio's an honest man.'
7 'I perchance am vicious in my guess'
8 'it is my nature's plague / To spy into abuses'
9 'O beware, my lord, of jealousy'
10 'cuckold'
11 'Who dotes, yet doubts, suspects, yet fondly loves?'
12 'the souls of all my tribe defend / From jealousy.'
13 'Look to your wife'
14 'observe her well with Cassio'
15 'She did deceive her father, marrying you'
16 'Foul disproportion'
17 'thoughts unnatural'
18 'Note if your lady strain his entertainment'
19 'Behold her topped'
20 'as prime as goats, as hot as monkeys'.

Move around the room, using all the available space. Speak your lines in different ways. For example, you might speak as if you are all spies passing on secrets, small children telling tales, neighbours gossiping.

b Form a large circle with one student in the centre, blindfolded (this helps to focus on the words). Those in the circle hiss their lines at the central person, sometimes very close to them, sometimes at a distance from them. Experiment with different ways of presenting your lines, perhaps devising a way of showing the progressive nature of the taunts (嘲弄).

c Individually, write an analysis of how skilfully you think Iago has played Othello during Act 3.

2 Sculptures of trust and jealousy

Issues of trust and jealousy are prominent throughout the act.

a In groups of three, one person takes on the job of sculptor again and the other two become the raw material. Create two sculptures, the first called 'Trust' and the second called 'Jealousy'.

b Talk together about how each of the themes of trust and jealousy are developed in Act 3. Choose two or three main characters and re-create your sculptures to reflect an appropriate type of trust or jealousy for that person. For example, how would a sculpture entitled 'Bianca's Jealousy' differ from one called 'Othello's Jealousy'? Remember, you are creating sculptures, not statues of real people. You could take photographs of these sculptures and create a classroom display. Add an appropriate quotation from the script as a caption for each sculpture.

3 Key moments in Act 3

Act 3 is the pivotal (关键) section of the play, where Iago's malevolent (恶毒) influence poisons Othello's mind irrevocably. The four photographs of Iago and Othello opposite show key moments in Act 3.

- Decide which moment each photo represents, and find an appropriate quotation. Write a short paragraph for each, explaining what is happening and why this is such a significant moment.

Iago encourages Othello's jealousy with increasingly graphic references to Desdemona's supposed infidelity. He teases Othello with mention of the handkerchief.

剧情简介： 伊阿苟为了让奥赛罗妒火中烧，益发绘声绘色地编造黛丝荻牟娜的不忠，再次提到那条手绢，调侃奥赛罗。

1 Role play (in pairs)

Iago's opening words in the scene suggest that he and Othello are part-way through a conversation, and that Iago continues to chip away (蚕食，逐步削弱) at Othello's grasp on reality.

- Speculate about what Iago might have been saying before the opening line in the script opposite. Role-play the dialogue you create, then read through to line 34, where Iago further stimulates Othello's imaginings of Desdemona and Cassio's sexual relationship.

2 Iago's lies (in fives)

a Iago tells Othello four separate lies in the first thirty lines of this scene, some prompting Othello to merely echo his words in response. Identify each of the lies.

b Look closely at the punctuation and you will see that a number of Iago's comments are either in the form of a question or of an unfinished sentence, marked by a dash (–). Talk together about the way Iago uses language here, and about the effect it has on Othello.

c For each of the lies you identified above, write down the specific words Iago uses. One person takes the role of Othello and the other four become Iago. Each Iago selects one of the lies from the script and memorises it. The person playing Othello memorises the line 'Think so, Iago?' (line 1). The four Iagos surround Othello and taunt him with their lies, repeating the words as many times as they like. Othello may only respond with his memorised line. Try saying the lines in different ways and at different speeds. How many kinds of dramatic effect can you create?

1	unauthorised	不正当
2	hypocrisy against the devil	假装正经却心存邪念
3	tempt heaven	考验上天
4	So = So long as	（只要）
5	venial slip	轻微过错
6	essence	存在
7	They … not	表面有名誉的人常常实际没有名誉
8	infected	染上瘟疫
9	Boding	预示厄运
10	abroad	到处
11	importunate suit	不断纠缠
12	voluntary dotage	主动献身
13	Convincèd or supplied	征服或满足了她们
14	But they must blab	他们一定会吹嘘

Language in the play 剧中语言

Animal imagery

In describing his obsession with the lost handkerchief (lines 19–22), Othello uses a simile based on the belief that a croaking raven (乌鸦) prophesied (预示) death to the inmates of a house, particularly in times of plague.

- Create a visual design that incorporates the image of the bird of ill omen and the handkerchief. Don't worry if your design is only rough – ideas are the most important element in this activity, not your artistic skills.

Act 4 Scene 1
Cyprus   A room in the castle

Enter OTHELLO *and* IAGO.

IAGO	Will you think so?
OTHELLO	Think so, Iago?
IAGO	What,
	To kiss in private?
OTHELLO	An unauthorised[1] kiss!
IAGO	Or to be naked with her friend in bed
	An hour or more, not meaning any harm?
OTHELLO	Naked in bed, Iago, and not mean harm? 5
	It is hypocrisy against the devil[2].
	They that mean virtuously and yet do so,
	The devil their virtue tempts, and they tempt heaven[3].
IAGO	So[4] they do nothing, 'tis a venial slip[5];
	But if I give my wife a handkerchief – 10
OTHELLO	What then?
IAGO	Why, then 'tis hers, my lord; and being hers,
	She may, I think, bestow't on any man.
OTHELLO	She is protectress of her honour too.
	May she give that? 15
IAGO	Her honour is an essence[6] that's not seen:
	They have it very oft that have it not[7].
	But for the handkerchief –
OTHELLO	By heaven, I would most gladly have forgot it.
	Thou said'st – O it comes o'er my memory, 20
	As doth the raven o'er the infected[8] house,
	Boding[9] to all! – he had my handkerchief.
IAGO	Ay, what of that?
OTHELLO	That's not so good now.
IAGO	What
	If I had said I had seen him do you wrong?
	Or heard him say – as knaves be such abroad[10], 25
	Who having by their own importunate suit[11]
	Or voluntary dotage[12] of some mistress
	Convincèd or supplied[13] them, cannot choose
	But they must blab[14] –

> Iago implies that Cassio has boasted about having sex with Desdemona. Othello is so upset that it appears to bring on an epileptic fit. Cassio enters but is persuaded by Iago to leave again.
>
> 剧情简介：伊阿苟暗示卡修曾自吹与黛丝荻牟娜有过云雨之情。奥赛罗痛心疾首，几乎引起癫痫发作。卡修上场，但被伊阿苟再次劝离。

1 Othello's breakdown (in pairs)

What effect does Othello's seizure (疾病发作) have on you as a reader or spectator? Discuss the following suggestions in turn with your partner, and decide which statements you most agree with. Make sure you can explain why.

- You wonder what kind of man is in charge of law and order in Cyprus.
- Your sympathy for Othello increases.
- It presents the audience with a stereotypical view of a black man who easily loses physical and mental control.
- Iago knows exactly where his victim's weak points are.
- It shows how much Othello loves Desdemona.
- It demonstrates how insanely possessive Othello is towards women.
- Even though Othello is a tough and powerful military leader, it exposes how deeply insecure he is.

As an extension to this activity, use the statements you have selected as a prompt for writing an analysis of this highly charged dramatic moment in the play.

1	unswear	发誓否认
2	belie	诽谤
3	fulsome	让人恶心
4	invest	使……沉浸于
5	shadowing passion	有风有影的冲动
6	instruction	提示，暗示
7	*trance*	昏迷
8	credulous	轻信
9	chaste	贞洁
10	reproach	耻辱
11	epilepsy	癫痫
12	temples	太阳穴
13	forbear	别动
14	lethargy	昏迷
15	have his quiet course	让它顺其自然
16	savage madness	疯狂撒野
17	withdraw yourself	您退避一下
18	on great occasion	在重要问题上

Language in the play 剧中语言
Dramatic grammar (whole class)

a To discover something about the state of Othello's mind, read lines 35–41 aloud while walking around the room. Change direction sharply at every punctuation mark. Increase the pace – go as fast as you dare! You'll find it's dizzying, underlining how Othello's tortured imaginings are accompanied by a breakdown in his language.

b Write a paragraph about the way Shakespeare structures language to reflect a character's state of mind in a dramatic way. Consider such things as sentence structure, sentence length, types of sentence (such as questions, exclamations, statements), and punctuation.

c Look back at Activity 2 on page 144, then write another paragraph about Iago's use of language.

Othello Act 4 Scene 1

OTHELLO   Hath he said anything?

IAGO   He hath, my lord; but be you well assured 30
No more than he'll unswear[1].

OTHELLO   What hath he said?

IAGO   Faith, that he did – I know not what he did.

OTHELLO   What, what?

IAGO   Lie –

OTHELLO   With her?

IAGO   With her, on her, what you will.

OTHELLO   Lie with her? Lie on her? We say lie on her when they belie[2] 35
her. Lie with her! Zounds, that's fulsome[3]! Handkerchief –
confessions – handkerchief! To confess and be hanged for his
labour. First to be hanged and then to confess. I tremble at it.
Nature would not invest[4] herself in such shadowing passion[5] without
some instruction[6]. It is not words that shakes me thus. Pish! Noses, 40
ears, and lips. Is't possible? – Confess? Handkerchief? O devil!

[He] falls in a trance[7].

IAGO   Work on,
My medicine, work! Thus credulous[8] fools are caught;
And many worthy and chaste[9] dames even thus,
All guiltless, meet reproach[10]. What ho, my lord! 45
My lord, I say! Othello!

Enter CASSIO.

How now, Cassio!

CASSIO   What's the matter?

IAGO   My lord is fallen into an epilepsy[11].
This is his second fit; he had one yesterday.

CASSIO   Rub him about the temples[12].

IAGO   No, forbear[13]. 50
The lethargy[14] must have his quiet course[15].
If not, he foams at mouth and by and by
Breaks out to savage madness[16]. Look, he stirs.
Do you withdraw yourself[17] a little while;
He will recover straight. When he is gone, 55
I would on great occasion[18] speak with you.

[Exit Cassio]

> Othello regains consciousness. Iago again assures him of the unfaithfulness of women, then instructs him to eavesdrop on a conversation in which Cassio will tell of his sexual intercourse with Desdemona.

 剧情简介：奥赛罗恢复知觉。伊阿苟再次向他保证，女人都是不忠的，并教他偷听卡修讲述他与黛丝荻牟娜私通之事。

Write about it 写作练习

'be a man' (in pairs)

a   Iago makes four jibes (嘲弄) at Othello's 'manhood' in the script opposite. Find the four comments and, in your pairs, agree what aspect of 'being a man' each comment refers to.

b   Discuss why Iago chooses to employ such terms of criticism. In doing so, it might help to think about the roles that Othello is trying to fulfil (soldier/war hero, husband, commander…). What is there about Othello, and the society that has formed him, that might make these terms of criticism particularly appropriate?

c   Together, write a couple of paragraphs about the ways in which Othello has tried to 'be a man' up to this point in the play.

1 Iago takes control

In lines 72–87, Iago swiftly sets out a course of action for Othello to follow. Earlier, he used insidious persuasive techniques, but now he is direct and unambiguous as he takes command of the situation.

- Take turns to speak the lines to bring out the urgency and seeming good sense of the plan Iago outlines. Emphasise words and phrases that will especially heighten Othello's fury.

1 hornèd man   头上长角的男人（即被戴了绿帽子的男人）
2 civil   有教养，文明
3 but yoked   没有套上轭（喻指不受婚姻约束的）
4 draw with you   和您一起拉车
5 unproper   不属于自己；不当
6 peculiar   自家的
7 spite   心病，耻辱
8 arch-mock   最大的嘲弄
9 lip   吻
10 wanton   荡妇
11 secure   安稳
12 a patient list   忍耐的限度
13 shifted him   把他打发走了
14 laid good scuse   编一个好理由（scuse = excuse）
15 ecstasy   昏迷
16 anon   很快
17 encave   躲，藏
18 the fleers … scorns   讥笑、嘲弄和明显的轻蔑
19 cope   与……私通
20 all in all in spleen   完完全全一时冲动、头脑发热
21 cunning   精明

	How is it, general? Have you not hurt your head?	
OTHELLO	Dost thou mock me?	
IAGO	I mock you? No, by heaven!	
	Would you would bear your fortune like a man!	
OTHELLO	A hornèd man's[1] a monster and a beast.	60
IAGO	There's many a beast then in a populous city,	
	And many a civil[2] monster.	
OTHELLO	Did he confess it?	
IAGO	Good sir, be a man:	
	Think every bearded fellow that's but yoked[3]	
	May draw with you[4]. There's millions now alive	65
	That nightly lie in those unproper[5] beds	
	Which they dare swear peculiar[6]. Your case is better.	
	O, 'tis the spite[7] of hell, the fiend's arch-mock[8],	
	To lip[9] a wanton[10] in a secure[11] couch	
	And to suppose her chaste! No, let me know;	70
	And knowing what I am, I know what she shall be.	
OTHELLO	O, thou art wise; 'tis certain.	
IAGO	Stand you awhile apart,	
	Confine yourself but in a patient list[12].	
	Whilst you were here, o'erwhelmèd with your grief –	
	A passion most unsuiting such a man –	75
	Cassio came hither. I shifted him[13] away	
	And laid good scuse[14] upon your ecstasy[15];	
	Bade him anon[16] return and here speak with me,	
	The which he promised. Do but encave[17] yourself,	
	And mark the fleers, the gibes, and notable scorns[18]	80
	That dwell in every region of his face;	
	For I will make him tell the tale anew,	
	Where, how, how oft, how long ago, and when	
	He hath and is again to cope[19] your wife.	
	I say but mark his gesture. Marry, patience,	85
	Or I shall say you're all in all in spleen[20]	
	And nothing of a man.	
OTHELLO	Dost thou hear, Iago?	
	I will be found most cunning[21] in my patience,	
	But – dost thou hear – most bloody.	

Othello hides and Iago reveals he will question Cassio about Bianca. Othello overhears part of their conversation about Cassio's love life. He wrongly thinks they speak of Desdemona.

剧情简介：奥赛罗藏起来，伊阿苟向观众透露他会向卡修询问碧昂卡。奥赛罗偷听到他们关于卡修情爱故事的一部分对话，错以为他们在说黛丝荻牟娜。

Stagecraft 导演技巧

Mime the 'eavesdropping' episode (in threes)

Lines 101–61 are often called the 'eavesdropping' episode, because in them Othello overhears (and misinterprets) Cassio's responses to Iago's questions and statements.

a Gain a first impression of this part of the scene by taking parts and running through the lines, adding some movement and gesture where appropriate.

b Prepare a 'silent movie' performance of these lines. Although your gestures are likely to be exaggerated, ensure they are clear to an audience. Make sure characterisation is communicated through the way people move, stand or position themselves. Create at least two captions (ideally, lines from the script) and either display them on large pieces of card or voice them at appropriate moments. Show your performance to the rest of your class.

1 keep time in all 把控自我；把控时机
2 strumpet's plague 娼妇的报应
3 unbookish 天真，无知
4 construe 理解
5 light 欢快
6 addition 头衔
7 Whose want 丧失它
8 speed 成功，发达
9 poor caitiff 可怜虫
10 poor rogue 可怜的东西
11 faintly 一点儿
12 importunes 催促
13 gives it out 宣称
14 Roman （凯旋的）罗马人
15 customer 娼妇
16 bear some charity 给一些善意（这里指信任）

▼ How would you set up the 'eavesdropping' episode so that the audience can see and hear Othello but he is still hidden from the other characters on stage?

IAGO	That's not amiss.
	But yet keep time in all¹. Will you withdraw? 90
	[*Othello withdraws.*]
	Now will I question Cassio of Bianca,
	A housewife that by selling her desires
	Buys herself bread and clothes. It is a creature
	That dotes on Cassio; as 'tis the strumpet's plague²
	To beguile many and be beguiled by one. 95
	He, when he hears of her, cannot refrain
	From the excess of laughter. Here he comes.

Enter Cassio.

	As he shall smile, Othello shall go mad;
	And his unbookish³ jealousy must construe⁴
	Poor Cassio's smiles, gestures, and light⁵ behaviours 100
	Quite in the wrong. How do you now, lieutenant?
CASSIO	The worser that you give me the addition⁶
	Whose want⁷ even kills me.
IAGO	Ply Desdemona well and you are sure on't.
	Now if this suit lay in Bianca's power, 105
	How quickly should you speed⁸!
CASSIO	Alas, poor caitiff⁹!
OTHELLO	[*Aside*] Look how he laughs already!
IAGO	I never knew a woman love man so.
CASSIO	Alas, poor rogue¹⁰! I think, i'faith, she loves me.
OTHELLO	[*Aside*] Now he denies it faintly¹¹, and laughs it out. 110
IAGO	Do you hear, Cassio?
OTHELLO	[*Aside*] Now he importunes¹² him
	To tell it o'er. Go to, well said, well said!
IAGO	She gives it out¹³ that you shall marry her.
	Do you intend it?
CASSIO	Ha, ha, ha! 115
OTHELLO	[*Aside*] Do you triumph, Roman¹⁴? Do you triumph?
CASSIO	I marry her? What! A customer¹⁵! I prithee, bear some charity¹⁶ to my wit. Do not think it so unwholesome. Ha, ha, ha!
OTHELLO	[*Aside*] So, so, so, so: they laugh that wins.

Othello continues to believe, wrongly, that Cassio speaks of Desdemona. He watches as Bianca meets Cassio and flings the handkerchief back in his face, supposing it had been given to him by some other woman.

剧情简介：奥赛罗继续误以为卡修说的是黛丝荻牟娜。他看见碧昂卡见到卡修时，把手绢甩在他脸上，就认为手绢是另一个女人给卡修的。

▼ Is this how you imagine Bianca to look and dress? What alternative interpretations of Bianca can you suggest? Think of an actor or famous person you would cast in a film version of *Othello* and the costume you would have them wear.

1 cry　谣传
2 scored me　给我打了烙印（伤害了我；坏了我的名声）
3 the monkey's own giving out　那猴崽子自己造的谣
4 flattery　自吹自擂
5 bauble　小贱货
6 imports　暗示
7 So … me　就这样黏着我，依偎着我，因我而哭泣
8 hales　拉扯
9 plucked　拉，拽
10 must leave her company　必须躲开她
11 Before me　见鬼了
12 such another fitchew　另一只臭鼬（指代妓女）
13 a perfumed one　（像妓女一样）抹了廉价香水的骚货
14 dam　母亲
15 piece of work　故事
16 hobby-horse　妓女，婊子
17 when … for　那就等下次再请你吧（即不会有下次了）

Characters　人物分析

Versions of Bianca (by yourself, then in pairs)

According to Iago, Bianca is a 'housewife' (pronounced 'huzif') or hussy (荡妇), who sells her 'desires' to earn a living. He goes on to make his meaning clearer by calling her a 'strumpet' (a whore). Some editors of *Othello* assume that Bianca is a prostitute, and refer to her in that way in the list of characters at the beginning of the play.

a Consider how accurate Iago is as a judge of women. Can you take his description at face value? Can you remember some of the things that Iago has said about other women so far in the play?

b With a partner, compare your findings on Iago's attitude to women. Talk together about what difference it makes to a production of the play if Bianca is unequivocally (毫不含糊) presented as a prostitute. Think about how it reflects on Cassio, and what general image of women is offered through the play. Remember, Bianca is one of only three women in the cast.

Othello Act 4 Scene 1
奥赛罗

IAGO	Faith, the cry[1] goes that you shall marry her.	120
CASSIO	Prithee, say true.	
IAGO	I am a very villain else.	
OTHELLO	[*Aside*] Have you scored me[2]? Well.	
CASSIO	This is the monkey's own giving out[3]. She is persuaded I will marry her out of her own love and flattery[4], not out of my promise.	125
OTHELLO	[*Aside*] Iago beckons me. Now he begins the story.	
CASSIO	She was here even now. She haunts me in every place. I was the other day talking on the sea-bank with certain Venetians, and thither comes this bauble[5] and, by this hand, falls me thus about my neck.	130
OTHELLO	[*Aside*] Crying 'O dear Cassio!' as it were. His gesture imports[6] it.	
CASSIO	So hangs and lolls and weeps upon me[7], so hales[8] and pulls me. Ha, ha, ha!	135
OTHELLO	[*Aside*] Now he tells how she plucked[9] him to my chamber. O, I see that nose of yours, but not that dog I shall throw it to!	
CASSIO	Well, I must leave her company[10].	
IAGO	Before me[11], look where she comes!	140
CASSIO	'Tis such another fitchew[12]! Marry, a perfumed one[13].	

Enter BIANCA.

What do you mean by this haunting of me?

BIANCA	Let the devil and his dam[14] haunt you! What did you mean by that same handkerchief you gave me even now? I was a fine fool to take it. I must take out the work? A likely piece of work[15] that you should find it in your chamber and not know who left it there! This is some minx's token, and I must take out the work? There, give it your hobby-horse[16], wheresoever you had it. I'll take out no work on't.	145
CASSIO	How now, my sweet Bianca! How now, how now!	150
OTHELLO	[*Aside*] By heaven, that should be my handkerchief!	
BIANCA	If you'll come to supper tonight, you may. If you will not, come when you are next prepared for[17]. *Exit*	

153

Cassio leaves to prevent further outbursts by Bianca. Othello determines to kill both Cassio and Desdemona, but is torn between violent hatred and love for his wife. Iago persuades him to put aside any remaining affection.

剧情简介：卡修离开，以免碧昂卡进一步发火。奥赛罗决心把卡修和黛丝荻牟娜都杀掉，但内心对妻子爱恨交织，十分煎熬。伊阿苟劝他把仅存的温情都放到一边。

Write about it 写作练习

'How shall I murder him …?'

Othello's immediate reaction is to plan a murder. As a reader or spectator, are you shocked by the brutality of the words? Write two paragraphs, one from a perspective that is sympathetic to Othello and his situation, and one that is highly critical of Othello. Include embedded quotations to back up your points.

- **Paragraph 1** Consider the way Iago has manipulated Othello. Could you argue that Othello has particular vulnerabilities? What has his life been like? Since Othello is a professional soldier, do you think he has been conditioned to react in violent ways? How has chance played a role in helping Iago's lies seem believable?
- **Paragraph 2** Think about how good a judge of character Othello appears to be. You might like to consider the secretive manner in which Othello courted Desdemona, and the disloyalty he showed Brabantio, one of his benefactors (恩人). Why is Othello so ready to believe his ensign, but not his ensign's wife, nor his own wife? In the end, just how believable *are* Iago's lies?

Stagecraft 导演技巧

In action (in threes)

a Explore different ways of reading lines 162–200, in which Iago cunningly deepens Othello's murderous impulses. Try, for example, whispering, ranting (咆哮), reasoning. You will find that Othello's feelings fluctuate, but Iago ensures that his hatred eventually triumphs.

b With two group members as Othello and the third as Iago, share Othello's lines according to the mood and attitude they reflect. Experiment with movement and positioning:

- the two Othellos standing back-to-back
- all three moving constantly around the room
- all three staying in the same place
- having Iago always behind Othello, whispering in his ear
- Iago standing on a higher level than the two Othellos
- the 'violent' Othello gradually gaining volume, stature, moving towards Iago.

1 rail　骂街
2 else　否则
3 sup　吃晚饭
4 fain　乐意
5 by this hand　我发誓
6 prizes　珍惜
7 nine years a-killing　杀上九年（相当于"千刀万剐"）
8 command him tasks　对他发号施令
9 your way　您的风格
10 plenteous = plentiful（丰富）
11 invention　想象
12 so gentle a condition　性情如此温和，如此有教养
13 too gentle　太温顺（容易被勾引）
14 fond over　痴恋
15 iniquity　罪孽
16 patent　特权
17 if … nobody　若您都不介意，别人更无所谓了
18 messes　碎肉

Othello Act 4 Scene 1
奥赛罗

IAGO	After her, after her!	
CASSIO	Faith, I must. She'll rail[1] in the streets else[2].	155
IAGO	Will you sup[3] there?	
CASSIO	Faith, I intend so.	
IAGO	Well, I may chance to see you; for I would very fain[4] speak with you.	
CASSIO	Prithee, come; will you?	160
IAGO	Go to; say no more.	

Exit Cassio

OTHELLO [*Coming forward.*] How shall I murder him, Iago?
IAGO Did you perceive how he laughed at his vice?
OTHELLO O, Iago!
IAGO And did you see the handkerchief? 165
OTHELLO Was that mine?
IAGO Yours, by this hand[5]. And to see how he prizes[6] the foolish woman your wife: she gave it him, and he hath given it his whore.
OTHELLO I would have him nine years a-killing[7]. A fine woman, a fair woman, a sweet woman! 170
IAGO Nay, you must forget that.
OTHELLO Ay, let her rot and perish, and be damned tonight, for she shall not live. No, my heart is turned to stone: I strike it and it hurts my hand. O, the world hath not a sweeter creature! She might lie by an emperor's side and command him tasks[8]. 175
IAGO Nay, that's not your way[9].
OTHELLO Hang her, I do but say what she is: so delicate with her needle, an admirable musician – O, she will sing the savageness out of a bear – of so high and plenteous[10] wit and invention[11] –
IAGO She's the worse for all this. 180
OTHELLO O, a thousand, thousand times – and then of so gentle a condition[12]!
IAGO Ay, too gentle[13].
OTHELLO Nay, that's certain; but yet the pity of it, Iago! O Iago, the pity of it, Iago! 185
IAGO If you are so fond over[14] her iniquity[15], give her patent[16] to offend; for if it touch not you, it comes near nobody[17].
OTHELLO I will chop her into messes[18]. Cuckold me!
IAGO O, 'tis foul in her.
OTHELLO With mine officer! 190
IAGO That's fouler.

Othello determines to follow Iago's suggestion to strangle Desdemona in her bed. Iago promises to kill Cassio that night. Lodovico brings Othello a letter from Venice, and asks about Cassio.

 剧情简介： 奥赛罗决心听从伊阿苟的建议，将黛丝荻牟娜掐死在床上。伊阿苟承诺当晚杀死卡修。劳德维寇从威尼斯带来一封给奥赛罗的信，并询问卡修近况。

Themes 主题分析

Justice

According to Othello, to strangle his wife in bed represents 'justice' (line 197). In Act 3, a false notion of proof was introduced in the dialogue between Iago and Othello, and since Othello believes that he has been supplied with the 'ocular proof' he demanded, he can now dispense 'justice' for crimes committed. In this way, the concepts of proof and justice have become completely distorted in the course of the play.

a Look up the word 'justice' in a dictionary, then attempt to write your own definition of the term. Give an example of what might be called 'justice' in daily life.

b Write a definition of the word 'justice' as three different characters from the play might understand it. Choose from Othello, Iago, Desdemona, the Duke, Brabantio and Roderigo.

Stagecraft 导演技巧

'Enter LODOVICO'

Step into role as director and write an outline of how you would stage Lodovico's entrance. Work out who would accompany him and how they would be dressed. Detail the advice you would give an actor playing Lodovico regarding his tone, manner and general bearing (举止). Add a justification for each of your decisions, and make some notes in your Director's Journal.

1 Two words (whole class)

Tiny sections of a play can be highly charged with significance. At line 212, Iago says only 'Lives, sir.' But how does he say it? And how does Lodovico (and everyone else) react?

- Four volunteers come to the front of the class and take the roles of Iago, Othello, Desdemona and Lodovico. Read the script from line 203 to line 214. In turn, volunteers from the rest of the class come forward as director and ask the actors to speak and show reactions in a variety of ways. Decide which is the most effective and why.

1. expostulate　讲理
2. unprovide　动摇我的决心
3. The justice of it pleases　这公平合理的做法让我满意
4. be his undertaker　做他的执行人（即干掉他）
5. I … pleasures　我欣然接受他们的任何指令
6. unkind breach　反常的争吵（unkind也可以理解为"绝情的"）
7. This … do　请您务必执行
8. in the paper　读信
9. division　观念分歧
10. T'atone them　让他们和解
11. Fire and brimstone!　烈火与硫黄！（即"下地狱吧！"传说死后下地狱的人要遭受硫黄烈火的炙烧）

OTHELLO	Get me some poison, Iago, this night. I'll not expostulate[1] with her, lest her body and beauty unprovide[2] my mind again – this night, Iago.	
IAGO	Do it not with poison; strangle her in her bed, even the bed she hath contaminated.	195
OTHELLO	Good, good! The justice of it pleases[3]; very good!	
IAGO	And for Cassio, let me be his undertaker[4]. You shall hear more by midnight.	
OTHELLO	Excellent good!	200

A trumpet [sounds within].

What trumpet is that same?

IAGO I warrant something from Venice.

Enter LODOVICO, DESDEMONA *and* ATTENDANTS.

'Tis Lodovico. This comes from the duke. See, your wife's with him.

LODOVICO	God save you, worthy general!	
OTHELLO	With all my heart, sir.	205
LODOVICO	The duke and senators of Venice greet you.	

[He gives Othello a letter.]

OTHELLO I kiss the instrument of their pleasures[5].

[He opens the letter and reads.]

DESDEMONA	And what's the news, good cousin Lodovico?	
IAGO	I am very glad to see you, signior; Welcome to Cyprus.	210
LODOVICO	I thank you. How does Lieutenant Cassio?	
IAGO	Lives, sir.	
DESDEMONA	Cousin, there's fallen between him and my lord An unkind breach[6]; but you shall make all well.	
OTHELLO	Are you sure of that?	215
DESDEMONA	My lord?	
OTHELLO	'This fail you not to do[7], as you will –'	
LODOVICO	He did not call; he's busy in the paper[8]. Is there division[9] 'twixt my lord and Cassio?	
DESDEMONA	A most unhappy one; I would do much T'atone them[10], for the love I bear to Cassio.	220
OTHELLO	Fire and brimstone![11]	
DESDEMONA	My lord?	

Lodovico reveals that the letter orders Othello to be recalled to Venice and Cassio be made governor of Cyprus. Desdemona says she is pleased. Othello strikes her in front of the Venetian delegation, and rages at her.

剧情简介：劳德维寇透露这封信将奥赛罗召回威尼斯，任命卡修为塞浦路斯总督。黛丝荻牟娜表示很高兴，奥赛罗当着威尼斯一行人的面打了她，并冲她大发雷霆。

1 'He strikes her' (in pairs)

Some nineteenth-century directors thought that Othello striking Desdemona was too shocking to show on stage, so they left this out.

- Talk together about what difference it would make to a production if this act of violence was omitted. Would you retain it? Give reasons for your decision.

1	Deputing Cassio in his government 让卡修接替他的职务
2	By my troth 我保证，说实话
3	'Tis very much 这太过分了
4	teem 受孕，繁育
5	prove 结果都变成
6	crocodile 鳄鱼（会流虚伪的眼泪）
7	Mistress （对妓院妓女的称呼）
8	turn 背过身去（也可指招待新客人）
9	obedient 顺从（含性暗示，来者不拒）
10	well-painted 装出来的

Stagecraft 导演技巧

Show the moment (in groups of five or six)

Create a tableau of line 231: 'I have not deserved this.' Make sure that the characters are recognisable from their reactions, their spatial relationships and their frozen gestures. Show your tableau to the rest of the class and ask them to guess who the different characters are. Ask individual characters to step out of the freeze-frame and explain what is going through their mind at that moment.

Characters 人物分析

Interpreting Desdemona (in pairs)

Some commentators suggest that in lines 202–31, Desdemona is deliberately provoking Othello in order to bring his increasingly disturbed behaviour out into the open.

- What do you think of that reading? Is there any evidence from the play so far that Desdemona is assertive enough to do this? Discuss this with a partner.

OTHELLO	Are you wise?	
DESDEMONA	What, is he angry?	
LODOVICO	Maybe the letter moved him;	225
	For as I think they do command him home,	
	Deputing Cassio in his government[1].	
DESDEMONA	By my troth[2], I am glad on't.	
OTHELLO	Indeed!	
DESDEMONA	My lord?	
OTHELLO	I am glad to see you mad.	
DESDEMONA	Why, sweet Othello?	
OTHELLO	Devil!	230

[*He strikes her.*]

DESDEMONA	I have not deserved this.	
LODOVICO	My lord, this would not be believed in Venice,	
	Though I should swear I saw't. 'Tis very much[3].	
	Make her amends; she weeps.	
OTHELLO	O devil, devil!	
	If that the earth could teem[4] with woman's tears,	235
	Each drop she falls would prove[5] a crocodile[6].	
	Out of my sight!	
DESDEMONA	I will not stay to offend you.	
LODOVICO	Truly, an obedient lady.	
	I do beseech your lordship, call her back.	
OTHELLO	Mistress[7]!	240
DESDEMONA	My lord?	
OTHELLO	What would you with her, sir?	
LODOVICO	Who? I, my lord?	
OTHELLO	Ay, you did wish that I would make her turn[8].	
	Sir, she can turn, and turn, and yet go on,	
	And turn again. And she can weep, sir, weep.	245
	And she's obedient[9]; as you say, obedient,	
	Very obedient – proceed you in your tears –	
	Concerning this, sir, – O, well-painted[10] passion! –	
	I am commanded home – get you away!	
	I'll send for you anon. – Sir, I obey the mandate,	250
	And will return to Venice. – Hence, avaunt!	

[*Exit Desdemona*]

Cassio shall have my place. And, sir, tonight
I do entreat that we may sup together.
You are welcome, sir, to Cyprus. Goats and monkeys! *Exit*

Lodovico expresses his horror to Iago at what he has just seen. Iago remarks that Othello is greatly changed. The next scene opens with Othello questioning Emilia about his wife's infidelity.

剧情简介：劳德维寇向伊阿苟表示，他对刚才看到的事情感到恐惧。伊阿苟说奥赛罗性情大变。下一场开场时，奥赛罗就妻子不忠一事询问艾蜜丽叶。

Language in the play 剧中语言
The man 'Whom passion could not shake' (in pairs)

Lodovico comments on how the Venetians had always considered Othello to be a man blessed with great self-control.

a Discuss whether or not you consider self-control to be an admirable quality in a man. Relate your discussion to Othello.

b Look carefully at Othello's syntax (sentence structure) in lines 243–54. What is different about his way of speaking here in comparison with his early speeches (for example, Act 1 Scene 3, lines 127–69)? Discuss what this comparison tells you about Othello's changing state of mind.

c Individually, write three paragraphs on the way Othello's language indicates the way he has changed since the beginning of the play. Use the ideas you discussed in the activity above. (Referring back to the 'Language' box on p. 146 may help you add some additional detail to your writing.)

Characters 人物分析
Iago's persuasive skill

Some readers have interpreted the character of Othello as rather stupid and gullible for having been taken in by Iago. On the other hand, Iago has succeeded in convincing everyone – including Lodovico at this point. It is testimony to Iago's acting skill that he has been so convincing to so many people. At line 273, Lodovico tells Iago with heavy (unconscious) irony, 'I am sorry that I am deceived in him' – meaning that he believes Othello has been misleading them.

a Examine each of Iago's comments to Lodovico in the script opposite. Assess the skill with which he imparts an opinion without seeming to do so.

b Think about why Iago adopts a very plain, down-to-earth way of speaking. What effect is this designed to have?

1 **all-in-all sufficient** 十分能干
2 **solid** 坚定，坚实
3 **shot ... chance** 意外事故的箭或偶然事件的飞镖
4 **Are his wits safe?** 他头脑清醒吗？
5 **light of brain** 脑子糊涂，神志不清
6 **breathe my censure** 悄悄说出我的看法
7 **If ... were.** = If he is not what he might be, I would to heaven he were what he might be.（他若不是他可能是的那种人，我倒巴不得他是。）
8 **yet ... worst** 但愿没有比打她更糟糕的事
9 **use** 习惯
10 **work upon his blood** 对他的血气起了作用
11 **courses** 行为
12 **denote** 暴露，显出
13 **I am deceived in him** 我看错他了

LODOVICO	Is this the noble Moor whom our full senate	255
	Call all-in-all sufficient[1]? Is this the nature	
	Whom passion could not shake? Whose solid[2] virtue	
	The shot of accident nor dart of chance[3]	
	Could neither graze nor pierce?	
IAGO	He is much changed.	
LODOVICO	Are his wits safe?[4] Is he not light of brain[5]?	260
IAGO	He's that he is; I may not breathe my censure[6]	
	What he might be. If what he might he is not,	
	I would to heaven he were.[7]	
LODOVICO	What! Strike his wife!	
IAGO	Faith, that was not so well; yet would I knew	
	That stroke would prove the worst[8].	
LODOVICO	Is it his use[9]?	265
	Or did the letters work upon his blood[10]	
	And new-create this fault?	
IAGO	Alas, alas!	
	It is not honesty in me to speak	
	What I have seen and known. You shall observe him,	
	And his own courses[11] will denote[12] him so,	270
	That I may save my speech. Do but go after,	
	And mark how he continues.	
LODOVICO	I am sorry that I am deceived in him[13].	

Exeunt

Act 4 Scene 2

Cyprus   Another room in the castle

Enter OTHELLO *and* EMILIA.

OTHELLO	You have seen nothing then?	
EMILIA	Nor ever heard, nor ever did suspect.	
OTHELLO	Yes, you have seen Cassio and she together.	
EMILIA	But then I saw no harm, and then I heard	
	Each syllable that breath made up between them.	5

Emilia states categorically that Desdemona is innocent. Othello sends for his wife. He dismisses Emilia, treating her as a brothel-keeper.

 剧情简介：艾蜜丽叶斩钉截铁地表示黛丝荻牟娜是无辜的。奥赛罗派人去叫妻子。他打发艾蜜丽叶走开，只当她是个妓院老鸨。

Themes 主题分析

Attitudes to women

Most people who come under Iago's influence begin to adopt offensively sexist language. Here, Othello refers to Emilia as a 'simple bawd' and Desdemona as a 'subtle whore'. He suggests that Emilia is a brothel-keeper and that Desdemona is a prostitute.

a Explain the three or four ways this image is used in lines 26–9.

b Note down other characters who have had their views and language debased (使粗俗) by Iago, particularly when they are talking about women.

c Pool your ideas with other students on a flipchart (挂图) or whiteboard, then discuss how important you consider this theme to be in the play so far.

d As an extension, you might like to consider Emilia's views about marriage, fidelity and men. Look back at Act 3 Scene 4.

1. durst = dare （胆敢）
2. wager　打赌
3. requite … curse　遭受那条蛇遭受的诅咒（《旧约全书》里提到蛇因为引诱亚当和夏娃吃禁果，上帝诅咒它"你必用肚子行走，终身吃土……"）
4. simple　愚蠢
5. bawd　老鸨
6. closet … secrets　肮脏秘密的保守者
7. Some of your function　您管的事（此处是把艾蜜丽叶当作老鸨使唤）
8. procreants　奸夫淫妇
9. Your mystery　您的营生
10. dispatch　去吧

Characters 人物分析

Othello in the hot-seat (whole class)

Look at the questions Othello asks Emilia (lines 1–18) and the answers she gives. Why does Othello not believe Emilia? And why do you think he asks the questions in the first place?

- One student steps into role as Othello in the hot-seat. The rest of the class asks questions about what he thinks of Desdemona, Emilia and Iago. What proof does he have that his wife is unfaithful? Why is he so convinced? Try to include short quotations in the questions and answers.

1 Desdemona's question

Only a little while earlier, Desdemona was struck and then angrily dismissed by Othello. Now she has been sent for, she enters and asks a question.

- Decide how Desdemona would behave and sound as she asks 'My lord, what is your will?' (line 23). Experiment, then make a directorial decision and justify it to the rest of the class. Once you have shared your ideas, add notes to your Director's Journal.

Othello Act 4 Scene 2
奥赛罗

OTHELLO	What! Did they never whisper?
EMILIA	Never, my lord.
OTHELLO	Nor send you out o'th'way?
EMILIA	Never.
OTHELLO	To fetch her fan, her gloves, her mask, nor nothing?
EMILIA	Never, my lord.
OTHELLO	That's strange. 10
EMILIA	I durst[1], my lord, to wager[2] she is honest,
	Lay down my soul at stake. If you think other,
	Remove your thought; it doth abuse your bosom.
	If any wretch have put this in your head,
	Let heaven requite it with the serpent's curse[3]! 15
	For if she be not honest, chaste, and true,
	There's no man happy. The purest of their wives
	Is foul as slander.
OTHELLO	Bid her come hither; go!

Exit Emilia

She says enough; yet she's a simple[4] bawd[5]
That cannot say as much. This is a subtle whore, 20
A closet lock and key of villainous secrets[6];
And yet she'll kneel and pray. I have seen her do't.

Enter DESDEMONA and Emilia.

DESDEMONA	My lord, what is your will?
OTHELLO	Pray, chuck, come hither.
DESDEMONA	What is your pleasure?
OTHELLO	Let me see your eyes.
	Look in my face.
DESDEMONA	What horrible fancy's this? 25
OTHELLO	[*To Emilia*] Some of your function[7], mistress:
	Leave procreants[8] alone and shut the door;
	Cough or cry 'hem' if anybody come.
	Your mystery[9], your mystery! Nay, dispatch[10]!

Exit Emilia

DESDEMONA	Upon my knees, what doth your speech import? 30
	I understand a fury in your words,
	But not the words.
OTHELLO	Why? What art thou?

Othello accuses Desdemona of gross dishonesty. She doesn't understand what he is talking about, but thinks his anger may be because he has been recalled to Venice by Brabantio's plotting.

 剧情简介：奥赛罗指责黛丝荻牟娜太不老实，她不明白他这话的意思，反而以为他发怒也许是因为他在布拉班修的密谋下被召回威尼斯。

1 Why does he not reply? (in pairs)

Spend five minutes discussing why you think Othello avoids answering Desdemona's direct questions: 'To whom …? With whom? How …?' (line 39). He merely responds with 'away, away, away!' How does this moment contribute to your understanding of Othello's character?

Language in the play 剧中语言

Othello's language: soliloquy? (in threes)

a Read through Othello's lines 46–68. Much of what he says is almost like a soliloquy. As one person reads, the other two echo any words or phrases connected with nature – for example, images of beauty or decay.

b Go through the speeches in more detail, sentence by sentence, and talk together about who you think he is addressing: the audience, himself, Desdemona or someone else? Explore ways in which each section of the speeches might be spoken on stage to give the audience insight into Othello's thoughts and feelings from moment to moment.

c Take turns to present a delivery to the class, explaining before or after your presentation how you hope to show Othello's mental state and emotions. Pinpoint what you consider to be the key words or phrases in contributing to the meaning.

Themes 主题分析

Images of nature (in threes)

Re-read lines 47–8, 60–1 and 65–6. Each pair of lines contains a strong visual image, all concerned in some way with the world of nature, but from a disturbing perspective.

- Create a collage or other visual display using these images as your inspiration. When you have finished, give the collage a title and create an exhibition of the completed artworks. Provide a paragraph of explanatory notes that can be fastened alongside your display.

---

1 one of heaven 天使
2 lost him 失去了他（这个岳父）
3 try 考验
4 Steeped 淹没
5 Given … hopes 剥夺我的自由和最大希望
6 The fixèd figure 固定的人物
7 time of scorn 蔑视的时代
8 To … at 一直被人指指戳戳
9 garnered up my heart 贮藏我的爱
10 fountain 源泉
11 current 溪流
12 cistern 水池，水塘
13 knot and gender 交配并繁衍
14 cherubin 小天使
15 grim 狰狞可怕
16 esteems 认为
17 shambles 屠宰场
18 quicken even with blowing 卵一产下就孵出苍蝇
19 ignorant 不明就里

DESDEMONA	Your wife, my lord; your true and loyal wife.
OTHELLO	Come, swear it; damn thyself;

                Lest, being like one of heaven[1], the devils themselves   35
                Should fear to seize thee. Therefore be double-damned:
                Swear thou art honest.

DESDEMONA   Heaven doth truly know it.
OTHELLO   Heaven truly knows that thou art false as hell.
DESDEMONA To whom, my lord? With whom? How am I false?
OTHELLO   Ah, Desdemon, away, away, away!   40
DESDEMONA Alas, the heavy day! Why do you weep?
                Am I the motive of these tears, my lord?
                If haply you my father do suspect
                An instrument of this your calling back,
                Lay not your blame on me. If you have lost him[2],   45
                I have lost him too.
OTHELLO   Had it pleased heaven
                To try[3] me with affliction, had they rained
                All kind of sores and shames on my bare head,
                Steeped[4] me in poverty to the very lips,
                Given to captivity me and my utmost hopes[5],   50
                I should have found in some place of my soul
                A drop of patience. But, alas, to make me
                The fixèd figure[6] for the time of scorn[7]
                To point his slow unmoving finger at[8]!
                Yet could I bear that too, well, very well;   55
                But there where I have garnered up my heart[9],
                Where either I must live or bear no life,
                The fountain[10] from the which my current[11] runs
                Or else dries up – to be discarded thence
                Or keep it as a cistern[12] for foul toads   60
                To knot and gender[13] in! Turn thy complexion there,
                Patience, thou young and rose-lipped cherubin[14];
                Ay, there look grim[15] as hell!
DESDEMONA I hope my noble lord esteems[16] me honest.
OTHELLO   O ay: as summer flies are in the shambles[17],   65
                That quicken even with blowing[18]. O, thou weed,
                Who art so lovely fair and smell'st so sweet
                That the sense aches at thee, would thou hadst ne'er been born!
DESDEMONA Alas, what ignorant[19] sin have I committed?

Othello calls Desdemona a whore to her face. He ignores her pleas of innocence, and continues to treat Emilia and Desdemona as if they work in a brothel.

 剧情简介：奥赛罗当面骂黛丝荻牟娜是婊子，不顾她自证清白的申诉，继续像对待妓院的人那样对待艾蜜丽叶和黛丝荻牟娜。

Language in the play 剧中语言

Exaggeration (in pairs)

Othello uses extravagant imagery of the heavens in his answer to Desdemona's innocent question, 'what ignorant sin have I committed?' (line 69). He focuses on the word 'committed', and states that 'Heaven stops the nose at it' (the smell of Desdemona's sin), 'the moon winks' (the moon refuses to look) and 'The bawdy wind, that kisses all it meets, / Is hushed within the hollow mine of earth / And will not hear it' (lines 76–9). He is saying that her sin is so revolting and so far-reaching that heaven, moon and wind are unable to bear it. This is a gross exaggeration if taken literally (the literary term is **hyperbole** [夸张]).

- What does such exaggeration suggest about Othello's state of mind and how he interprets his wife's behaviour? Discuss this with a partner.

Write about it 写作练习

Emilia's version (in pairs)

In his last two encounters with Emilia, Othello has persisted in addressing her as if she is a 'madam' and Desdemona is one of her prostitutes. At line 92 he tells Emilia, 'We have done our course' (finished our business) and then proceeds to pay her.

What does Emilia make of all this? Write a letter in which she shares her version of all that has happened since their arrival in Cyprus, and how she thinks events might unfold in the future. What details does she reveal honestly? Are there any facts that she decides not to mention? Does she ask her friend for advice? Step into role and consider including the following:

- surviving the storm
- the wedding celebration between your 'mistress' and 'the Moor'
- Cassio losing his job and Desdemona's attempt to get him reinstated
- giving your husband Desdemona's lost 'napkin'
- Othello's sudden mood swings and inexplicable jealousy
- any suspicion you have about what your husband is up to.

Try to include some of Emilia's phrases or lines from the script.

---

1 **What committed!** 你犯了什么罪!?
2 **commoner** 人尽可夫的娼妇
3 **make … cheeks** 我的面颊羞红得如同火炉一般
4 **stops the nose** 捂住鼻子
5 **winks** 闭上眼睛
6 **bawdy wind** 流里流气的风
7 **hollow mine** 空矿洞，深处
8 **Impudent strumpet!** 无耻的婊子!
9 **vessel** 身体
10 **cry you mercy** 请您原谅（带讽刺意味）
11 **took you** 误解了你
12 **Saint Peter** 圣彼得（看守天堂之门的圣徒，这里奥赛罗讽刺他的妻子没有守住自己的圣洁之门）
13 **done our course** 干完了我们的好事
14 **keep our counsel** 为我们保密
15 **conceive** 想象，猜疑
16 **How do you** 您怎么了
17 **half-asleep** （被惊得）晕头转向

OTHELLO	Was this fair paper, this most goodly book,	70
	Made to write 'whore' upon? What committed!¹	
	Committed? O thou public commoner²!	
	I should make very forges of my cheeks³	
	That would to cinders burn up modesty	
	Did I but speak thy deeds. What committed!	75
	Heaven stops the nose⁴ at it, and the moon winks⁵;	
	The bawdy wind⁶, that kisses all it meets,	
	Is hushed within the hollow mine⁷ of earth	
	And will not hear it. What committed?	
	Impudent strumpet!⁸	
DESDEMONA	By heaven, you do me wrong.	80
OTHELLO	Are not you a strumpet?	
DESDEMONA	No, as I am a Christian.	
	If to preserve this vessel⁹ for my lord	
	From any other foul unlawful touch	
	Be not to be a strumpet, I am none.	
OTHELLO	What, not a whore?	
DESDEMONA	No, as I shall be saved.	85
OTHELLO	Is't possible?	
DESDEMONA	O, heaven forgive us!	
OTHELLO	I cry you mercy¹⁰ then:	
	I took you¹¹ for that cunning whore of Venice	
	That married with Othello. You, mistress,	
	That have the office opposite to Saint Peter¹²,	90
	And keeps the gate of hell! You, you, ay, you!	

Enter Emilia.

	We have done our course¹³; there's money for your pains.	
	I pray you turn the key, and keep our counsel¹⁴.	*Exit*
EMILIA	Alas, what does this gentleman conceive¹⁵?	
	How do you¹⁶, madam? How do you, my good lady?	95
DESDEMONA	Faith, half-asleep¹⁷.	
EMILIA	Good madam, what's the matter with my lord?	
DESDEMONA	With who?	
EMILIA	Why, with my lord, madam.	
DESDEMONA	Who is thy lord?	
EMILIA	He that is yours, sweet lady.	100

Desdemona expresses her distress and bewilderment at Othello's treatment of her. She cannot speak the word 'whore'. Emilia speculates it is all the trick of a villain seeking promotion.

 剧情简介： 面对奥赛罗对她的态度，黛丝荻牟娜既难过又困惑。她说不出"婊子"这个词，艾蜜丽叶揣测这都是某个恶棍为了升官而使的诡计。

1 Desdemona's soliloquy (in small groups)

Many modern readers of the play have found Desdemona's submissiveness (顺从) in the face of severe provocation rather frustrating. However, others have argued that in previous centuries, her behaviour might have been regarded as exemplary for a married woman.

a Lines 106–8 are Desdemona's only soliloquy in the play. It is conventional that in a soliloquy a character always speaks truthfully. What 'truths' does Desdemona utter in these three lines?

b What advice would you give to the actor playing Desdemona in the way she should deliver these lines? First, think about who she is addressing the lines to. Then consider her tone of voice, pace and volume. Add these thoughts to your Director's Journal.

c Attitudes towards domestic violence have changed a lot since Shakespeare's time. Carry out some research into seventeenth-century beliefs about men's rights over women. Share your findings with other groups.

2 'some eternal villain' (whole class)

Emilia's guess that 'some eternal villain' is responsible for the 'slander' (lines 129–32) is extremely accurate. The dramatic irony is made even more acute by the fact that Iago is present. Has Emilia finally recognised the truth? Or is it just a case of unconscious irony?

a As a whole class, nominate one student to play Iago, who comes to the front of the class. While someone reads out Emilia's words, 'Iago' shows how he reacts. Freeze on 'I'll be hanged else'.

b Then bring forward two volunteers to play Emilia. One performs the role as if unconscious of the truth; the second performs it as if she is beginning to realise her husband is at the root of the trouble. Which works better? Can you explain why?

c Predict what Iago's next line will be and write it down. Then turn the page and find out what response Iago actually makes at this moment of high dramatic tension.

---

1 But ... water 只有应该用泪水表达的回答
2 that ... misuse 招致他如此误解我的行为
3 a child to chiding 不习惯于被人责骂
4 bewhored her 骂她是娼妇
5 despite and heavy terms 轻蔑和辱骂
6 in his drink 喝醉的
7 callet 淫妇
8 forsook 放弃
9 Beshrew 诅咒
10 trick 错觉，妄想
11 eternal 该死的
12 busy and insinuating rogue 爱管闲事、巴结钻营的无赖
13 cogging, cozening slave 招摇撞骗的奴才
14 I'll be hanged else 我宁可被绞死也不背弃我的观点

DESDEMONA I have none. Do not talk to me, Emilia.
I cannot weep, nor answers have I none
But what should go by water[1]. Prithee tonight
Lay on my bed my wedding sheets, remember;
And call thy husband hither.
EMILIA   Here's a change indeed!   *Exit*   105
DESDEMONA 'Tis meet I should be used so, very meet!
How have I been behaved that he might stick
The smallest opinion on my least misuse[2]?

Enter IAGO *and Emilia.*

IAGO What is your pleasure, madam? How is't with you?
DESDEMONA I cannot tell. Those that do teach young babes   110
Do it with gentle means and easy tasks.
He might have chid me so; for, in good faith,
I am a child to chiding[3].
IAGO   What is the matter, lady?
EMILIA Alas, Iago, my lord hath so bewhored her[4],
Thrown such despite and heavy terms[5] upon her   115
As true hearts cannot bear.
DESDEMONA Am I that name, Iago?
IAGO   What name, fair lady?
DESDEMONA Such as she said my lord did say I was.
EMILIA He called her whore. A beggar in his drink[6]
Could not have laid such terms upon his callet[7].   120
IAGO Why did he so?
DESDEMONA I do not know; I am sure I am none such.
IAGO Do not weep, do not weep! Alas the day!
EMILIA Hath she forsook[8] so many noble matches,
Her father, and her country, and her friends,   125
To be called whore? Would it not make one weep?
DESDEMONA It is my wretched fortune.
IAGO   Beshrew[9] him for't!
How comes this trick[10] upon him?
DESDEMONA   Nay, heaven doth know.
EMILIA I will be hanged if some eternal[11] villain,
Some busy and insinuating rogue[12],   130
Some cogging, cozening slave[13], to get some office,
Have not devised this slander; I'll be hanged else[14].

Emilia continues to suggest that a villain has poisoned Othello's mind. She reminds Iago that he has suspected her of infidelity with Othello. Desdemona professes her undying love for Othello, whatever happens.

剧情简介：艾蜜丽叶接着提出，是某个恶棍毒化了奥赛罗的心灵。她提醒伊阿苟说，他曾怀疑自己的妻子与奥赛罗有染。黛丝荻牟娜表白，不管发生什么事情，自己对奥赛罗的爱都矢志不渝。

1 'Here I kneel': intercut two scenes (in threes)

At line 150, Desdemona kneels to Iago to enlist (争取) his help. Not only is this heavy with irony, it also parallels the scene where Othello kneels before Iago to swear vengeance (Act 3 Scene 3, line 451).

a Read through these two incidents and the relevant sections of surrounding script. Copy and complete the table below. Some of Othello's key words and images are listed in the left-hand column. Pick out clear echoes from Desdemona's speech and add them to the right-hand column. What are the similarities and what are the differences? (For example, both mention heaven, but from different perspectives.)

Othello kneels (Act 3 Scene 3)	Desdemona kneels (Act 4 Scene 2)
'blood, blood, blood'	
'icy current … compulsive course'	
'bloody thoughts'	
'violent pace'	
'ne'er ebb to humble love'	'ever will … love him dearly'
'revenge'	
'marble heaven'	'this light of heaven'
'sacred vow'	

b In your groups, experiment to find a way of performing these speeches, intercutting the two episodes where husband and wife both kneel unwittingly before their tormentor. The actions are similar, but what differences exist between the two?

▶ What might Iago make of Emilia's telling description of the 'scurvy fellow' who might be behind Othello's uncharacteristic behaviour?

1 **halter** 绞索
2 **keeps her company** 被当作她的情人
3 **form** 外表；方式，办法
4 **companions** 流氓，无赖
5 **unfold** 揭露
6 **within door** 小声
7 **squire** 先生（意指小人）
8 **the seamy side without** 丑里子外穿（指被搞得晕头转向，不辨是非）
9 **suspect me** 怀疑我（与摩尔人私通）
10 **by this light of heaven** 凭这天堂之光发誓
11 **in … deed** 在思想或行动上
12 **beggarly divorcement** 乞丐般的离婚
13 **Comfort forswear me!** 让我永无幸福之日！
14 **abhor me** 让我恐惧
15 **vanity** 荣华富贵
16 **humour** 一时之气
17 **does him offence** 冒犯他，让他生气
18 **chide with** 斥责

IAGO	Fie, there is no such man; it is impossible.
DESDEMONA	If any such there be, heaven pardon him.
EMILIA	A halter[1] pardon him and hell gnaw his bones! 135
	Why should he call her whore? Who keeps her company[2]?
	What place, what time, what form[3], what likelihood?
	The Moor's abused by some most villainous knave,
	Some base notorious knave, some scurvy fellow.
	O heaven, that such companions[4] thou'dst unfold[5], 140
	And put in every honest hand a whip
	To lash the rascals naked through the world,
	Even from the east to th'west!
IAGO	Speak within door[6].
EMILIA	O fie upon them! Some such squire[7] he was
	That turned your wit the seamy side without[8] 145
	And made you to suspect me[9] with the Moor.
IAGO	You are a fool, go to.
DESDEMONA	O good Iago,
	What shall I do to win my lord again?
	Good friend, go to him; for, by this light of heaven[10],
	I know not how I lost him. Here I kneel: 150
	If e'er my will did trespass 'gainst his love
	Either in discourse of thought or actual deed[11];
	Or that mine eyes, mine ears, or any sense
	Delighted them in any other form;
	Or that I do not yet, and ever did, 155
	And ever will – though he do shake me off
	To beggarly divorcement[12] – love him dearly,
	Comfort forswear me![13] Unkindness may do much,
	And his unkindness may defeat my life,
	But never taint my love. I cannot say 'whore': 160
	It does abhor me[14] now I speak the word;
	To do the act that might the addition earn
	Not the world's mass of vanity[15] could make me.
IAGO	I pray you be content; 'tis but his humour[16].
	The business of the state does him offence[17], 165
	And he does chide with[18] you.
DESDEMONA	If 'twere no other –
IAGO	It is but so, I warrant.

Emilia and Desdemona go off to dinner with the Venetian visitors. Roderigo is fed up with Iago, accusing him of tricking him out of jewellery that was meant to have been passed on to Desdemona. He threatens Iago.

 剧情简介：艾蜜丽叶和黛丝荻牟娜离开，与威尼斯访客共进晚餐。若德瑞苟受够了伊阿苟，指责他骗其金银珠宝，那些本来是要送给黛丝荻牟娜的。他威胁伊阿苟。

1 What happened at dinner? (in groups of six or seven)

After the highly emotional episode of marital strife, Desdemona is called to a formal dinner to entertain her Venetian guests. The scene is not included in the play, but there are strong dramatic possibilities in such an artificially polite and formal occasion, with seething (涌动的) undercurrents of highly charged emotional discord.

- Improvise or write the imagined scene, giving due consideration to how Othello, Desdemona, Emilia and Lodovico might speak and behave towards one another in public.

Stagecraft 导演技巧

Playing the scene (in pairs)

The final part of Scene 2 brings in Roderigo, who bitterly complains that he is being exploited and cheated by Iago, and has no prospect of winning Desdemona. Iago displays his usual quick-wittedness, and his initially brief replies incite Roderigo's anger and a threat of a duel ('seek satisfaction'). On the next page of the script, Iago flatters Roderigo and devises a murderous plan to kill Cassio, thus enabling Roderigo to win Desdemona. This episode between Iago and Roderigo has been interpreted in different ways by commentators and directors. Some see it as continuing to raise the tension. Others believe it has strong comic possibilities to temporarily lower the tension.

a Take parts and read lines 171–235, then discuss how you would play the episode in two or three different ways. Try out different readings. Decide which works best, and why.

b Annotate an enlarged copy of the script, making precise suggestions about how you think it should be acted. Then write a paragraph outlining the reasons for your decisions. You might like to refer to:

- your knowledge of the two characters so far
- the situation at this point in the story, including Iago's complex balancing act with all the lies he is telling
- the need to lighten the mood at this point in the play (or not)
- the need to heighten the tension even further (or not).

---

1 stay the meat 等待用餐
2 daff'st me 搪塞我
3 device 借口
4 conveniency 机会
5 endure it 忍耐下去
6 put up in peace 默默忍受
7 performances 行为
8 no kin together 不一致
9 naught = nothing
10 I ... means 我的钱要花光了
11 half 轻易
12 votarist 修女
13 expectations 鼓励
14 sudden respect 即刻关注
15 fopped 被愚弄
16 solicitation 求爱
17 seek satisfaction of you 找您算账
18 You have said now? 您说完了?

Othello Act 4 Scene 2
奥赛罗

        [*Trumpets sound within.*]
Hark how these instruments summon to supper!
The messengers of Venice stay the meat[1].
Go in, and weep not; all things shall be well.   170
           Exeunt Desdemona and Emilia

        Enter RODERIGO.

    How now, Roderigo?
RODERIGO   I do not find that thou deal'st justly with me.
IAGO   What in the contrary?
RODERIGO   Every day thou daff'st me[2] with some device[3], Iago, and rather, as it seems to me now, keep'st from me all conveniency[4] than suppliest me with the least advantage of hope. I will indeed no longer endure it[5]. Nor am I yet persuaded to put up in peace[6] what already I have foolishly suffered.   175
IAGO   Will you hear me, Roderigo?
RODERIGO   Faith, I have heard too much; for your words and performances[7] are no kin together[8].   180
IAGO   You charge me most unjustly.
RODERIGO   With naught[9] but truth. I have wasted myself out of my means[10]. The jewels you have had from me to deliver to Desdemona would half[11] have corrupted a votarist[12]. You have told me she hath received them, and returned me expectations[13] and comforts of sudden respect[14] and acquaintance, but I find none.   185
IAGO   Well, go to; very well.
RODERIGO   Very well, go to! I cannot go to, man, nor 'tis not very well. By this hand, I say 'tis very scurvy and begin to find myself fopped[15] in it.   190
IAGO   Very well.
RODERIGO   I tell you 'tis not very well. I will make myself known to Desdemona. If she will return me my jewels, I will give over my suit and repent my unlawful solicitation[16]; if not, assure yourself I will seek satisfaction of you[17].   195
IAGO   You have said now?[18]

Iago promises Roderigo that Desdemona will be available for him soon. He plots that Roderigo shall kill Cassio that night as Cassio leaves Bianca's house.

剧情简介：伊阿苟向若德瑞苟保证，黛丝荻牟娜很快就是他的了。他策划让若德瑞苟当晚趁卡修离开碧昂卡家时杀掉他。

Characters 人物分析

Iago the manipulator

What information does Iago (kneeling in the picture below) choose to pass on to Roderigo (sitting) about Othello's next posting (任命；派驻) and about Cassio's forthcoming promotion? What reward is Roderigo promised for 'knocking out [Cassio's] brains'?

- Write a paragraph describing the way in which Iago works to manipulate other characters – and how quickly he thinks on his feet (脑子反应快).

1. protest intendment 宣称要做的事
2. there's mettle in thee 你有些胆量了
3. just exception 有道理的投诉
4. It hath not appeared 看起来并不是这样
5. devise engines for my life 设计要我的命
6. compass 可能的范围
7. Mauritania 毛里塔尼亚（北非古国名）
8. abode be lingered 延迟停留
9. determinate 确定的
10. harlotry 妓女
11. honourable fortune 幸运（即升职）
12. his going thence 当他离开时
13. fashion 安排，促成
14. fall out 发生
15. second 帮助，策应
16. necessity 需要
17. put it on him 除掉他
18. grows to waste 快过去了
19. About it! 去做准备吧！

174

Othello Act 4 Scene 2
奥赛罗

RODERIGO   Ay, and said nothing but what I protest intendment[1] of doing.

IAGO   Why, now I see there's mettle in thee[2], and even from this instant do build on thee a better opinion than ever before. Give me thy hand, Roderigo. Thou hast taken against me a most just exception[3]; but yet I protest I have dealt most directly in thy affair.

RODERIGO   It hath not appeared[4].

IAGO   I grant indeed it hath not appeared; and your suspicion is not without wit and judgement. But, Roderigo, if thou hast that in thee indeed, which I have greater reason to believe now than ever – I mean purpose, courage, and valour – this night show it. If thou the next night following enjoy not Desdemona, take me from this world with treachery, and devise engines for my life[5].

RODERIGO   Well, what is it? Is it within reason and compass[6]?

IAGO   Sir, there is especial commission come from Venice to depute Cassio in Othello's place.

RODERIGO   Is that true? Why, then Othello and Desdemona return again to Venice.

IAGO   O no, he goes into Mauritania[7] and takes away with him the fair Desdemona, unless his abode be lingered[8] here by some accident; wherein none can be so determinate[9] as the removing of Cassio.

RODERIGO   How do you mean 'removing' of him?

IAGO   Why, by making him uncapable of Othello's place – knocking out his brains.

RODERIGO   And that you would have me to do?

IAGO   Ay, if you dare do yourself a profit and a right. He sups tonight with a harlotry[10], and thither will I go to him. He knows not yet of his honourable fortune[11]. If you will watch his going thence[12] – which I will fashion[13] to fall out[14] between twelve and one – you may take him at your pleasure. I will be near to second[15] your attempt, and he shall fall between us. Come, stand not amazed at it, but go along with me. I will show you such a necessity[16] in his death that you shall think yourself bound to put it on him[17]. It is now high supper-time and the night grows to waste[18]. About it![19]

RODERIGO   I will hear further reason for this.

IAGO   And you shall be satisfied.

Exeunt

Othello bids goodnight to Lodovico after their dinner, and orders Desdemona to go to bed to await him. She talks with Emilia of her love for Othello, of death, and of Barbary, her mother's maid.

剧情简介： 奥赛罗晚饭后向劳德维寇道晚安，命黛丝荻牟娜上床等他。黛丝荻牟娜跟艾蜜丽叶谈到自己对奥赛罗的爱，谈到死亡，谈到她母亲的侍女芭波蕊。

1 Inner dilemmas/outward politeness (in sixes)

In lines 1–9 of Scene 3, all three characters are troubled by what they have seen or heard recently, yet all maintain a veneer (假象) of calm politeness.

- Three people take on the roles of Lodovico, Desdemona and Othello. The remaining three represent each character's innermost thoughts. Perform the script, punctuating each line with what you think is really going on in the mind of the speaker.

Characters 人物分析

Emilia and Desdemona (in pairs)

Scene 3 is often referred to as the 'willow' scene. It focuses on Emilia and Desdemona, and provides a quietly moving final moment, in contrast to the recent turmoil.

a Take parts and read from line 10 to the end of the scene (line 101). As you read, think about the relationship between the two women. Is it a close friendship, or that of mistress and servant. What evidence can you find in the script to back up your view? Look, for instance, at the terms of address used (if any). Who gives commands or asks questions? Who gives advice, and in what terms?

b Write two paragraphs describing the relationship between Emilia and Desdemona at this point in the play. How has it developed from the beginning of Act 2?

2 Foreboding (预兆)

In this scene, there is a general sense of foreboding. Devise a diagram or collage to show how each of the following contributes to the ominous atmosphere, in the context of Iago's earlier suggestion that Othello should 'strangle her in her bed' and Othello's desire for 'blood, blood, blood':

- bedsheets
- the order to dismiss Emilia
- Barbary's story and the willow song
- Desdemona's complete obedience.

In each case, add a quotation from the play. Your diagram or collage should help others to understand the dramatic effect of this part of the play.

---

1 on th'instant 马上，立刻
2 forthwith 当即，很快
3 incontinent 立马，立即
4 nightly wearing 睡衣
5 So would not I 我不愿这样
6 approve 珍视
7 checks 责骂
8 unpin 解开扣，摘下发簪
9 grace and favour 风度和可爱之处
10 All's one 都一样，没关系
11 you talk 您瞎说
12 proved mad 结果变了心
13 forsake 抛弃
14 willow 柳树（旧时为失恋情人的象征）
15 An old thing 一首老歌
16 fortune 命运
17 I … / But … 我发现自己难以……
18 hang … side 把自己的头歪向一边

Othello Act 4 Scene 3 奥赛罗

Act 4 Scene 3
Cyprus   A room in the castle

Enter OTHELLO, LODOVICO, DESDEMONA,
EMILIA *and* ATTENDANTS.

LODOVICO	I do beseech you, sir, trouble yourself no further.
OTHELLO	O, pardon me; 'twill do me good to walk.
LODOVICO	Madam, good night. I humbly thank your ladyship.
DESDEMONA	Your honour is most welcome.
OTHELLO	Will you walk, sir? O, Desdemona. 5
DESDEMONA	My lord?
OTHELLO	Get you to bed on th'instant[1]. I will be returned forthwith[2]. Dismiss your attendant there. Look't be done.
DESDEMONA	I will, my lord.

Exeunt [*Othello, Lodovico and Attendants*]

EMILIA	How goes it now? He looks gentler than he did. 10
DESDEMONA	He says he will return incontinent[3]; He hath commanded me to go to bed And bade me to dismiss you.
EMILIA	Dismiss me?
DESDEMONA	It was his bidding; therefore, good Emilia, Give me my nightly wearing[4], and adieu. 15 We must not now displease him.
EMILIA	I would you had never seen him.
DESDEMONA	So would not I[5]: my love doth so approve[6] him That even his stubbornness, his checks[7], his frowns – Prithee, unpin[8] me – have grace and favour[9] in them. 20
EMILIA	I have laid those sheets you bade me on the bed.
DESDEMONA	All's one[10]. Good faith, how foolish are our minds! If I do die before thee, prithee shroud me In one of those same sheets.
EMILIA	Come, come, you talk[11].
DESDEMONA	My mother had a maid called Barbary: 25 She was in love, and he she loved proved mad[12] And did forsake[13] her. She had a song of willow[14]; An old thing[15] 'twas but it expressed her fortune[16], And she died singing it. That song tonight Will not go from my mind. I have much to do 30 But[17] to go hang my head all at one side[18]

Desdemona sings a sad song from her childhood as she prepares for bed. She and Emilia discuss their differing attitudes to marriage and fidelity.

 剧情简介：黛丝荻牟娜准备就寝时，唱起一首儿时唱的哀伤的歌。她和艾蜜丽叶谈起对婚姻和忠贞的不同看法。

1 'a proper man' (in pairs)

Desdemona refers to Lodovico as being 'a proper man' (a good-looking man) and someone who 'speaks well'. Emilia agrees.

- Spend about five minutes discussing why Desdemona says this. What interpretations of this comment are possible? As director, how would you want Desdemona to say this in order to encourage an audience to share your interpretation? Add a short note to your Director's Journal.

Stagecraft 导演技巧
The Willow Song

The first edition of the play (published in 1622) omits the song altogether. Perhaps the boy actor who played Desdemona at that time couldn't sing!

- From your reading of the script, and/ or viewing of either a live or filmed performance, what was your reaction to the song? What effect did it have on you? List what a performance would gain or lose if the song were omitted. Compare your feelings with those of other students.

▶ Explore ways of presenting the Willow Song to create a moving and dramatic effect between the two women at this point in the play.

1	dispatch	快点儿
2	touch of his nether lip	吻他一下（nether = lower）
3	sycamore tree	野无花果树（这种树常与忧郁的恋人联系起来）
4	Lay by these	把这些收起来
5	hie thee	快点儿
6	garland	花环
7	moe = more	
8	couch	睡觉
9	bode	预示
10	'Tis … there	那是不相干的
11	in conscience	诚实
12	abuse	欺骗，背叛
13	In such gross kind	如此卑鄙
14	heavenly light	月光

	And sing it like poor Barbary – prithee, dispatch[1].	
EMILIA	Shall I go fetch your nightgown?	
DESDEMONA	No, unpin me here.	
	This Lodovico is a proper man.	
EMILIA	A very handsome man.	
DESDEMONA	He speaks well.	35
EMILIA	I know a lady in Venice would have walked barefoot to Palestine for a touch of his nether lip[2].	
DESDEMONA	[Sings]	

    The poor soul sat sighing by a sycamore tree[3],
        Sing all a green willow;
    Her hand on her bosom, her head on her knee,   40
        Sing willow, willow, willow;
    The fresh streams ran by her and murmured her moans;
        Sing willow, willow, willow.
    Her salt tears fell from her and softened the stones –
Lay by these[4].
        Sing willow, willow, willow –   45
Prithee, hie thee[5]; he'll come anon.
        Sing all a green willow must be my garland[6].
        Let nobody blame him; his scorn I approve –
Nay that's not next. Hark, who is't that knocks?   50

EMILIA	It's the wind.	
DESDEMONA	[Sings]	

    I called my love false love, but what said he then?
        Sing willow, willow, willow;
    If I court moe[7] women, you'll couch[8] with moe men –
So get thee gone; good night. Mine eyes do itch –   55
Does that bode[9] weeping?

EMILIA	'Tis neither here nor there[10].	
DESDEMONA	I have heard it said so. O, these men, these men! Dost thou in conscience[11] think – tell me, Emilia – That there be women do abuse[12] their husbands In such gross kind[13]?	
EMILIA	There be some such, no question.	60
DESDEMONA	Wouldst thou do such a deed for all the world?	
EMILIA	Why, would not you?	
DESDEMONA	No, by this heavenly light[14].	
EMILIA	Nor I neither by this heavenly light; I might do't as well i'th'dark.	

Emilia says she would commit adultery if it gained her husband the world. Desdemona can't believe this. Emilia asserts that husbands are to blame, and argues for equality and mutual respect in marriage.

剧情简介：艾蜜丽叶说她愿意犯下私通之罪来给丈夫赢得整个世界。黛丝荻牟娜觉得不可思议。艾蜜丽叶声称该责怪的是男人，婚姻中男女应该平等，互相尊重。

▲ Role-play Emilia and Desdemona. Justify their views, making reference to their respective social positions, their experience of men and married life.

1 In troth　说实话
2 undo't　弥补
3 joint-ring　情侣戒指，廉价戒指
4 measures of lawn　几匹布
5 exhibition　钱财
6 Ud's = God's
7 venture purgatory　甘受炼狱之苦
8 to th'advantage　此外
9 store　住满
10 played　赌博；卖身
11 slack their duties　疏于他们的职责（指性爱）
12 pour … laps　将属于我们的温存倾注到别的女人身上
13 Throwing restraint upon us　把枷锁套在我们身上
14 scant　削减
15 our former having　我们曾经拥有的
16 in despite　出于怨恨
17 galls　胆量（去报复）
18 sport　寻欢作乐
19 Is't … errs?　是薄弱意志让他们犯错的吗？
20 use us well　善待我们
21 ills　错事
22 pick　学习
23 by bad mend　引以为戒

Characters　人物分析

Emilia and Desdemona's contrasting views (in pairs)

a Compare the two women's views of men and marriage. With a partner, discuss what the women say to each other in lines 57–101. Would you agree that one is a romanticised view, whilst the other is much more practical? What difference does each woman's social position make to their separate views?

b To develop your discussion, look at the production photographs of Emilia and Desdemona here and on pages 170, 178 and 183. What does each photograph suggest about their relationship (look at positioning, expressions and direction of gaze, costume, lighting)? Add some notes to your Director's Journal to explain how you think these two women characters should be played.

DESDEMONA   Wouldst thou do such a deed for all the world?
EMILIA   The world's a huge thing; it is a great price
            For a small vice.
DESDEMONA   In troth¹, I think thou wouldst not.
EMILIA   In troth, I think I should, and undo't² when I had done it. Marry, I would not do such a thing for a joint-ring³, nor for measures of lawn⁴, nor for gowns, petticoats, nor caps, nor any petty exhibition⁵. But for all the whole world! Ud's⁶ pity, who would not make her husband a cuckold, to make him a monarch? I should venture purgatory⁷ for't.
DESDEMONA   Beshrew me, if I would do such a wrong for the whole world.
EMILIA   Why, the wrong is but a wrong i'th'world; and having the world for your labour, 'tis a wrong in your own world, and you might quickly make it right.
DESDEMONA   I do not think there is any such woman.
EMILIA   Yes, a dozen; and as many to th'advantage⁸ as would store⁹ the world they played¹⁰ for.
                But I do think it is their husbands' faults
                If wives do fall. Say that they slack their duties¹¹
                And pour our treasures into foreign laps¹²,
                Or else break out in peevish jealousies,
                Throwing restraint upon us¹³; or say they strike us,
                Or scant¹⁴ our former having¹⁵ in despite¹⁶ –
                Why, we have galls¹⁷, and though we have some grace,
                Yet have we some revenge. Let husbands know
                Their wives have sense like them: they see, and smell,
                And have their palates both for sweet and sour
                As husbands have. What is it that they do
                When they change us for others? Is it sport¹⁸?
                I think it is. And doth affection breed it?
                I think it doth. Is't frailty that thus errs?¹⁹
                It is so too. And have not we affections,
                Desires for sport, and frailty, as men have?
                Then let them use us well²⁰; else let them know
                The ills²¹ we do, their ills instruct us so.
DESDEMONA   Good night, good night. God me such uses send,
            Not to pick²² bad from bad, but by bad mend²³!

                                                                Exeunt

Othello
奥赛罗

Looking back at Act 4 第4幕回顾
Activities for groups or individuals

1 The focus of Act 4

Act 4 takes on a much narrower, more domestic focus than the previous three acts, and it is worth considering how Act 4 furthers the action of the play.

- As a first step, draw a table similar to the one below and compile a summary of each act so far, suggesting (as far as you know) where each scene is set.

	Summary of events	Where set
Act 1	Iago and Roderigo tell Brabantio that his daughter has secretly married Othello. Brabantio takes his complaint to the Duke of Venice. Othello (and Desdemona) defend themselves in front of the Senate; the Duke allows the marriage. News that Cyprus is under threat from a Turkish attack means that Othello must set sail immediately and command the troops.	Venice: **a** in the streets **b** in the Senate
Act 2		Cyprus: **a** the quayside **b** …
Act 3		
Act 4		

- Suggest some ideas about staging, set designs, sound and lighting that could help to emphasise this movement from public to private affairs. What would you highlight as key dramatic moments in Act 4?

2 Abuse of Desdemona

The following lines are all spoken by Othello directly to Desdemona's face:

- 'thou art false as hell'
- 'look grim as hell!'
- 'O, thou weed'
- 'Was this fair paper … / Made to write "whore" upon?'
- 'O thou public commoner!'
- 'Impudent strumpet!'
- 'Are not you a strumpet?'
- 'What, not a whore?'
- 'I took you for that cunning whore of Venice'
- 'We have done our course'.

a In large groups, each person learns one of the lines above. Move around the room, and every time you encounter another student, shout, hiss or sneer your line in their face.

b Stand in a long line, all facing one way. Go swiftly down the row, spinning round one by one so that you are facing the next person, and snap your lines harshly. Then try standing in a tight circle with one student kneeling in the middle – volunteers only! Hurl your lines of abuse at them.

c Use the physical experience of the activities above to help you write a short essay analysing Othello's motives for such language, and Desdemona's feelings in response to it.

3 Private thoughts

At the end of Act 4, each of the main characters is poised on the brink of a significant event.

- Choose three from the following characters: Roderigo, Desdemona, Iago, Othello, Emilia. In role, write down one sentence for each that you feel best encapsulates (概括) their hope or wish at this moment. Then share these sentences with the rest of the class, by reading out in role.
- Discuss any variations, and talk about why some of you may have interpreted characters and their motivation in different ways at this point in the play.

Iago positions Roderigo for the murder. He hopes both Cassio and Roderigo will die. Roderigo fails to kill Cassio, who wounds him instead. Iago leaps out of hiding, strikes Cassio and runs off.

 剧情简介： 伊阿苟布置若德瑞苟杀人，希望卡修和若德瑞苟都死掉。若德瑞苟未能杀死卡修，反被卡修打伤。伊阿苟从藏身处跳出，刺伤卡修后逃走。

Language in the play 剧中语言
Count the commands
How many commands can you find in the opening five lines of Iago's conversation? What does the repeated use of the imperative ('Stand!' 'Be bold!') emphasise about the relationship between Iago and Roderigo?

1 Intrigue again
Act 5 opens in a very similar way to Act 1, with Iago and Roderigo plotting villainy in the streets late at night. What other similarities are there with that opening scene – and what key differences?

- Create a poster or display to explore the parallels between the opening of this scene and of Act 1 Scene 1. Include some short quotations (words, phrases or lines) that you believe to be significant. Display your poster in the classroom.

Characters 人物分析
Iago: motiveless malignity (恶毒)? (in pairs)
The nineteenth-century poet and writer Samuel Taylor Coleridge was intrigued by the character of Iago, whose activities he described as arising out of 'motiveless malignity' (wickedness that cannot be explained). Iago himself has already given several reasons for his vendetta (积怨) against Othello and Cassio, but these seem rather flimsy (站不住脚) and inconsistent.

a Read through Iago's aside in lines 11–22. What reason does he give here for his behaviour?

b What other reasons has Iago already given for his hatred of Othello and Cassio?

c Discuss what you think is meant by Iago's comment 'He hath a daily beauty in his life / That makes me ugly' (lines 19–20).

d Write a paragraph outlining your thoughts about Iago's motivation (or lack of it) to do harm to others.

1 bulk 墙柱（墙体凸出部分）
2 rapier 长剑
3 bare 拔出鞘的
4 put it home 深深刺中
5 at thy elbow 在你身旁
6 It … us 成败与否，在此一举（mars：毁灭）
7 resolution 决心
8 miscarry 失手
9 take thy stand 你站好
10 retires 退至幕后
11 quat 疖子，脓包（喻指窝囊废）
12 almost to the sense 快熟透了
13 makes my gain 对我有利
14 Live Roderigo = If Roderigo lives
15 calls me to a restitution 找我索赔
16 bobbed 蒙骗
17 unfold 揭露
18 soft 嘘
19 his gait 他的步态
20 coat 外套（指里面套着铠甲的衣服）
21 make proof of 试试

Act 5 Scene 1
Cyprus   A street at night

Enter IAGO *and* RODERIGO.

IAGO	Here, stand behind this bulk[1], straight will he come.
	Wear thy good rapier[2] bare[3], and put it home[4].
	Quick, quick, fear nothing; I'll be at thy elbow[5].
	It makes us or it mars us[6]; think on that,
	And fix most firm thy resolution[7]. 5
RODERIGO	Be near at hand; I may miscarry[8] in't.
IAGO	Here, at thy hand; be bold, and take thy stand[9].

[*He retires*[10].]

RODERIGO	I have no great devotion to the deed,
	And yet he hath given me satisfying reasons.
	'Tis but a man gone. Forth my sword! He dies! 10
IAGO	[*Aside*] I have rubbed this young quat[11] almost to the sense[12],
	And he grows angry. Now, whether he kill Cassio,
	Or Cassio him, or each do kill the other,
	Every way makes my gain[13]. Live Roderigo[14],
	He calls me to a restitution[15] large 15
	Of gold and jewels that I bobbed[16] from him
	As gifts to Desdemona.
	It must not be. If Cassio do remain,
	He hath a daily beauty in his life
	That makes me ugly; and besides, the Moor 20
	May unfold[17] me to him – there stand I in much peril.
	No, he must die. But soft[18], I hear him coming.

Enter CASSIO.

RODERIGO	I know his gait[19]; 'tis he. Villain, thou diest!

[*He lunges at Cassio.*]

CASSIO	That thrust had been mine enemy indeed
	But that my coat[20] is better than thou think'st. 25
	I will make proof of[21] thine.

[*He wounds Roderigo.*]

RODERIGO	O, I am slain!

[*Iago wounds Cassio in the leg and exit*]

CASSIO	I am maimed forever. Help, ho! Murder, murder!

Enter OTHELLO.

Othello hears the scuffles and, satisfied Cassio is dead, goes off to kill Desdemona. Lodovico and Gratiano cautiously investigate the cries of the two wounded men. Iago arrives to help.

  剧情简介：奥赛罗听到打斗声，满心以为卡修已死，便前去谋杀黛丝荻牟娜。劳德维寇和格拉奇阿诺小心查看两名呼救的伤者。伊阿苟前来帮忙。

1 Who's doing what, and when? (in pairs)

There is a great deal of action in the first fifty-five lines of Scene 1. As you can imagine, on stage it is both fast-moving and exciting. Below is one person's idea for staging it at the Globe Theatre (now rebuilt on London's Bankside). The drawing shows different characters at different moments, and the events are numbered in the order in which they occur in the script.

- Identify each person in the drawing, then work out which moment in the script is being represented in each case. Find a suitable quotation for each one (five in all). Copy and complete the table below.

	Character	Moment	Quotation
1			
2			
3			
4			
5			

1 Minion 我的甜心（含轻蔑意）
2 dear 情郎
3 unblest 受诅咒的
4 hies 很快就到
5 Forth of my heart 从我心里
6 blotted 抹去
7 watch 巡夜人
8 passage 路人
9 mischance 意外
10 direful 可怕，吓人
11 heavy 黑暗
12 counterfeits 骗子
13 think't 假定它
14 come in to the cry 到呼救现场
15 in his shirt 穿着衬衣（衬衫式长睡衣）
16 spoiled 完了
17 undone 受伤

OTHELLO	[*Aside*] The voice of Cassio: Iago keeps his word.	
RODERIGO	O villain that I am!	
OTHELLO	[*Aside*] It is even so.	
CASSIO	O help, ho! Light! A surgeon!	30
OTHELLO	[*Aside*] 'Tis he. O brave Iago, honest and just,	
	That hast such noble sense of thy friend's wrong!	
	Thou teachest me. Minion[1], your dear[2] lies dead,	
	And your unblest[3] fate hies[4]. Strumpet, I come!	
	Forth of my heart[5] those charms, thine eyes, are blotted[6];	35
	Thy bed, lust-stained, shall with lust's blood be spotted.	

Exit Othello

Enter LODOVICO *and* GRATIANO.

CASSIO	What, ho! No watch[7]? No passage[8]? Murder, murder!	
GRATIANO	'Tis some mischance[9]; the cry is very direful[10].	
CASSIO	O, help!	
LODOVICO	Hark!	40
RODERIGO	O, wretched villain!	
LODOVICO	Two or three groan. It is a heavy[11] night.	
	These may be counterfeits[12]: let's think't[13] unsafe	
	To come in to the cry[14] without more help.	
RODERIGO	Nobody come? Then I shall bleed to death.	45
LODOVICO	Hark!	

Enter Iago, with a light.

GRATIANO	Here's one comes in his shirt[15], with light and weapons.	
IAGO	Who's there? Whose noise is this that cries on murder?	
LODOVICO	We do not know.	
IAGO	Did you not hear a cry?	
CASSIO	Here, here; for heaven's sake, help me!	
IAGO	What's the matter?	50
GRATIANO	This is Othello's ancient, as I take it.	
LODOVICO	The same indeed, a very valiant fellow.	
IAGO	What are you here that cry so grievously?	
CASSIO	Iago? O, I am spoiled[16], undone[17] by villains!	
	Give me some help.	55

In pretending to investigate what has happened, Iago secretly stabs the injured Roderigo. Cassio is discovered to have a severe leg wound. Bianca arrives to see what has happened, and Iago insults her.

剧情简介：伊阿苟装模作样调查事情的原委，暗地里捅了受伤的若德瑞苟一刀。卡修被发现腿部严重受伤。碧昂卡前来看出了什么事，结果被伊阿苟羞辱一番。

Stagecraft 导演技巧

Darkness – and Iago's play-acting (in pairs)

In Shakespeare's time, the play would have been acted at the Globe in broad daylight, so Shakespeare provides his actors with language and action to suggest that this scene takes place at night. Audiences would have been familiar with such dramatic presentations, and accepted them willingly, ready to suspend their disbelief.

- What examples can you find in the script opposite of words or phrases that act as signals to the actors and the audience that it is very dark and difficult to make out what is happening?

Shakespeare continues to present Iago as a cunning manipulator, ready to seize any opportunity under cover of darkness to further his own interests. He plays the innocent, honest soldier yet again, calling in Lodovico and Gratiano to help, and even binding Cassio's wound with his shirt to show friendship. But he also takes advantage of the darkness to stab Roderigo, whose last words are: 'O damned Iago! O inhuman dog!'

- Read through Iago's lines in the script opposite, pausing after every sentence. In the pause, the other person describes what impression Iago is attempting to create through his words.

1 **make away** 逃走
2 **As you shall prove us** 您会认得我们
3 **praise** 判断，评判
4 **notable** 臭名昭著
5 **may you suspect** 您是否能猜出来
6 **mangled** 伤害

Language in the play 剧中语言

Sentence structure (in small groups)

a The script is full of short, simple sentences. To catch the mood and the speed of the action, try these ways of reading lines 56–84:

- Read around the group, with each person exclaiming a single sentence before handing on.
- Repeat the exercise, but this time exclaim only one word – the one you think most important – in each sentence.
- Repeat both exercises, but as quickly as possible.

Identify which of these are questions, statements or exclamations.

b Talk together about the speed at which you think the lines should be spoken, and why Shakespeare chose to use so many short sentences here.

IAGO	O me, lieutenant! What villains have done this?	
CASSIO	I think that one of them is hereabout	
	And cannot make away¹.	
IAGO	O, treacherous villains!	
	[*To Lodovico and Gratiano*] What are you there? Come in,	
	and give some help.	
RODERIGO	O, help me here!	60
CASSIO	That's one of them.	
IAGO	O murderous slave! O villain!	
	[*He stabs Roderigo*.]	
RODERIGO	O damned Iago! O inhuman dog!	
	[*He faints*.]	
IAGO	Kill men i'th'dark? Where be these bloody thieves?	
	How silent is this town! Ho, murder, murder!	
	[*Lodovico and Gratiano come forward*.]	
	What may you be? Are you of good or evil?	65
LODOVICO	As you shall prove us², praise³ us.	
IAGO	Signior Lodovico?	
LODOVICO	He, sir.	
IAGO	I cry you mercy. Here's Cassio hurt by villains.	
GRATIANO	Cassio?	70
IAGO	How is't, brother?	
CASSIO	My leg is cut in two.	
IAGO	Marry, heaven forbid!	
	Light, gentlemen. I'll bind it with my shirt.	

Enter BIANCA.

BIANCA	What is the matter, ho? Who is't that cried?	
IAGO	Who is't that cried?	75
BIANCA	O, my dear Cassio, my sweet Cassio!	
	O, Cassio, Cassio, Cassio!	
IAGO	O notable⁴ strumpet! Cassio, may you suspect⁵	
	Who they should be that have thus mangled⁶ you?	
CASSIO	No.	80
GRATIANO	I am sorry to find you thus; I have been to seek you.	

Iago accuses Bianca of involvement in the affray. He pretends to be surprised at identifying Roderigo as Cassio's attacker. He shows great concern for Cassio, and has him carried off to receive treatment.

剧情简介：伊阿苟指控碧昂卡参与滋事。他假装认出是若德瑞苟袭击了卡修而大吃一惊，对卡修表示极为关心，派人把他抬走，接受治疗。

Write about it 写作练习
Clever Iago? Or helped by chance?

Iago continues to play the role of the concerned friend. He bustles about (四下忙碌), accusing Bianca, feigning (佯装) distress at discovering Roderigo, and calling for a chair for Cassio. Iago seems to have avoided personal disaster very narrowly, through a combination of chance and his own skill. However, if Lodovico and Gratiano had immediately and properly investigated the screams from the street (line 37), the scene might have unfolded in a very different way.

a Write a paragraph explaining which aspects of this incident you think are down to Iago's skill. Then write a second paragraph outlining how you think chance works in Iago's favour at this point.

b Write about another incident in the play where chance has helped Iago and he has been lucky to get away with his scheme without anyone discovering what he's up to. What general observations can you make about the relationship between chance and intention in the play?

1 garter （长筒袜的）袜带（防止袜筒脱落）
2 a chair 滑竿，担架
3 trash 贱货
4 be a party in 参与
5 Save you your labour 就不劳您大驾了
6 bear … o'th'air 把他抬进屋去（当时认为新鲜空气对伤口不利）

Themes 主题分析
Attitudes to women (by yourself)

Iago immediately casts doubt on Bianca, calling her 'this trash' (language similar to that used by Cassio in Act 4). He even insinuates that Bianca might be an accessory to the murder attempt (lines 105–10). Iago can rely on other characters sharing his insulting view of women. Bianca becomes an easy target for Emilia, too, who calls her a 'strumpet' (whilst Cassio is thought of as a poor victim!).

- Read up to line 129, noting the way Iago and others treat Bianca, and how she responds. Then imagine you are Bianca, arrested on suspicion of being accessory (从犯) to murder. In role, write a short statement defending yourself against Iago's charge of being 'a party in this injury'. Explain how you know Cassio, what your movements have been this evening, how you came to be in the street at that time, and what you heard or saw. Practise reading it in role, and then share it with the rest of the class, who can question Bianca once she has read her statement.

Othello Act 5 Scene 1
奥赛罗

IAGO	Lend me a garter¹: so. O for a chair²
	To bear him easily hence!
BIANCA	Alas, he faints!
	O, Cassio, Cassio, Cassio!
IAGO	Gentlemen all, I do suspect this trash³ 85
	To be a party in⁴ this injury.
	Patience awhile, good Cassio. Come, come,
	Lend me a light. Know we this face or no?
	Alas, my friend and my dear countryman!
	Roderigo? No – yes, sure – O, heaven, Roderigo! 90
GRATIANO	What, of Venice?
IAGO	Even he, sir; did you know him?
GRATIANO	Know him? Ay.
IAGO	Signior Gratiano! I cry your gentle pardon.
	These bloody accidents must excuse my manners
	That so neglected you.
GRATIANO	I am glad to see you. 95
IAGO	How do you, Cassio? O, a chair, a chair!
GRATIANO	Roderigo?
IAGO	He, he, 'tis he.

[*Enter* ATTENDANTS *with a chair.*]

O, that's well said, the chair!
Some good men bear him carefully from hence.
I'll fetch the general's surgeon. [*To Bianca*] For you, mistress, 100
Save you your labour⁵. – He that lies slain here, Cassio,
Was my dear friend. What malice was between you?

CASSIO   None in the world, nor do I know the man.
IAGO   [*To Bianca*] What, look you pale? – O, bear him out o'th'air⁶.

[*Cassio is carried off; Roderigo's body is removed*]

Iago accuses Bianca of looking guilty. He explains to Emilia what has happened, and she verbally abuses Bianca. Iago sends Emilia to Othello with the news.

剧情简介：伊阿苟指责碧昂卡面露愧疚之色。他向艾蜜丽叶讲述事情的经过，艾蜜丽叶大骂碧昂卡。伊阿苟让艾蜜丽叶去给奥赛罗报信。

1 'I am no strumpet' (in pairs)

The embedded directions for the actor playing Bianca here are to specifically look 'pale' with 'gastness of eye' (lines 105–6). Yet she is strong enough to mount (展开) a robust defence, ironically telling Iago and Emilia that she leads as honest a life as her accusers.

a Traditionally, Bianca has not been depicted as a sympathetic character. Discuss the ways a director can influence the sympathies of an audience at moments like this.

b Emilia is quick to support her husband's view of Bianca as a prostitute. Why do you think she does this?

Stagecraft 导演技巧

Fast forward (in groups of eight to ten)

For this activity you need to work in a large, clear space as you will be rushing around. Make sure that it is safe for your needs.

a Think of old silent movies when the action gets ridiculously fast-moving, and is usually accompanied by breathlessly rapid music. Or consider what happens when you hold down the fast-forward control when watching a movie and the action becomes comically frenetic (疯狂). Try staging Act 5 Scene 1 as if it is being played like that. You will find the need for speed adds to your understanding of the sequence of events.

- Share out parts; each person will need to familiarise themselves with the script so that they feel confident in reading it very quickly.
- Agree on a way to 'block' the basic moves.
- Act it out as fast as you can – keep going even if someone makes a mistake.
- If you do it properly, you should be completely out of breath at the end! To make it more fun, find some suitable musical accompaniment, for example old silent-movie chase music.

b While you are still catching your breath, sit in a circle and launch immediately into a reading of the next scene. This way you'll gain an appreciation of how Shakespeare effects a dramatic change in tone and pace between Scenes 1 and 2.

1 gastness 恐惧的神情
2 if … anon 你要是瞪眼看着（这是内疚的表现），我们很快就会让你如实招来
3 'Las = Alas （哎呀）
4 set on 袭击
5 'scaped = escaped
6 Go know of 去打听
7 I therefore shake not 因此我并不发抖
8 dressed 包扎好伤口
9 tell's another tale 对我们如实讲来
10 happed = happened
11 afore 在前面
12 fordoes me quite 彻底毁了我

	Stay you, good gentlemen. Look you pale, mistress?	105
	Do you perceive the gastness¹ of her eye?	
	[*To Bianca*] Nay, if you stare, we shall hear more anon².	
	Behold her well; I pray you, look upon her.	
	Do you see, gentlemen? Nay, guiltiness	
	Will speak, though tongues were out of use.	110

Enter EMILIA.

EMILIA   'Las³, what's the matter? What's the matter, husband?
IAGO   Cassio hath here been set on⁴ in the dark
　　　　By Roderigo and fellows that are 'scaped⁵.
　　　　He's almost slain and Roderigo dead.
EMILIA   Alas, good gentleman! Alas, good Cassio!   115
IAGO   This is the fruits of whoring. Prithee, Emilia,
　　　　Go know of⁶ Cassio where he supped tonight.
　　　　[*To Bianca*] What, do you shake at that?
BIANCA   He supped at my house, but I therefore shake not⁷.
IAGO   O, did he so? I charge you go with me.   120
EMILIA   O, fie upon thee, strumpet!
BIANCA   I am no strumpet, but of life as honest
　　　　As you that thus abuse me.
EMILIA   　　　　　　　　　As I? Foh! Fie upon thee!
IAGO   Kind gentlemen, let's go see poor Cassio dressed⁸.
　　　　Come, mistress, you must tell's another tale⁹.   125
　　　　Emilia, run you to the citadel
　　　　And tell my lord and lady what hath happed¹⁰.
　　　　Will you go on afore¹¹? [*Aside*] This is the night
　　　　That either makes me, or fordoes me quite¹².

　　　　　　　　　　　　　　　　　　　　　　　Exeunt

Othello reasons why Desdemona needs to die and that the dead cannot be restored to life. He kisses her and nearly abandons his intent to kill her, but resolves that she must die.

 剧情简介：奥赛罗左右思量为何黛丝荻牟娜该死，而人死不能复生。他亲吻她，差点放弃杀她的念头，但最后他铁了心，她非死不可。

Language in the play 剧中语言

Othello's soliloquy (in pairs)

a Read through Othello's soliloquy (lines 1–22), swapping the reading at each full stop, colon or semi-colon. Discuss what you think Othello means in this speech.

b Rewrite this soliloquy in modern English, without using any euphemisms (委婉语), metaphors or imagery.

c Talk about Othello's language in the original script. What are the key differences between your plain version and Shakespeare's? What effects do you think such language might have at this moment in the play? How might it position the audience to respond?

d A soliloquy can be seen as a form of internal dialogue, where a character develops an argument focused on a core dilemma. Consider ways of performing this speech as if it is a conversation. Experiment with ways of dividing up the speech, and how to say the words to create different effects. Decide how you might stand, move, use different volumes and so on.

e In your Director's Journal, write some notes advising the actor playing Othello on how to deliver the lines. Then share your ideas with the rest of the class, either presenting the speech as a 'two-hander' (两个演员的一场戏) or with a single person speaking the lines.

1	It	（指通奸）
2	whiter … snow	比雪还白的肌肤
3	alabaster	雪花石膏（用作室内雕塑）
4	betray	不忠于
5	flaming minister	燃烧的火炬
6	Should	= If
7	cunning'st	最精致
8	pattern	典范
9	Promethean heat	普罗米修之火（希腊神话中普罗米修窃取天火送给了人类）
10	relume	重新点燃
11	balmy	芬芳
12	Justice	正义女神
13	sword	剑（天平和剑是正义的象征，天平代表公平，剑代表惩罚）
14	It … love	爱她，所以杀了她

1 Othello's 'cause' (in small groups)

Othello repeats the word 'cause' three times in the opening three lines of the scene. This word could carry several meanings:

- an action that prompts a reaction (Desdemona's infidelity)
- a morally justifiable end that one is pursuing, 'all in a good cause' (Othello wishing to protect 'more men' and restore moral order)
- a legal usage describing an accusation brought against someone in court (Othello sees himself as an agent of impartial justice – but at lines 16–17, as he kisses her, his emotions threaten to reject his role as a minister of 'justice').

Take the phrase 'It is the cause' and illustrate the three meanings above in a way that relates to Othello's situation and state of mind at this point in the play. Use whatever dramatic method of presentation seems appropriate to you (for example, mime, tableaux, improvisation).

Act 5 Scene 2
Cyprus   Desdemona's bedchamber

Enter OTHELLO, *with a light, and* DESDEMONA *in bed.*

OTHELLO   It[1] is the cause, it is the cause, my soul:
Let me not name it to you, you chaste stars.
It is the cause. Yet I'll not shed her blood,
Nor scar that whiter skin of hers than snow[2]
And smooth as monumental alabaster[3] –   5
Yet she must die, else she'll betray[4] more men.
Put out the light, and then put out the light:
If I quench thee, thou flaming minister[5],
I can again thy former light restore,
Should[6] I repent me; but once put out thy light,   10
Thou cunning'st[7] pattern[8] of excelling nature,
I know not where is that Promethean heat[9]
That can thy light relume[10]. When I have plucked thy rose,
I cannot give it vital growth again;
It needs must wither. I'll smell it on the tree.   15
             He kisses her.
O balmy[11] breath, that dost almost persuade
Justice[12] to break her sword[13]! One more, one more!
Be thus when thou art dead, and I will kill thee
And love thee after. One more, and this the last.
So sweet was ne'er so fatal. I must weep.   20
But they are cruel tears: this sorrow's heavenly –
It strikes where it doth love[14]. She wakes.

Desdemona wakes. Othello orders her to confess her sins before her death. Desdemona, fearful, replies that her only sin is in loving him.

 剧情简介：黛丝荻牟娜醒来，奥赛罗命她死前忏悔自己的罪孽。黛丝荻牟娜恐惧万分，说她唯一的罪孽是爱他。

1 Desdemona's last moments (in pairs)

a Desdemona is apparently lying asleep in her bed when Othello enters. In some productions, she passively awaits her fate; in others, she puts up a spirited struggle, physically fighting back as Othello finally smothers (闷死) her. Discuss what your instructions to the actor would be.

b The photograph below suggests a moment of quiet desperation. To gain a first impression of this final dialogue between husband and wife, take roles as Othello and Desdemona and read lines 23–85, adding movement and action at appropriate points (the script hints at facial expressions and other reactions).

1	bethink yourself	记得
2	Unreconciled	还未得到宽恕
3	Solicit for it straight	立刻为之祈求宽恕吧
4	I will walk by	我会走到一旁（给你一点儿隐私空间来祈祷）
5	unprepare̍d	未做升天准备
6	forfend	禁止
7	Hum!	哼！
8	fatal	可怕
9	They … you	我的罪孽就是爱您
10	for loving	因为爱
11	very frame	这身体
12	portents	不祥的征兆
13	point on	针对

196

DESDEMONA	Who's there? Othello?	
OTHELLO	Ay, Desdemona.	
DESDEMONA	Will you come to bed, my lord?	
OTHELLO	Have you prayed tonight, Desdemon?	
DESDEMONA	Ay, my lord.	25
OTHELLO	If you bethink yourself[1] of any crime	
	Unreconciled[2] as yet to heaven and grace,	
	Solicit for it straight[3].	
DESDEMONA	Alack, my lord, what may you mean by that?	
OTHELLO	Well, do it, and be brief: I will walk by[4]:	30
	I would not kill thy unprepared[5] spirit;	
	No – heaven forfend[6]! – I would not kill thy soul.	
DESDEMONA	Talk you of killing?	
OTHELLO	Ay, I do.	
DESDEMONA	Then heaven	
	Have mercy on me!	
OTHELLO	Amen, with all my heart!	
DESDEMONA	If you say so, I hope you will not kill me.	35
OTHELLO	Hum![7]	
DESDEMONA	And yet I fear you, for you're fatal[8] then	
	When your eyes roll so. Why I should fear I know not,	
	Since guiltiness I know not, but yet I feel I fear.	
OTHELLO	Think on thy sins.	
DESDEMONA	They are loves I bear to you[9].	40
OTHELLO	Ay, and for that thou diest.	
DESDEMONA	That death's unnatural that kills for loving[10].	
	Alas, why gnaw you so your nether lip?	
	Some bloody passion shakes your very frame[11]:	
	These are portents[12]; but yet I hope, I hope	45
	They do not point on[13] me.	

Othello accuses Desdemona of giving her handkerchief to Cassio. She denies this, yet Othello is convinced he has enough proof. He tells her that Cassio has confessed to sexual relations with Desdemona, but is now dead.

 剧情简介：奥赛罗指责黛丝狄牟娜将手绢送给卡修。她否认此事，但奥赛罗坚信自己有充分证据。他告诉她说，卡修已承认与她有染，但卡修已经死了。

Themes 主题分析

'Justice'? (in pairs)

Desdemona's request to 'Send for the man and ask him' (line 50) is reminiscent of Act 1, when Othello calls for Desdemona to support his testimony when Brabantio accuses him of abduction (诱拐). In that case, the Duke agreed to send for Desdemona, who was able to corroborate (证实) Othello's story. Here, Othello cannot hear what the key witness (Cassio) has to say, and he merely accuses Desdemona of 'perjury'. Othello's view of justice and of evidence has changed in the course of the play.

a There is much legal language in this bedroom episode, almost as if it were some kind of courtroom in session, with Othello taking on the roles of both judge and executioner (行刑者). Read through the script (lines 47–76) and pick out any examples of legal-sounding language you can find. Identify what constitutes the case for the prosecution, what the case for the defence, and what is presented as evidence.

b Perform a version of this section of the scene as if it is taking place in a court of law. Play with the script as much as you like, but retain fragments of the original language. Try playing it in different styles and tones (for example, as a parody of a television courtroom drama). This experiment may help you decide on effective ways of performing the episode on stage.

1 be still   别动；停止
2 perjury   伪证
3 but not yet to die   还不至于死
4 article   指控
5 choke   窒息，压制
6 conception   恶念
7 do groan withal   为之痛苦
8 But … love   有的只是上天允许的那种人间之爱
9 stone my heart   使我心硬如石，使我变得铁石心肠
10 Send for him hither   叫他来这里
11 used thee   享用过你（即发生过性关系）
12 his mouth is stopped   他的嘴被闭上了
13 tane order for't   已奉命行事
14 interprets   猜到
15 Had … lives   他即使有他的头发那么多条命

Characters 人物分析

Othello the executioner

Othello asks Desdemona the questions he should have asked her in Act 3 or 4. Yet he is on the verge of killing her, and appears not to be interested in any answer that does not match his view of events.

a How do you read Othello's mood? Do you agree with critics who argue that his tone is calm and rational?

b In what ways have directors interpreted this scene? View two movie versions of this scene and try reading Othello's part in different ways (is he calm, quiet, resigned, angry, frustrated?) Write some notes in your Director's Journal, suggesting what advice you would give to the actor playing Othello.

OTHELLO   Peace, and be still[1]!
DESDEMONA I will so. What's the matter?
OTHELLO   That handkerchief which I so loved and gave thee,
           Thou gav'st to Cassio.
DESDEMONA   No, by my life and soul!
           Send for the man and ask him.
OTHELLO   Sweet soul, take heed.   50
           Take heed of perjury[2]: thou art on thy death-bed.
DESDEMONA Ay, but not yet to die[3].
OTHELLO   Yes, presently.
           Therefore confess thee freely of thy sin;
           For to deny each article[4] with oath
           Cannot remove nor choke[5] the strong conception[6]   55
           That I do groan withal[7]. Thou art to die.
DESDEMONA Then Lord have mercy on me!
OTHELLO   I say, Amen.
DESDEMONA And have you mercy too! I never did
           Offend you in my life; never loved Cassio
           But with such general warranty of heaven   60
           As I might love[8]. I never gave him token.
OTHELLO   By heaven, I saw my handkerchief in's hand.
           O perjured woman! Thou dost stone my heart[9],
           And mak'st me call what I intend to do
           A murder, which I thought a sacrifice.   65
           I saw the handkerchief.
DESDEMONA   He found it then;
           I never gave it him. Send for him hither[10];
           Let him confess a truth.
OTHELLO   He hath confessed.
DESDEMONA What, my lord?
OTHELLO   That he hath used thee[11].
DESDEMONA   How? Unlawfully?   70
OTHELLO   Ay.
DESDEMONA He will not say so.
OTHELLO   No, his mouth is stopped[12]:
           Honest Iago hath tane order for't[13].
DESDEMONA O, my fear interprets[14]! What, is he dead?
OTHELLO   Had all his hairs been lives[15], my great revenge   75
           Had stomach for them all.

In spite of her pleas, Othello suffocates Desdemona. He is disturbed by Emilia calling from outside the door.
剧情简介：尽管黛丝荻牟娜一再恳求，奥赛罗还是闷死了她。门外艾蜜丽叶的叫门声搅乱了奥赛罗。

1 Action – avoiding melodrama (情景剧；通俗剧)
(in threes)

Take parts and act lines 77–106. Make decisions about the pace, timing of stage directions, positioning and delivery of words to suit the dramatic effect you wish to achieve. Think about the way Othello interprets Desdemona's ironically innocent words: 'Alas, he is betrayed, and I undone.' How do you avoid the scene becoming melodramatic, and therefore bordering on the ridiculous? Share your version with one other group, then discuss any differences of interpretation.

Stagecraft 导演技巧
'He smothers her' (whole class)

The photographs below demonstrate two very different interpretations of the stage direction: *'He smothers her.'*

- Discuss how these dramatisations differ in terms of dramatic focus (on Desdemona or on Othello?), force and level of brutality. If you had to choose just one picture to illustrate this page of script, which one would it be, and why?

1 undone　完了
2 Out　呸
3 but = only
4 Down　去死吧
5 Being … pause　动手了就不能停下
6 by and by　来了
7 'Tis like　有可能
8 high = loud
9 insupportable　我受不了了
10 globe　全球，全世界
11 yawn　裂开（像地震一样）
12 alteration　（黛丝荻牟娜之死带来的）改变
13 the curtains draw　幕布合拢（在环球剧场的戏台上，床可能设在后台的凹室里，见第186页插图；这里是奥赛罗把代表床帘的幕布拉上）

DESDEMONA	Alas, he is betrayed, and I undone[1].	
OTHELLO	Out[2], strumpet! Weep'st thou for him to my face?	
DESDEMONA	O banish me, my lord, but[3] kill me not!	
OTHELLO	Down[4], strumpet!	80
DESDEMONA	Kill me tomorrow; let me live tonight!	
OTHELLO	Nay, if you strive –	
DESDEMONA	But half an hour!	
OTHELLO	Being done, there is no pause[5].	
DESDEMONA	But while I say one prayer!	
OTHELLO	It is too late.	
DESDEMONA	O, Lord, Lord, Lord!	85

                      He smothers her.

EMILIA	(*Within*) My lord, my lord! What, ho! My lord, my lord!	
OTHELLO	What noise is this? Not dead? Not yet quite dead?	
	I that am cruel am yet merciful;	
	I would not have thee linger in thy pain.	
	So, so.	
EMILIA	(*Within*) What, ho! My lord, my lord!	
OTHELLO	Who's there?	90
EMILIA	[*Within*] O, good my lord, I would speak a word with you.	
OTHELLO	Yes – 'tis Emilia – by and by[6]. – She's dead.	
	'Tis like[7] she comes to speak of Cassio's death:	
	The noise was high[8]. Ha! No more moving?	
	Still as the grave. Shall she come in? Were't good?	95
	I think she stirs again. No. What's best to do?	
	If she come in, she'll sure speak to my wife –	
	My wife, my wife! What wife? I have no wife.	
	O insupportable[9]! O heavy hour!	
	Methinks it should be now a huge eclipse	100
	Of sun and moon, and that th'affrighted globe[10]	
	Should yawn[11] at alteration[12].	
EMILIA	[*Within*] I do beseech you	
	That I may speak with you. O, good my lord!	
OTHELLO	I had forgot thee. O, come in, Emilia.	
	Soft, by and by. Let me the curtains draw[13].	105
	Where art thou?	

                      [*He unlocks the door.*]
                      What's the matter with thee now?

Emilia reports that Roderigo is dead but Cassio lives. Desdemona revives briefly, only to protect her husband in her dying breath. Othello confesses to Emilia and attempts to explain.

剧情简介：艾蜜丽叶报告说，若德瑞苟死了，但卡修还活着。黛丝荻牟娜苏醒了片刻，虽然只剩最后一口气，还竭力维护丈夫。奥赛罗向艾蜜丽叶承认自己的作为，并试图加以解释。

Characters 人物分析

Desdemona's death (in small groups)

Even in her dying breath, Desdemona supports her husband. She tells a lie on her death-bed, in an attempt to protect him from a murder charge. Do you admire her for her faithfulness, or do you find her action difficult to believe – even within the social and historical context of the play? Is it possible to regard Desdemona as a dramatic construct rather than as a 'real' person or character?

a Discuss your attitudes to the way Desdemona has been portrayed in Scene 2. Focus your discussion on:
- how twenty-first century readers might react to Desdemona
- how a reader's gender and culture might affect the way he or she sees Desdemona
- how Desdemona reflects early seventeenth-century attitudes to women and marriage (the research you did as part of Activity 1 on p. 28 may help with this)
- how Desdemona as a dramatic figure embodies or relates to the play's themes and concerns (see also pp. 224–5)
- whether it is possible to reconcile the earlier Desdemona of Act 1 with the one here in Act 5.

b Present your views to the rest of the class and explore any differences of opinion.

Themes 主题分析

Contrasts and opposites (in pairs)

The script opposite contains a number of sharply contrasting images:
- angel/devil
- false/true
- water/fire
- hell/heavenly
- sweet/harsh.

Locate each pair and explore ways of presenting them through movement only (mime). After this physical activity, talk together about the significance of each pair of contrasts in their dramatic context (e.g. what they suggest about characters, themes or mood).

1 yonder's 那儿有
2 error of the moon 月亮的失误（即月亮偏离轨道，过去人们认为月亮的这种失误能使人疯癫）
3 was wont 惯常
4 out of tune 出了错
5 Commend … lord 代我向我温柔的夫君致意
6 like a liar 就像骗子
7 folly 不忠
8 belie 污蔑
9 false as water 水性杨花（谚语）

Enter EMILIA.

EMILIA   O, my good lord, yonder's[1] foul murders done.
OTHELLO   What? Now?
EMILIA   But now, my lord.
OTHELLO   It is the very error of the moon[2]:
         She comes more nearer earth than she was wont[3]
         And makes men mad.
EMILIA   Cassio, my lord, hath killed a young Venetian
         Called Roderigo.
OTHELLO   Roderigo killed?
         And Cassio killed?
EMILIA   No, Cassio is not killed.
OTHELLO   Not Cassio killed! Then murder's out of tune[4],
         And sweet revenge grows harsh.
DESDEMONA   O, falsely, falsely murdered!
EMILIA   O Lord! What cry is that?
OTHELLO   That? What?
EMILIA   Out and alas, that was my lady's voice!
         [*She draws the bed-curtains.*]
         Help, help, ho, help! O, lady, speak again!
         Sweet Desdemona, O sweet mistress, speak!
DESDEMONA   A guiltless death I die.
EMILIA   O, who hath done this deed?
DESDEMONA   Nobody; I myself. Farewell.
         Commend me to my kind lord[5]. O farewell!   *She dies*
OTHELLO   Why, how should she be murdered?
EMILIA   Alas, who knows?
OTHELLO   You heard her say herself it was not I.
EMILIA   She said so; I must needs report the truth.
OTHELLO   She's like a liar[6] gone to burning hell:
         'Twas I that killed her.
EMILIA   O, the more angel she,
         And you the blacker devil!
OTHELLO   She turned to folly[7], and she was a whore.
EMILIA   Thou dost belie[8] her, and thou art a devil.
OTHELLO   She was false as water[9].
EMILIA   Thou art rash as fire to say
         That she was false. O, she was heavenly true!

Othello reveals that Iago gave him the details of Desdemona's infidelity. Emilia increasingly questions Iago's part in Othello's story and curses them both. She is unmoved by Othello's threats and calls for help.

 剧情简介：奥赛罗透露是伊阿苟给他提供了黛丝荻牟娜不忠的种种细节。艾蜜丽叶一步步追问伊阿苟在奥赛罗故事中扮演的角色并诅咒他们俩。她不惧奥赛罗的威胁，大声呼救。

Write about it 写作练习

'honest, honest Iago' (in threes)

Emilia's shocked response, and the ten repetitions of the word 'husband', culminate in (以……告终) Othello's exclamation: 'My friend, thy husband, honest, honest Iago.'

a Produce a series of tableaux based on your interpretation of line 153. Take digital photos of each.

b Using the three photographs from the activity above as stimulus, write three paragraphs about 'honest' Iago in his roles as:
- husband
- friend
- colleague.

1 'Ha!'

Speed-write (five minutes only) what you think Othello means by his exclamation 'Ha!' at line 157. Compare your notes with others and discuss what led to your interpretation.

1 top her 骑上了她
2 else 你若不信
3 damned … hell 惩罚我下九重地狱
4 But = Except
5 just grounds 正当理由
6 extremity 终极刑罚
7 false to wedlock 出轨
8 entire 纯粹
9 chrysolite 黄晶石（一种宝石）
10 told me on 告诉我关于
11 slime 黏液（暗指精液）
12 iterance 重复
13 made mocks with 奚落了
14 pernicious 邪恶的
15 half a grain a day 每天一星半点儿，非常缓慢
16 to th'heart 完全
17 too fond of 太迷恋，太痴情于
18 filthy bargain 肮脏的下贱东西（比喻她选择这样一个丈夫代价惨重）
19 no more worthy heaven 天理不容
20 Peace, you were best 您最好住口
21 gull 笨蛋
22 dolt 白痴
23 I … sword 别想用你的剑威胁我

OTHELLO	Cassio did top her[1]: ask thy husband else[2].	
	O, I were damned beneath all depth in hell[3]	
	But[4] that I did proceed upon just grounds[5]	
	To this extremity[6]. Thy husband knew it all.	140
EMILIA	My husband?	
OTHELLO	Thy husband.	
EMILIA	That she was false to wedlock[7]?	
OTHELLO	Ay, with Cassio. Nay, had she been true,	
	If heaven would make me such another world	
	Of one entire[8] and perfect chrysolite[9],	
	I'd not have sold her for it.	
EMILIA	My husband?	145
OTHELLO	Ay, 'twas he that told me on[10] her first;	
	An honest man he is, and hates the slime[11]	
	That sticks on filthy deeds.	
EMILIA	My husband?	
OTHELLO	What needs this iterance[12], woman? I say thy husband.	
EMILIA	O mistress, villainy hath made mocks with[13] love!	150
	My husband say that she was false?	
OTHELLO	He, woman;	
	I say thy husband. Dost understand the word?	
	My friend, thy husband, honest, honest Iago.	
EMILIA	If he say so, may his pernicious[14] soul	
	Rot half a grain a day[15]! He lies to th'heart[16].	155
	She was too fond of[17] her most filthy bargain[18].	
OTHELLO	Ha!	
EMILIA	Do thy worst.	
	This deed of thine is no more worthy heaven[19]	
	Than thou wast worthy her.	
OTHELLO	Peace, you were best[20].	160
EMILIA	Thou has not half that power to do me harm	
	As I have to be hurt. O gull[21]! O dolt[22]!	
	As ignorant as dirt. Thou hast done a deed –	
	I care not for thy sword[23] – I'll make thee known,	
	Though I lost twenty lives. Help! help! ho, help!	165
	The Moor hath killed my mistress. Murder, murder!	

Montano, Gratiano and Iago come to investigate Emilia's cries of murder. She challenges Iago about what he has told Othello about Desdemona. Iago orders her home.

 剧情简介：芒塔诺、格拉奇阿诺和伊阿苟上场，查看艾蜜丽叶呼喊谋杀是怎么回事。艾蜜丽叶质疑伊阿苟对奥赛罗说的关于黛丝荻牟娜的话。伊阿苟命她回家。

1 Four key moments (in sixes)

Imagine freezing the action on stage at four key moments:
- 'Disprove this villain, if thou be'st a man.' (line 171)
- 'O monstrous act!' (line 189)
- 'What, are you mad?' (line 193)
- 'thou hast killed the sweetest innocent / That e'er did lift up eye' (lines 198–9).

Take roles, and for each 'moment' create a still picture that you can hold for at least thirty seconds. Within each tableau, select a key character who can step out and describe their thoughts or fears at that precise moment. Present your four moments to the rest of the class in a sequence.

1 lay … neck   把杀人的罪名加在您头上
2 my heart is full   我满心愤懑
3 apt   有可能
4 odious   令人作呕
5 charm your tongue   闭嘴
（charm：用符咒封住）
6 set the murder on   嗾使凶杀
7 strange   让人难以置信的
8 smell't   嗅到此事
9 'Tis proper   应该，照理
10 roar   号啕大哭

Language in the play 剧中语言

Repetition: dramatic effect (in pairs)

Throughout this part of the script, characters have a tendency to repeat certain words or phrases (for example, 'lie' and 'villainy').

a Talk together about the dramatic effect of each repetition.

b The interjection, 'O', is used eight times in the script opposite (uttered by Emilia, Montano, Othello – and even chorused [异口同声] by everyone on stage at one point). Find all these instances and experiment with how it might be said on each occasion. Look in particular at Othello's 'O! O! O!' at line 197. What might 'O' mean here? Does each 'O' mean the same thing?

Characters 人物分析

Emilia's rebellion

''Tis proper I obey him, but not now', declares Emilia at line 195. Increasingly in this scene, Emilia takes centre stage.

a Using the knowledge you've gained about acceptable wifely behaviour, what social and financial repercussions (后果) would this act of rebellion carry for Emilia?

b Not only does Emilia show great courage (for example, 'I care not for thy sword', line 164), but she is also the one character who has worked out what's been going on. What does this episode add to your understanding of her character?

Othello Act 5 Scene 2
奥赛罗

Enter MONTANO, GRATIANO *and* IAGO.

MONTANO What is the matter? How now, general?
EMILIA O, are you come, Iago? You have done well,
That men must lay their murders on your neck[1].
GRATIANO What is the matter? 170
EMILIA Disprove this villain, if thou be'st a man.
He says thou told'st him that his wife was false.
I know thou didst not, thou'rt not such a villain.
Speak, for my heart is full[2].
IAGO I told him what I thought, and told no more 175
Than what he found himself was apt[3] and true.
EMILIA But did you ever tell him she was false?
IAGO I did.
EMILIA You told a lie, an odious[4] damnèd lie:
Upon my soul, a lie, a wicked lie! 180
She false with Cassio? Did you say with Cassio?
IAGO With Cassio, mistress. Go to, charm your tongue[5].
EMILIA I will not charm my tongue; I am bound to speak:
My mistress here lies murdered in her bed.
ALL O, heavens forfend! 185
EMILIA And your reports have set the murder on[6].
OTHELLO Nay, stare not, masters; it is true indeed.
GRATIANO 'Tis a strange[7] truth.
MONTANO O monstrous act!
EMILIA Villainy, villainy, villainy!
I think upon't, I think – I smell't[8] – O villainy! 190
I thought so then; I'll kill myself for grief.
O villainy, villainy!
IAGO What, are you mad? I charge you get you home.
EMILIA Good gentlemen, let me have leave to speak.
'Tis proper[9] I obey him, but not now. 195
Perchance, Iago, I will ne'er go home.
OTHELLO O! O! O!
Othello falls on the bed.
EMILIA Nay, lay thee down and roar[10],
For thou hast killed the sweetest innocent
That e'er did lift up eye.

Othello confesses the murder to Gratiano, who says that Brabantio is dead. Emilia reveals that Iago persuaded her to steal Desdemona's handkerchief and give it to him. Iago tries to silence her.

 剧情简介： 奥赛罗向格拉阿诺承认自己杀了人。格拉奇阿诺说布拉班修已死。艾蜜丽叶揭发，伊阿苟曾说服她把黛丝荻牟娜的手绢偷来给他。伊阿苟试图让她闭嘴。

Themes 主题分析
Attitudes to women (in pairs)

What do you think of Gratiano's response at lines 203–5 on discovering that Desdemona has just been murdered (remember, Gratiano is a relative of Desdemona)? Some commentators have expressed surprise that he seems more preoccupied with Brabantio's death than Desdemona's. They interpret this as meaning that he blames Desdemona for Brabantio's death. How do you interpret his words?

Write about it 写作练习
What was 'confessed'?

Othello claims that Desdemona committed 'the act of shame' many times with Cassio, and that 'Cassio confessed it'. Remind yourself exactly what Cassio 'confessed' to, and in what circumstances. There are three versions of this 'confession': Iago's, Othello's and Cassio's. Turn back to Act 4 Scene 1, lines 72–153, to remind yourself of the 'evidence' involved.

- Write three paragraphs – one each for Cassio, Othello and Iago. Each paragraph begins: 'This is what I believe happened in the eavesdropping episode in Act 4 Scene 1.'

1 Dramatic moment (whole class)

At line 221, the stage direction reads: '*Iago draws his sword and threatens Emilia.*' Think about the action on stage at this precise moment. A group of five volunteers comes to the front of the class. All take roles, ready to create a tableau. A sixth volunteer steps forward as director and positions the actors. Consider the following:

- Who is looking at whom?
- What are their facial expressions?
- How much distance should there be between specific characters – and why?

New volunteer directors from the rest of the class may step forward in turn to alter positions and explain why they have done so.

1. I scarcely did know you 我几乎没认出您来
2. uncle 叔父（格拉奇阿诺应当是布拉班修的兄弟）
3. shows 看起来
4. grim 冷酷，残忍
5. mortal 致命
6. Shore … twain 把他年久的生命线一切为二（即要了他的老命）
7. Did he live now 他要是还活着
8. do a desperate turn 不顾一切地拼命（turn：举动，行为）
9. curse … side 把他的守护天使从他身边赶走
10. fall to reprobance 自绝于上帝，甘愿下地狱
11. act of shame 苟且之事（指通奸）
12. gratify 回报
13. amorous works 云雨之事
14. recognisance 信物
15. 'Twill out 真相会大白
16. north 北风
17. cry shame against me 骂我不要脸
18. dull 愚蠢
19. by fortune 凑巧

OTHELLO	[*Standing up*.] O, she was foul!	
	I scarce did know you[1], uncle[2]; there lies your niece,	200
	Whose breath indeed these hands have newly stopped.	
	I know this act shows[3] horrible and grim[4] –	
GRATIANO	Poor Desdemon, I am glad thy father's dead:	
	Thy match was mortal[5] to him, and pure grief	
	Shore his old thread in twain[6]. Did he live now[7],	205
	This sight would make him do a desperate turn[8],	
	Yea, curse his better angel from his side[9]	
	And fall to reprobance[10].	
OTHELLO	'Tis pitiful; but yet Iago knows	
	That she with Cassio hath the act of shame[11]	210
	A thousand times committed. Cassio confessed it,	
	And she did gratify[12] his amorous works[13]	
	With that recognisance[14] and pledge of love	
	Which I first gave her. I saw it in his hand:	
	It was a handkerchief, an antique token	215
	My father gave my mother.	
EMILIA	O God! O heavenly God!	
IAGO	Zounds, hold your peace!	
EMILIA	'Twill out[15], 'twill out. I peace!	
	No, I will speak as liberal as the north[16];	
	Let heaven, and men, and devils, let them all,	
	All, all cry shame against me[17], yet I'll speak.	220
IAGO	Be wise and get you home.	
EMILIA	I will not.	
	[*Iago draws his sword and threatens Emilia.*]	
GRATIANO	Fie,	
	Your sword upon a woman!	
EMILIA	O thou dull[18] Moor, that handkerchief thou speak'st of	
	I found by fortune[19] and did give my husband,	
	For often, with a solemn earnestness –	225
	More than indeed belonged to such a trifle –	
	He begged of me to steal it.	
IAGO	Villainous whore!	

Othello attempts to kill Iago, but is prevented by Montano. Iago stabs Emilia and then escapes. Emilia dies speaking of Desdemona's purity. Othello finds another sword and calls to Gratiano.

  剧情简介： 奥赛罗想杀死伊阿苟，但被芒塔诺拦住了。伊阿苟刺了艾蜜丽叶一剑后逃走。艾蜜丽叶死去，口中仍说黛丝荻牟娜是清白的。奥赛罗找到另一把剑，招呼格拉奇阿诺过来。

Stagecraft 导演技巧

Slow motion (in groups of five or six)

Iago's abuse of Emilia ('Filth, thou liest!') does not stop her telling the truth, and the scene erupts in a flurry (一阵混乱) of action.

a Act out the stage direction at line 233 in slow motion. Decide how to make the best use of the space you have available, and experiment with different ways of performing this intensely dramatic episode.

b Turn to the picture of an Elizabethan theatre on page 186 and plot the same action in that space. Make notes in your Director's Journal.

1 'honour outlive honesty' – what do you think?

Think about Othello's comment: 'why should honour outlive honesty?' (line 243).

- Write a paragraph explaining what you understand by these words and why they might be considered significant in the context of the whole play.

Themes 主题分析

Attitudes to women (in pairs)

One commentator points out that the men on stage do nothing to save Emilia's life; indeed, when Montano disarms Othello, he inadvertently saves Iago at Emilia's expense. In her dying words Emilia asks to be laid next to Desdemona's body, but there is no stage direction to indicate whether this happens or not. No one mentions Emilia again.

- How significant do you think this is in light of the theme of attitudes to women? If you were directing the play, how would you want Emilia's final movements and her death to be staged? How would you instruct each of the men on stage to respond? Would Emilia get her final wish to be laid next to Desdemona? If so, how would this be effected (and by whom)?

1 coxcomb 蠢货
2 stones 霹雳
3 Precious 十足的（表示加强语气）
4 notorious 彻头彻尾的
5 recovered 夺下
6 without 从外边
7 pass 逃走
8 puny whipster 无足轻重的小人物
9 honour outlive honesty 名声比正直更能长久
10 play the swan 做一只天鹅（据说天鹅临死前会发出美妙的鸣叫）
11 come my soul bliss 愿我的灵魂得到拯救
12 of Spain 西班牙制造的（质量一流的剑）
13 ice-brook's temper 放在冰水里淬过的钢
14 perforce 所以
15 suffer 受伤
16 Look in upon me 进来看看我
17 naked 赤手空拳

EMILIA　　　She give it Cassio! No, alas, I found it
　　　　　　And I did give't my husband.
IAGO　　　　　　　　　　　　　Filth, thou liest!
EMILIA　　　By heaven, I do not, I do not, gentlemen.　　　　　　　　230
　　　　　　O murderous coxcomb¹, what should such a fool
　　　　　　Do with so good a wife?
OTHELLO　　　　　　　　　　Are there no stones² in heaven
　　　　　　But what serves for the thunder? Precious³ villain!
　　　　　　[*Othello runs at Iago; Montano disarms him; Iago stabs Emilia from*
　　　　　　　　　　　　　behind and exit.]
GRATIANO　　The woman falls; sure he hath killed his wife.
EMILIA　　　Ay, ay; O, lay me by my mistress' side.　　　　　　　　　235
GRATIANO　　He's gone, but his wife's killed.
MONTANO　　'Tis a notorious⁴ villain. Take you this weapon,
　　　　　　Which I have here recovered⁵ from the Moor.
　　　　　　Come guard the door without⁶; let him not pass⁷,
　　　　　　But kill him rather. I'll after the same villain,　　　　　　240
　　　　　　For 'tis a damnèd slave.
　　　　　　　　　　　　　　Exeunt Montano and Gratiano
OTHELLO　　　　　　　　　I am not valiant neither,
　　　　　　But every puny whipster⁸ gets my sword.
　　　　　　But why should honour outlive honesty⁹?
　　　　　　Let it go all.
EMILIA　　　　　　　　　What did thy song bode, lady?
　　　　　　Hark, canst thou hear me? I will play the swan¹⁰　　　　245
　　　　　　And die in music: [*Sings*] 'Willow, willow, willow.'
　　　　　　Moor, she was chaste; she loved thee, cruel Moor;
　　　　　　So come my soul to bliss¹¹, as I speak true;
　　　　　　So speaking as I think, I die, I die.　　　　　　　*She dies*
OTHELLO　　I have another weapon in this chamber;　　　　　　　　250
　　　　　　It was a sword of Spain¹², the ice-brook's temper¹³.
　　　　　　O, here it is. – Uncle, I must come forth.
GRATIANO　　(*Within*) If thou attempt it, it will cost thee dear;
　　　　　　Thou hast no weapon, and perforce¹⁴ must suffer¹⁵.
OTHELLO　　Look in upon me¹⁶ then, and speak with me,　　　　　255
　　　　　　Or naked¹⁷ as I am, I will assault thee.

Othello, now fully realising that he has murdered an innocent woman, expects the punishments of hell. Lodovico and the others return with Iago, and Othello attacks him.

 剧情简介：奥赛罗现在完全明白自己谋杀了一个无辜女人，期待自己得到下地狱的惩罚。劳德维寇和其他人将伊阿苟押回来，奥赛罗刺向伊阿苟。

Language in the play 剧中语言
Othello's speech

Some commentators have said that the broken Othello is here attempting to use language to reclaim his former glory as a renowned military leader. This is reflected in his use of:

- metaphor
- hyperbole (exaggeration)
- simple, powerful monosyllables
- grand, poetic language.

a Identify examples of each of these features in lines 257–79. Make notes on the dramatic effectiveness of each. Consider which of these features link to other parts of the play, and make notes explaining these thematic and verbal connections.

b Othello's speech is structured in three parts, corresponding with the three stages of his life: Othello the great warrior; Othello the murderer at his life's end; and Othello tortured in hell. His life's journey is imagined as a sea voyage. Choose one of the following:

- Devise a group presentation, exploring the structure of the speech and its images. Employ whatever dramatic method of presentation seems appropriate to you (words and movement, tableaux, mime or some other form).
- Produce a poster or collage based on the speech, using a sea voyage as the organisational frame.

1	A … thigh	挂在战士大腿上的匕首，没有一把比它好
2	your stop	你们的警卫力量
3	weaponed	武装
4	butt	目标
5	sea-mark	航标
6	utmost sail	最远的航行
7	'Tis a lost fear	没什么好怕的
8	Man but a rush	只用一根灯芯草刺
9	retires	向后退缩
10	ill-starred	煞星临头（旧时认为人的命运受星宿影响）
11	smock	罩衣（女士的内衣）
12	compt	审判日
13	slave	奴才（奥赛罗在说自己）
14	steep-down gulfs	万丈深渊
15	viper	毒蛇，阴险小人
16	his … fable	(传说认为魔鬼的脚是偶蹄)

1 Lodovico's entrance: Venetian law restored

With the entrance of Lodovico and Cassio, the controlling force of Venetian law is reintroduced. Lodovico calls on the two defendants as if in a court of law, and presides as if he is a high court judge. But Othello's violence towards Iago momentarily disturbs that order.

- Work out how you would stage the entrance of Lodovico and the others in a way that suggests this return to Venetian authority, following the script in lines 275–84. Block the moves and positioning, either as a class or on your own, using the picture of an Elizabethan theatre on page 186. Write a paragraph justifying your choices in your Director's Journal.

Othello Act 5 Scene 2
奥赛罗

[*Enter Gratiano.*]

GRATIANO What is the matter?
OTHELLO   Behold, I have a weapon:
A better never did itself sustain
Upon a soldier's thigh¹. I have seen the day
That with this little arm and this good sword   260
I have made my way through more impediments
Than twenty times your stop². But, O vain boast!
Who can control his fate? 'Tis not so now.
Be not afraid, though you do see me weaponed³:
Here is my journey's end, here is my butt⁴   265
And very sea-mark⁵ of my utmost sail⁶.
Do you go back dismayed? 'Tis a lost fear⁷:
Man but a rush⁸ against Othello's breast,
And he retires⁹. Where should Othello go?
[*He goes to the bed.*]
Now, how dost thou look now? O ill-starred¹⁰ wench!   270
Pale as thy smock¹¹! When we shall meet at compt¹²
This look of thine will hurl my soul from heaven
And fiends will snatch at it. Cold, cold, my girl,
Even like thy chastity.
O cursèd, cursèd slave¹³! Whip me, ye devils,   275
From the possession of this heavenly sight!
Blow me about in winds! Roast me in sulphur!
Wash me in steep-down gulfs¹⁴ of liquid fire!
O Desdemon! Dead Desdemon! Dead! O! O!

Enter LODOVICO, *Montano,* CASSIO *in a chair, Iago in the charge of*
OFFICERS.

LODOVICO Where is this rash and most unfortunate man? 280
OTHELLO   That's he that was Othello: here I am.
LODOVICO Where is that viper¹⁵? Bring the villain forth.
OTHELLO   I look down towards his feet; but that's a fable¹⁶.
          If that thou be'st a devil, I cannot kill thee.
[*He wounds Iago.*]

213

Lodovico takes control and investigates the case. Othello asks Cassio's pardon. Letters found in Roderigo's pockets tell of Iago's plot to kill Cassio and of Roderigo's threat to expose Iago. Iago refuses to give any explanation of his conduct.

 剧情简介：劳德维寇控制局面，调查案件。奥赛罗请求卡修原谅。他们在若德瑞苟衣服口袋里找到信件，信中说明伊阿苟如何密谋杀死卡修，以及若德瑞苟如何威胁告发伊阿苟。伊阿苟拒绝对自己的行为做任何解释。

Characters 人物分析
Iago: 'I bleed, sir, but not killed'

a Iago's line could be uttered in a variety of ways. How would you advise an actor to say those words? Consider the following suggestions to help in your decision:

- Iago is playing for sympathy.
- He is bitterly sarcastic.
- He is resigned to his fate.
- He is detached and neutral.
- He is utterly defeated, in pain and wants to die.
- He is triumphant, taunting Othello.
- He is chillingly inhuman, hinting at his own indestructibility.

b Watch at least two movie versions of this scene and discuss how each actor cast as Iago plays this line.

c As an additional challenge, discuss why Iago refuses to speak further. Write a paragraph explaining possible reasons for his silence.

1. in my sense 我感觉
2. practice 计策，圈套
3. ensnared 陷害
4. Torments 拷打，酷刑
5. ope = open
6. thou dost best 你最清楚
7. heathenish 野蛮
8. discontented paper 充满怨恨的信
9. belike 很可能
10. in the nick 瞬间
11. Came in 介入
12. satisfied him 给了他满意的解释
13. caitiff 恶棍，卑鄙小人

1 'An honourable murderer' (in pairs)

Othello claims that he is 'An honourable murderer … / For naught did I in hate, but all in honour.' (lines 291–2). What do you make of this paradox – can a murderer be honourable?

- Role-play an imaginary interview between Lodovico and Othello, in which Othello is asked to defend this statement.

Write about it 写作练习
Two letters

Lodovico reports that two letters have been found in Roderigo's pocket, both helping to explain Iago's plotting. The first is probably written by Iago and 'imports / The death of Cassio' (in other words, laying out instructions and reminding Roderigo why the murder needs to happen). The second is a 'discontented paper' written by Roderigo, probably to Iago or Othello, complaining about the way he has been treated, and wanting to recover the money he has lost.

- Write the two letters.

LODOVICO	Wrench his sword from him.	
IAGO	I bleed, sir, but not killed.	285
OTHELLO	I am not sorry neither; I'd have thee live,	
	For in my sense¹ 'tis happiness to die.	
LODOVICO	O, thou Othello, that wert once so good,	
	Fallen in the practice² of a damnèd slave,	
	What shall be said to thee?	
OTHELLO	Why, anything:	290
	An honourable murderer, if you will;	
	For naught did I in hate, but all in honour.	
LODOVICO	This wretch hath part confessed his villainy.	
	Did you and he consent in Cassio's death?	
OTHELLO	Ay.	295
CASSIO	Dear general, I never gave you cause.	
OTHELLO	I do believe it, and I ask your pardon.	
	Will you, I pray, demand that demi-devil	
	Why he hath thus ensnared³ my soul and body?	
IAGO	Demand me nothing; what you know, you know.	300
	From this time forth I never will speak word.	
LODOVICO	What! Not to pray?	
GRATIANO	Torments⁴ will ope⁵ your lips.	
OTHELLO	Well, thou dost best⁶.	
LODOVICO	Sir, you shall understand what hath befallen,	
	Which, as I think, you know not. Here is a letter	305
	Found in the pocket of the slain Roderigo,	
	And here another: the one of them imports	
	The death of Cassio, to be undertook	
	By Roderigo.	
OTHELLO	O villain!	
CASSIO	Most heathenish⁷ and most gross!	
LODOVICO	Now here's another discontented paper⁸,	310
	Found in his pocket too; and this, it seems,	
	Roderigo meant to have sent this damnèd villain,	
	But that, belike⁹, Iago, in the nick¹⁰,	
	Came in¹¹ and satisfied him¹².	
OTHELLO	O the pernicious caitiff¹³!	
	How came you, Cassio, by that handkerchief	315
	That was my wife's?	

Cassio tells how he found the handkerchief, and how Iago used Roderigo. Lodovico pronounces Othello's arrest and Cassio's instatement as governor. Othello asks that his whole story should be truthfully told. He stabs himself.

 剧情简介：卡修告诉大家他是怎么发现手绢的，伊阿苟又是如何利用若德瑞苟的。劳德维寇宣布逮捕奥赛罗，卡修就任总督。奥赛罗请求人们如实讲述他的故事，然后拔剑自尽。

Write about it 写作练习

Othello's obituary (讣告)

Othello's last major speech in the play is in resonant, controlled verse, and amounts to his own obituary (a biographical account celebrating someone's life soon after they have died). He follows the conventions of obituary writers and includes the following elements:

- his service in Venetian colonial exploits (line 335)
- his emotional/love life (line 340)
- his downfall (lines 341–4)
- his last moments (lines 344–7)
- a past great deed (lines 348–52).

Some readers find it difficult to accept all aspects of Othello's own interpretation of his life. He claims he 'loved not wisely, but too well' and that he was 'one not easily jealous but, being wrought, / Perplexed in the extreme'. Both are contentious (引起争议的) remarks, open to challenge. And while his claim to have served the state well may be true, that 'truth' is from the point of view of Venetians rather than their foreign subjects.

a Speak lines 334–52 aloud. Familiarise yourself with the language, and experiment with how it might be acted, depending how you interpret Othello's mood and tone at this point.

b Make some brief notes summarising what Othello says about each of the key areas of his life.

c Find published examples of obituaries of famous people in newspapers. Using these as models, write Othello's obituary. Remember, it should celebrate the great general's achievements. Decide which aspects of his life you would emphasise, and which aspects you might choose not to mention. As an additional challenge, try to embed some short quotations from the play in your writing (for example, complimentary comments other characters say about Othello, particularly earlier in the play).

d If you want a further challenge, write an *alternative* obituary. Follow the conventions of obituary writers, but write from the point of view of a Turk (Othello's 'enemy'). Where would it be critical of Othello, and how might the Turkish writer deal with Othello's attitudes: e.g. 'circumcisèd dog'?

1 but even now 就在刚才
2 wrought to his desire 实现他的图谋
3 upbraids 责怪
4 Brave 蔑视，欺负
5 upon the watch 在我值夜的时候
6 set him on 怂恿他，挑唆他
7 forsake 离开
8 hold him long 让他长久忍受折磨
9 close prisoner rest 受到严密看押
10 Soft you 且慢
11 unlucky 不幸
12 relate 讲述
13 nothing extenuate 丝毫不开脱
14 set down 记下
15 wisely 明智，审慎
16 wrought 被煽动，被挑拨
17 Perplexed in the extreme 彻底不知所措
18 base Indian 卑劣的印第安人（当时美洲印第安人完全不懂得黄金和珠宝的价值）
19 subdued 认罪服输
20 Albeit ... mood 尽管不习惯哭泣
21 Aleppo 阿勒颇（古时土耳其城市）
22 malignant 心怀恶意
23 turbaned 扎包头的
24 traduced 中伤，诽谤
25 circumcisèd dog (指穆斯林士兵；circumcisèd: 受过割礼的)
26 smote 刺杀

OTHELLO ACT 5 SCENE 2
奥赛罗

CASSIO	I found it in my chamber;
	And he himself confessed but even now[1]
	That there he dropped it for a special purpose
	Which wrought to his desire[2].
OTHELLO	O fool, fool, fool!
CASSIO	There is besides in Roderigo's letter	320
	How he upbraids[3] Iago, that he made him
	Brave[4] me upon the watch[5], whereon it came
	That I was cast; and even but now he spake –
	After long seeming dead – Iago hurt him,
	Iago set him on[6].	325
LODOVICO	You must forsake[7] this room and go with us.
	Your power and your command is taken off
	And Cassio rules in Cyprus. For this slave,
	If there be any cunning cruelty
	That can torment him much and hold him long[8]	330
	It shall be his. You shall close prisoner rest[9]
	Till that the nature of your fault be known
	To the Venetian state. Come, bring him away.
OTHELLO	Soft you[10]; a word or two before you go.
	I have done the state some service and they know't:	335
	No more of that. I pray you, in your letters
	When you shall these unlucky[11] deeds relate[12],
	Speak of me as I am; nothing extenuate[13],
	Nor set down[14] aught in malice. Then must you speak
	Of one that loved not wisely[15], but too well;	340
	Of one not easily jealous but, being wrought[16],
	Perplexed in the extreme[17]; of one whose hand,
	Like the base Indian[18], threw a pearl away
	Richer than all his tribe; of one whose subdued[19] eyes,
	Albeit unusèd to the melting mood[20],	345
	Drops tears as fast as the Arabian trees
	Their medicinable gum. Set you down this;
	And say besides that in Aleppo[21] once
	Where a malignant[22] and a turbaned[23] Turk
	Beat a Venetian and traduced[24] the state,	350
	I took by th'throat the circumcisèd dog[25]
	And smote[26] him thus.
	He stabs himself.

Othello dies beside Desdemona. Lodovico awards Othello's possessions to Gratiano, and orders Cassio to decide Iago's punishment. Lodovico leaves to report in full to the Venetian state.

 剧情简介：奥赛罗死在黛丝荻牟娜身边。劳德维寇将奥赛罗的财产判给格拉奇阿诺，并命卡修决定如何惩处伊阿苟。劳德维寇将回威尼斯，向城邦完整禀报此事。

Write about it 写作练习
Lodovico's report

Lodovico states his intention of going immediately to Venice to make his formal report of events to the Senate. Write his report.

1 'he was great of heart' (in pairs)

In lines 334–52, Othello imagined what his obituary would be like. Here, Cassio's words about the dead Othello are the closest anyone comes to a real obituary or eulogy (悼词). Othello is hardly mentioned in the closing lines of the play and attention is drawn to Iago.

- Talk together about the dramatic effect of this decision to focus on Iago.

Stagecraft 导演技巧
A final image (in large groups)

What last image would you want an audience to be left with in a production of Othello? The final stage direction ('*Exeunt*') is for all the remaining actors to go off, but there are important choices for a director to make. For example, would you have them all leaving together? Would you want the bodies on the bed to be spot-lit or obscured by curtains – and where does Emilia's corpse lie? Might you wish to end with a tableau involving all or some of the remaining characters? Should there be some music or other sound effects, or complete silence? Discuss, and stage your final image.

1 period 结局
2 great of heart 内心强大
3 Spartan dog 斯巴达狗（传说古斯巴达猎狗非常凶猛）
4 fell 凶残
5 The object poisons sight 这情景惨不忍睹
6 keep 待在
7 seize upon 接收
8 they succeed on you 它们由您来继承
9 censure 审判
10 hellish 魔鬼般的
11 Myself will straight abroad 我直接上船（回威尼斯）
12 act 事件

▼ How does this staging of the final moments of the play compare with your own interpretation?

LODOVICO	O bloody period[1]!
GRATIANO	All that's spoke is marred!
OTHELLO	I kissed thee ere I killed thee: no way but this,
	Killing myself, to die upon a kiss. 355

He [falls on the bed and] dies

CASSIO	This did I fear, but thought he had no weapon,
	For he was great of heart[2].
LODOVICO	[*To Iago*] O Spartan dog[3],
	More fell[4] than anguish, hunger, or the sea,
	Look on the tragic loading of this bed:
	This is thy work. The object poisons sight[5]; 360
	Let it be hid.

[*The bed-curtains are drawn.*]

Gratiano, keep[6] the house
And seize upon[7] the fortunes of the Moor,
For they succeed on you[8]. To you, lord governor,
Remains the censure[9] of this hellish[10] villain:
The time, the place, the torture, O, enforce it! 365
Myself will straight aboard[11], and to the state
This heavy act[12] with heavy heart relate.

Exeunt

OTHELLO 奥赛罗

Looking back at the play 本剧回顾
Activities for groups or individuals

1 Fifteen-minute version

Split into five groups, with each group taking one act of the play. Produce a three-minute version of your chosen act, using only words from the script. When you are ready, put each of the five acts together in turn to create a fifteen-minute version of the whole play. As a variation, you could try performing each act in a different style (soap opera, documentary, slapstick comedy [闹剧], melodrama).

2 Production matters

Imagine you are planning a production of *Othello*. In groups, discuss and then execute the following tasks:

- At what point in the play would you have the interval? Explain your decision.
- What music will you play as the audience settles in at the start, or as people leave at the end of the play? Justify your choices.
- Design a poster, publicity material (flyers) and a programme cover.
- Write the programme notes for your production.
- Draw up a cast list, indicating which characters could 'double up' their parts.

3 Coroner's (验尸官) investigation (written version)

Three or four corpses – one suicide and three suspected murders – all in the space of one evening! The coroner in Cyprus would be kept busy investigating the full circumstances of each of the deaths.

- Compile the coroner's dossier (卷宗). It includes eye-witness statements, psychiatric reports, post-mortem (尸体解剖) reports, and any other relevant documentation about the deceased. Include mock-ups of army personnel files, newspaper cuttings and personal letters. Use your imagination! Work in small groups and produce a large display of the various examples of written 'evidence'. (See also pp. 228–9.)

4 Production photographs

Look through all the photographs in this edition, including those in the photo gallery at the start. Choose three or four images that most appeal to you. Consider costume, style and colour. Use them as inspiration for a piece of analytical writing, explaining what you find interesting about their interpretations of characters or particular moments of the play. Include key quotations from the script to support your points.

5 The myth of the handkerchief

a How significant is Desdemona's 'napkin', which Emilia finds and gives to Iago in Act 3 Scene 3? Trace its history and meaning as it is passed from person to person in the course of the play. (See Act 3 Scene 3, lines 288–330; Act 3 Scene 4, lines 48–96; Act 4 Scene 1, lines 142–91.)

b Each person takes one of the following roles:

- Bianca
- Egyptian charmer
- Iago
- Cassio
- Othello
- Othello's mother
- Desdemona
- Emilia.

Pass an appropriately decorated handkerchief or tissue from person to person in the correct order; when the 'napkin' is passed to you, state who you are, how you got it and what you believe to be its significance.

c Discuss how far the napkin serves merely as a plot device, or whether it becomes richly symbolic as the play progresses. Also, discuss how it links the female characters in the play.

Othello 奥赛罗

Perspectives and themes 视角与主题

What is the play about?

Traditionally, answers to this question have focused on characters or themes. Themes are ideas or concerns that are dramatically explored or presented in different ways as the play develops. In *Othello*, such themes include: jealousy; appearance versus reality; reputation; public versus private concerns; and racism. In recent years, developments in literary theory have led to several different ways of approaching Shakespeare, and each of these provides different answers to the question 'What is *Othello* about?'

Cultural materialist criticism – this argues that the play offers a subversive (颠覆性) critique of the social and political beliefs of Shakespeare's time (and shows how changing beliefs have shaped subsequent readings). For example, racism and sexism in *Othello* are seen as inherent in the way early (and late) capitalist society is structured, rather than simply located in individuals.

Feminist criticism – this emphasises the importance of the three female characters, and explores the limits imposed on their freedom to act. It shows how gender has constructed traditional (male) readings of the play, accusing it of having a 'domestic' focus. So, traditional criticism tends to idealise Desdemona as a submissive wife, whilst diminishing the roles of Emilia and Bianca.

New historicist criticism – this places the play firmly in its historical context, and explores ideas about society and power that were current in Shakespeare's time. New historicists may be interested in apparent acts of subversion, and the way these moments of disorder are contained within the action of the play. One focus, therefore, might be on Othello as a self-made man, who represents a move away from the medieval belief in humans' fixed place in society.

Performance criticism – this explores *Othello* as performance text, analysing past and present theatrical productions. Through the centuries, different productions have reflected changing interpretations of *Othello*. In more recent years, this also encompasses (包含) film and other moving-image performances.

Post-colonial criticism – this exposes European colonial attitudes towards race and difference as reflected in literary texts. It explores cultural assumptions of superiority and what it is to be 'civilised', highlighting, for example, the way Othello is presented as both intriguingly exotic and threateningly savage.

Post-modernist criticism – here, the focus is on the script itself, rather than on its context. Post-modernist criticism stresses how meaning is hard to pin down, as in the concepts of 'honesty' and 'justice', for example.

Psychoanalytical criticism – this focuses on undercurrents of desire, and repressed sexuality. For example, Iago's attitudes to sex and women offer a productive starting point for analysis, with some commentators suggesting latent homosexuality (潜在同性恋) as an explanation of his behaviour towards Othello.

At the heart of modern forms of criticism is the belief that all interpretation carries certain assumptions (for example, about society, literature, political issues in the play). No interpretation is the 'correct one', and in each case, evidence must be sought to illustrate the reading.

◆ Choose a critical approach from the list above, then pick at least two scenes or dramatic moments from *Othello* and explain how they can be interpreted in a way that supports your selected reading. Write five paragraphs arguing why the play should be read in this way.

Characters 人物分析

This section offers a number of activities that will help you explore different views of 'character'. These combine more traditional ideas about characterisation with broader considerations of the thematic, dramatic and political functions of the characters in *Othello*.

Traditional approaches to 'character'

Character analysis has traditionally been regarded as the key to understanding any Shakespeare play. One of the most influential writers about Shakespearean tragedy, A. C. Bradley, said that the plays told universal truths about human existence.

Early twentieth-century criticism therefore tended to focus on Othello as a tragic hero. Critics have applied ancient Greek ideas on tragedy (notably those of Aristotle), and assumed that the tragic hero is a mixture of admirable qualities and a fatal tragic flaw. Much twentieth-century criticism was dominated by debates about whether Othello's 'flaw' is jealousy (triggered by the malevolent Iago) or his inherent egotism (自负) and self-centredness. This approach usually treats characters as if they were living people, with real feelings, thoughts and lives that go beyond the confines of the play.

However, there are problems with such readings. It has been argued that Elizabethan and Jacobean playwrights were not concerned with constructing psychologically consistent 'characters'. Indeed, there is evidence that certain 'character traits' would be conveyed to audiences on Shakespeare's stage through 'stock' (惯用的，老套的) gestures and signalled by types of costume, so when it came to dramatic roles, 'realism' was highly unlikely. It may be that the fascination with tragic heroes emerged some time during the nineteenth century — the time of the great Victorian actor-managers, famed for their starring roles — and further influenced by the kind of characterisation developed in the novels of the time. Some critics and historians have suggested that Victorian moralists were interested in using Shakespeare's characters as examples for moral guidance.

◆ In small groups, discuss how you might apply the idea of the tragically flawed noble hero to Othello. Give examples of things Othello says and does that might be termed 'noble' or 'heroic', then describe what goes wrong for him. How far can his downfall be ascribed to (归结于) external factors (such as a hostile society or Iago's hatred), and how far should it be blamed on a 'flaw' in his own character?

◆ In 1693, Thomas Rymer (the earliest recorded critic of *Othello*) suggested that the play's central lesson was that 'maidens of quality' should not 'run away with Blackamoors'. What 'moral lesson' could you draw from the play today?

Alternative approaches to character

Shakespeare was writing at a time of rapid change — socially, politically and economically. Today, many critics argue that his audiences were more concerned with the interplay between characters and the exchange of ideas in the plays.

Much recent literary theory assumes that the most important aspect of a character is his or her dramatic function within the social and political context of the play. As such, characters embody the themes and wider concerns of the play, and they exist only while on stage, within a dramatically created world. (See the activity on Roderigo's role on p. 227 for a further exploration of this idea.)

Othello 奥赛罗

Themes most commonly identified in *Othello* include: appearance and reality; opposites (such as loyalty and disloyalty, honesty and dishonesty, light and dark); the position of women; the importance of reputation; alienation/belonging; justice.

◆ Consider which characters most contribute to an understanding of each of the themes above and in what way. In pairs, create a poster for a classroom display.

The representation of women

Nowhere in Shakespeare are relations between males and females more searchingly, painfully probed.

Marilyn French, 1982

There are only three women in the play, and each of them is bound up in a relationship with a man. Only one survives.

◆ In small groups, consider the roles of the three women. Discuss the following list of statements in turn, deciding which you agree or disagree with:

a All three women are presented according to men's interpretations.
b The women are completely passive.
c Each woman is defined in terms of her male partner.
d Women are fully emancipated in the play.
e Each woman stands for an aspect of 'womanhood' – romantic idealist, practical realist and sex object.
f Each relationship provokes jealousy in one partner.
g Women's roles in the play are ambiguous.
h The women are all portrayed as stupid.
i Men hold all the power in Venetian society.
j Each woman comes from a different social class, and that is significant.
k Women talk the most sense in the play.
l The women are bonded by a notion of 'sisterhood'.
m The women are more trusting than the men.
n The men use abusive terms to refer to women; women don't use abusive terms back.
o All three women have identical attitudes to men and relationships.

◆ Select the three statements you most agree with and write a short paragraph for each, explaining your reasons. Then choose the statement you most disagree with, and write a further paragraph giving your arguments.

◆ Choose two or three quotations from the play that seem to say something important about the presentation of one or all of the women characters. Put the lines together into a short oral, dramatic or written presentation that sums up your conclusions. Think about the way language 'normalises' gender roles.

- In the UK there is a long-running BBC radio programme called Woman's Hour, in which all sorts of women's issues are discussed, including current news events. Imagine that Emilia, Desdemona and Bianca have been invited on to the Venetian version of Woman's Hour to discuss their views on marriage, immediately after the announcement that society beauty Desdemona has independently arranged her own marriage to Othello. Find all the key scenes where the three women air their contrasting views. The table below will help you locate some of these.

Character	Scene
Desdemona	Act 1 Scene 3, lines 244–55; Act 2 Scene 1, lines 100–60; Act 3 Scene 3, lines 45–89
Emilia	Act 2 Scene 1, lines 100–60; Act 3 Scene 4, lines 97–100; Act 3 Scene 4, lines 153–6
Bianca	Act 3 Scene 4, lines 163–95

- In groups of four, improvise the studio discussion. Try to incorporate some of each woman's actual words from the play, and aim to bring out their contrasting views. For example, how might Desdemona and Emilia relate to Bianca?

- Some critics believe that each woman's love for their man is much stronger than the love or loyalty they feel for each other as women. All three are underestimated and abused by the men they love. Use your experience of *Othello* to write an essay on the claim that: 'The real tragedy for Desdemona, Emilia and Bianca is that their marital and emotional bonds take precedence over (优先于) their common cause as women.'

Othello
奥赛罗

How Othello changes

In the course of the play, Othello apparently changes from the 'noble Moor' to a 'devil' and a 'murderous coxcomb'. In Act 1 Scene 2, he speaks with calm authority: 'Keep up your bright swords, for the dew will rust them' (line 59). By the start of Act 4, he is suffering from tortured confusion: 'Pish! Noses, / ears, and lips. Is't possible? – Confess? Handkerchief? O devil!' (lines 40–1).

◆ In groups of five, each person takes one act of the play and researches Othello's role by completing the activities below:

  a Briefly summarise Othello's actions during the course of the act.

  b Note down any significant descriptions of Othello made by other characters.

  c Describe how Othello relates to one other character – pick out a short piece of dialogue that seems significant, and explain why. Look carefully at the language used.

  d Pick out one or two of Othello's speeches that you consider to be particularly dramatic. Are they in verse or prose? What effect does this have?

◆ When each person has completed their individual investigation, pool (汇总) your research. Discuss any changes you see in Othello in terms of action, relationships and language. Present your findings as graphs, flow diagrams or a storyboard.

◆ Consider whether this research provides all the evidence that you need to show how Othello changes over the course of the play. Does it tell the 'full story'? What other aspects of Othello's development might you have investigated?

Iago – the malcontent (牢骚满腹的人)

Iago is a malcontent, a man with a grudge. He puts on the outward appearance of a bluff (直爽), honest soldier, but behind that false exterior he manipulates, mentally tortures and betrays Othello. Yet for over four hundred years this deeply malicious figure has fascinated audiences. The following activities invite you to think about him in today's world.

◆ In groups, play around with the character of Iago. If he was a real person, what:

  a would be his favourite movie?
  b would be his favourite book?
  c would be his favourite TV programme?
  d would be his favourite type of music?
  e daily newspaper would he read?
  f football (or other sports) team would he support?
  g would he do for a living?
  h would his leisure activities be?
  i political party might he support?
  j would be his views of key current affairs?

Present your group's ideas to the rest of the class. Be prepared to explain why you made those choices for Iago.

◆ In pairs, create a 'photograph' of Iago with one other character (like the one on the right). The second person's identity should be obvious from their posture, position and facial expression. Show your 'photograph'. The rest of the class guesses who Iago's companion is.

◆ When all pairs have shown their 'photographs', hold a class discussion on why some characters were easier to guess than others, and what all the photographs reveal about Iago (e.g. whether there were differences in the way he was portrayed by each pair).

Cassio – a press conference

- One student takes the part of Cassio; others play government advisers (perhaps Montano and Lodovico) and at least one spin-doctor (媒体顾问). Prepare a formal statement for Cassio to read out at a press conference, following the deaths of Othello and Desdemona. Prepare answers to questions that journalists are likely to ask. (Which questions might Cassio refuse to answer?)

- Other students take on the roles of newspaper and television reporters. Prepare questions about recent events, Cassio's view of Othello and others, his military career, his motivation, interests, feelings, private life and so on. What kind of information will your readers/viewers be interested in? Organise the press conference and role-play the event as a whole class. You could even video it.

Roderigo's role

Shakespeare based *Othello* on a story by a sixteenth-century Italian writer, Giraldo Cinthio, in which a wicked ensign falls in love with a Moorish captain's wife, Disdemona. The ensign grows bitter when she refuses to return his advances, so he tells lies to make the captain believe his wife has been unfaithful. Cinthio's story is much longer and more complicated than Shakespeare's taut (紧凑), focused version, but the character of Roderigo is entirely Shakespeare's invention and does not exist in the original source.

- Write at least three paragraphs exploring what dramatic function Roderigo serves in the play. Think about:

- the various things Iago asks Roderigo to do. Which of these help further the plot, and in what ways?

- what sense you gain of Roderigo from his manner of speaking and how he relates to others

- the ways in which Roderigo provides a contrast to Iago, Othello and Cassio

- the points in the play when Roderigo appears – for example, does each appearance raise or lower the dramatic tension?

The characters – a summary

- Make a list of all the 'main' characters in the play (first, you should agree who you would include or exclude in this category). Look back over all the production photographs in this edition, including the photo gallery at the beginning of the book.

- When you have made your list, take each character in turn and say what characteristics are emphasised in the various images, making sure you consider age, ethnicity, physical features, facial expressions, clothes and props as appropriate.

- For each character, decide which photo best fits your idea of how the role should be portrayed and defend your choice. Feed back to the rest of the class.

▼ Who do you think is the other person with Iago in the production photograph below?

Othello
奥赛罗

Coroner's investigation 验尸官的调查

A role-play activity for the whole class

Time: a month after Othello's death.
Place: a coroner's court in Venice.

Create a whole-class role-play around an imaginary coroner's investigation. It provides plenty of scope for getting everyone imaginatively involved in an active investigation of characters' relationships, motivations and the public and private aspects of the play.

The following notes will help focus each participant's preparation for the role-play. Take time to prepare your character and their side of the story, then set the room out as a court. The coroner presides over the hearing (听证会) and assesses the evidence at the end of the role-play.

Coroner
- Work in a small group with the assistant/usher(s) ([法院] 传达员), etc.
- What questions will you put to each character?
- What concrete evidence exists? Any exhibits (物证) to use in court (e.g. weapons/letters)?
- Consider how you will shape your questions to elicit full answers (as opposed to 'yes'/'no' replies).

Coroner's assistant
- Assist coroner in running the proceedings (诉讼).
- Establish an order of events and present it on paper.
- Keep a record of the proceedings of the court.

Montano
- What contact did you have with Othello/Cassio/Iago? What impressions did you get of them?
- Did you witness any important/significant events at first hand?
- Did Othello live up to his reputation?

Duke of Venice
- How will you behave in court?
- Which characters did you know well?
- What relevant evidence do you have for the court?
- How do you now see your position in relation to the whole Cyprus venture?
- Do you feel any sense of responsibility for what has happened?

Iago
- Will you offer any defence? Why might you be persuaded to talk?
- What motivation exists for your acts? (Look up your major speeches and soliloquies.)
- Why do you think Cassio got the job of Othello's second-in-command instead of you?
- What do you think of other characters?

Bianca
- What contact did you have with any of the main characters?
- Were there any significant events you witnessed at first hand?
- How do you regard your position in this society?

Coroner's investigation

Lodovico
- What is your considered opinion about the cause of the deaths?
- What do you think of Othello's behaviour in the time you knew him?
- What relevant events were you present at?
- How do you see your position in relation to the whole Cyprus venture?

Roderigo
- Yes – you live! (See Act 5 Scene 2, lines 323–4 – you might be walking with difficulty.)
- What happened at your meetings with Iago?
- What was your part in his plots?
- What do you now think of Iago, Desdemona, Cassio, Othello?
- What did you say to Cassio before the brawl?
- Where have you been for the past month?

Cassio
- What is your version of events?
- Who seems to blame?
- What is your opinion of Othello now?
- What was Othello like to serve under?
- Why did you get promoted over Iago?
- What do you look forward to?

A Gentleman of Cyprus
- At what important event were you present?
- Why were you there?
- Give your version of the occasion.
- What is your reaction to the tragic deaths, and how do you feel about the continuation of Venetian rule?

Clown
- Who employed you?
- What messages were you given and to whom were you sent?
- What was your impression of the people you came into contact with?
- How would you describe their changing moods?
- Consider how you might act/speak in court (terrible puns, for instance).

Gratiano
- How do you feel about the deaths of your brother and niece?
- How has your family in Venice reacted?
- Could you have done anything to prevent the tragedy?
- What eye-witness accounts can you offer the court?

Other roles (if needed)
Jury members, court ushers – could be involved in helping others to prepare their roles, or be responsible for creating exhibits (letters, etc.)

OTHELLO
奥赛罗

The language of *Othello* 《奥赛罗》的语言

Dramatic language

Shakespeare was writing for theatre conditions that were very different from those common today – open-air stages with no electric light. There was little in the way of scenery, and few props. Playwrights therefore had to create atmosphere, mood and setting almost entirely through language.

- Below are some examples of this kind of language in *Othello*. In each case, identify where the quotation comes from and who is speaking. Then find other examples of each feature in the script:

- Embedded stage directions: 'Look where she comes!'; 'Iago beckons me'.

- Setting the scene: 'What from the cape can you discern at sea?'; 'on the brow o'the sea / Stand ranks of people'; 'Strike on the tinder, ho!'; 'Light, I say, light!' (indicating it's night-time).

- Voicing a character's 'thoughts': this could be done through asides or soliloquies. For examples of how a soliloquy might be staged see pages 44 and 88. A number of asides reveal inner thoughts and sometimes emphasise dramatic irony: 'I am not merry, but I do beguile / The thing I am by seeming otherwise'; 'He takes her by the palm'; 'By heaven, that should be my handkerchief!'.

Verse and prose

Like most playwrights at the time, Shakespeare wrote poetic drama, mostly in **iambic pentameter** (抑扬五音步) – lines that are made up of a basic five-beat rhythm. This rhythm is thought to be the one that most closely echoes everyday speech patterns (da DUM, da DUM, da DUM, da DUM, da DUM), and when spoken aloud a line is said to last as long as a normal human breath. However, Shakespeare also varied the way he wrote lines of his scripts, playing around with the five beats, sometimes using **rhyming couplets**, sometimes using prose, depending on the effect he wanted to create.

Verse

Shakespeare traditionally gave verse to his high-status characters. Othello's early speeches are in iambic pentameter. Lines are often run on (**enjambement** [跨行]) as ideas are developed in a coherent and confident way (e.g. Act 1 Scene 3, lines 76–94). In contrast, Iago's speeches are often **end-stopped** (尾断行) or have a mid-line **caesura** (停顿处) (pause). This suggests he is a plain-speaking man.

Prose

Prose is commonly used by comic or low-status characters – for example, the Clown and the Musician speak in prose. (Surprisingly, the Herald's announcement at the beginning of Act 2 Scene 2 is not in prose.) However, Shakespeare sometimes alternates between verse and prose in order to change the mood and tone of a scene. An example is when Othello and Cassio speak in verse together at the beginning of Act 2 Scene 3, but as the scene progresses and Cassio becomes more drunk, he switches to prose. Iago, of course, skilfully switches between the two. His use of prose gives the impression of informal talk, taking others into his confidence, whereas his soliloquies are in verse.

- Trace Othello's speeches through the course of the play. Where does his syntax (sentence structure) begin to fall apart? How is his state of mind reflected in his language? To help you, look at two or three of his major speeches. For example: his first full speech in front of the Senate (Act 1 Scene 3, lines 76–94); his 'general camp' speech to Iago (Act 3 Scene 3, lines 346–58); his speech directly before he falls into a trance (Act 4 Scene 1, lines 35–41). As an extension, go on to consider what happens to Othello's language right at the end of the play, once he has realised the truth and has – too late – shaken off Iago's influence (Act 5 Scene 2, lines 334–52).

- Look carefully at two scenes in which Iago speaks in prose. At what point does he switch to verse? Present your ideas about the effect of this.

The language of Othello

Imagery

Imagery conjures up (唤起) vivid pictures or associations in the mind and adds a symbolic and visual dimension to the play. Shakespeare's language is rich in imagery, and he particularly makes repeated use of similes (明喻) and metaphors. In Othello, certain image clusters recur, which are outlined below.

Animals

- Usually insulting, especially when used by Iago: 'an old black ram / Is tupping your white ewe'; 'Plague him with flies'.
- As Othello comes under Iago's influence, he echoes Iago's choice of image: 'I had rather be a toad / And live upon the vapour of a dungeon'; 'as prime as goats, as hot as monkeys'.
- Exposed as a villain, Iago is called 'inhuman dog' and 'viper'.

Poison and disease

Disease reflects the supposed corruption of Venetian society, and becomes a metaphor for the corruption of Othello's mind.

- Iago's words act as poison in the play: 'poison his delight'; 'pour this pestilence into his ear'.
- Othello's jealousy acts like poison: 'If there be cords or knives, / Poison or fire … / I'll not endure it.'
- Othello asks Iago for real poison: 'Get me some poison, Iago, this night'.
- Ironically, in Act 1 Othello is falsely accused by Brabantio of drugging Desdemona: 'corrupted / By spells and medicines'.

Hell and the devil

The play resonates with numerous references to hell and damnation.

- Iago to Brabantio: 'the devil will make a grandsire of you'.
- Brabantio to Othello: 'Damned as thou art, thou hast enchanted her'.
- Iago about himself: 'Divinity of hell! / When devils will the blackest sins put on, / They do suggest at first with heavenly shows / As I do now.'
- Othello on vengeance: 'Arise, black vengeance, from thy hollow cell'.
- Othello on Desdemona: 'the fair devil'.
- Emilia to Othello: 'thou art a devil'.
- Iago is revealed to be 'that demi-devil'; 'this hellish villain'.

Seeing and not seeing

Sight, or seeing things as they really are, works on an increasingly metaphorical level throughout the play, infusing (全面影响) the language and driving the plot.

- At the beginning of the play, Desdemona is very clear about what she sees in Othello: 'I saw Othello's visage in his mind, / And to his honours and his valiant parts / Did I my soul and fortunes consecrate'. She disregards outward appearances, for example his black skin.
- Act 2 begins with people staring out to sea, waiting to see the arrival of ships.
- Othello, though he demands 'ocular proof', is frequently convinced by things he does not see.
- After Othello has killed himself, Lodovico says to Iago: 'Look on the tragic loading of this bed: / This is thy work. The object poisons sight; / Let it be hid'.
- Even at a public level, seeing is portrayed as a very misleading sense: in Act 1 Scene 3, a senator suggests that the Turkish retreat to Rhodes is 'a pageant / To keep us in false gaze'.

◆ In small groups, create a collage that captures key images in the play. You can use any found pictures that you think are appropriate, or combine images and words. Be prepared to explain and/or analyse your collage to other groups, with close reference to the text.

Othello
奥赛罗

Images: is Othello avoiding reality?

Othello's 'cause' speech, uttered as he enters Desdemona's bedchamber, about to kill her (Act 5 Scene 2, lines 1–22), is rich in visually striking images. One writer has suggested that Othello cannot face the reality of his own role, the living woman before him and his intended act, so he finds symbols for each in an attempt to idealise his situation.

◆ Explore this interpretation by locating the following images and explaining briefly the effect of each one.

Image	How it is being used
A carved alabaster effigy (雕像) on a tomb	
Light	Metaphor for life. 'Snuff out' = killing. Desdemona is personified as light – opposite to hell.
A rose	
The figure of Justice (usually depicted with sword and scales)	

◆ Create a series of tableaux that visually capture the speech.

◆ Look again at Othello's final speech (Act 5 Scene 2, lines 334–55). Identify the images he uses and explain their effect. Talk together about whether you think his imagery here may be another example of avoiding the reality of his situation.

◆ Using Othello's 'cause' speech and one other speech of your choice, write an analysis of Othello's language in the play. Pay close attention to verse and imagery, providing quotations to support your comments. How does the language reflect the themes of the play, suggest something about the 'character' speaking, and provide dramatic moments which might move an audience emotionally? Aim to write at least five paragraphs, including an introduction and conclusion.

Race and culture in *Othello*　《奥赛罗》里的种族和文化

Is *Othello* a racist play?

The central character of this play could be said to be:

- mentally unstable
- physically aggressive
- sensual (好色)
- insanely jealous
- highly gullible (易上当).

His main action in the play is to strangle a white woman. He is black.

A clear example of offensive racial stereotyping?

Certainly, there is some historical evidence of racial stereotyping in Shakespeare's England. There were enough black residents (mainly from Africa) to prompt Elizabeth I to express her discontent at the great numbers of 'Negars and blackamoors which are crept into the realm', and to proceed to expel (驱逐出境) some from the country. Popular travel books portrayed the natives of Africa as barbarous, lawless and 'a people of beastly lyvinge'. One contemporary writer on the history and people of Africa claimed that:

> *Whomsoever they finde but talking with their wives they presently go about to murther them ... by reason of jealousie you may see them daily one to be the death and destruction of another.*

One source Shakespeare appears to have used when composing *Othello* is Leo Africanus's *A Geographical History of Africa*, published around 1600. It is typical of the contemporary attitudes and assumptions:

> *Those which we named the inhabitants of the cities of Barbarie are somewhat needie and covetous (贪婪), being also very proud and high-minded (高傲), and woonderfullly addicted unto wrath; insomuch that (according to the proverbe) they will deeply engrave in marble any injurie be it never so small, & will in no wise (决不) blot it out of their remembrance ... Their wits are but meane, and they are so credulous, that they will beleeve matters impossible, which are told them.*

▲ The Moorish ambassador to Queen Elizabeth I, 1600–01.

'The Moor'

The word 'Moor' has its roots in the name of a people originating from North Africa (roughly what is now Morocco and Algeria). In Shakespeare's time, however, it could also be used as a generic term to describe anyone from the African continent. Othello is variously described as 'a Barbary horse' (suggesting he is Arabic), or 'black' and 'thick-lips', indicating he is darker skinned from sub-Saharan Africa. Critics have argued for centuries over Othello's precise ethnicity, but why should this matter?

OTHELLO
奥赛罗

What some critics have said

In *A Short View of Tragedy* (published in 1693), Thomas Rymer drew comparisons between the imagined Venetian society of the play and seventeenth-century England:

> With us a Blackamoor might rise to be a trumpeter … With us a Moor might marry some little drab (荡妇), or Small-coal Wench … certaynly never was any Play fraught like this of Othello with improbabilities.

Just over a century later, Samuel Taylor Coleridge expresses a similar view:

> It would be something monstrous to conceive this beautiful Venetian girl falling in love with a veritable (真正的) negro.

Such attitudes continued to be expressed even in the twentieth century. Several influential writers on *Othello* concentrated on debating Othello's precise ethnic origins, taking great pains to prove that he would have been Arabic in appearance (see the illustration on p. 233). A. C. Bradley (*Shakespearean Tragedy*, 1904) explains why he considered this to be a particularly important point:

> Perhaps if we saw Othello coal-black with the bodily eye, the aversion (厌恶) of our blood … would overpower our imagination.

It was assumed that it would be less uncomfortable for white audiences to watch a lighter-skinned Othello having physical contact with Desdemona than an actor portrayed as black.

F. R. Leavis (*The Common Pursuit*, 1952) echoes some of the early Renaissance attitudes towards men of African descent when he ascribes 'voluptuous (体态丰满的) sensuality' and 'sensual possessiveness, appetite' to the central character, and comments that 'the stuff of which he is made begins … to deteriorate and show itself unfit'. In other words, there is something inherently unstable about Othello, a man who is naturally prone to uncontrollable sexual urges and jealousies. Leavis's view was highly influential during the latter half of the last century, and dominated ways of thinking about *Othello* until serious challenges were mounted (展开) by critics coming from more politically aware traditions from the 1980s onwards (see pages 238–9 for some examples).

Is the play about 'race'?

When Shakespeare wrote the play, it is unlikely that this concept was at the forefront of people's consciousness. However, this question has fascinated critics over the past fifty years.

The Caribbean writer C. L. R. James famously asserted that *Othello* was not a play about 'race', and that if all racist references were removed the basic plot would remain the same. Instead, he said, it is a play about jealousy, and the ethnic origins of the leading characters are irrelevant.

In contrast – and having originally agreed with this view – the Nigerian poet and novelist Ben Okri wrote that he changed his mind after watching a live performance in a London theatre as 'practically the only Black person in the audience'. Okri draws a parallel between his own feeling of isolation in the audience with Othello's visible isolation as a black man on stage. Okri goes on to say:

> Any Black man who has gone out with a white woman knows that there are a lot of Iagos around … If it did not begin as a play about race, then its history has made it one.

◆ Make a list of all the elements in the play that you would argue are directly linked to issues of race and racism. Divide them up into: verbal references (what characters actually say); implied references; and what are likely to be visual references (for example, on stage the visible contrast between black and white characters is strongly marked at all times, whereas on the page it is less noticeable).

◆ Discuss with a partner whether you agree that the play would not be changed very much if all direct verbal references to race/ethnicity were removed. Could Othello then be played by a white actor?

'Far more fair than black'

On page 12, you were asked to explore the way that language carries and reinforces the prejudices of the dominant social group. It is easy to recognise the blatant (公然的) and intentional racist abuse in much of Iago's and Roderigo's dialogue, but language often works more subtly in carrying meaning. The activities that follow explore more fully how language can be culturally loaded (有文化内涵).

Definitions

◆ Working in pairs, look up the word 'black' in a dictionary. Note down how many different uses there are of the word. Now do the same for 'white' and 'fair'. Divide the definitions into positive and negative uses. See if you can find the earliest recorded dates of particular usages. Discuss your findings in class, making links and comparisons between the three sets of definitions and, if possible, constructing a timeline of historical usage.

◆ Compile a list of sayings that use the various meanings of the words 'black', 'fair' or 'white'. For example, a 'whitewash' can refer to glossing over (掩饰) negative associations in a report; giving someone a 'black look' means looking at someone in an unfriendly way; 'black Wednesday' is a term used to refer to the day the stock markets crashed … and so on. Discuss how the various meanings of these words informs the way we use everyday language, then move on to a consideration of the ways language works in *Othello*.

Meanings

◆ In groups of three, discuss in what sense the Duke is using the word 'black' when he says: 'If virtue no delighted beauty lack, / Your son-in-law is far more fair than black.' (Act I Scene 3, lines 285–6).

◆ Identify other uses of 'black' in the play and discuss their meanings in the context of who uses the word and when.

Othello
奥赛罗

Portrayals

The conventional image of hell is of a place of evil, torture and darkness. In early Christian church paintings, devils were always portrayed as black (see the picture below). The connotation of evil is very evident in Emilia's raging at Othello for killing Desdemona: 'O, the more angel she, / And you the blacker devil!' (Act 5 Scene 2, lines 131–2). Iago also explicitly links blackness with sinfulness: 'When devils will the blackest sins put on' (Act 2 Scene 3, line 318).

In Shakespeare's *Macbeth* there are other examples of the way blackness is linked with evil. The three witches are called 'secret, black, and midnight hags (老妖婆)', and the tyrant Macbeth himself is referred to as 'black Macbeth'.

◆ In pairs, make a collection of similar references in *Othello* that link blackness with the devil. Which characters make these references most?

◆ Now find references to 'fair', 'angels' and 'heaven'. Who uses theses terms and when? How often are fair and dark terms set up in opposition to each other?

Black and white imagery

At the heart of the play is the marriage of a black man and a white woman, seen by many of the play's characters to be 'against all rules of nature'. Black and white imagery emphasises this opposition throughout the fabric of the play's language. In the cultural and historical context of the play, black and white can be equated with dark and light, hell and heaven, good and bad. The contrast between black and white is further intensified by Shakespeare's use of **antithesis** (对偶): the setting of word against word, or phrase against phrase (as in 'fair' against 'black', 'black ram' against 'white ewe'). Shakespeare uses this device frequently in all his plays, probably because antitheses express conflict, and conflict is usually at the heart of all drama. It is used in different ways throughout *Othello* (as when 'hand' is set against 'heart' and in Othello's 'sweet revenge grows harsh'). But it is the insistent opposition of black against white that powerfully pervades the whole play.

In Shakespeare's day, black characters were not usually cast as the 'hero' and it is likely, therefore, that his audiences would automatically make negative associations. Black-skinned Othello is often referred to by his colour or ethnicity ('the Moor', 'sooty bosom') and linked to evil, yet expectations are reversed within the actions of the play in that it is white-skinned Iago who turns out to be evil, and who immerses himself in images of hell and night. In contrast, Desdemona's fairness is emphasised and, even at the end of the play, Othello refers to her as a 'pearl' and as 'light'.

Race and culture in Othello

The first scene of the play, where Iago's plan is first hatched, takes place at night. The play moves through storm into daylight, then moves back to night for the final tragic events. The drunken barracks party, where Iago's scheming really begins to take off, occurs at night, drawing Othello and Desdemona from their bed-chamber on what should be their wedding night.

Some commentators have suggested that Othello's inherent bravery and virtue mean that at the beginning of the play he is able to overcome colour prejudice. Then, he is comfortable in his position as a general, and speaks with calm authority, even when challenged by Brabantio in front of the Senate. But away from the civilised confines of Venice, he is corrupted by Iago. As his relationship with Desdemona is 'blackened' by lies, Othello becomes more conscious of himself as black, and begins to conform to racist stereotypes. He, too, comes to regard 'black' as a negative term: 'Her name, that was as fresh / As Dian's visage, is now begrimed and black / As mine own face.'

◆ Using only black-and-white illustrations, photos, display paper and other resources, create a collage out of words, quotations and pictures that explores the central opposition between black and white in the play. Mount a display of your collages on the wall and compare your interpretations. Pick out the key differences and discuss the reasons for these.

◆ Using the information in this section, and your collages, write an analytical essay entitled, Othello: 'Far more fair than black', exploring the ways in which black and white are set in opposition to each other on both a literal and a metaphorical level.

Venice and Venetian culture

Shakespeare's choice of Venice as a setting is significant. For an English audience in 1604, Venice was a byword (代名词) for thriving capitalism. It was a republic where the wealthier merchant classes controlled the state, buying powerful military forces to protect their colonial exploits (掠夺，剥削). In contrast, England had only just started

increasing overseas trade in Africa, India and elsewhere, and was on the brink of massive colonial enterprise in the New World. It is likely that English merchants would recognise in Venice the mercantile (商业的，贸易的) and colonial force that they wanted to see England become.

The Venetian state employed mercenary soldiers (雇佣军). It was a cosmopolitan state, so a black military leader is quite a believable figure. Othello, an ex-slave, is revered (尊敬) by the Venetian Senate simply because he very effectively defends their interests. He is, however, not entirely 'one of them', especially not when it comes to marrying one of their daughters. Desdemona is described as a stolen jewel because Brabantio feels he has been robbed by someone who was employed to protect his possessions! The non-feudal society of Venice confers power on Othello – but not status. This provides a rich source of dramatic tension.

Othello 奥赛罗

Critics' forum 评论家论坛

On these two pages are extracts from influential Shakespeare critics, writing about *Othello*. You will discover that the readings offered are very different, and in some cases quite contradictory.

Working in small groups, read through each extract and summarise the main points. Then think about what evidence from the play the writer in each case might go on to use in support of their view. Try to suggest what assumptions underpin (支持) the readings, what other influences each reader brings to their interpretation of the play (for example, Christianity, empire) and what theoretical perspective they might be adopting (see p. 222).

Imagine *Critics' Forum* is a late-evening television arts programme, chaired by Melanie Bookworm. In it, a group of professional critics with very differing views is brought together for a discussion on a particular work of literature. Tonight it is *Othello*. One student (as Ms Bookworm) chairs the debate, the rest choose a critical stance from the extracts given, and each argues their case. Remember, you'll have to know the play really well and do thorough preparation beforehand.

Focus on character (and Othello's exoticism)

> [Othello] does not belong to our world, and he seems to enter it we know not whence — almost as if from wonderland. There is something mysterious in his descent from men of royal siege (王族); in his wanderings in vast deserts and among marvellous peoples; in his tales of magic handkerchiefs and prophetic Sibyls (女先知); in the sudden vague glimpses we get of numberless battles and sieges in which he has played the hero and has borne a charmed life; even in chance references to his baptism, his being sold to slavery, his sojourn (旅居) in Aleppo. And he is not merely a romantic figure; his own nature is romantic. So he comes before us, dark and grand, with a light upon him from the sun where he was born.
>
> A. C. Bradley, 1904

Focus on character and his language

> Othello, in his magnanimous (大度，宽宏) way, is egotistic. He really is, beyond any question, the nobly massive man of action, the captain of men, he sees himself as being ... In short, a habit of self-approving, self-dramatisation is an essential element in Othello's make-up, and remains so at the very end. It is, at the best, the impressive manifestation of a noble egotism ... This self-centredness doesn't mean self-knowledge: that is a virtue which Othello, as soldier of fortune, hasn't had much need of.
>
> F. R. Leavis, 1952

Focus on the poetry

> Among the tragedies of Shakespeare *Othello* is supreme in one quality: beauty. Much of its poetry, in imagery, perfection of phrase, and steadiness of rhythm, soaring yet firm, enchants the sensuous imagination. Othello is like a hero of the ancient world in that he is not a man like us, but a man recognised as extraordinary. He seems born to do great deeds and live in legend. He has the heroic capacity for passion. But the thing which most sets him apart is his solitariness. He is a stranger, a man of alien race, without ties of nature or natural duties.
>
> Helen Gardner, 1955

Critics' forum

Focus on the message *Othello* carries for us today

The action of Othello opens out to include the audience, and their perception of the struggle of good and evil. They do not go home hoping they will never meet an Iago, but rather understanding something of the nature of evil and how soon bright things come to confusion ... We no longer feel, as Shakespeare's contemporaries did, the ubiquity (无处不在) of Satan, but Iago is still serviceable to us, as an objective correlative of the mindless inventiveness of racist aggression. Iago is still alive and kicking and filling migrants' letterboxes with excrement (粪便).

Germaine Greer, 1986

Focus on society and culture

In loving and marrying each other, Othello and Desdemona instinctively act according to principles of racial equality and sexual freedom which are still not normative, still far from generally accepted and practised even in our own day, let alone in Shakespeare's. Shakespeare's tragic protagonists are all overpowered by the prevailing social and ideological tides which sweep them unawares out of their depth, rather than by some metaphysically predestined misfortune or by some flaw, whether culpable (应受责备), haphazard (偶然) or innate, in the composition of their characters.

Kiernan Ryan, 1989

Focus on attitudes to 'race' and culture

From the opening scenes of the play, we quickly note how Othello experiences his identity in contradictory terms set by the Venetians ... Generations of Western critics largely ignored these ideological underpinnings of Othello's identity and focused instead on the Moor's character in terms of psychological realism. However, as the literary history of the play testifies (证明), they had difficulty in reconciling Othello's role as a tragic hero with his blackness ... Othello self-destructively internalizes the prevailing racism, while Desdemona ... remains an idealized, virtuous woman – keeping alive the image of a besieged, white femininity so crucial to the production of the black man as a 'savage'.

Jyotsna Singh, 2004

Focus on ideology – then and now

The relation between violence and the ideological power of the state may be glimpsed in the way Othello justifies himself, in his last speech, as a good Venetian: he boasts of killing someone. Not Desdemona ... but a 'malignant and a turban'd Turk' who 'Beat a Venetian and traduc'd the state'. Othello says he 'took by the throat the circumcised dog / And smote him thus'. And so, upon this recollection, Othello stabs himself, recognizing himself, for the last time, as an outsider, a discredit (耻辱) to the social order he has been persuaded to respect.

Alan Sinfield, 2004

Focus on carnival and burlesque (荒诞) elements

The abusive language, the noisy clamour (喧嚣) under Brabantio's window, and the menace of violence of the opening scene of Othello link the improvisations of Iago with the codes of a carnivalesque disturbance or charivari (喧闹) organized in protest over the marriage of the play's central characters ... In staging the play as a ceremony of broken nuptials, Iago assumes the function of a popular festive ringleader (主谋) whose task is the unmaking of a transgressive (违犯社会规约的) marriage. As the action of Othello unfolds, the audience is constrained to witness a protracted and diabolical (恶魔般的) parody of courtship leading to a final, grotesquely distorted consummation in the marriage bed.

Michael D. Bristol, 2004

Othello in performance

There is no substitute for seeing a live performance of the play at the theatre, as well as watching different movie versions, in order to gain an appreciation of the living play as opposed to simply reading the script.

Since its first recorded performance in 1604, *Othello* has remained a popular stage play, gripping (扣人心弦) in its focused intensity. During the 1700s, for example, *Othello* was performed on a London stage for all but seven years of the whole century. However, one of the earliest critics of the play, Thomas Rymer (1693), dismissed it as 'a Bloody Farce' because he thought that too much hinged upon (依赖于) 'so remote a trifle as a handkerchief'.

Key critical discussion in the twentieth century tended to focus upon whether it is Iago or Othello who commands the greatest stage presence. Largely, this debate was bound up with competing interpretations of *Othello*, shaped by the critical writings of A. C. Bradley (1904) and F. R. Leavis (1937). In brief, Bradley argued that Othello was essentially noble and was brought down by Iago's villainy. In contrast, Leavis saw Othello as self-centred and self-dramatising, all too ready to believe Iago's hints and lies. Bradley viewed Iago as the more complex, fascinating character, but Leavis asserted that Iago 'is not much more than a necessary piece of dramatic mechanism'. In reality, Iago has nearly one-third of the lines of the play – many more than Othello. The success or otherwise of productions is often measured by a director's ability to attain a dramatic balance between these two characters.

Since the late twentieth century, critical attention has been increasingly directed towards cultural, post-colonial and feminist/gendered readings of the play influenced by developments in literary theory (see pp. 222, 238 and 239).

《奥赛罗》的演出

Shakespeare's stage

Open-air playhouses in Shakespeare's day meant that the experience of going to see a play was very different from today. There were no stage lights, so performances took place in daylight. The large audience surrounded the stage on three sides, with those standing on the ground floor pressed against the edge of the stage itself (see p. 6 for a photograph of the modern Shakespeare's Globe, which was built on the site of the original theatre in 1997). With three tiers (层) of seating, open-air acoustics (音效), noisy bustling audiences and a lack of lights, it is likely that actors adopted an exaggerated acting style, with big gestures and 'stock' ways of standing to suggest certain moods or character types. Costumes would carry vital clues about the wearer (and don't forget that women's parts were played by boys because women were not allowed to act on stage until much later in the seventeenth century). Movements and facial expressions had to be visible from three floors up.

Theatre companies like The King's Men (Shakespeare's company) were expected to perform a range of plays from a repertoire (可表演剧目) at any one time, presenting a different play each day of the week. This would mean little rehearsal time and the necessity of learning lines very quickly. Actors would not get a copy of the whole play – just their own lines (literally, their 'part') with the addition of preceding cues. Embedded stage directions would therefore contain vital clues to each actor about what was going on and where it was happening. To make this process even more complicated, plays often included more speaking parts than actors in the company. Therefore actors doubled up and played more than one role.

Othello in performance

- In small groups, choose any key scene from *Othello* and talk about how it might have been staged at the Globe. Have a go at acting the parts, using grand gestures and stylised (程式化) ways of speaking the lines.

- What would be the major challenges for boys playing the parts of Emilia, Desdemona and Bianca?

Casting

From Shakespeare's day right up to the 1980s, Othello was played on the London stage by white actors 'blacked up'. Perhaps the most famous example was Laurence Olivier's performance in 1964 (below left), which is still regarded by many critics as the definitive (最佳) Othello.

Heavily influenced by F. R. Leavis's reading of the play, Olivier portrayed Othello as a sensuous and barely civilised egotist. However, this view has been challenged in recent times. Modern understandings of 'race' and cultural politics have led to less favourable criticisms of Olivier's performance, which is now regarded by many as relying on racist stereotypes.

Two famous black actors challenged the tradition of white actors taking the role, one in the nineteenth century and one in the twentieth. Ira Aldridge, an African-American actor, was the first black actor to play major Shakespeare roles. Aldridge's performances in the 1850s could not help but carry political resonance (特殊意义, 共鸣), coming as they did at a time when the anti-slavery movement was gathering pace (迅速发展).

The African-American actor Paul Robeson's performance as Othello in the 1930s and 1940s (below right) has come to be regarded as the antithesis of Olivier's, in that it emphasised 'noble', sympathetic aspects of Othello. Robeson, the son of a former slave, was a singer and political activist. A campaigner for civil rights in the United States, he interpreted the role of Othello as an outsider who takes a fierce pride in his culture. Robeson was at first wary of being cast as Othello, in case he was perceived in a stereotypical way. He did not receive a wholly positive reception on the London stage, but in a later production he took Broadway (New York) by storm.

Othello
奥赛罗

Nowadays, audiences expect to see a black actor playing Othello, and it would be regarded as potentially racist to cast a white actor in the role, given the struggle experienced by black actors to gain equal access to leading roles in the professional theatre. Blacking up carries memories of racist 'minstrel' (吟游歌手) routines and it is unlikely that a director would contemplate this now. An interesting experiment, however, was the 'photonegative' (如同底片的；负光电) staging by the Washington Shakespeare Theatre (1997), where Othello was played by a white actor and all other parts by black actors, deliberately reversing the construction of 'outsider'.

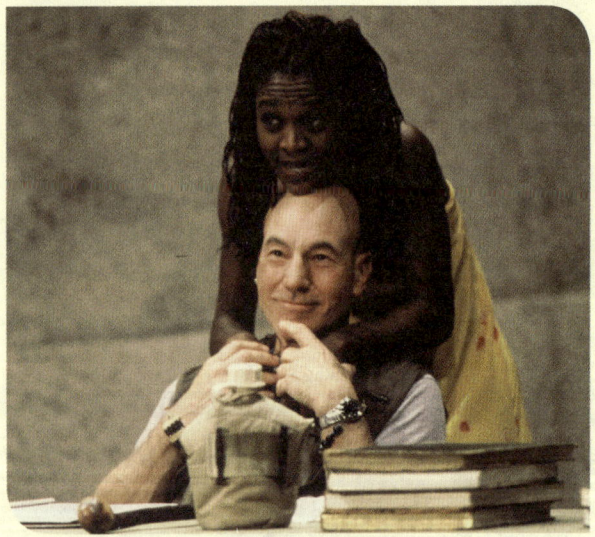

◆ In small groups, discuss what effect you think different casting decisions might have on the way a modern audience 'reads' a performance of *Othello*. For example, in the last two decades the part of Bianca has often been played by a black actor (see p. 225). Why do you think several directors have done this? What difference would it make if Emilia was black (see the image on p. 178)? Could you envisage a black Iago? Increasingly, a 'colour-blind' approach is taken to casting professional Shakespeare productions (for example, a black actor played Henry V at the National Theatre in London in 2003). Could Othello be played successfully by a white actor or is the play too specific about 'race' for that to work?

◆ Search the Internet for images of Othello taken from recent productions. Also look again at the photographs in this edition of black and white actors playing Othello and other characters. Summarise your discussion, make some notes, then compare your ideas with other groups.

Openings

As a skilled playwright, Shakespeare knew he had to catch the interest of his audience right at the start of each play. Therefore in most plays we find vigorous dialogue, intriguing situations and conflict introduced in the first scene. Scene 1 of *Othello* is no exception, opening as it does in the middle of a heated argument.

◆ Consider how the opening moments are portrayed in three different screen versions of *Othello*. For example:

◆ Trevor Nunn's 1990 RSC production starts briefly with an empty stage in half-light; a striking visual contrast is immediately established with Iago in dark military uniform and Roderigo dressed in a light-coloured linen suit and panama hat.

◆ Oliver Parker's 1995 Hollywood film opens with a lengthy title sequence (片头), the camera tracking a gondola's journey through night-time Venice, establishing time and place. A shrouded pair of figures is seated close together; the woman's face is occasionally glimpsed, but the man is masked. The scene cuts to the Senate where war is being discussed. Cut back to a secret wedding scene, Iago and Roderigo as two surreptitious (鬼鬼祟祟) onlookers. It is only now that some of Iago's opening dialogue is introduced.

◆ Orson Welles chose to begin his 1952 black-and-white film version with Othello's funeral procession, overlooked by a caged Iago; in this version, the play is visually framed by its tragic outcome, the main action becoming a kind of flashback.

Othello in performance

- Imagine you are making a new movie of *Othello*. How will your film begin? Where (and when) will it be set? What music or sound effects will you use? What atmosphere are you seeking to create? Will you want to reorder/cut the script? Storyboard the opening of the play. If you have access to cameras, film the opening three or four minutes of the play and share with other groups in your class. Which is the most successful and why?

Adaptations

In the eighteenth century, it became popular to rewrite certain of Shakespeare's tragedies in order to give them a happy ending.

- Imagine you are a stage adapter and have been asked to give *Othello* a happy ending. How will you do it? Which characters need to survive for it to be regarded as 'happy'? Which characters do not need to survive — why not? At what point in the play do you have to begin to make changes? Does a happy ending demand that Iago is punished or not? Make notes outlining your alterations, including some examples of your new script.

A number of modern writers and directors have taken the core elements of the *Othello* story and created a modern drama out of it. Tim B. Nelson's 2001 film version, *O*, transferred the action to a modern American high school. Othello becomes OJ, star of the basketball team and the only black student in the school. He has a relationship with Desi, the principal's daughter.

In a made-for-television adaptation (first screened in the UK in 2001), scriptwriter Andrew Davis transposed (改变地点) the story to modern London. Ben Jago, deputy Metropolitan Police Commissioner, is passed over for promotion in favour of his black colleague, John Othello. Michael Cass is assigned bodyguard duties when Othello and his beautiful wife, Dessie, are racially harassed.

▲ The movie *O* gave the *Othello* story a modern setting, in which jealous teenager Hugo deliberately drives a wedge between (离间，挑拨) high-school couple OJ and Desi.

- Compile a file of ideas for a made-for-television drama based upon the Othello story.
- Summarise the new storyline in approximately 500 words and include a list of characters.
- Describe the setting and time (the present, the past or the future); suggest a series of locations, matched to specific scenes.
- Cast your production with known actors, film stars or other celebrities. Explain your choices.
- Take the key 'temptation' scene (Act 3 Scene 3) and explain how you will adapt this to fit your own version.
- Draw some costume designs, or use pictures taken from magazines or the Internet.

Othello
奥赛罗

Silent Othello, triplicate (三个) Iago

The Russian-American company Synetic Theater specialise in silent adaptations of Shakespeare plays, which rely on choreographed dance (编排舞蹈), athletic physical movement, vividly designed costumes and screen projections to convey the drama. In their production of *Othello* three performers simultaneously took the role of Iago, creating the effect that he is everywhere whispering, listening or interfering in the action (see picture below).

◆ Choose one scene from Act 3 and decide how you could make a 'triple Iago' enhance the tension.

Political *Othello*

Othello challenges apartheid (种族隔离)

Although some critics have argued that *Othello* is not a play primarily about race, in certain 'post-colonial' contexts this aspect of the play is unavoidably highlighted and the whole play becomes politically charged. One such production was directed by Janet Suzman in 1980s South Africa – in defiance of the apartheid regime there. The Market Theatre of Johannesburg production included a black actor as Othello, not only appearing alongside his white colleagues, but kissing a white woman on stage in a society where such conduct was punishable by imprisonment. The production drew international notice, and became a political weapon against the apartheid government.

Othello and the Metropolitan Police

On a smaller scale, Andrew Davies's modern adaptation (see picture opposite) was made in the context of accusations of racism against the London Metropolitan Police. Eammon Walker, who starred as police chief John Othello, emphasised the political context of the play when interviewed:

> Andrew Davies … was dealing with a London problem: the Metropolitan Police and death within custody. This is a big issue for Britain … Now, I don't know if you can hope that something can be changed by this particular production, but what you can hope for is that you plant a seed in somebody's brain – maybe a person of power who is able to do something about it. You can hope that they can turn around and make a difference in the society that we are living in. That's basically what we do as playwrights, as directors, as actors: We shine a mirror on to society for them to look into. If they see something they don't like, then it's up to them to change it.

Othello in postcolonial India

In the late 1990s, *Othello* was adapted for a Kathakali style of production in India. Kathakali is a traditional form of Indian theatre, using masks, dance moves and formalised gestures. Arjun Raina, who played Othello, said in an interview that for him there were clear parallels between

◀ The three Iagos in Synetic Theater's 2010 production.

Othello in performance

Othello's situation and that of Indians searching for their identity in the context of their colonial past under British rule.

◆ Debate with others in your class whether it is ever possible to read a Shakespeare play without filtering its meaning through our own current cultural and political understandings.

Othello on stage and on film

Seeing a performance of any play you are studying is vitally important in helping you to understand the way it works as a drama. A good way to develop ideas about different ways in which *Othello* might be interpreted is to watch more than one production. A live performance will provide you with a very different experience than watching a movie version. However, you are most likely to have access to a film version. A number of activities in this book have suggested that you look at key scenes in different film versions.

▼ Andrew Davis's television adaptation was released at a time when the police force was being accused of racism.

There are a number of ways in which you might work with a movie:

a Look at the date it was made and consider how the film is a reflection of its social and cultural history (e.g. fashions in hair styles, clothes; attitudes to women, to 'race'; style of acting; sophistication of editing technology, and so on).

b Watch the whole movie and see if you can identify any changes the screenwriter has made (cutting the original script, omitting minor characters, changing the order of any scenes).

c Take a key scene and examine the way it has been constructed. For instance, look at:
  • camerawork (shot type, movement, camera angles)
  • editing (the way shots are cut)
  • sound (dialogue, music, sound effects)
  • lighting (light, dark, sources of light)
  • costumes, props, setting and locations; use of colour.

d Press the pause button and freeze the action at a key moment. Analyse the mise en scene (舞台调度) (in other words, whatever you can see in the frame including many of the items listed above).

e Compare two or more movie versions at the same point in the plot. How do they differ and which do you find the most effective? Explain your reasons.

Write a review

◆ Look at full-length film or theatre reviews in a newspaper or online. Familiarise yourself with the style of writing and the way each critic analyses aspects of the production. Write a review of a live theatre production if you are lucky enough to be able to see one; or write a review of one of the movie versions you have viewed. How has the director approached the play? How is the relationship between Othello and Iago presented? What kind of a woman is Desdemona? Is the turning of Othello by Iago convincing?

OTHELLO
奥赛罗

Writing about Shakespeare 笔论莎士比亚

The play as text

Shakespeare's plays have always been studied as literary works – as words on a page that need clarification, appreciation and discussion. When you write about the plays, you will be asked to compose short pieces and also longer, more reflective pieces like controlled assessments, examination scripts and coursework – often in the form of essays on themes and/or imagery, character studies, analyses of the structure of the play and on stagecraft. Imagery, stagecraft and character are dealt with elsewhere in this edition. Here, we concentrate on themes and structure. You might find it helpful to look at the 'Write about it' boxes on the left-hand pages throughout the play.

Themes

It is often tempting to say that the theme of a play is a single idea, like 'death' in *Hamlet*, or 'the supernatural' in *Macbeth*, or 'love' in *Romeo and Juliet*. The problem with such a simple approach is that you will miss the complexity of the plays. In *Romeo and Juliet*, for example, the play is about the relationship between love, family loyalty and constraint; it is also about the relationship of youth to age and experience; and the relationship between Romeo and Juliet is also played out against a background of enmity between two families. Between each of these ideas or concepts there are tensions. The tensions are the main focus of attention for Shakespeare and the audience; this is also how the best drama operates – by the presentation of and resolution of tension.

Look back at the 'Themes' boxes throughout the play to see if any of the activities there have given rise to information that you could use as a starting point for further writing about the themes of the specific play you are studying.

Structure

Most Shakespeare plays are in five acts, divided into scenes. These acts were not in the original scripts, but have been included in later editions to make the action more manageable, clearer and more like 'classical' structures. One way to get a sense of the structure of the whole play is to take a printed version (not this one!) and cut it up into scenes and acts, then display each scene and act, in sequence, on a wall, like this:

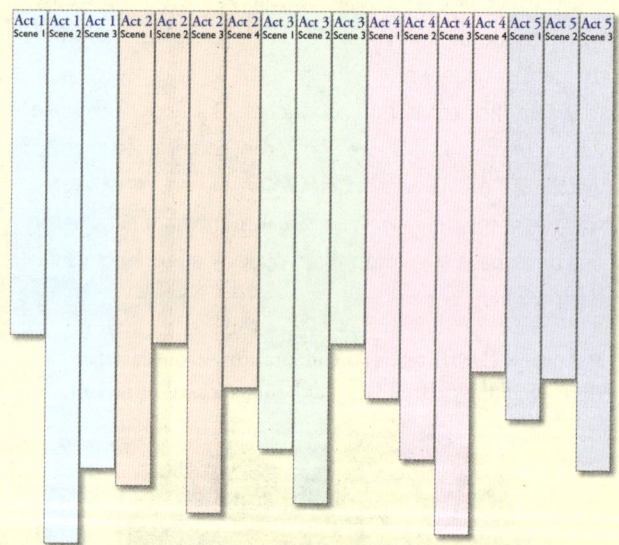

As you set out the whole play, you will be able to see the 'shape' of each act, the relative length of the scenes, and how the acts relate to each other (such as whether one act is shorter, and why that might be). You can annotate the text with comments, observations and questions. You can use a highlighter pen to mark the recurrence of certain words, images or metaphors to see at a glance where and how frequently they appear. You can also follow a particular character's progress through the play.

Such an overview of the play gives you critical perspective: you will be able to see how the parts fit together, to stand back from the play and assess its shape, and to focus on particular parts within the context of the whole. Your writing will reflect a greater awareness of the overall context as a result.

The play as script

There are different, but related, categories when we think of the play as a script for performance. These include *stagecraft* (discussed elsewhere in this edition and throughout the left-hand pages), *lighting*, *focus* (who are we looking at? Where is the attention of the audience?), *music and sound*, *props and costumes*, *casting*, *make-up*, *pace and rhythm*, and other *spatial relationships* (e.g. how actors move around the stage in relation to each other). If you are writing about stagecraft or performance, use the notes you have made as a result of the 'Stagecraft' activities throughout this edition of the play, as well as any information you can find about the plays in performance.

What are the key points of dispute?

Shakespeare is brilliant at capturing a number of key points of dispute in each of his plays. These are the dramatic moments where he concentrates the focus of the audience on difficult (sometimes universal) problems that the characters are facing or embodying.

First, identify these key points in the play you are studying. You can do this as a class by brainstorming what you consider to be the key points in small groups, then debating the long-list as a whole class, and then coming up with a short-list of what the class thinks are the most significant. (This is a good opportunity for speaking and listening work.) They are likely to be places in the play where the action or reflection is at its most intense, and which capture the complexity of themes, character, structure and performance.

Second, drill down at one of the points of contention and tension. In other words, investigate the complexity of the problem that Shakespeare has presented. What is at stake? Why is it important? Is it a problem that can be resolved, or is it an insoluble one?

Key skills in writing about Shakespeare

Here are some suggestions to help you organise your notes and develop advanced writing skills when working on Shakespeare:

- Compose the title of your writing carefully to maximise your opportunities to be creative and critical about the play. Explore the key words in your title carefully. Decide which aspect of the play – or which combination of aspects – you are focusing on.
- Create a mind map of your ideas, making connections between them.
- If appropriate, arrange your ideas into a hierarchy that shows how some themes or features of the play are 'higher' than others and can incorporate other ideas.
- Sequence your ideas so that you have a plan for writing an essay, review, story – whichever genre you are using. You might like to think about whether to put your strongest points first, in the middle, or later.
- Collect key quotations (it might help to compile this list with a partner), which you can use as evidence to support your argument.
- Compose your first draft, embedding quotations in your text as you go along.
- Revise your draft in the light of your own critical reflections and/or those of others.

The following pages focus on writing about *Othello* in particular.

Othello 奥赛罗

Writing about *Othello* 笔论《奥赛罗》

As you will have seen from the pages dealing with *Othello* in performance, directors have interpreted the play in a number of different ways. It is likely that the specific versions you have watched either on the stage or on film will shape the way you respond to the play. Reading any piece of literature is an active process on the part of the reader, in which your own experiences, values and beliefs help you to make sense of the text. That is one of the reasons why we all read texts in different ways (and why critics argue about what each play 'means'). When you come to write about *Othello*, it is important that you think carefully about what the play means to you personally.

Conventional essays

You may have to write an essay about *Othello* that will be formally assessed. These essays often follow a set structure and need to fulfil the specific requirements of the examination syllabus (大纲) you are studying. You will need to decide what your opinion is, then plan out a carefully constructed argument that lays out your points in a logical order, supporting each point with reference to the text, sometimes giving precise quotations. Make sure you do not just retell the story of the play.

The following titles are typical examination essays based on *Othello*:

a Choose two or three central themes and explain how each is developed linguistically and dramatically through the play.

b Discuss Othello's relationship with Desdemona. Do you believe he truly loves her?

c Write a detailed character study of Desdemona that is sympathetic to her; now write a second version that is unsympathetic. Write approximately one page for each. The first part will argue that she is a completely innocent participant in the tragedy; the second part will argue that she makes a number of wrong decisions and is partly responsible for what happens.

d In the story on which Shakespeare based *Othello*, the characters sailed to Cyprus on a calm sea. Why do you think Shakespeare adds a mighty storm at the beginning of Act 2 Scene 1?

e How far is Othello's tragic downfall brought about because he is an outsider?

f Within the world of the play, is Othello's love for Desdemona 'against all rules of nature', as Brabantio says?

g Some commentators have said that the focus of *Othello* is not the title character (主人公), as is the case with Shakespeare's other great tragedies. Instead, the play should have been called *Iago*. Do you agree?

h Comment on the time-scheme of the play, where realistically not enough time could have elapsed on Cyprus for Desdemona to have committed adultery. Examine the problem of time in *Othello* and the possible dramatic reasons behind this 'double time-scheme'.

i Write about an aspect of language that interests you in *Othello*.

Pick at least two of these essay titles and sketch out an essay plan for each. Find between five and ten relevant quotations from the script that you can match to specific points on each plan. Swap plans with two other students in your class and give constructive feedback. Make suggestions for improvements.

Select the two essay titles that you think are the most difficult to answer. Try to pinpoint what aspects of the questions you find most challenging. Talk together with a partner and share ideas. Based on your selected essay titles, draw up some revision notes on each topic.

Research projects

The better you understand Shakespeare's times and the social context in which he was writing, the better you will understand *Othello*. Choose one of the following topics and undertake some detailed research, using library resources and the Internet. Make sure you select information carefully from your sources (don't just copy) and always check that as far as you can tell you are using a reliable source. Present your information in as clear a manner as you can – the exact written format is up to you.

a Venice in the seventeenth century

b Shakespeare's London

c playhouses and Shakespeare's acting companies

d attitudes to women in Shakespeare's time (you might like to look for examples of seventeenth-century sermons [说教] that outline how to be a good wife)

e overseas exploration, travel writing and the beginning of colonial expansion

f the main sources Shakespeare used when composing *Othello*.

Creative responses

Throughout the left-hand pages of this book, you have been encouraged to be creative in your responses to *Othello*, particularly through drama-based activities and visual display work. Sometimes for school assessments you are asked to write creatively, for example, by creating missing scenes, or by composing stories inspired by events, characters or themes. Here are some ideas for creative writing (feel free to think of some alternative activities yourself):

a Roderigo claims to be hopelessly in love with Desdemona. We learn that Brabantio had banned him from the house. Imagine that Roderigo writes two love letters to Desdemona – one delivered to her house before the news of her marriage to Othello, and one following their arrival on Cyprus that remains undelivered. Write the letters.

b Othello and Desdemona's marriage takes place off stage, before the play opens. Decide who would have been present in addition to the couple themselves, then write the missing scene.

c Write the scene where Othello tells Desdemona what has just happened in the barracks and why he has had to dismiss Cassio.

d What happens to Cassio and Bianca after the play ends? Write Bianca's story.

e Who owns the handkerchief at the end of the play? Compose a story that focuses on the new owner and what happens to him or her.

f Recast (改写) the murder scene in Desdemona's bedchamber (Act 5 Scene 2, lines 22–107) as an extract from a novel. Use third-person narrative, decide what action will be described by the narrator and what dialogue you want to keep. End on a cliff-hanger (悬念) as Emilia comes into the room.

And finally …

Write a reflective account of your time spent studying *Othello*. What did you initially expect the experience of studying Shakespeare to be like? (Try to pinpoint where those assumptions came from.) Were your expectations fulfilled – or challenged? What aspects of studying the play did you find most difficult and what helped you overcome them? What did you like best about the play? What was your favourite activity from this book and how did it transform your understanding of an aspect of the play?

Othello
奥赛罗

William Shakespeare 莎翁年表
1564–1616

1564	Born Stratford-upon-Avon, eldest son of John and Mary Shakespeare.
1582	Marries Anne Hathaway of Shottery, near Stratford.
1583	Daughter Susanna born.
1585	Twins, son and daughter Hamnet and Judith, born.
1592	First mention of Shakespeare in London. Robert Greene, another playwright, described Shakespeare as 'an upstart crow beautified with our feathers'. Greene seems to have been jealous of Shakespeare. He mocked Shakespeare's name, calling him 'the only Shake-scene in a country' (presumably because Shakespeare was writing successful plays).
1595	Becomes a shareholder in The Lord Chamberlain's Men, an acting company that became extremely popular.
1596	Son, Hamnet, dies aged eleven. Father, John, granted arms (acknowledged as a gentleman).
1597	Buys New Place, the grandest house in Stratford.
1598	Acts in Ben Jonson's *Every Man in His Humour*.
1599	Globe Theatre opens on Bankside. Performances in the open air.
1601	Father, John, dies.
1603	James I grants Shakespeare's company a royal patent: The Lord Chamberlain's Men become The King's Men and play about twelve performances each year at court.
1607	Daughter Susanna marries Dr John Hall.
1608	Mother, Mary, dies.
1609	The King's Men begin performing indoors at Blackfriars Theatre.
1610	Probably returns from London to live in Stratford.
1616	Daughter Judith marries Thomas Quiney. Dies. Buried in Holy Trinity Church, Stratford-upon-Avon.

The plays and poems

(no one knows exactly when he wrote each play)

1589–95	*The Two Gentlemen of Verona, The Taming of the Shrew, First, Second* and *Third Parts* of *King Henry VI, Titus Andronicus, King Richard III, The Comedy of Errors, Love's Labour's Lost, A Midsummer Night's Dream, Romeo and Juliet, King Richard II* (and the long poems *Venus and Adonis* and *The Rape of Lucrece*).
1596–99	*King John, The Merchant of Venice, First* and *Second Parts* of *King Henry IV, The Merry Wives of Windsor, Much Ado About Nothing, King Henry V, Julius Caesar* (and probably the Sonnets).
1600–05	*As You Like It, Hamlet, Twelfth Night, Troilus and Cressida, Measure for Measure,* **Othello***, All's Well That Ends Well, Timon of Athens, King Lear.*
1606–11	*Macbeth, Antony and Cleopatra, Pericles, Coriolanus, The Winter's Tale, Cymbeline, The Tempest.*
1613	*King Henry VIII, The Two Noble Kinsmen* (both probably with John Fletcher).
1623	Shakespeare's plays published as a collection (now called the First Folio).

Acknowledgements 鸣谢

Cambridge University Press would like to acknowledge the contributions made to this work by Rex Gibson.

Picture Credits

p. iii Donmar Theatre 2007, Johan Persson/ArenaPAL; p. v: Shakespeare's Globe 2007, © Marilyn Kingwill/ArenaPAL; p. vi left: Theatre Royal, Northampton 2003, © Donald Cooper/Photostage; p. vi right: RSC/Barbican Theatre, London 2000, © Donald Cooper/Photostage; p. vii top: The Royal Opera/Royal Albert Hall, London 1997, © Donald Cooper/Photostage; p. vii bottom: RSC, Stratford-upon-Avon 1999, © Ben Christopher/ArenaPAL; p. viii top: RSC/Barbican Theatre, London 2000, © Donald Cooper/Photostage; p. viii bottom: Crucible Theatre, Sheffield 2011, © Johan Persson/ArenaPAL; p. ix top: Young Vic Theatre, London 1984, © Donald Cooper/Photostage; p. ix bottom: Northern Broadsides and West Yorkshire Playhouse/Trafalgar Studios 2009, © Donald Cooper/Photostage; p. x top: Northern Broadsides and West Yorkshire Playhouse/Leeds 2009, © Nobby Clarke/ArenaPAL; p. x bottom: RSC/The Other Place, Stratford-upon-Avon 1989, © Donald Cooper/Photostage; p. xi top: RSC/Barbican Theatre, London 2000, © Donald Cooper/Photostage; p. xi bottom: Northern Broadsides and West Yorkshire Playhouse, Leeds 2009, © Donald Cooper/Photostage; p. xii: Donmar Theatre 2007, Johan Persson/ArenaPAL; p. 6: Chicago Shakespeare Theater/Shakespeare's Globe 2012, © Donald Cooper/Photostage; Shakespeare's Globe 2007, © Johan Persson/ArenaPAL; p. 16: Pennsylvania Shakespeare Festival 2006, © Pennsylvania Shakespeare Festival; p. 18: RSC/Royal Shakespeare Theatre 1985, © Donald Cooper/Photostage; p. 20: 'Grand Procession of the Doge, Venice' (16th century illustration), © Lifestyle Pictures/Alamy; p. 24: Birmingham Repertory Theatre 1993, © Donald Cooper/Photostage; p. 36: RSC/Barbican Theatre, London 2000, © Donald Cooper/Photostage; p. 42: Donmar Theatre 2007, Johan Persson/ArenaPAL; p. 44: Crucible Theatre, Sheffield 2011, © Geraint Lewis; p. 47 The Doge's Palace, Venice, © Dmitri Ometsinsky/Shutterstock; p. 52: Donmar Theatre 2007, Johan Persson/ArenaPAL; p. 56: RSC/Barbican Theatre, London 2000, © Donald Cooper/Photostage; p. 58: Northern Broadsides and West Yorkshire Playhouse, Leeds 2009, © Donald Cooper/Photostage; p. 62: RSC/Barbican Theatre, London 2000, © Donald Cooper/Photostage; p. 64: Ludlow Festival 2010, © Donald Cooper/Photostage; p. 68: Synetic Theater 2011, © Graeme Shaw/GBS Photography; p. 70: RSC/Royal Shakespeare Theatre 1985, © Donald Cooper/Photostage; p. 72: RSC/Barbican Theatre, London 2000, © Donald Cooper/Photostage; p. 86: Synetic Theater 2011, © Graeme Shaw/GBS Photography; p. 91 top: Regent's Park Open Air Theatre 1979, © John Timbers/ArenaPAL; p. 91 bottom: Ludlow Festival 2010, © Donald Cooper/Photostage; p. 102: Donmar Theatre 2007, © Donald Cooper/Photostage; p. 108: Crucible Theatre, Sheffield 2011, © Donald Cooper/Photostage; p. 112: RSC/The Other Place, Stratford-upon-Avon 1989, © Donald Cooper/Photostage; p. 114: Northern Broadsides and West Yorkshire Playhouse Leeds 2009, © Donald Cooper/Photostage; p. 116 RSC/Swan Theatre 2004, © Donald Cooper/Photostage; p. 122; RSC Tour/Warwick Arts Centre 2009, © Donald Cooper/Photostage; p. 132: Synetic Theater 2011, © Graeme Shaw/GBS Photography; p. 134: Birmingham Repertory Theatre 1993, © Donald Cooper/Photostage; p. 143 top: Crucible Theatre, Sheffield 2011, © Donald Cooper/Photostage; p. 143 middle left: RSC/Royal Shakespeare Theatre 1979, © Donald Cooper/Photostage; p. 143 middle right: Paul Robeson and Peggy Ashcroft in *Othello* 1930, Bettmann/Corbis; p. 143 bottom: Northern Broadsides and West Yorkshire Playhouse Leeds 2009, © Donald Cooper/Photostage; p. 148: RSC/Swan Theatre 2004, © Geraint Lewis; p. 150: Ludlow Festival 2010, © Donald Cooper/Photostage; p. 152: RSC/Barbican Theatre, London 2000, © Donald Cooper/Photostage; p. 158: RSC Tour/Warwick Arts Centre 2009, © Geraint Lewis; p. 170: RSC/Barbican Theatre, London 1986, © Donald Cooper/Photostage; p. 174: Crucible Theatre, Sheffield 2011, © Johan Persson/ArenaPAL; p. 178: Cheek by Jowl/Riverside Studios, London 2004, © Donald Cooper/Photostage; p. 180: Ludlow Festival 2010, © Donald Cooper/Photostage; p. 183 top: RSC/Royal Shakespeare Theatre 1985, © Donald Cooper/Photostage; p. 183 bottom: Donmar Theatre 2007, © Geraint Lewis; p. 196: Synetic Theater 2011, © Graeme Shaw/GBS Photography; p. 200 left: Northern Broadsides and West Yorkshire Playhouse Leeds 2009, © Donald Cooper/Photostage; p. 200 right: Cheek by Jowl/Riverside Studios, London 2004, © Donald Cooper/Photostage; p. 204: Ludlow Festival 2010, © Donald Cooper/Photostage;

Othello
奥赛罗

p. 218: RSC/Barbican Theatre, London 2000, © Donald Cooper/Photostage; p. 221: RSC/Swan Theatre 2004, © Donald Cooper/Photostage; p. 224: RSC/Barbican Theatre, London 1986, © Donald Cooper/Photostage; p. 225 top: Shakespeare's Globe 2007, © Johan Persson/ArenaPAL; p. 225 bottom: RSC/Barbican Theatre, London 2000, © Donald Cooper/Photostage; p. 227: Northern Broadsides and West Yorkshire Playhouse Leeds 2009, © Donald Cooper/Photostage; p. 232: Donmar Theatre 2007, Johan Persson/ArenaPAL; p. 233: Moorish ambassador, © University of Birmingham Collections; p. 234: Glyndebourne Festival Opera 2001, © Donald Cooper/Photostage; p. 236: 'Descent of Christ into Limbo' by Jacopo Bellini, © DEA/A. Dagli Orti/Getty Images; p. 237: Crucible Theatre, Sheffield 2011, © Johan Persson/ArenaPAL; p. 241 left: Laurence Olivier and Maggie Smith in Othello 1964, © Topfoto/ArenaPAL; p. 241 right: Paul Robeson in Othello 2006, © Topfoto; p. 242: Patrick Stewart as Othello with Patrice Johnson as Desdemona in the Shakespeare Theatre Company's Othello (1997), Photo by Carol Rosegg; P. 243: Still from the film O 2001, © Miramax/Dimension Films/The Kobal Collection/Bob Basha; p. 244: Synetic Theater 2011, © Graeme Shaw/GBS Photography; p. 245: Keeley Hawes and Eamonn Walker in Othello 2001, © AF Archive/Alamy.

Sources

The quotations in the Critics' forum section are from the following sources:

Extract from 'Lecture V: Othello' from Shakespearean Tragedy by A. C. Bradley, 1904, Macmillan and Co.; extract from 'Diabolic intellect and the noble hero' from The Common Pursuit by F. R. Leavis, 1952, Chatto & Windus; extract from The Noble Moor by Helen Gardner, Proceedings of the British Academy, volume LXI, 1955; extract from Shakespeare by Germaine Greer, 1986, Oxford University Press; extract from Shakespeare by Kiernan Ryan, 1989, Pearson Education Ltd; extract from 'Othello's identity, postcolonial theory and contemporary African rewritings of Othello' by Jyotsna Singh and from 'Cultural materialism, Othello and the politics of plausibility' by Alan Sinfield in Lena Cowen Orlin (ed.), Othello, New Casebook series, 2004, Palgrave Macmillan; extract from 'The pathos of Western modernity: Charivari' in Big-time Shakespeare by Michael D. Bristol, 1996, Routledge.

Produced for Cambridge University Press by White-Thomson Publishing
+44 (0)843 208 7460
www.wtpub.co.uk

Managing editor: Sonya Newland
Designer: Clare Nicholas
Concept design: Jackie Hill